James Grant

Harry Ogilvie

The Black Dragoons

James Grant

Harry Ogilvie
The Black Dragoons

ISBN/EAN: 9783337122058

Printed in Europe, USA, Canada, Australia, Japan

Cover: Foto ©Andreas Hilbeck / pixelio.de

More available books at **www.hansebooks.com**

HARRY OGILVIE

OR

THE BLACK DRAGOONS

BY

JAMES GRANT
AUTHOR OF "THE ROMANCE OF WAR"

———————

LONDON
GEORGE ROUTLEDGE AND SONS
BROADWAY, LUDGATE HILL
GLASGOW AND NEW YORK

CONTENTS.

HARRY OGILVIE;

OR,

The Black Dragoons.

CHAPTER I.

OF MY BOYHOOD.

An hour before daylight, on a morning in December, in the **year** 1632, the bell at the gate of the University of Glasgow was rung furiously, and the despairing cry of a woman was heard echoing among the heavy balconies and dark quadrangles of the edifice; old Nehemiah Spreul, the porter, started in dismay from his box-bed, and undeterred by the energetic warnings of his cosy helpmate, Hannah, threw a plaid over his shoulders, snatched up a broadsword, for the times were perilous, and hastily opened the eyelet hole of the deeply-arched and richly-carved gate, which faces the High-street.

The morning was dark and cold; the sharp sleet pattered heavily on the lofty-windows, the ponderous stone balconies, the steep roofs and pointed towers of the college; but, save the howling of the winter wind, all was still in the quaint street, which is overshadowed by the *Auld Pedagogie* of Bishop Turnbull.

Cautiously honest Nehemiah unbarred the wicket, and gathering courage, peeped out to discover what " that eldritch yell" might mean. Then, great was his horror to perceive a woman prostrate on the pavement, with the blood flowing from her bosom in a long red current over the white snow; one hand was still upraised as if it had just relinquished the knob of the bell, which had given a summons so startling; the other clasped to her breast a poor little child about a year old—blue with cold, and half dead of privation and exposure.

Reader, this child was—MYSELF!

Nehemiah's shout for help brought his trembling spouse to

his side, and *her* outcries, when united to those of certain carlins at the adjacent closeheads, soon aroused the inmates of the University; and the Lord Chancellor, the Lord Rector, the Dean, Principal Zephaniah Bogle and the Professors, who, as well as the students, *all* lived then within the college walls, came hurrying to the spot; and if their commiseration was earnest, it was noisy and active too; for while the elder gentlemen bore the body of my mother—who was found to be quite dead of a wound in her heart—into the house of a lecturer, the younger betook them to bilbo and dagger, and with little more attire than their hastily donned scarlet gowns and slippers, they scoured all the High-street, the Gardens, the Trongate, the Candleriggs, and the Drygate, as far as " the Bell of the Brae;" but searched in vain for the perpetrator of this outrage, for the snow fell so fast that the footsteps of the assassin left no track upon the street to indicate the way he had fled.

My mother, for such I believe this unfortunate to have been, was supposed to be a lady, by the whiteness of her hands and the delicacy of her person. She seemed to be under thirty years of age, and was clad in the tattered remnants of garments which had once been rich and luxurious, but now were sorely soiled and worn. On her finger was a marriage ring; one of that old fashion which was used before the plain hoops were adopted. It had two ruby hearts surmounted by a little coronet of diamonds. This was preserved by the venerable principal, together with a gold medal, which was attached to my neck by a riband, and bore the letters H. O., E. F., and a scutcheon bearing a lion passant, crowned with the crown of Scotland, and collared with an open one, the heraldic bearing of the clan Ogilvie, and in corroboration thereof, the name *Henry Ogilvie* was found written upon my little garments, probably by the hand of the poor being in whose now cold bosom I had nestled.

The rector, the dean, and others, armed with these proofs of gentle birth, made every inquiry to discover who this unhappy person might be, but in vain. Scotland was then a wild and disturbed country; there were no serials or journals like the *Mercurius Caledonius* of later years, and no means of circulating a description of the foundling or offers of reward, otherwise than by the voice of town-drummers and bellmen. Thus, after futile inquiry, far and near, throughout the three wards of Clydesdale, the principal sealed up, and carefully locked in his cabinet, the medal and the ring, and I was consigned to the care of Hannah Spreul, the porter's wife; the remains of my poor mother were interred with respect in the burying-ground of the cathedral; the event soon became forgotten, or ceased to be spoken of, and every thing went on as before.

A woman was murdered and her child lost; yet neither were ever sought or inquired for. Her grave lay beside the wall of the ancient church in a secluded spot, between two buttresses. I know the place well, for old Nehemiah often led me there by the hand in after years, and told me the story again and again, omitting no part or portion of my mother's aspect and attire in his narrative, till the whole has been impressed upon my memory with terrible distinctness; and as I grew in years, the yearning to discover her destroyers, her name, and my father's family, became so strong within me, as to warp my feelings and usurp the place of every other thought.

And oft when roughly chidden—for old Nehemiah was somewhat crusty—I have rushed away from the gloomy college which had now become my home, to seek the burying-ground, which was shaded then by many lofty trees, and there I have sat for hours beside her grave, gleaning away the weeds and nettles, gazing wistfully on the silent turf, and speaking to myself of her who slept below, till the old porter, or at times the older and kinder principal himself, would come to fetch me back; for that half flattened mound, where the dock and nettle waved, seemed to me the home and resting-place of all my race—at least of all I had ever known.

I strove to remember her—my mother! and I repeated " mother—mother"—what magic there was in the name! I strove to embody her figure, and it rose before me, in idea, not as I could recal it, but as the janitor described it, pale and beautiful, with her long black hair mingling with the blood that stained her pure white bosom. In fancy, I saw her smile upon me, unfriended and alone in the world, with such a smile as never beamed on the heart of a motherless child; then the powerful vision would fade away, and I saw only the long grass waving in the wind beside the old grey wall. And many a bitter and many a lonely tear I have shed, when other boys spoke of their happy homes, of their mother's love and their father's protection; of their little brothers and kind sisters—for I had none of these. I was a poor little waif floating on the irresistible current of events; and I would creep thoughtfully to my nest in a garret of the old college, draw a rug over my head, pray to God and my mother, and cry myself asleep. But enough of this! what has a rough soldier like I to do with all this tender regret?

My life slipped quietly away for a few years, save when I received a beetling from the janitor's wife, when I lingered at times on the errands she sent me; for often when the good woman, with horn barnacles on her hooked nose, was waiting impatiently for the last *Bawbee* pamphlet on godliness, by the Reverend Zachary Boyd, I was solacing myself by whipping a top, or play-g with cherry paips on the sunny side of the Trongate, with other callants as ragged, and perhaps as friendless as myself; but generally the poor woman was kind to me as a mother could be, perhaps, for other parent I never knew one, except by name; and she thriftily shaped and cut down her husband's wide slops, or knee-breeches, to fit me, while there was always some kind fellow or wild buck among the students, who gave me his cast gown, and now and then a crown, as a reward for delivering his letters to certain kind dames who dwelt in the Gallowgate and other places there adjacent. And as I received crowns, kisses, and bon-bons from these, I had a very ample, though not very select circle of acquaintance.

Thus, till I was ten years old, my life was happy enough—poor little devil! I then began to blush for wearing old Nehemiah's sad coloured slops, though I was not a little proud of the guy scarlet doublets Hannah fashioned for me out of the academic gowns. Thus, I may say with truth, that the first coat I ever wore was a red one.

Now came the year 1638.

The reverend principal, who, of course, was a clergyman, had found his hands more than full enough with the national discontents that followed the accession of King Charles, whose obstinate and absurd interference with the government of Scotland made our troops invade England, and cut his forces to pieces at Newburnford; the dreadful riot which ensued on the 23rd of July, when Lucky Geddes flung her stool at a bishop's head in the Kirk of St. Giles; the concoction and signing of the solemn league and covenant, abjuring the rites and doctrines of the Romish church which were classed with those of the newly imposed liturgy and canons,—a covenant resembling those which God made of old with the children of Judah, and which was subscribed by thousands, yea, hundreds of thousands of the Scottish people on the first day of March, 1638, sworn to, on bended knees, with weeping eyes and hands and swords uplifted—a glorious sight, and a memorable epoch! The reverend principal, I have said, whose mind had been as fully occupied by all these events, as if he had been the Earl of Argyle himself, that boasted pillar of the kirk and all godliness, in the summer of that year, began to interest himself in my affairs, with which I had hitherto conceived he had no business whatever.

However, it pleased the good man to send me to school at his own expense. One day, having patted me on the head, when I was playing cherrypit in the quadrangle, and asked me what I should like to be, I replied, " Principal of Glasgow College," for, to my mind, it seemed a brave thing to live in a fine house, to have a sleek ambling horse to ride on, with holsters at its saddle, to have a pretty housemaid to warm one's bed in the cold winter nights, and to have everyone standing aside and vailing his bonnet, when one rode through the streets.

"A laudable and noble ambition, my gude bairn," said he, "and this day shalt thou begin the first step of the ladder I have clambered."

This was the prelude to my sorrows; on that very evening I found myself seated on a hard stool in the old Grammar School, which stood in a gloomy and dingy alley known as the Grey-friars' Wynd, spelling my way through the *Auld Prymar;* and such was the ill-will of the callants to my red coat, that I had to fight many a battle, and shed much blood from the nose in defence of it, for they stigmatized it as the college livery.

This institution was the ancient High School of Glasgow—a foundation coeval with the University itself; the good old Principal paid my expenses—one of which, I remember, was ten shillings Scots per quarter for writing, and then I had a bannock and a luggie of milk for luncheon; but the old janitor here had an especial spite at me, as I never had halfpence to give him, and for the most trivial error, or no error at all, he would beat me without mercy, until one day, when I turned upon him like a lion, and in presence of the whole school—about three hundred boys —tore his gown to rags, wrenched away his baton, and flung it into the fire.

From thenceforward I was never molested; but his taunts made me blush for my poverty; thus, the more I learned, the less philosophy I acquired on that point.

In those days there was a yearly collection made in all Scottish schools, denominated *bleeze-silver*—a gratuity presented to the teachers by their scholars; he who gave most was named a *king.* And though I was always dux of my class, I was never king of the Candlemas offering—for so it was named, owing to the time it took place, being a relic of some old Catholic custom; and my total inability to contribute anything made some of my task-masters severe at one time and inattentive at others. Yet was ever in front of my class, and was never behind any boy in anything, from conjugating a verb, to robbing an orchard or clark; but the bleeze-silver was the yearly bane of my existence. *Vivat!* was the cry in school which greeted an ordinary fee, and *Gloriat!* for a guinea or more.

On the first Candlemas-day after the signing of the Solemn League and Covenant, when godliness, religious fervour, and enthusiasm were at their zenith, we were to be visited by certain patrons of the school, and this year I had resolved not to be behind my class-fellows in my offering, even if I should rob a church for it,

In my tribulation I bethought me of a famous courtezan, called Mally-with-the-black-eyes, who dwelt in a pretty house near the shooting butts, and who had always been kind to me when I brought her love-gifts and messages from the studeuts— for Mally was the empress of the university. I visited her— told my story, and received a kiss and five guineas.

"Oh, madam," said I, overpowered by the sight of so much money, "they will accuse me of stealing! Where shall I say I got it?"

"From black-eyed Mally, at the butts."

"I fear me, madam, that winna protect me."

"Go-to," said she, kissing me again, for I was considered a pretty lad; "say the Earl of Argyle is in my house, and that he will protect you."

On this, she and all her rouged companions laughed.

Five guineas!—I had never seen so much money before; and they were all fresh and bright from the mint at Edinburgh.

Candlemas came, and my heart beat high under my ragged coat, for I now knew that I should put to shame every boy and braggart in the school.

Our visitors arrived; they were an imposing group of richly-dressed lords and lairds, with several long-visaged clergymen clad in sad-coloured garments. Among them were Zachary Boyd, author of the "Last Battel of the Soule;" and the Reverend David Dickson, Professor of Divinity. Thus a long examination of us ensued, but principally on points of doctrine and scripture; but being somewhat defective in my answers, I received from Messieurs Dickson and Boyd a severe rebuke; and though I had already fought my way right through the then standard Latin grammar of old Carmichael, the minister of Haddington, I did not receive one half the credit awarded to some hypocritical little varlets who could snuffle a few texts of scripture through their noses; and to each of these, a gentleman, who had long yellow hair hanging on his shoulders, and a silver star sparkling on his breast, gave a crown-piece, and I administered a hearty cuffing when the school was dismissed.

The examination concluded, and the long ladle went round for the bleeze silver. Every boy gave all he could spare, and the hall rang with alternate shouts of "Vivat" and "Gloriat." It came before me at last, and the grim, sour-visaged janitor placed it almost under my nose, with an impudent grin on his hard features.

My heart beat, and I dashed in my five guineas, with the air of a Roman saving his country, or a Scottish lord selling it.

"Five guineas!" stammered the thunderstruck janitor— "five guineas frae ragged Harry Ogilvie!"

Old Nehemiah, my patron, and the principal, who were in the

school, grew pale at this exclamation. The surprise of my class-fellows was great, and every eye was fixed on me, as my contri-bution had been the last one.

"This is a braw largess to come from such as *you*, my man-nie," said the head-master; "came ye by it honestly?—tak' hold o' him, janitor!"

The janitor did so, readily. My heart swelled, and my cheek blushed, for never had so many eyes been on me before, and I felt like a criminal.

" You have an unco' look o' guilt about ye, sir—where got *you* sae muckle to spend?" asked the rector of the school.

" I got it from a friend who is ever kind to me," said I, ready to weep at my own friendless condition.

" A friend," resumed the rector, relaxing his stern and ter-rible brow; "who may that friend be?"

" Mally-with-the-black-eyes," said I; then some of the older scholars laughed; the janitor grinned, and glances of horror were exchanged between Zachary Boyd, the yellow-haired per-sonage, and their friends in the sad-coloured garments.

" Mally—who is she?" thundered the rector, who had better reasons for knowing her, than he chose to acknowledge; " can any one tell?"

" A neer do weel lass, sir," said the janitor; " a weel kenned light o' love in the Gallowgate, and a braw friend for a growing callant to boast o' "

" You are a saucy auld carle," said I, boldly; " and you had better keep a civil tongue in your head, lest it be cropped out by the Earl of Argyle, who was in Mally's house this morning, and will protect both her and me."

Had a bombshell fallen through the roof at that moment, the visages of those around me could not have exhibited more con-sternation than they did at these words. The horrified divines drew back, and the tall thin gentleman, with his silver star glit-tering on the breast of his black velvet cassock-coat, and with a diamond-hilted rapier, hanging in a blue silk sash, stood before me. Parted in the centre of his head, his long yellow hair fell in elf locks over his shoulders; his features were harsh, stern, and forbidding; his lips were thin; his teeth sharp as those of a cat; his eyes were keen and lowering in expression, and one of them had a hideous squint. His whole air was commanding, grim, and ascetic, and I felt my boyish heart shrink beneath the terror of his presence.

Heaven alone knows what emotion it was that stirred within me then, or by what magic this strange man's presence so be-wildered me,

" Look up, boy," said he, gravely; " I am Archibald, Earl of Argyle "

Thus I found myself face to face with him who was esteemed the mirror of religion, of piety, purity, and presbyterianism. His son Archibald, Lord Lorn, a proud but sly-looking young man, with a shock head of red hair, accompanied him, and was clad in the same kind of sad-coloured garments.

As the Earl looked at me, with the eye of one who would wither up whatever he gazed on, his brow suddenly relaxed; his expression changed, and something akin to surprise and alarm spread over it; but veiling all under a bland exterior, he turned to the rector, saying—

" Reverend sir, how is this boy named?"

" Harry Ogilvie, my lord."

The Earl started as if a wasp had stung him, and, child as I was, I could see the strange glance he exchanged with his son the Lord Lorn.

" How came he here—and who are his parents?" were the next stern queries.

In a very subdued manner the rector of the school led forward Mr. Bogle, the principal of the college, and he in turn brought forward Nehemiah Spreul, the gate-ward, for all seemed to tremble in speaking to Argyle, and the mournful story of my mother's fate was told to the Earl, who heard it with calm composure, and without one word of pity, for sternness and asceticism had spread a crust over all his heart (if, indeed, he ever had one), and taught him to veil every emotion under an immoveable gravity of demeanour. Thus Nehemiah, being a testy old man, concluded his story in a burst of anger, at the little interest it seemed to excite in the noble listener, while, bonnet in hand, I stood trembling between them; but the Earl drank in every word, and an undercurrent of secret thoughts was passing under his stealthy eyes; child as I was, I could read that, too!

" Ken ye the bairn, my lord," asked the gate-keeper.

" How should I, sirrah?" retorted the Earl, frowning.

" Ye glowre at him sae," was the tart reply.

" Have a care, sir!" said the rector, in great alarm at this indiscretion.

" A strange story this, sirs," said the Earl.

" If a true one," added Lord Lorn; " but whose son can he be?"

" His father's," said Nehemiah, testily.

" The most of children are so," said a military-looking man, whom I afterwards understood to be Marshal Sir Alexander Leslie, General of the armies of the covenant; " unless the father is long abroad, and then they are sometimes the children of other people. Such cases happened to some among us in the Low Country wars."

At this dull jest no one laughed but Nehemiah, who was duly rebuked by Zachary Boyd, and told that loud laughter was ungodly, and the sign of a wicked heart.

"And an abomination in the sight of the Lord," added the Earl. "And so you have never discovered a clue as to who the mother of this poor boy may have been?"

"Never, my Lord—her fate is involved in mystery," replied the principal.

"Doubtless she hath been the victim of some barbarity."

"A martyr, my Lord."

"Yea, a martyr," snuffled the preaching nobleman, willing, apparently, to misunderstand the reverend principal, or to adopt anything he said; "but why should we regret her—the blood of the martyrs is the seed of our kirk; the more they are oppressed. the more they grow, like the children of the Israelites in Egypt."

"Oh the callant grows brawly," said old Nehemiah, patting my head; "and proud would your mother be to see you to-day, my bonnie man."

"But the green fruit was spared, and the ripe taken," mumbled Argyle: for it was a canting time, when men stuffed their dialogue with more texts of Scripture than I now can dare to think of. "Let us not repine or impugn divine justice; we live to die that we may die to live, as our very reverend friend, Mr. Boyd, saith in his admirable work, the *Last Battel of the Soule.*"

In reply to this remark, Mr. Zachary made a profound bow; and the Earl struck his gold-headed cane emphatically on the floor, and while giving me a keen, deep, and bitter glance from his squinting eye—a glance that I never forgot—turned to leave the school, with all his company; and so ended this examination. But the affair of the Candlemas offering did not end here, for I was severely rebuked, and had hard tasks given me, so hard, indeed, that but for the natural emotions of gratitude to my nurse Hannah, her spouse Nehemiah, and my patron, the principal, I would assuredly have run off and joined the wandering tinkers, or Egyptians, who travelled through the country selling pots, pans, and spurtles, spoons, and luggies, and whose free, roving life, and jovial demeanour, had often excited my envy and admiration.

Moreover, poor Mally, natheless her black eyes, her wiles, smiles, and many admirers, after being placed on the cutty-stool in the Laigh Kirk, and hearing a moving discourse from Mr. Zachary Boyd, was ducked in the Clyde, for having taken in vain the name of the Lord Argyle; she had her pretty ears nailed

to the market cross, and thereafter was drummed out of
Glasgow, and banished that city for ever. So my bleeze silver
cost the poor girl dear.

CHAPTER II.

I BECOME A STUDENT, AND AM KIDNAPPED

I MADE such progress at the High School in the Greyfriars'
Wynd, that I was soon removed by the kind principal to the
University, where he gave me, or procured for me, a bursary,
which supplied me with means of pursuing my studies, and
enabled me to provide myself with that which had long been the
object of my ambition—a rapier from the booth of a Dalmascar;
after which I began to wink at the girls, cock my bonnet, and
ruffle it with other gallants on the green, or swagger with a
terrible air of effrontery in the Trongate.

I was placed in *Natio Glottiana sive Clydesdalæ*, one of the
four nations into which the students are divided, and which
comprehends the natives of Lanark, Renfrew, and Dunbarton,
and all from the source of the Clyde to the Rock of Balclutha.

There were then only six classes in the University—logic,
moral and natural philosophy, Greek, divinity, and humanity;
and I made my way through the three former to the satisfaction of my good patron, though there were many other affairs
in which I became involved, beyond the college walls, which
were not quite so pleasing to him.

I remember well my little wainscotted room. It overlooked
the High-street, and was hung in some places with tapestry,
having moral sentences issuing from the mouths of all the
figures, to which my predecessors had added beards, mustachios,
tobacco-pipes, and other appendages, by the artistic application
of a burnt cork.

When I was sixteen, I exchanged at times my coarse red
student's gown for a cloak of drab-de-Berri; I learned to dance
—put a feather in my hat—planted a hand in the bowl-hilt of
my spada—and, with my pumps well flowered with ribbons, was
wont to swagger out in the evening to seek adventures, and I
soon encountered one that was anything but pleasing; but of
that anon.

In such times, and among such a class of fiery young fellows
as the students attending a Scottish university, sheer necessity
compelled all to acquire the noble science of defence; and I
applied myself to it with such ardour, that I soon attained the

se of every species of weapon, from backsword and dagger to
the musket and pike.   This enabled us to ruffle it bravely on the
Green and in the Trongate, and to show how we—the *men* of
Glasgow—looked down on the Greenock "folk," and Paisley
bodachs."

I became one of the best shots at the Butts,* where the
weaponshaws were held, near the Gallowgate; and there, before
I was eighteen, I could beat the best masters of fence, either
with blunt foils or sharp rapiers—'twas all one to me.   I punched
more holes in their pyne doublets than I could afford to pay for;
and in all these sports, whether leaping, wrestling, and tossing
the bar, Patrick, Master of Oliphant, and William Linn, of
Linn, two of the handsomest young men iu the city, were ever
with me, among the foremost; and having no rivalry, as we
were equal, a warm friendship existed between us.   I am proud
to record this; for one was the heir of Lord Oliphant, of Aberdalgie; the other was a gentleman of that ilk, and I but a poor
and nameless dependent on the bounty of the principal.

We were often involved in brawls and street quarrels, for we
broke windows o' nights, wrenched off door-risps, rang the alarm-
bell, and snatched away the wigs of respectable Saltmarket burgesses, or broke the lanterns with which they or their female
servants lighted them home after dusk; and we were wont to
make a terrible uproar regularly every 29th of June, St. Peter's
day, when Glasgow fair is held: and *anent* these proceedings
three special proclamations were fulminated at tuck of drum by
the Lord Provost, John Grahame.

For such pranks we were frequently fined by the rector's
court, a tribunal which had the power of life and death over the
students; and once I was arraigned before it for the heinous
crime of singing a chanson on Christmas eve.   I was publicly
rebuked, for it was a gloomy and fanatical age; and I was told
by the principal, that "when merry, I ought to solace myself
and relieve my exuberance of spirits by a psalm."

"But such, sir," said I, "would not be the first impulse of the
happy."

"Go to!" said he, with a frown; "read my friend Zachary
Boyd's *Last Battel of the Soule*, and ye will agree with me,
that before death no man can be happy."

I bowed, paid my fine, which the Master of Oliphant lent me,
and mentally bequeathing them all to the devil, walked off,
feeling not a little disgusted at the gloom, which scemed to
increase year by year with the political discoutents of the
time.

With all their crooks and poverty, my college days were very

* Now the site of the Infantry Barracks.

happy ones. Linn, the Master, and I, were three inseparables, though I was a hard student, and they knew more of the "Hundred Merry Tales," or the dramas of Shakspeare the Englishman, than of Nepos, Sallust, and Livy; and on holidays, such as the anniversary of the Gowrie conspiracy, or so forth, when we were all entertained in the wainscotted hall with cakes and ale, despite the black-gowns, the Geneva bands and solemn visages of Zephaniah Bogle and the professors, there was never a crew of merrier cocks than the students of old St. Mungo; and the merriest of them all were the Laird of Linn and the Master of Oliphant, whose kindness enabled me to share their recreations; so when not studying, my life was a round of horse-racing, hawking, golfing, and archery, chess, wine, wassail, and such fun and frolic, as these old courts had not witnessed since the great and gallant Montrose, afterwards Captain-General of Scotland, studied there, some twenty years before.

So slipped away the time; and after I passed my sixteenth year, I wrote an essay to prove that the heart was the seat of love, and *not* the liver, as our jolt-headed ancestors hitherto believed. This production made some noise at the time; and though I was vehemently complimented by Zachary Boyd, I made myself the foe for ever of all the barber-chirurgeons in the town; and they taunted me as one who had no more brains than a snipe; as a swasher, who handled the rapier better than the pen, as most of them found to their cost, when one night Linn and I tore down all their brass basons and painted poles, and flung them into the Clyde. A student of sixteen is a man!

The passage of that great presbyter, the Earl of Argyle, through Glasgow, on his way to a meeting of the General Assembly of the Kirk of Scotland, had brought to my recollection the story of poor Mally-with-the-black-eyes and her five guineas; and in a chamber of the *Cat and Bagpipes* (a famous resort of students in the Trongate) I made Linn and Oliphant laugh loud and long at the affair, as we sat over a bottle of Bourdeaux, playing at wide-ruff and the sharp old game of trumps, and totally heedless of three taciturn and well-armed strangers who occupied an opposite table.

One bottle followed another; we took to playing shovelboard with the broad pieces of King James; and the night wore on, till the ringing of the Tron-bell, at ten o'clock, warned us away; when, taking our swords and cloaks, we set out for the college, near which we all lodged. As we departed, the three strangers arose and followed us; but I gave no heed to the circumstance then. The night was dark, for the month was November; a thick haze obscured the unlighted thoroughfares; there seemed to be none abroad but ourselves; and as we heard our feet echoing far along the silent street, we began to sing in chorus—

> " Far owre yon moss, far owre yon muir,
>   Far owre yon bonnie bush o' heather ;
> O a' the lads that e'er may be,
>   Shew me the lad o' Galawater."

Then we heard a sweet voice at an open window, close by, taki up the next verse—

> • ' Lords and lairds came here to woo,
>   And gentlemen with sword and dagger ;
> But the black-eyed lass of Galashiels
>   Loves but the lad of Galawater."

"Gloriat!" exclaimed the Master of Oliphant, waving his bonnet; "by my faith, pretty lass—but ye deserve a kiss for that."

"Fie," said she; "is this a fashion for a discreet gentleman to speak P"

"Nay, I cry you mercy, pretty one; I am no discreet gentleman; but a student, as you may see by my scarlet gown. And these gentlemen with me are the reverend principal and Mr. Zachary Boyd."

"So you are a student, eh !" said the girl, laughing.

"At your service, madam."

"And what do you study P"

"The art of love," said I.

"Is that the principal or Mr. Boyd who spoke P" asked the lady from the window.

"Oh, the principal—the principal, of course," replied Linn.

"That art of love must be the most pleasing of studies," said the lady.

"But unfortunately it is not in the curriculum here," replied Linn.

"Dullard," said the Master, "is this an age for studying the gentle art of love, when the lady is taught that marriage alone is the grand aim and object of her life P"

Some more absurd and bantering conversation ensued between us and this gay fair one, who was joined by a companion. Both, we could perceive, were very pretty, with long piked stays, which exhibited rather more of their fine bosoms than the rigid fashions of the time allowed.

"Come away," I whispered; "they are only a couple of cozening queans—two polecats in fardingales; so beware."

But the Master sprang through the open window into the room; and Linn leaped in after him, to expostulate, I have no doubt; but immediately upon this the casement and its shutters were closed, and I found myself alone in the dark street.

After hesitating a moment, I was about to kick at the door in student-fashion; but remembering that my two companions were quite able to take care of themselves, and, moreover, being now aware that three dusky and footpad-like fellows were hovering near me, I turned and walked away.

On this my three shadows came gliding close behind me. Placing a hand in the hilt of my rapier, I stepped on a little way, but growing tired of being dogged thus, I turned boldly and confronted them. They were tall, stout men in buff coats, each with a case of Scottish pistols in his belt, a good hanger by his side, and a black velvet mask on his face. All this was rather alarming for a lad of sixteen; but then I was bolder than I may have been in after years.

"God give you all good even, sirs," said I; 'but what seek you here?"

"Certes, my little man, the king's causeway is as free to us as it is to you," said one, gruffly.

"Pass on, then, and begone," said I, with rising anger.

"That will be as we, not as you, please." said another, whose voice did not sound unfamiliar to me; though, like his companions, he spoke with a strong West Highland accent.

"If you are bent upon a quarrel, sirs, you are come to the right quarter." said I, keeping my hand upon my bilbo, which was of matchless edge and elasticity; "but three men with swords and pistols might have had the courage to make the assault before my friends left me."

"Enough of this, my beau coq," said the first, with an insolent laugh, making a snatch at my hilt; "yield up that toasting-fork, or it will prove the worse for you."

But before the words were well out of his mouth, the said toasting-fork had flashed from its scabbard, and been run right through his better arm. Uttering a cry of rage, he drew, and with the blood dripping over his hand, fell furiously on me.

"Here's a coil with a vengeance!" exclaimed the second.

"A brave young hawk, though!" said the third, with a gruff laugh, as they also drew and surrounded me; but I defended myself with great vigour, shouting all the while—

"Hue and cry! armour—armour! murder and fire!"

On hearing this, and the clashing of swords, the window which had been closed so suddenly was dashed open, and William Linn and Patrick Oliphant, minus cloaks and ruffs, leaped out, with sword and dagger, to my aid.

"Fie, cowards—three to one!" they exclaimed, and bravely fell on, like gallant gentlemen; but, notwithstanding their skill and courage, their youthful strength could never compete with that of our taller assailants. Linn was hurled senseless to the ground, and the gallant young Master was run right through the body. I was so paralysed by this sudden and terrible catastrophe, that I forgot to defend myself; my antagonists passed my point, closed with me, and I was at once disarmed, knocked down and gagged by means of a scarf. My arms were then pinioned by a cord, and with great brutality I was dragged through an adjacent close towards the river.

Half stunned and wholly horrified, I was incapable of resistance, and believed that I was in the hands of mohawks or footpads, who might rob, strip, and then throw me, pinioned as I was, into the Clyde. A cold perspiration came over me, when, issuing from the gloomy street, they dragged me towards its bank, and I could see the lights in the Gorbals opposite, and the still, calm flow of the glassy stream, as it chafed against the piers of the ancient bridge, which was built by Bishop Rae, in 1345.

They came to the edge, and grasping me by the hands and heels, one said—

"Heave now, and with a will, sirs!"

"God help and receive me!" I cried, on finding myself thrown roughly—not into the river, as I expected—but into a boat. The assassins, for such I believed them to be, now leaped in after me.

"Dougal," said one, "whereabout is thy foster-brother's ship?"

"In the mid-stream," replied he whom I had wounded, and who sat growling and muttering in the stern, while the other two betook them to their oars, and pulled down the river among the shipping.

CHAPTER III.

"THE GOOD INTENT," OF GLASGOW.

A few strokes brought them alongside of a large merchant-ship, which lay in the mid-channel, with her sails loose and ready for sea.

My heart swelled within me, and I strove to burst the bands which confined my limbs, and to make one effort to free myself from these kidnappers.

"Ardmohr, has the blood ceased to flow from that arm of thine?" asked one, through his mask.

"Yea," replied he, who sat in the stern; "but I have lost more than the Lord Argyle can ever repay me for."

"Peace, fool—hush!" cried the other, placing a hand roughly over the speaker's mouth.

"By the God of Israel, you had better keep your hands to yourself, my Lord Lorn," exclaimed the wounded man, rising with sudden fury gleaming in his eyes, which shone like two red coals through the holes in his mask.

"Argyle, Lorn, and Ardmohr!" thought I: "these are name

to remember; now I know my enemies. Oh for a sword and one hand free, to kill them all."

By the seamen I was roughly dragged on board; then the boat was shot away from the vessel, and it disappeared in the midnight obscurity which involved the river and its shipping. Through the side-rail of the vessel, which, as usual then with merchantmen, was without bulwarks, I could discern the whins waving on the lonely Broomielaw, and the dusky outline of the High-street, the towers of the cathedral, and the spires of the Cross and Tron.

Perceiving that I was almost suffocated, one of the seamen, a rough fellow, muffled in a coarse gaberdine, relieved my mouth from the scarf which gagged it.

"Take thy last look of them, my braw lad,—spire and hill, bridge and river," said he, laying a heavy hand on my shoulder, for the next land thou seest will be the coast of Virginia, and the Cripple Creek, where the *lead mines* are. A fine place for malignants and enemies of the kirk to reflect on their errors and come to their senses."

" What ship is this—and what villain are you?"

" No villain at all, lookye, my young master, so you had better keep a civil tongue in your head, for I have a rope's end here, and the iron bilboes below. I am Duncan Campbell, captain and owner of this ship—the snow, *Good Intent*, pinck-built, as you may see, and carrying eight 12-pounders, with a crew of fifty men, in the Virginia trade, of which you will ken a wee bit mair, my braw lad, by this time twelvemonth. I fight my own way upon the high seas, and fear neither buccanier nor Beelzebub. Forecastle ahoy! Man the windlass forward there—heave short on the anchor."

My heart sank within me on finding that I was helpless and about to be kidnapped for the English plantations, and to be sold to that people as a slave, to work in their lead mines. Amid all my anxiety for myself I was not without sorrow for the two brave friends who had fallen in defending me, and who were then lying dead, perhaps in the Trongate.

Finding that it would be unavailing to storm and rail at fortune or my captors, I asked—

" Who were those that brought me here?"

" I know not," replied the skipper, looking aloft, and whistling.

" What! you know not the name of your rascally employers?"

" May be I do—and may be I dinna; but the least said is soonest mended—let fall the foretack there!"

" Fie upon thee for a dishonest knave—but shall I name them?"

" Square the yards and sheet home, my lads! name them? do so if you can," said he, with a grin under his broad bonnet.

"Argyle, your worthy chief, his son the Lord Lorn, and your foster brother, Dougal Campbell of Ardmohr."

"Where got ye this information?" he asked, with angry surprise.

"From their own lips, as one smote the other and they quarrelled."

"It is false, and you are a young fool," said he, angrily, and added to the seamen—"take him below; the chield's clean daft —so make him fast under hatch."

I was flung into a dark and dirty cabin, the close atmosphere of which was rendered more obnoxious by the combined odour of bilge water, tar, grease and rancid butter, ham and stale herrings, which prevailed there.

The tumult and bitterness of my thoughts confused me; my head swam, and my wrists and ancles were swollen and benumbed by their fastenings. Powerless and in the dark, I lay on the hard lower deck, just where the men of this ruffian skipper, the minion of some powerful enemy, flung me; while near, I heard the water rippling against the outer sheathing, and this, united to the creaking of the ship's timbers, announced that the *Good Intent* was under weigh, and dropping down the river on her voyage to the far and foreign plantations of Virginia.

Anger, fear, and mortification of the deepest and bitterest kind, filled my breast; and while I sorrowed for the poor old principal, whose kind face I might never see again, and sorrowed also for the sour visaged janitor Nehemiah Spreul, and for the solemn quadrangle, the dusky chambers and the quaint courts of the old university, which had been my home in infancy, I re-called all that was known of my mother's fate, and began to marvel within myself whether my present predicament had not some mysterious connexion with her terrible and obscure death? I thrust away the thought, it seemed too absurd. And yet, I had never wronged any man that I could remember of, and there was not one in the realm of Scotland who, I believed, could have an interest in my life or death.

Quarrels I had, of course, at times, in the College gardens or Glasgow Green; but they were only such as were fairly finished by a handy blow, or a bout with rapiers which were sheathed on the first blood being drawn. Save Oliphant, Linn, the princi-pal, and old Nehemiah or his gudewife, I had few friends to regret me; but I thought of them all with the keenest sorrow, and of the old haunts I might never see more; while every im-pulse of a nature generally just and generous, led me to resent and revolt from so atrocious an invasion of my personal rights and liberty; and the knowledge that every ripple over which the vessel glided was increasing the distance between me and my home, between me and freedom, between me and the chances of escape. roused within me an agony and emotion that were almost suffocating.

Some hours passed away.

I was still in darkness, and the silence on deck informed me that this ship—this infernal snow, the *Good Intent*—with her eight twelve-pounders, had no doubt waited for my being brought on board, and was now far down the river. I resolved for the hundredth time to make an effort to unfetter my stiff and swollen hands. How often had I attempted it already!

In vain I tugged and wrenched; I was powerless; my flesh was swollen and almost cut by the tightness with which the cords had been so barbarously drawn; but in my struggle I found that the knot had fortunately come round to the upper side, and at once I applied my teeth to it.

After an effort or two it began to loosen, and then my heart beat fast and wildly!

By my teeth alone I unfastened three tight knots, on this hard cord, and, though deadened and swollen, my hands at last were free! But I had still much to achieve. My powerless fingers long refused to untie the other end of this hateful cord which bound my ankles, for my assailants had trussed me up like a market calf on a carrier's cart.

At last I stood erect and stretched my limbs, and clenched my hands, while my chest expanded and my heart beat with the wildest emotions of anger, joy, anxiety, eagerness, and hope to baffle my tormentors. In the defence of my freedom, I felt myself equal to the achievement of anything, but how to leave the cabin in which I was confined, and how to quit the ship and reach the shore, from which she might be I knew not how far!

Groping in the dark, I felt with outstretched hands the bulkheads and sides of the little den into which I had been flung; and after stumbling over several barrels, boxes, and piles of Westphalia hams and Goudah cheeses, I discovered the sliding door of the cabin, and pushing it softly aside, found that it opened behind the companion ladder, *on which* (by the faint light of a lamp that swung in the cabin beyond) I could perceive a seaman armed with a poignard and cudgel, stretched at full length, with his feet planted on the deck.

On discovering this sentinel my hopes began to sink, and in my desperation I sighed for a weapon—anything from a claspknife to a Lochaber-axe—that I might encounter him. He was a powerful and muscular fellow, with a red snub nose and wide mouth surrounded by a forest of ragged hair. His brawny hands, with their swollen joints. resembled a bundle of hard

knots; and then the size and weight of the cudgel he carried
might have appalled any man.

His sturdy bulk occupied the entire breadth of the ladder,
which was the only means of access to the deck, and through the
open hatch above I could inhale the pure air of the river, and
see the blue stars shining aloft. The sky was yet dark, but
dawn could not be far distant.

A long-drawn snort announced that this well-whiskered
Cerberus was sound asleep; and, as there was not a moment to be
lost, I drew off my boots and slipped out softly, with a heart tremulous with anxiety and fear, for I felt myself so helpless and
unaided.

Climbing up the under side of the ladder, and clinging with my
hands, I soon reached the top, but in coming round to the upper
side I unfortunately planted my left foot full upon the up-turned
visage of the seaman, who uttered a cry, or something between
a snort and a roar, as he awoke in a moment, on being thrust at
full-length sprawling on the floor.

I now sprang up the companion-hatch like a hare; crossed
to the vessel's side by one bound, and, with a triumphant shout
of "Gloriat!" plunged headlong into the river.

CHAPTER IV.

THE CASTLE OF ARDMOHR.

I must have sunk to the bottom, and in a place where the water
is deep; but, notwithstanding the fierce excitement under which
I laboured, I preserved my breath for a few seconds, and after
swimming under water, as from childhood I had been an expert
diver in the pool near the green banks of the Broomielaw, I
rose to the surface more than a hundred yards from the *Good
Intent,* and luckily astern of her; thus the space between us
increased rapidly. So little did Dougal Campbell, her worthy
skipper, concern himself about my fate, that he neither burned a
light nor backed his mainyard, nor threw over a coop or spar to
save me, but bore on, with all his sails filled to the yardheads
by a soft east wind; and the ship loomed large between me and
the star-studded sky, while I floated for a time on the water to
recover my breath, to recal my energies, and to consider what
point of land to make for.

My position was a perilous one!

At this place I found the river more than four miles broad;
but, fortunately, the *Good Intent* had been steering close in on
the Argyleshire coast, and by the clear twinkling of the stars

aided by the pale yellow flush of dawn in the east, I could perceive the familiar outline of the hills which look down on the
Gairloch, and the light that burned on the topmost turret of the
ancient castle of Ardincaple, beaming afar off like a red spark
among the distant woods: and thus I knew that I was not more
than twenty miles from Glasgow.

In my inmost heart I thanked Heaven for my sudden and
glorious escape; but I was not yet safe, being a full mile from
the beach, and I might never reach it.

"Sink or swim," thought I, while striking boldly out for the
shore, "I'll make the effort; better drown at once in the dear
old Clyde than pine and die as a slave of the English planters in
Virginia."

The river was lonely, there were but few vessels on it, and
these were scattered far apart; the chill mist of November was
rolling on its surface, and its banks seemed dim and distant; but
a yellow gleam began to steal along the mountain tops, as the
morning light spread upward and the rays of the sun, though he
was yet far below the horizon, played in long and wavering lines
upon the ragged edges of the clouds.

I swam carefully and vigorously, husbanding my strength and
resting at times, but my progress was slow, and I felt my limbs
becoming chilled; occasionally I sank so low that the difficulty
of breathing became great, while my heart fluttered and there
was a cold, rushing wind in my ears. Meantime the warm
morning sun came up in his ruddy splendour; his red rays
pierced the dim November mist, and the river rippled around me
in long and glittering lines of light.

I still swam bravely on.

Afar off, abruptly cutting the line of the cold blue sky, rose
the rugged peaks of the Argyleshire mountains, with their dun
sides of heath, in some places already flecked by the snows of
the coming winter. In the foreground stretched a broad and
low peninsula, covered by thick dark pines or half stripped
coppice, above which, and jutting close upon the water, a
square baronial fortress reared its corbelled battlement above
the stone-coped towers of its barbican. To the westward lay
Roseneath, clothed with mountain firs, and half veiled in summer
haze.

I frequently waved a hand above my head, and sent a shout
for aid across the shining water, in the desperate hope that some
one in this lonely castle on the promontory might see the signal
or hear the cry: but the former was unseen, and the latter too
faint to obtain attention; yet I could perceive figures moving
about on the green sward before the gate, though the hour was
early, and the dark smoke of the freshly-heaped fires rolled in

dusky volumes from the great square chimneys of the kitchen, the bakehouse, and hall.

Power was passing away from me, and I was only a pistol-shot distant from the shore!

Finding myself half blind and exhausted, the dread of drowning, the despair of dying when so close to the beach, became strong within me. This extreme sense of danger served, I fear, to lessen my energies; so sighing forth a last faint cry to Heaven for mercy and to man for help, the water closed above me; there was a terrible rushing in my ears, and all became darkness and oblivion in a moment.

I must have lost my senses for a time.

On again becoming conscious I found my head above water, and felt the great rough paws of some animal paddling beside me, while its hot, panting breath fanned my cheek; and in half a minute more I was drawn over the gravelly beach. Desperately I clung to it and drew myself close up, while my preserver, a stalwart Highland stag-hound, shook the water like mist from his shaggy grey coat, and barked and bounded about me with delight.

I soon recovered, and staggered up. At a short distance rose the barbican and square tower of the fortalice—a grim-looking place, all loopholed for musketry, with windows heavily grated on every side, and six pieces of cannon frowning over the gate and river. Close by were pines and copsewood growing to the water edge, and near me was a young girl about seventeen, whose rank was announced by the fashion of her dress, which was one of those enormous piked boddices then in fashion, with the high, rough, and stiff-brocaded skirt. These had been quite the rage since Henrietta Maria brought them among us.

She was without a head-dress, having apparently just run out of the barbican wicket, which was wide open, and she stood irresolute whether to address me or take to flight; for the sudden apparition of her great dog fishing a half-drowned person out of the river had scared the roses from her pretty cheek.

From me the dog now bounded to her, and bayed with his deep voice as he crouched beneath her tiny hand and licked it.

"Down, Corrie, down!" said she; and the noble dog wagged his long tail, and looked up in her face with his fiery hazel eyes full of intelligence. He was one of those gallant dogs which have been famous in the Scottish annals of the chase since the days of the King of Selma.

"But for your dog, sweet mistress," said I, bowing low with joy and gratitude, "I had never reached the land: to its efforts, and your most fortunate presence, I owe my life."

The young girl smiled, while the colour came and went in her rounded cheek; her dark hazel eyes filled with pleasure and pity, and she looked beautiful and graceful as a fairy, notwithstanding the enormous stays and fardingale in which her slender form was imprisoned.

"You must be weary, hungry, and cold," said she. "Come with me—breakfast is just over; but the butler and pantler shall attend you."

"Cold, wet, and weary, I am indeed; but I never was less inclined to eat in my life," I added, with a sigh of sorrow and bitterness, as I thought of my two friends, who had probably been slain in my defence; of all I had endured and all I had escaped overnight; and of the fine bilbo I had lost—for it was only procured by me after long and hard saving; and such was the turbulence of the time, and the rumours of strife then current, that I can assure thee, my friend and reader, that a good bilbo blade was a piece of valuable property to a poor bursar of Glasgow College.

"How came you, sir, to be swimming in the water?"

"I fell overboard from a ship," said I, cautiously.

"And did not the sailors stop their ship to pick you up?" she asked, while her large brown eyes dilated with fresh pity and wonder.

"No——"

"Cruel and wicked!" said she, as we entered the court of the castle, over the gate of which I observed a large coat of arms—the boar's head, and lymphads, carved. "Oh! pray tell me all about this."

"A great misfortune happened to me—a deadly wrong was done me overnight; but, please God, I shall yet be avenged!" I exclaimed, furiously.

The little lady shrunk from me.

"Oh! if you should be a malignant!" she exclaimed, eyeing me with an expression of fear.

"I might be worse, lady," said I; "for in my soul I have ever admired the high chivalry of those brave cavaliers of Montrose who are struggling for the king against our Scottish government."

"Worse—oh! who can be worse than a malignant?"

"A crop-eared English roundhead, or his canting Scottish comrade—God confound them both!" said I.

"Oh! hush," said she, in great terror, as we entered the hall; "surely you know not where you are!"

This exclamation made me silent; for my speech was both rude and unwary; but I was highly excited, and moreover rash.

A large fire was blazing on the hearth of the hall, and thus my wetted garments were soon dried. Food and a jug of spiced ale were set before me, and the old butler and pantler both grumbled under their beards because I fell to work upon their viands without the invariable preliminary of a long grace; and I am certain they used the (then) obnoxious term "malignant" more than once.

"Nay, nay," said I, "I am no malignant, but a half-famished student of Glasgow College. Believe me, carle butler, we seldom get such ale as this at the Auld Pedagogie."

"Then it deserves the better thanksgiving," snuffled the butler, who was a west-country Highlander. "God forgie us our sins and bless our enemies!"

"Bless your own, if you please," said I; "but I reserve to myself the privilege of wishing mine in Heaven, or *elsewhere* forth the kingdom of Scotland."

"Nurse vengeance against none," continued the other, turning up the whites of his eyes with that absurd affectation of devotion with which all men had now become affected.

"Trust me, master butler, I will nurse it—yea, foster it as the only property I possess—yet I am no malignant—and one day I shall have the full measure of it."

"How much may that be, my young birkie?" asked the pantler.

"Four feet, eight inches."

"How——"

"The length of my bilbo—a good blade—lost last night in the streets of Glasgow in an encounter with three villanous kidnappers."

"Malignants, doubtless—excommunicated of God and kirk. Alake! sirs, the land is fu' o' them; for it hath pleased Heaven to sow many tares among the wheat."

"Another farl of cakes, and please to fetch me one more jug of ale. Many thanks, good butler; I have made the repast of a king."

At last I was satisfied with a meal which my pretty little hostess had superintended. The fragments were removed, and I was commanded to appear before the lady of the fortalice in her own chamber, as she was anxious to hear all about me. I would rather have spent an hour with my charming young friend in the long boddice, for her prattle had delighted me during my repast; while I envied the great rough dog Corrie, on whose shaggy neck she nestled her bright face and soft curling hair.

"And who is the noble lady by whom I am so honoured, and who seeks this interview?" I asked.

"The Lady of Ardmohr," said my little protectress.

"The lady who?" I repeated, in a breathless voice.

"Do you not know where you are?" she asked, while laughing

~ my bewilderment. "Are you unaware that this is the castle of Colonel Dougal Campbell, of Ardmohr? Did you not observe the lymphads and the boar's head of *the Great Clan* above the gate? Well, 'tis his mother who wishes to hear your story."

I stood silent and confounded.

"Do you not hear me?" asked the young girl with winning kindness, as she took my hand in hers.

"Yes—oh! yes—and the Laird?"

"Is gone with the Lord Argyle to a meeting of the General Assembly; but he will return *to day*—indeed, the lady looks hourly for her son."

Here was a pleasant piece of intelligence!

"What is your name, sweet lady?"

"Flora."

"Flora—Flora; I shall ever remember it!"

"And yours, sir?"

I dared not answer, and so I asked—

"Is Ardmohr your father?"

"No," she replied, with a proud smile; "my father is the chief of greater men than he."

"Thank Heaven! he is not your relation."

"Who—Ardmohr?"

"Yes."

"But why?"

"Because I hate him!"

"Hush! here is his mother—*my aunt.*"

I found myself in a dangerous vicinity, and so intense was my anxiety to begone, that I have but a faint recollection of what followed.

I can remember, however, finding myself before a thin and grim-looking gentlewoman, clad in a sad-coloured velvet sacque. She sat in a high-backed chair, with silver barnacles on her hooked nose, and the Pastor of Kilwinning's recent work upon the "Vnlawfulnesse and Danger of Limited Episcopacie," before her. Her whole aspect was as stern, grave, and antiquated as that of her chamber, which was hung with dark and faded arras. She asked me innumerable questions, and inquired particularly about the state of my soul, and my ideas of doctrine. She then requested me to join her in prayer for my enemies, which I flatly refused to do; and after submitting to a great deal of perplexing curiosity and trembling at every sound, lest it might be her devil of a son returned; after telling twenty stories to deceive her, I thanked Heaven when I found the barbican gate of Ardmohr shut behind me; and after kissing the pretty hand of the hazel-eyed Flora, found myself away on the high road to Glasgow, though minus bonnet, sword, cloak, and purse. But what mattered these? I was free, unfettered, and with a whole skin.

CHAPTER V.

THE COURT OF THE LORD RECTOR.

In this unpleasant plight I travelled on foot towards Glasgow, by the road which crosses the Leven at Dunbarton, and carefully avoided every man I saw on horseback, lest he might prove to be this Laird of Ardmohr, who took such an unwarrantable interest in my affairs, and of whom I had a wholesome dread, and against whom I cherished no small amount of cordial hatred; for although I was altogether unconscious of having wronged him, I had suffered deeply at the hands of him and of those who were leagued with him. Being but a boy, my passions, at all times easily roused, were almost ungovernable in this matter; yet among my chief regrets were the loss of my daintily-laced cloak and steel-hilted rapier.

These sorrows were somewhat alleviated, when, on my reaching the university about night-fall, I found the missing articles hanging on their pegs as usual in my chamber, having been found by the civic guard—a patrol of thirty armed burghers, whose duty it was to watch the streets—and by whom my two gallant companions, Linn of Linn, and the Master of Oliphant, had been borne to their lodgings, and had their wounds (happily they were only wounded) bound up and attended to.

A fight in the streets with sword and dagger, between two or more gentlemen; or a skirmish with muskets and pistols, axe and claymore, between two adverse families, clans, parishes, or towns—in short, any species of squabble, however noisily and blood-thirstily maintained, was a matter of comparatively little moment in my young days; for all Scotland was in arms, as the reader will soon be informed. Thus, when a brawl took place overnight, the dead were buried in the morning, and swords were carefully wiped, and buff coats hung up; and until another fray ensued, the good men of Glasgow thought no more on the subject.

But the reverend principal, who had long been severe upon me for what he was pleased to term my " godless, shameless, malapert, and hellicate course of life," had all the particulars of the late brawl sifted by the lord rector's court, which was solemnly assembled a day or two after, and it sat in awful state, with long visages, black caps, and black gowns, the lord chancellor, the lord rector, the dean, principal, lecturers, and all, placed row above row, with all their taciturnity and inquisitorial terror to awe a poor scapegrace into a state of nonentity.

They met in the public hall of the college.

This apartment, which occupies the middle story of the street front, is of great length and solemn aspect, being pannelled with oak blacker than ebony, and deriving an additional shade of gloom by the faintness of the light that struggles through the ponderous framework of its windows, which overlook a quaint and narrow thoroughfare. Above the chair of the chancellor were the arms of the college—viz., a crowned mace, with a bell on one side and a tree on the other, having a bird in its branches; in base, a salmon with the ring of King Ewen in its mouth, and everywhere was emblazoned the motto *Via Veritas Vita*.

Feeling conscious that I was the injured party, it was with no small emotion of wrath I found myself arraigned a prisoner before this rectorial court, every member of which was prepared to prejudge and punish me, almost without a hearing; but I was at great pains to smother the spirit of rebellion that glowed within me.

The worthy old principal Zephaniah Bogle, without asking for my defence, after accusing me of general misconduct, of bullying the citizens on the Green, and kissing sundry honest women at various times, of which they had authentic evidence, and of fighting like a footpad or lawless Highland limmer in the public streets, gave me a grave and solemn harangue, interlarded with many scriptural quotations and metaphors, informing me that I was a brand foredoomed to the burning; one of the seed that had fallen on barren places; one of the many tares among the good wheat; and that if ever again my name was brought before the lord rector, either through my own misconduct, or by the misconduct of others, I should be stripped of my gown, and cast forth as one beyond redemption.

"Instead of Christian meekness and godliness," said the chancellor, "your mouth is filled with idle laughter and profligate songs."

"Lay to heart the words of the blessed psalmist, thereanent," began the lord rector.

"'They that sow in tears shall reap in joy,'" quoth the dean, taking up the quotation.

"Study the 'Battel of the Soule,' or the 'Canterburian's Self-Conviction,'" said the senior professor; "for by my troth, young birkie, your conduct better beseemeth a bellicate malignant of the Lord Montrose than a God-fearing lad, whom our worthy principal designeth for the sacred office of the ministry."

"True, true," added the principal; "but, to my sorrow, he hath become a haunter of taverns, a ruffler, a dancer, and a bully."

"Thou shouldst go to rest with the sun and rise with him," said the senior lecturer, taking up the burden of this objurgatory cantata; "all the philosophers of the ancients—all the great and learned of Athens, Egypt, and Judea—even Solon and Lycurgus, went to bed betimes."

"The rules which suited a couple of dull-witted pedants like Solon and Lycurgus, wont suit a student of St. Mungo," said I, losing all patience. "Moreover, the ancients of Athens and Judea, with all their rules, were a set of blockheads, who may go to the devil for me!"

The old blackcaps frowned terribly at this irreverend remark, which was deemed rank heresy; but I found it beyond all endurance to be assaulted, sword-in-hand, in the street; to have my two companions run through the body; to be bound with cords, and flung, like a bale of cotton, into a ship's hold; narrowly to escape kidnapping, more narrowly to escape drowning, and then to be rebuked in this fashion.

"My lords and reverend sirs," said I, swelling with passion and grief, "I have done no wrong; and he who says so lies! I never liked my studies, though I have fought my way from class to class, and from honour to honour, because my pride revolted at being beaten in anything by clodpoles whom I despised; but I am sick of cant and sick of hypocrisy; hence will I rather hang myself than study divinity, as I have no more vocation for the ministry than I have for becoming a Brahmin."

All started to their feet at these words; the chancellor, the rector, the principal, the dean, the six professors, and the six lecturers, as if appalled and confounded by my contumacy; for this court had the power of imprisonment, life and death.

I was scared by my own boldness in braving them. I remember only an indistinct muttering, and seeing two-and-thirty indignant eyes, scowling at me under sixteen black caps; and perceiving the hand of the lord rector stretched out, as he sentenced me to close and solitary confinement on bread and water during the pleasure of the court; and in an hour thereafter, I found myself in a small and gloomy apartment overlooking the pleasure ground, which sloped down to the brink of the Molindinar burn, and had a few scattered trees, partly blighted and blackened by the smoke of the city; for although the population was then only fourteen thousand in number, it was a busy one.

The sloping ground was the garden of the college.

A truckle bed with a mattress lay in one corner of my new apartment; a fauldstool stood in another; and on a stone shelf stood a black jack full of pure water as my beverage, and a Breeches Bible for my perusal.

The window was so small, and so high from the ground, that it was left ungrated; a pear tree trained up the wall spread its

half leafless branches round it.   Opposite were the spires of the
cathedral and the wooded brow of the Fir Park, which rose above
the straggling dwellings of the Drygate, and shone in the warm
glow of the setting sun.

Weary with all I had undergone, separated from my two
wounded friends, who had been conveyed to their own homes
(one to Perthshire, and the other to Lothian), I endeavoured to
forget my loneliness, my wrongs, and sorrows, and stretching
myself on the pallet, strove to sleep, or, boy like, to remember in
dreams only the sweet little maid of Ardmohr.

But events which succeeded soon obliterated *her* from my
memory.

CHAPTER VI.

BREAD AND WATER.

OLD Nehemiah Spreul, who acted as my jailor, one night, when
bringing to me the usual supper, a half bannock of barley-
meal, and a jack filled with water, made those inquiries into the
recent brawl, which the rector's court considered itself too lofty
to make.

"I have three enemies — the Earl of Argyle, his son, the
Lord Lorn, and the Laird of Ardmohr;—three Campbells : men
whom I never wronged," said I, passionately; "but I shall
slay them all, Nehemiah, for the manner they have invaded my
liberty, and the deadly wrong they have done me."

At this time, the name of Argyle in Scotland was armed with
as many terrors as ever that of Cromwell bore in England;
and the cynical Nehemiah, while he smiled at the idea of that
powerful western lord finding an object for his wrath in a
poor bursar of Glasgow, nevertheless was terrified by my vehe-
mence, for in Scotland, he who doubts the purity, probity, and
righteousness of the house of Argyle, does not believe in heaven.

The pertinacity with which I adhered undeviatingly to my
own story, did not fail to impress the old man at last, and he
inquired,—

"Did the Master of Oliphant hear their names?"

"No."

"Why?"

"He was left bleeding and senseless on the causeway.   Poor
Patrick Oliphant!"

"Or the young Laird of Linn?"

"No; he, too, was stretched upon the street, and it was only
when my foul abductors quarrelled among themselves, and when

Lorn rashly smote Ardmohr upon his black masque, that I learned who they were."

"Weel, then, tak' ye an auld man's advice, Harry Ogilvie; be silent, and mairatour be wary in this matter, for ye are owre unfriended to enter the lists against one wha is esteemed the greatest peer in Scotland and the starkest pillar o' her kirk."

"The hypocrite! In what way can a poor lad like I have crossed the path or purpose of one so great, so rich, so titled, and so powerful?"

"Remember the affront anent black-eyed Mally and the five guineas," whispered Nehemiah, glancing stealthily about, for the name of Argyle was too terrible and too sacred to be treated of lightly; "he is ane Hielandman, and of course never forgets or forgies an affront."

"I tell you, Nehemiah," I exclaimed, starting up in a fresh gust of passion, "I will have the lives of both Argyle and Lorn if they set on me again!"

"Alake, puir laddie!" replied the janitor, shaking his white head, and smiling; "what can you essay against the powerful lord, who crushed the great Montrose, who burned the house of Airlie, who destroyed the Earls of Hartfell and Findourie, and by ae wag o' his finger cut the head off the commissary o' Dunkeld? Bairn, ye are as ane who is daft."

I was silent, for the truth of this speech oppressed me; my neart was full of wrath at the strange magnitude of the punishment projected for a wrong so trivial, as the scene which had occurred so long ago in the grammar school; and, moreover, I was exasperated by the injustice and severity of the rectors, and resolved to desert the university on the first convenient opportunity. I had long considered the necessity of this movement, but my window was too high from the ground, and I was not so lost to all sense of decency or gratitude as to lay violent hands on old Nehemiah, my first patron and second father, when once in each day he brought me the meagre fare prescribed for me by the sour-featured whigs of the rector's court.

Day after day passed monotonously away, and I begged hard that a few books might be given me, to lighten the tedium of the weary hours which were passed in watching the smoke curling from the blackened chimnies of the Drygate, or the shadows changing on the cathedral spires and the banks of the Molendinar burn; but the answer I invariably received was, that my Bible was with me, and I required no other book.

My pertinacity, however, induced Nehemiah to apply to the librarian in my behalf, and one day, to my joy, he returned with an armful of volumes, on which I sprang with delight, and opened in succession; but, alas! they consisted only of the current literature of that godly epoch.

"What is this?" I asked, with strong disgust. "'An Antidote against Arminianisme.' Tut! The next, 'Anabaptisme the True Fountaine of Independencie;' the next, 'A Shove to Heavy-Doupit Christians;' 'Zion's Flowers, or Christian Poemes for Spiritual Edification;' 'The Last Battel of the Soule.' Grant me patience! Dost thou think I am mad, Nehemiah Spreul?" I exclaimed, flinging them all about the room. "Away with all this rubbish to the snuff-wife, and if the rector will not let me have the 'Hundred Merry Tales,' 'Blind Harry's Wallace,' 'Ovid,' or 'Amadis de Gaul,' he may go to Jehanum and be hanged to boot, for a sulky old bear!"

Nehemiah gave me a long and grave look, expressive of indignation at the profane literature I preferred to the sanctified armful he had brought me; and respectfully picking up the volumes, he groaned in spirit, and withdrew. Whether or not he delivered my impudent message, I cannot tell; at all events, no other books were sent me, and I had no other resort for amusement than to watch the sun rise and set, or listen to the eternal croaking of the venerable colony of rooks, which cawed in the trees behind the college, where they had probably been since the days of Bishop Turnbull, for crows, we are told by some naturalists, will live for two hundred years, and all the world knows of the deep-witted savan who put one in a cage to test the fact.

With a piece of chalk I caricatured the chancellor, rector, and the six professors on the four walls of my chamber, giving them all an amplitude of nose, with learned scrolls, tobacco-pipes, and tavern jokes issuing from their mouths; but I gained nothing by this display of spite and artistic skill, save an additional month's imprisonment, and thereupon reflecting seriously that I had been already caged up about six weeks, I began strictly to reconnoitre the window, and finding the pear tree stout and tough, and that its branches were firmly nailed to the wall, I conceived the possibility of levanting in the night, when suddenly I discovered a species of solace which made my imprisonment a *little* more endurable.

Winter had come, and departed early.

It was now the first month of spring, when the soft influence of that delightful season makes the heart expand, we scarce know why. But man rejoices when the green buds burst, when the bright flowers open their cups to the sun, the trees put forth their tender leaves, and at early dawn and dewy evening the birds sing on every hedge and spray, for their happy voices are the heralds of the opening year. of the coming summer, and the glowing harvest. I am inclined to linger a little over these early recollections, as the reader will have enough of the incidents of war, the march, the battle, the siege, and the sack ere long.

Well—it was gentle spring, and the mavis and merle, the joys of the copsewood, filled the air with melody. I was seated at my open window, weaving plans for the future, and building castles in the air, when the voice of a young girl singiug in the garden below arrested my attention, as it was very unusual to hear a merry lilt now in the oppressive atmosphere of godliness that surrounded me. She was culling flowers immediately under my window, and singing a lively air; then she paused, and began a slower and an older song,—

> " There was a fair May, and to milking she went,
> With her red rosy cheeks and her coal-black hair"—

Here she paused again; so I finished the stanza.

> " And she met a Black Dragoon riding over the bent,
> With a double and adieu to thee May fair !"

She started, and looked upward, while something of alarm blended with merrimeut in her pretty face.

This young girl was charming !

A mass of wavy chesnut hair shaded her soft and sweetly feminine face; she had a bright Aurora smile, and grace in all her motions. On her head, and jauntily tied on one side, was a very small but conical hat, of a fashion much worn by ladies of the Puritan party. She wore a long boddice of dark blue velvet, sleeved to the wrist, while her ruff came close round her throat. I was just about to open the trenches by some pretty compliment, when, after looking timidly and hurriedly about her, she said,—

"So, so, sir, you are Mr. Ogilvie, the wild student, who has been warded by the rector's court."

"Because he escaped being killed in the streets," said I; "exactly, madam; I am that distinguished personage, and your very humble servant. But I cry you mercy; surely I do not look so *very* wild ?"

"No, in sooth, you look rather pale; but you must have beeu very wicked to incur the anger of the doctors of the university."

"Not at all; one has only to be jolly, to have them as enemies for life."

"And you offended my good uncle, the principal, in particular."

"So, my pretty one, you are the principal's niece. Would to heaven he were my uncle! I am not wicked," said I, in my most insinuating tone, and quite delighted to find this sudden aud charming acquaintance likely to be further developed; "but I shall ever deem myself most unhappy if my unfortunate position lowers me in the estimation of one so kind and so beautiful."

She bowed and blushed at this compliment.

"And it was you," she continued, "who wrote the strange essay on love, was it not?"

"Yes, and I now know practically that the heart is the true seat of the passion."

She blushed again, and stooped over the flower-bed.

"And so you are the niece of my dear friend, Doctor Zephaniah Bogle?" I asked.

"Yes, the daughter of his sister."

"And your name is—"

"Margaret Muir."

"What!" I exclaimed, with well-feigned astonishment, "are you that beautiful and amiable Margaret Muir, of whom I have heard so much?"

"Yes," she replied simply, though I had never heard of her until that moment, but was resolved to make the most of the occasion. "But now I must go."

"Ah, why?"

"Lest I am seen speaking with you."

"And whom will it concern if you are seen?"

"I fear you are very wicked and wild, like all students."

"I assure you, on my honour, that I am not," said I, with great earnestness; "I am mild as a lamb, if I only get my own way."

"Why, then, are you here?"

"Because, as I told you, I narrowly escaped, firstly, being run through the body; secondly, being kidnapped; and thirdly, being drowned;—three heinous crimes in the eyes of our wise senators. I know of no other reason."

"A strange one truly," said she, laughing and moving away.

"Ah, don't leave me yet awhile," said I; "I am very lonely, caged up here in this dam—I mean dreary room; but you will come hither and speak with me sometimes, will you, dear Madame Margaret?"

"Perhaps," said she, as she kissed her hand with a kind but waggish smile, and hastened down the garden walk, where I saw her join the solemn, sombre, and portentous Zachary Boyd, who was sitting under a yew tree, with his sturdy legs, which were cased in black silk breeches, crossed one over the other, and twirling his thumbs, with his eyes turned upward, and his thoughts exalted above all sublunary things.

Taking her little white hand in his huge rough paw which

had never known a glove, he kissed it and led her away between
the thick hedges, which grew in long, shady, and close-clipped
rows in the old college garden.

"What the deuce does *he* want with her?" thought I; "he
will bore the poor girl to death with his 'Last Battel of the
Soule,' no doubt."

I watched anxiously for my new friend next day, and much
about the same hour she appeared in the garden, as she seemed
very fond of flowers, and particularly of those which grew under
my window. We conversed on various subjects, and always
recurred to ourselves as the most pleasant we could discourse
upon. I paid her innumerable compliments, and declared that
if she did not contrive some means to procure me a stout rope,
by which I might be enabled to drop from my apartment, I
would fling myself out at her feet, and then she would have my
death to answer for. At this she laughed merrily, and affected
to busy herself with her flowers, while singing of the Fair May
and the Black Dragoon who interrupted her milking.

Again and again she came, and my prison became alternately
more bearable or insupportable, according to the visions love and
ambition kindled in my boyish heart; for these two emotions
almost deprived me of sleep, and my enthusiastic mind became
inflated by new hopes and a new ardour, and fell into tender and
undefinable reveries.

I began, as usual, to erect various handsome fabrics in the
air; I recalled all that I had read in romances bearing on my
case; I remembered the Knight's tale in Chaucer, where Palamon
and Arcite fall in love with Émilia, whom they saw in the garden
of their prison; and I thought of Scotland's royal bard, the
captive James, and the fair "young floure" of Windsor, the beautiful Jane Beaufort; and so finding the cases all parallel, I made
up my mind to fall in love with Maggie Muir, and did so accordingly.

The manners and spirit of this young creature, who could **not**
have been more than my own age, were very winning. My
mind became full of her; and in my dreams her bright sunny
face came before me, and I thought all the happiness of earth
would be concentrated in one kiss of her ripe and pouting lips.

We soon fall in love at the age I was then, and though we
just as soon fall out of it again, we love with great ardour and
enthusiasm while the passion lasts.

I know not whether the pretty Margaret guessed my secret,
for I dared not tell her—as a love declaration would be sadly
deficient in point if delivered over a third story window—but
my eyes must have told all that my lips dared not utter; besides,
she laughed so much when I paid her insinuating compliments,

that the stolid gravity she displayed when with the ponderous author of the "Last Battel of the Soule," on whose arm I saw her leaning daily, was, I am sure, all assumed. The pretty little hypocrite!

My new passion conflicted with my anxiety to revenge myself upon the Rector's Court by leaving the college with all its learned lumber, and plunging into the whirl of life that lay beyond its walls; for within the shaded courts of old St. Mungo the world seemed to stand still, and the clocks to forget to strike.

If once beyond the precincts, I could easily contrive means to see and converse with the pretty Margaret, who was far too attractive to be in the immediate vicinity of so many enterprising youths as are usually to be found about a university.

CHAPTER VII.

A USE FOR A PEAR TREE.

I NOW bethought me of the long-forgotten pear tree, which grew up to my window, and which I thought was sufficiently strong to *bear* me, though heavier than the jargonelles it usually bore; and I knew that, if once in the garden, I would place the wall of the precincts and the waters of the Molendinar burn between me and the petty tyrants of the rector's court in less than three minutes.

My window was on the third story of the buildings; it was a dormer rising above the slates, and surmounted by a pediment full of grotesque carvings; its sill was about five and twenty feet from the ground; so, one night in March, after Nehemiah had locked me up and deposited the black jack of water and invariable half bannock, I resolved to essay the long-cherished attempt to escape, and raised my window with an agitated heart.

The night was dark and stormy; thick masses of cloud floated rapidly across the sky, and red lightning was gleaming beyond the spires of the cathedral, and flashing for a moment on the windows of the quaint university, the buildings of which were buried in dusky obscurity, save where an occasional ray glimmered through a half-closed window, as if to indicate where some student or professor yet lingered over the incubrations of the learned, or it might be his bowl of Glasgow punch.

The clock in that tall square tower which stands between the outer and inner quadrangle, and has so much of the gothic character in its belfry and balustrade, struck ten; and after the last note died away, I heard only the soughing of the wind as it shook the old trees, and moaned in the courts and arcades of the college.

I passed through the narrow window with ease. I caught the topmost branches of the stout tree, which was so carefully trained against the wall by the principal (who had a mighty love for fine and luscious jargonelles), and the branches, as they stood straight out on each side, formed an easy and convenient ladder; thus, while descending with every safety and facility, I blamed my own timidity which had delayed an escape so long.

As I passed—softly, of course—the window of the chamber below the one I had left, a light shining through the half-parted shutter prompted me to peep in, and I saw—what?

My pretty Margaret in the most seducing little nightcap, under which all her chesnut hair was smoothly braided; her fine bust divested of the high ruff and hideous stomacher, and two plump, white, dimpled arms placed behind her, as she was in the act of unlacing her stays, and singing all the while to herself like a linnet.

I was escaping—going away to begin a life of wandering, of vagabondism perhaps, and I might never see her more. To resist the desire, or let pass the opportunity of speaking with her, were impossible, and quietly raising her window I pushed one shutter open.

Intent upon her song, and on regarding the charming vision of herself as revealed in the mirror, she heard me not. Raising higher the sash, I entered softly, and noiselessly approached her. Then I paused, and trembled at my own temerity, for I had never been so near her before, and never touched her.

"Margaret," said I, in a subdued voice.

She uttered a half-suppressed cry of terror and sprang away, alarm and astonishment impressed on her pretty face; but before she could reach the door my hand was round her soft warm neck, and I implored her to pardon and to hear me; "for never again," said I, "will my voice fall on your ear."

"But say, sir—madcap or worse—what brings you here, like a thief in the night, into my room—my bedchamber? If you are seen—if we are overheard—"

"I cannot be seen, nor shall we be overheard; but we must speak low. I am escaping, Margaret, and going—"

"Where?"

"Alas! I know not, for I have neither home nor hold—kith nor kin—in all the wide, wide world that is before me; and I could not depart, perhaps never to see you more, without—"

"What, sir—what?" said she, blushing and throwing a garment over her white shoulders.

"Without telling you in plain words, that which I dared not do before—that I love you—love you very much—oh, I cannot say how much!" I continued, trembling, for this was the honest

avowal of a boy's impassioned heart.   "Oh, yes, dear Margaret,"
I continued, slipping my arms round the fine figure which the
half-laced boddice yet compressed, and which I felt palpitating
under my embrace; "one kiss, Margaret—only one!"

"Oh, Harry Ogilvie," she whispered, blushing crimson as my
trembling lips were pressed to her beautiful shoulder, and my
heart seemed leaping to my mouth.

"Margaret, you are a sweet, sweet tempter."

"Oh, do not—do not speak to me of love," she exclaimed,
repelling me with both her hands; "see how I am trembling all
over, Harry—in pity go away.   I am promised to—"

"To whom?" I demanded.

"Zachary Boyd."

"To Zachary Boyd—*you?*"

"Yes," said she, casting down her fine eyes with a coy smile
of sadness.

"Impossible! impossible! you cannot mean it."

"It is so—but why impossible?"

"Is he not old, and starched, and grim, and gloomy, with all
his musty quotations and devilish *Battel of the Soule!*"

"To me he is young and beautiful," said Margaret, pouting.

She was sitting on the edge of her little bed, and was endeavouring to refasten the string of her boddice, but her rosy fingers
trembled very much.

Her neck, her arms, and ancles were perfection.

"Oh, Margaret," said I, "this is both absurd and terrible."

"To me," she replied, with downcast eyes, "to me his gloom
is piety; his grimness the decent gravity which becometh a
minister; but doubtless you would have me to marry a bullyrook
student—a ruffling gallant, like—"

"Like myself, dear Margaret," I added, forgetting, alas! that
I was only a lad, and had not a tester in the world.

"Now do not come near me again, but go," she said, imploringly; "go, before your discovery here ruins us both—or
me at least; for who would protect me then?"

"One so gentle and so modest as you, Margaret, requires no
other protection than her own purity."

"Grant me mercy, sir, what would my uncle think—oh, heavens! let go my waist—what will the people say?"

"Ah, why were you thrown like a temptation in my path?"
said I, giving way to an irrepressible gush of sadness, and feeling
piqued, as most men do, to find a pretty girl placed beyond my
reach.

"My uncle the principal would never believe that I could love
a student—a mere boy."

"Why not, Margaret—you are but a girl?"

"It matters not now; I have given my troth-plight, and by Lammas-tide shall wed."

"Alas, that you should tell me so."

"I am sorely grieved for you, poor Harry Ogilvie; but what I have undertaken, that will I perform. The minister, Zachary, was kind as a son to my poor mother, after my three dear brothers were killed by the English at the battle of Newburnford. He nursed her on her death-bed, and when dying, she placed my hand in his. I was very sad and heartbroken, but kind Zachary in his own quaint way consoled me, and taught me to remember that my good mother was not lost, but only gone before me, to the place where we must all follow her. So, since then, he has been father, brother, and lover, all in one to me; but pardon me, Harry, do these tidings make your heart heavy?"

"Yes—heavy as lead, sweet Margaret; yet it feels lighter by the avowal I have made you. I could not have gone forth with the untold secret, that I loved you, in my breast."

"And where are you going, Harry?" she asked, anxiously.

"Alas—I know not—I am but a bubble on the current of events; a poor waif on the shores of time! I go to France to fight the Imperialists and Lorrainers—or, it may be, to the Lowlands of Holland, for I must become a soldier now, Margaret, a wandering soldier of fortune. The battlefield is the poor Scotsman's best inheritance."

Her eyes filled with tears.

"Poor Harry Ogilvie!" said she.

"Give me one parting kiss, Margaret," said I, full of tenderness, for love begetteth love, and my lonely heart yearned unto all who were kind to me, "one only, and I will go, never again to cross your path, but with the earnest prayer that every blessing may attend you."

She seemed to think there was no harm in granting my gentle request, and bent her flushed face towards me. I pressed my lip to her cheek; she was the first woman I had ever kissed (in solemn earnest, at least), and throwing an arm round her, I was about to steal one more, when—O, horror! close by us towered the dark figures of the principal and Zachary Boyd, clad in their sad-coloured doublets and Geneva cloaks, their faces begrimed by snuff, by wrath and righteous indignation at such unholy proceedings; for, in those days of excessive godliness, when Argyle was king of the western Pharisees, it was an awful violation of propriety to kiss a pretty girl at any time; but such an act perpetrated in her own room, at midnight, was enough to rend the veil of the temple, and cause an earthquake in the land.

We had been too unwary, and our voices had awakened the curiosity of the two divines, who had been sitting cosily by the fire in an adjacent chamber, discussing the "Vnlawfulnesse of Episcopacie," through the mellowing medium of various tankards of mulled sack.

Poor little Margaret uttered a cry, as if caught in the commission of a crime, and covered her pale face with her hands.

Sternly the principal regarded us through his horn rimmed spectacles, and swelling with an indignation which was undoubtedly just,

"A red plague upon thee, Harry Ogilvie," he exclaimed, "what make ye here, sir?"

"Love," I was strongly tempted to auswer; but pity for Margaret, and the respect I had for the old man, repressed the spirit of mischief.

"I was escapiug, reverend sir, and coming down the pear tree, I missed my way, and am here."

"A sorry excuse; Harry Ogilvie, thou art a graceless villain!" exclaimed Zachary Boyd, in great wrath.

"And *thou*, minx," scowled the principal; "wherefore raised you not an outcry?"

"My dear uncle!" sobbed Margaret.

"Dear me not, madam! why—I shall choke! Oh, brother Zachary, this affliction came not out of the ground."

"Verily no," snarled Zachary; "for to you it came in at the window. Hear me, thou son of Judas——"

"Mr. Boyd," exclaimed Margaret, hysterically, through her tears; "he has done no harm, believe me—we were only conversing——"

"Very fine, madam—very fine!—sitting on the edge of your couch, with his arm round you—your shoulders bare, and a night coif on," continued Mr. Bogle; "is this becoming the child of him who was a minister of God's word? Doth it beseem my niece, or the betrothed of him who penned the " Last Battel of the Soule?"

"Oh, Maggie," groaned Mr. Boyd, reproach in his large eyes and in his deep voice; "is it modest or discreet?"

"Oh, mercy, sirs, have mercy!" sobbed the poor girl, wringing her hands, while I glanced once or twice at the window, thinking it high time to decamp.

"And what did this young ruffian tell thee?"

"That he loved me, dear uncle, that was all."

"Of course—of course."

"As if love could live in a godless heart," said Mr. Boyd.

"But *you*, Mr. Zachary, have told me the same thing a hundred times—that you loved me."

"Simpleton," thundered the principal, "he alone hath a right to do so; moreover, he visits by the door, and not by the lattice,

like a Hieland limmer or Border Hamesüken ; but come, sir, get
you gone, and to-morrow the lord rector's court——"

" Will find that I despise its authority, and will rather die
than submit to it again."

" We shall see, sir—we shall see," said the principal.

" And so you told her that you loved her, my young birkie,"
said Mr. Boyd, with a sour smile on his broad hard face ; " oh,
that I could smite thee, even as Paul smote Elymas !"

I cast down my eyes, being conscious that I had in some sort
wronged this good man too.

" Spoke ye of love ? speak, ingrate !" said the principal.

" Alas—yes."

" A strange love, yours, sir," said Mr. Boyd, with a mixture
of pity and spite in his tone ; " to take her away from the broad
bosom of an honest man and sincere Christian, who loved her
first ; who reared and tended her ; to take her from him, I say,
and to offer her the passing fancy of a rattle pated fop—poverty,
rags, dependence, and regret, in lieu of comfort, position, and
the happiness of a minister's manse. A black shame upon ye,
sir !"

" Reverend and well-beloved brother," groaned the principal,
" ye say well."

" Mr. Boyd," said I, thinking this scene had lasted quite long
enough ; " I can bear your reproaches, sir, because you are my
senior by many years, and are, moreover, an ordained minister of
God's word ; and I can bear *your* taunts, most reverend principal,
because you have been as a father, a protector, and a guide to me.
As such you shall ever hold an honoured place in my heart, and
deserve its warmest gratitude ; but never again will I submit to
the rules of the rector's court, and so must bid you all a kind
farewell. Good bye, dear Margaret—another time, perhaps, you
may hear of me, when fortune gives me a better coat than this
red gown, which here I solemnly bequeath to the devil !"

With these words I threw off my student's mantle, which was
of scarlet cloth.

" A long adieu," said I, and kissed Margaret again.

" Shoo—away with you !" cried Mr. Boyd, losing all patience
at this reiterated proceeding : and I sprang through the window,
descended by the pear tree into the gardens, passed through
them like a hare, cleared the wall of the precincts by one bound,
and soon placed the water of the Molendinar burn between me
and the towers and courts of the old university.

Thus, in one hour, I found myself without a home ; *sans* purse
and sword ; *sans* means of subsistence ; and, more than all, I
had lost my pretty mistress to boot.

A cold wind swept through the hollow ; the burn brawled

ever its stony bed; the sky was dark and dreary, for midnight
brooded over Glasgow and her slumbering thousands; but
darker and more dreary seemed the cloud that hovered on the
horizon of my fortunes, and my poor heart was full of dim forebodings.

CHAPTER VIII.

THE RECRUITING PARTY.

MORNING dawned on the grey cathedral city—a beautiful morning
of spring. The sky was serene, and the sunshine bright and
warm. Around me, the trees were budding, and the birds in full
song; but while my heart beat high with scarce known wishes,
and sighed for unattainable things, amid the gilded castles I
had woven in the air, and amid the joyous consciousness of that
perfect freedom which makes the soul of every youth expand
within him, it was not without its own fears for the future.

I found myself homeless, because I neither would nor could
return to college. I found myself penniless, because my sole
dependance had been on the liberality of the principal, and on
my bursary, which I had forfeited, or on the lecturers, when I
acted as their drudge and amanuensis, in writing their dreary
orations to dictation; I found myself friendless, because none
seemed to care for me now, so warped were the hearts of all who
knew me, by fanaticism and gloom, canting, prayer, and that
pharisaical pretence of meditation and sanctimoniousness, in
which all men imitated and strengthened each other.

Hence it was evident, that to one who was homeless, penniless,
and friendless, there was a necessity for immediate action.

William Linn of Linn, or the Master of Oliphant, would no
doubt have assisted and advised me; but I knew not where they
were, or whether they had survived those wounds received in my
defence, three months ago.

I had long wished to be a soldier, and my heart bounded with
a noble ambition to imitate the brilliant career of those Scottish
cavaliers of fortune who, under the banners of Gustavus Adolphus, of Christian IV., and of the Empire, had filled all Europe
with the fame of their exploits. Still more did I long to imitate
the daring chivalry of that small band of gallant clansmen, who,
under the baton of the great Marquis of Montrose, Captain-
General of Scotland, had routed the well-disciplined armies of
the Scottish Parliament at the decisive battles of Tippermuir
Aberdeen, and Fyvie; by the shores of the Lochy; at Auldearn,
Alford, and Kilsyth, until his star fell to rise no more in that
terrible cavalry engagement in the Vale of Philiphaugh. But

I had never dared to speak of this secret wish at the university; for there, the mighty marquis—the great cavalier—was stigmatised as a malignant and oppressor of the just in Israel. I had no money to take me abroad, and I knew no one who would give me letters to any of the Scottish gentlemen who commanded the armies of the Continent, or in Germany, where at that time sixty fortified cities were governed, and in many instances, garrisoned by Scots alone.

Fortunately for me, my native country had a strong and admirably well-organized army of her own, which for the last ten years had been commanded by field marshals the Earls of Leven and Callendar, who—as Patrick Gordon records—had brought back with them from Germany well-trained Scottish officers, sufficient to discipline a force of fifty thousand men; and this army had before it every prospect of a severe and protracted war. Thus I could not lack congenial employment long, or an opportunity for high enterprise.

Full of these thoughts, I wandered along the burnside, till I reached the Gallowgate, which was then bordered by a street of straggling houses, and by turning to the right I soon found myself amid the bustle of the sunny Trongate; and though I was without breakfast, and had not a halfpenny to procure one, my heart seemed to grow lighter as I repeated to myself, *I will be a soldier*, and strode along whistling the " Old Scot's march;" and Heaven that day opened up a brilliant path to me !

I had few sources of personal regret. I certainly deplored that the amiable old principal should think so vilely of me, and that, after all his kindness, we had parted in anger; but I was not without an emotion of spite and disappointment at the result of my affair with little Margaret Muir; but that soon passed away; for if she was a waggish girl who had trifled with me as a youth, it was that very youth which prevented me from suffering too deeply. Then, the only two comrades I ever had were gentlemen of family and estate, while I was but a poor bursar, whom perhaps they had forgotten already.

Dreamily I sauntered along the Trongate. It was fortunate that I had no appetite, for my hands went far into my pockets, and found nothing there.

It is a quaint street of old houses, of massive architecture. There the citizens of St. Mungo dwell, and have dwelt for ages, in peace and contentment—pleased with the same accommodation that pleased their frugal forefathers in the days of the third and fourth Jameses.

Near the Tron steeple I espied the Reverend Zachary Boyd stepping sedately along in his sad-coloured breeches, his sable Geneva cloak, and on his head a velvet calotte cap, from which his hair flowed lank and straight on his stiffened bands and collar; and I shrunk into a turnpike stair to avoid him, for in truth I felt somewhat ashamed to meet the good man face to face.

As usual at this hour—about nine in the forenoon—the street was crowded by the rich old mercantile noblesse of Glasgow: I mean that proud class which existed in those and other days, when they were generally the sons of westland lairds who had scrolls and scutcheons carved in stone above their dwellings in the Saltmarket, and who, in their prosperity, comported themselves with less of decent pride, perhaps, than courtly pomp.

They had a particular side of the Trongate left to themselves, and usually wore fine scarlet cloaks, trimmed with broad lace, doublets, and small clothes of Genoese velvet; and as they carried walking swords in silver sashes, and struck their gold-headed canes emphatically on the pavement, it was as much as any poor man's beef and bread—perhaps his bones—were worth, to presume to address or jostle them; and if a "puir buithhalder" (*i. e.*, shopkeeper) was accosted in the open street by one of these opulent traders with the English plantations or the far-off isles of the west, he was deemed a happy man for life, and in a fair way to fortune.

As I walked along, a new impetus was given to my thoughts by the sound of martial music; and then, surrounded by a dense crowd of gaping rustics and craftsmen, a party of troopers, with their helmets and cuirasses shining, and long rapiers glittering in the sun, wheeled round from the High-street and rode along the Trongate, with kettle-drums beating, their brass trumpets sounding, and long cockades of blue and white ribbons—the national colours—streaming from their plumes.

They were about forty in number, and were nearly all sergeants and corporals, being the staff of a cavalry regiment which had just entered Glasgow, beating up for recruits.

My heart bounded—it seemed to rise to my mouth with every blare of the glorious trumpet, every clash of the cymbals, and crash of the kettle-drums, and I scarcely knew where I was. The Trongate seemed to widen and the sky to brighten as the glow of military ardour kindled in my breast; and I marched with the troopers along the densely crowded and dusty streets, gazing on the novel sight with joy and hope.

They were all strong and soldierlike men; they rode powerful horses, and were completely accoutred after the fashion of our Scottish heavy dragoons at that time, with triple-barred helmets, gorgets, breast and back-pieces, pauldrons, plate-sleeves, gauntlets, and tassettes of black unpolished iron. Each had a good sword and pair of holster pistols, and a carbine, and was jack-

\..)sted to the thigh.   Each wore over his right shoulder a white
-carf.   Their horses had large black saddle-cloths, with the royal
crest of Scotland in the corner; and their whole aspect was
sombre, soldierly, and service-like.

The kettle-drums ruffled; tan-ta-ra-ra-ra went the trumpets;
the black horses paced proudly, and shook the white froth from
their fierce nostrils and chain bridles, as the troop drew up in line
near the cross; and after a flourish of music, Sergeant Gideon
Glanders rode to the front, and began a long and oily harangue,
full of the old staple promises of glory, glitter, and honour, not
forgetting Sir John Hepburn the musketeer, who became a
marshal of France, and John Middleton, once a pike-man, who
was then an earl and lieutenant-general of Scottish horse, a rank
attained by his own bravery and the glorious fortune of war.

The sergeant, who was a cunning and jolly fellow, with an
enormous moustache that stuck out in every direction, a red nose,
somewhat disfigured by a sword-cut, and carbuncular cheeks, the
result of good living, hard service, and hard drinking, gave
a flowery oration on the pleasure of riding a fine horse, presented to you by his sacred majesty; of being a commissioned
officer in less than a month, and heading a band of gallant fellows
like himself, with trumpets sounding, drums brattling, and
colours flying—the foe before you, with glory, rank, wealth, and
pretty women in the background—showers of soft kisses and hard
cash.   But in the spirit of the time, he invited some of the stout
fellows about him to enlist under the banner of a true covenanted
king—to wit, his sacred majesty Charles II., now residing at
Breda; to mount and ride against the English in defence of
Christ's crown and the kirk of Scotland—for fifty men were now
wanted for the worthy regiment of Black Dragoons, raised ten
years ago by Field-Marshal Leslie—the victors of the day at
Newburnford—and now quartered in the Gallowgate of Glasgow,
under the command of the most noble colonel, Count Ogilvie, of
Mariburg, lately Governor of Altona, Knight of the Dannebrog,
and major-general of horse in Lower Saxony :—God save the kirk
and king!   Hurrah!

" Hip, hip, hurrah!" cried the crowd; and a thousand blue
bonnets were waved in the air, and tan-ta-ra-ra-ra went the
trumpets again.

The enthusiasm was great, for the high military spirit of the
Scottish people was at its zenith, while religious ardour was nobly
blended with a patriotic desire to defend the kingdom against the
English republicans, and to shield it from those armed encroachments in which their protector seemed likely to rival the late
king.   Several young men were pressing forward, when I thrust

a passage through the crowd, and reaching the non-commissioned officer, said—

"Give me a cockade, sergeant—if you will take me for a soldier."

"That will I blythely, my lad; but we are all stout fellows, and tall too, in the Black Dragoons, while thou seemest but a youth, yet straight as a pike and growing too, I warrant," said the burly sergeant. "There is courage in that eye—a young buck of spirit!"

"He'll command a troop in a week, and bid his soldiers come and go, like the centurion of old," said a corporal with a wink, for which I cared little.

"The lassies will be pulling each other's hair for him when he dons the buff coat and jack boots," said a third.

Tan-ta-ra-ra-ra rang the trumpets, and all the recruiting party laughed.

"Come on, my lad," said an old sergeant, pinning on my cockade; "when I was thine age I was poor—so I said, better sell my sword to the Swede than beg, and I became a captain of Swart Ruyters till Scotland required me again; and now I ride in her ranks but a poor sergeant of dragoons."

"Set your chin to my holster-flap," said Sergeant Glanders, for this seemed to be the gauge of height. "'Tis all right, my lad: thou shalt be a Black Trooper," he added, clapping me on the shoulder. "Thou'st been a ruffler, I warrant, and the exchequer's run out—eh?"

"I am a bachelor of the university."

"How—"

"A hellicate student," snivelled a voice in the crowd. "I had like to ken wha but he wad be sae ready to wear breeks made out o' sheet iron."

"How!" resumed the sergeant; "what manner of bachelor is that?"

"A student in his third or fourth year. Another month would have seen me laureate—a master of arts; but it matters not, I must e'en follow the drum sith 'twill no better be!"

"And could you follow aught better?" cried the sergeant, brandishing his long sword "When I rode in the Swedish Leif regiment of horse, commanded by Colonel MacDougal, I have seen the Austrian burgomasters of three towns on their knees, with silver keys, golden purses, and foaming pots of wine before me, sirs—yea, though I was but a corporal: but that was under Gustavus Adolphus, the friend of the pious soldier and the bulwark of religion—God rest him!"

My example was speedily followed, and no less than nineteen other young men were selected from the crowd, who pressed forward to enlist; and so elated was the worthy Sergeant Glanders with his morning's success, that he marched the whole party, with swords drawn and trumpets sounding, to that famous old rendezvous of the wild bucks of the university, the " Cat and Bagpipes," kept by Adam Wilson in the Trongate; and then, after beating the " point of war," the troopers dismounted, and we all clattered and crowded into the common hall of the tavern, where tables stood ready for dicing or drinking, and where the walls were pasted over with proclamations and warnings " anent" malignants and cavaliers, risings-in-arms, and I know not what more.

Here a bailie of Glasgow was in attendance (for in those days of trooping and civil war, a sergeant of Black Dragoons was too great a personage to attend upon a magistrate) to swear us all in; and we were accordingly sworn to be leal men and true— not to the king, but wisely *to the Parliament and Estates of Scotland;* for we can never trust to rulers who live in London —and this we swore, as we should be answerable to Heaven at the day of doom.

" Hollo, gudewife," cried our noisy covenanting sergeant, as he jangled his spurs through the paved hall, on the floor of which his iron-heeled boots and long basket-hilted sword were jarring; " kill ye the fatted calf, and if there be no fatted calf to kill, desire thy pantler to bring us a farl of bannocks and stoups of the auld brown cow to every man round. Let us drink and be merry; for lo! I bring twenty brave recruits to serve the gude auld cause, and the king's most sacred majesty !"

" Who shall reign till he hath put his enemies under his feet —*first* Corinthians," said Corporal MacSnaffle, through his nose; but whether in piety or derision, I was then uncertain, as all men canted in the same fashion.

" Yea," vociferated Sergeant Glanders, striking his gauntletted hand on the table, " the king, who shall reign until he hath blown all their infernal brains out—*second* Corinthians, first troop—or verse is it ?

> " So mount, my tall fellows, ' to horse,' is the cry,
> For glory and guilders we are ready to die !

Aye, aye! I have sung that old song many a day on the long, dusty, and d—nable marches in Silesia and Lower Saxony, where we fought under the noble Marquis of Hamilton. Your healths, gentlemen and comrades. God bless the king, and all our noble selves !"

This merry and boisterous sergeant poured the stoup of ale through his long and wiry mustachios; then he wiped off the froth with the back of his gauntlet, and while beating time on the board with the pot, began to sing the old camp song of Scoto-swedes, altering it to the occasion.

> " All brave lads raise up your spirits!
>   Honor abides you, attended by fame,
> All are rewarded according to merits,
>   Honour begetteth, who winneth the same.
> O, vivat *King Charles*, I pray God protect him !
> Send *Cromwell* to hell, for it doth expect him !
>   Charge, lads, charge ! and close in around,
>   Till Cæsar shall give ground !
>   O, hark how the trumpets sound.
>   Tan-ta-ra-ra-ra !"

At this point of our sergeant's noisy song, a solemn-looking figure in Geneva cloth, with lank hair hanging on each side of a long visage, was seen making his way towards him; and my breast swelled with mingled emotions on recognising Mr. Zachary Boyd.

CHAPTER IX.

THE CAT AND BAGPIPES.

I WAS rather surprised to see this sombre, pious, and learned divine in such a place as the " Cat and Bagpipes ;" but he immediately explained that he was there by an order of the Privy Council and Commission of Assembly, to catechise the recruits, in absence of the regimental chaplain, who was suffering from a pistol shot received at the battle of Invercarron.

"Catechise !" reiterated Sergeant Glanders, with an oath, sworn, however, in Low Dutch ; " such nonsense was never heard of in the Swedish army; yet never did a more pious king than the great Gustavus ride to battle ; and he never omitted to thank Heaven for a victory or escape."

" And did ye not do so likewise ?" asked Zachary, pressing his large hands together.

" Why—once, perhaps—when a six-pound shot missed my leg and carried away my holsters, as I rode with Sir James Ramsay, the Black Colonel, in the vanguard of Scots at Leipzig."

" Verily," mumbled Corporal MacSnaffle, " a wonderful instance o' God's providence !"

" Wonderful instance of a rascally gleed gunner," added the sergeant; " for I carried our troop standard, with the crosses of Scotland and Sweden interlaced—and that should have been mark enough."

" And dost thou never pray, sergeant ?" asked Zachary, coldly pushing aside the frothing pot, which our bluff non-commissioned officer tendered him.

"We have but little time for that, I assure you, sir," grumbled Sergeant Glanders. "Moreover, praying is the parson's work, and why does our chaplain get major's pay, if his duty is to fall on the rank and file? These last ten years of service I have seen, after leaving the Swedish army for the Scottish, have been sharp as any. Zounds, sir, in that time, I have been in eight pitched battles in Britain, and six of these were fought on Scottish ground, where Scot met Scot as stoutly and as well as ever I saw them sweep the Imperialists from the Rhine to the Elbe. But as for praying,—lookye, reverend sir, what with having my duty, my horse, my accoutrements and harness to look after— yea, having to wash and mend my own shirts—having my billet to hunt for, and a pretty wench to run after occasionally, I have very little time for that."

"Verily, verily, Gideon Glanders," said Corporal MacSnaffle, through his nose, "I say unto thee, thou art a reprobate."

"Silence, corporal," retorted the red-faced sergeant; "silence, or, by the God of Jacob—to speak in thine own fashion—I will crack the iron utensil that covers thine empty pate. Nay, reverend sir, I am no reprobate withal. No man needeth prayer more, or hath less time for it, than the poor private soldier; and believe me, he who faces death every day—who in the morning rides bravely in his saddle, and, ere night, may be mangled and buried in a ditch, hath no need of homilies to remind him that he is mortal. There was a time when I prayed—yea, prayed devoutly; but that was when I was a wee bit bairnie, and on my knees, wi' uplifted hands, I prayed every night, for my father and mother, for myself and the auld house dog, Hector—for even he wasna forgotten," continued the sergeant, sliding into his native dialect as his eyes filled. "But I have seen mickle to harden the heart since then; for by many a deep trench, filled to the brim with Austrian dead; by many a blazing town; by many a deadly breach and bloody field, on the shores of the Vistula, the Rhine, and the Oder, hath my path in life been cast; and I am not ashamed to say, that I bless Heaven for its great kindness, that in my fortieth year I find myself at hame in auld Scotland—sound, wind and limb, and a sergeant of the Black Dragoons! At times, I may swear a little, Mr. Zachary, or laugh and be jolly; then you will say I forget my God. It may be so; but then I am assured that HE never forgets me—a poor soldier though I am. And being no reprobate, am ready to run any man through the body who says so. A hint for you, corporal."

Still Mr. Boyd declined the proffered pot of ale.

"It matters not, sir," said the sergeant, proudly, as he drained it himself; "one who has shared his canteen with the immortal King of Sweden and the gallant Marshal Hepburn, may easily pocket such an affront from thee."

Rough though his bearing, and boisterous his manner, there was much in this veteran sergeant that I esteemed and admired; he was never rude or uncivil, and seldom canted, save when he slyly wished to make fun of Corporal Bezaleel MacSnaffle, who being an old and true blue Covenauter, inveterately interlarded every sentence with scriptural phraseology.

Silence being proclaimed, and the ale pots drained, the soldiers planted their elbows on the table, and eyed each other knowingly, while the reverend catechist examined all the recruits on various doctrinal points and the creed of the Kirk of Scotland; and as every one of them knew the matter in hand, and was as well able to argue any point as the divine himself, their answers were satisfactory, save one or two, which displeased the patient Zachary exceedingly.

"Your words savour of Arianism, young man," said he to one named Carlourie; "and yours of Latitudinarianism; but I doubt not you will become a clever aud efficient vessel, under judicious training."

"Aye, aye," said Sergeant Glanders, "once under the hands of our rough rider, and we shall soon make a man of him."

The learned author of the "Last Battel of the Soule" changed colour visibly when I appeared before him, and his face expressed anger, pain, and mortification, while I remembered, with something of pique and hostility, the interview of last night, and the pitiful result of my love affair with pretty Margaret Muir.

"With you and for you I have no words," said he, gravely. "My opinion of you, Master Ogilvie, hath been formed long ago —yea, formed with sorrow. You are as a brand foredoomed to the burning; and neither in this world nor the next, cau come to good, I fear me. I deem you as a lost sheep, and need say no more. You have brewed an evil draught, oh Harry Ogilvie, and must drink the bitter dregs thereof. Farewell. You have sown an evil crop, and have now naught to reap but nettles, weeds and tares, thorns and brambles, spread over pitfalls and precipices."

"Then I shall rush my horse at them all the more boldly," said I, with a proud air, as he turned away with undisguised sadness, and left me.

"Thou hast spoken like a man," said the sergeant; "but this is a sorry account of thee, Master Ogilvie; yet I think not the less of thee for all that."

I thought very much the less of myself, however; and with a sorrow, not unmixed with anger, I long remembered the parting words of the good but quaint Zachary Boyd.

The sergeant now gave to each recruit a pound sterling, or equal to eighteen pounds Scots, as a bounty or largess. I spent all mine in wine and ale, entertaining the party and their friends, and drank to drown dull care. In this oblivious spirit I felt merry, even joyous, and sang songs of love and war to please Sergeant Glanders, and joined the pious corporal in a hymn, about hanging our harps by the waters of Babel, while the soldiers beat time with their quart pots or the iron heels of their jack-boots. I thumped the gudeman, Adam Wilson, between the shoulders, until I nearly choked him; I kissed his daughter Annie (of whom more anon), I rumpled the silken gown of his buxom gudewife, and was soon the idol of the recruiting party, and felt myself able for anything, from toying with a pretty lass, to haranguing the right reverend and right honourable the General Assembly.

"Well, young cockerel," snivelled the corporal, "art happy at last?"

"Yes," said I, as I sat on the table with one hand on a pot of ale, and the other round the waist of the landlady's daughter; "gloriat—happy as a king!"

"What the sum total of that happiness may be," said the sergeant, "I know not, as I never was a king; but pass the black-jack, Trumpeter Tom."

"Alake!" said the corporal, turning up the whites of his eyes, "there is no happiness on earth."

"Is there not?" cried the sergeant: "well-a-day! of all the canting, croaking, miserable, infernal old—"

"Hush—hush!" cried several of the dragoons.

"Happy as a king indeed," continued the covenanting corporal, with a grim smile; "I should like to hae questioned King Charles anent that happiness when the English lurdanes spat in his face, or when he was sawing through the grating of his window in the Castle of Carisbrook."

"And I should have liked one fair shot with my holster pistol at that same Major Hobson of Cromwell's, who was watching the poor man below—d—n his eyes for a crop-eared cur—amen! Tom, pass that jack here again, and blow to horse."

In ten minutes after this the dragoons were once more mounted, and preceded by their trumpets, kettle-drums, and recruits, they marched to the quarters of our colonel, where all the standards and the captains of troops were lodged in the ancient mansion of the Lairds of Silvercraig in the Saltmarket.

I wondered if pretty Margaret would feel sad when her grave betrothed related the step I had taken.

I felt assured that she would; for every woman feels, to the last, a gentle interest in the fate and fortune of one who has loved her, even though his love be unrequited.

CHAPTER X.

THE SOLEMN LEAGUE AND COVENANT.

In the ardour with which I have pursued the relation of my own adventures, I have seldom recurred to the great events of that stirring epoch—events in which I was soon to take an active, if not rather a prominent part.

While I had been quietly following my studies at the University of Glasgow, and been buried among the musty lore of its library, which was founded in the fifteenth century, the kingdoms of Scotland and England had each been shaken to its centre.

In defiance alike of the law of the land, of the civil and religious rights of the people, and regardless of their wishes, Charles I., influenced by evil counsellors, introduced the English liturgy into Scotland, where it was extensively circulated; but its principal vendors were the dealers in snuff and bon-bons. I had more than one copy myself, but they were used as lining for my trunk. Tumults immediately broke out in Scotland, and the students and regents of old Glasgow were the first to testify their aversion to the prelatic ritual by withdrawing from all religious ordinances rather than kneel at the sacrament, as enjoined by the obnoxious Articles of Perth. The entire nation were averse to the royal supremacy in spiritual matters, and to the governing of the church by bishops, as being unauthorised in Scripture. Moreover, as Scotsmen, we were determined that even the anointed king himself should not dictate to us, and annul those charters which had been written in the blood of our people; nor should he infringe those laws and liberties which our fathers had bequeathed to us from many a hard-fought field.

The Solemn League and Covenant, one of the most necessary and formidable documents ever known in Scottish history, was prepared and signed by the entire nation; St. Andrew's cross was unfurled, and the men of the realm were summoned to arms.

"We'll have no *tulchan* bishops!" was the cry; this term was in great vogue in those days, when the prelates were set up as stuffed calves, and the Scottish placemen—an infamous class in all ages—*milked* their benefices. Petitions against the liturgy were presented to the king in London.

"I declare my willingness to grant a pardon for the past; but I require the quiet adoption of the liturgy," he replied, "and implicit obedience for the future."

But the Earls of Rothes, Cassilis, Eglinton, Home, Lothian, Wemyss, and Argyle; the Lords Lindesay, Yester, Balmerino, Cranston, Loudon, and other leaders of the presbyterians, scorned to accept of pardon on such conditions; and as *all petitions from Scotland*, on any subject, have ever been so much waste paper, unless the people have their swords on the grindstone to enforce attention to their demands, they called an assembly of the church, and this most important meeting was held in Glasgow. Two hundred and sixty commissioners from presbyteries, universities, and burghs attended, and the godly Alexander Henderson was chosen moderator; but the convocation was dissolved by the king's order, and then ARMS alone could defend the liberties of Scotland!

War was declared against Charles; Field-Marshal Sir Alexander Leslie, of Balgonie, the friend and comrade of Gustavus Adolphus, was summoned from Sweden to lead the Scottish army; Leith was fortified; in one week every stronghold in Scotland was stormed and garrisoned anew by the people. Still the king was madly resolved on enforcing the liturgy, and marched from London with twenty thousand men, while a fleet of twenty ships of war with another English army came round by sea. The latter force was commanded by a Scottish noble, for it would almost seem an ordinance of God that every act of political infamy or national perfidy should be performed by one of our peers.

The Scottish army, consisting of twenty-five thousand infantry, with its horse and artillery, took up a position on Dunsclaw, where all the best rules of discipline and duty were adopted and enforced by its officers, the veterans of the thirty years' war. A great and decisive conflict between the king and his people— a strife the memory of which must have fallen like a shadow on ages yet to come—would assuredly have been fought then, had Charles not been disheartened by the result of a cavalry encounter on the 3rd of June, 1639, when the Scottish dragoons under Count Ogilvie, of Mariburg, totally routed the English near Kelso.

Then Charles endeavoured to negotiate; the Earl of Dunfermline brought a last petition from the camp of the Scots, imploring the king to hear them before every tie which bound them to him was cut asunder by the sword; and this petition was graciously received; for on Dunselaw were five and twenty thousand blue bonnets drawn up in order of battle, all good men and true, and the lighted matches shone by the muzzles of forty pieces of cannon.

Without these fine accessories the petition would have been received as petitions from Scotland usually are; but I would ever have my countrymen to bear in mind, that grape and canister are brave appendages to such a legal document.

Commissioners were appointed on both sides, and after a sullen and suspicious armistice, both armies retired into their own countries; but the Scottish Parliament maintained the staff and officers of all their regiments on full pay, so that no sudden invasion of the kingdom could take place. Their demands were simple and just.

Pure and unmingled presbytery, triennial parliaments, and full freedom of debate.

But instigated by Laud, Strafford, and others, Charles, who thought that his ill-defined prerogatives were about to be swept away, once more prepared for a war with Scotland, and, by compulsory loans or otherwise, resorted to every means of raising money in England and Ireland for this purpose. York was his new muster place; the Earl of Northumberland was his general, the Earl of Strafford his lieutenant-general, and Lord Conway commander of his cavalry.

Anticipating all this, the Scottish army under Marshal Leslie crossed the Tweed and marched into England, there to fight the foe on his own ground.

At Newburnford on the Tyne they found General Lord Conway, with six thousand infantry, the English life-guards, and several batteries of heavy cannon, prepared to defend the passage of the river. The cannonade of the Scottish artillery soon destroyed the redoubts of Conway, and the noble Marquis of Montrose was the first man of the Scottish army who crossed the river, by plunging in, sword in hand, at the head of his own battalion of musketeers, who marched through, girdle deep, under a heavy fire of cannon and musket shot. Colonel Count Ogilvie followed at the head of the Black Dragoons; and there, on the memorable 28th of May, 1640, the English were totally routed, their royal standard taken, and their life-guards cut to pieces.

This was worth a million of petitions to the Throne!

Charles was now forced to respect the covenant, to conform himself, when in Scotland, to the presbyterian church, and to create the covenanting leader, Marshal Sir Alexander Leslie, a peer, by the title of Earl of Leven and Lord Balgonie, placing a coronet on his head in the parliament-house at Edinburgh.

Then followed the civil wars in England, and once more our army marched into that country, to make common cause with our old enemies against the unhappy king. Then came the exploits of the gallant Montrose, and his glorious battles, during which he passed like a whirlwind over the Highlands; then followed the Assembly at Westminster; the delivery of Charles to the English by the shameless cozening of Argyle and five other Scotsmen. Far less dishonourable had it been to their memory and to us, had they tried their native prince by a court-martial and shot him before their camp at Newcastle; but to yield him up to his judicial murderers—oh, it was a deed well worthy of Gillespie the ill-favoured! Then followed the defeat and butchery of Montrose—a butchery which Argyle, with the Lord and Lady Lorn, beheld from their windows with exultation; and the latter, though a lady of high birth, with an amount of hatred, venom and cruelty, such as never before swelled up in a woman's heart, spat in the face of the fallen hero, as he ascended that scaffold on which he perished—he, the great cavalier—with the fortitude of a soldier and the resignation of a Christian.

The reader will pardon this brief recurrence to the terrible events of my own time, which now bring me down to the year 1650.

I was then about eighteen years of age.

At this time the neighbouring kingdom of England was in a wretched condition. Quakers rode about the highways naked, or clad only in white sheets ; brewers sang psalms, tailors taught, watermen expounded, and soldiers preached. A musketeer, named Melchisedeck Makepeace, went into the church of Walton-on-Thames, bearing five lighted candles, and declaring to the people that he had a message from God to proclaim the abolition of the sabbath, of the clergy, and of the Bible, which he con-sumed with the fifth candle. In short, the blasphemies and absurdities of the English were almost incredible. At Dover a woman beheaded her child, believing in a command, like Abraham. At York, in '47, a woman crucified her aged mother, and a man named Precisian knocked the head off a barrel of beer, for presuming to work on the sabbath-day ; nor was my own country much behind England in the race of folly and fanaticism.

Alas for Scotland ! she was now no longer an united nation, but a people rent into three wretched factions, of whose mutual hatred, England, according to her ancient use and wont, hastened to take a wicked advantage.

The *first* of these were the rigid presbyterians, who acknow-ledged Argyle as their leader, and who had the supreme direction of affairs, with the government of the realm in their own " holy" hands. They wore sad-coloured garments, and had their hair hanging straight on their shoulders; they usually walked with the whites of their eyes turned up, and texts of Scripture on their tongues.

The *second* were the moderate presbyterians, who were justly indignant at the base betrayal of the king, and whose leader was the noble Duke of Hamilton and Chatelherault.

The *third* party were the loyal cavaliers, or absolutists, the followers of the dead Montrose, of Huntly, Airlie, and the Highland chiefs—men who blindly adhered to the king in victory or defeat, in sunshine and in storm, and who perished on the scaffold for the right divine, with that joyous courage and mag-nanimity in which no martyrs ever surpassed our Scottish Jaco-bites. These cavaliers were vilified by the other parties as Malignants, Philistines, Amalekites, Egyptians, and Troublers of

Israel; but they were all brave gallants, who dressed themselves gorgeously, strode, swaggered, and swore, diced and drunk, to show their scorn of ghostly advice and sour-visaged sanctity.

In one point alone did these three parties agree—viz., acknowledging the sovereignty of Charles, a sentiment very distasteful to the Earl of Argyle, who in the autumn of 1648, after assuming the significant title of Dictator of Scotland, had invited Cromwell, the Protector of England, to Edinburgh, where he feasted him royally in the great hall of the castle; and where they recently held secret meetings, at Lady Home's house in the Canongate, and made their mutual arrangements for the execution of the king, and the substitution of a divided republic for two united crowns.

But notwithstanding these secret treaties, and this mutual understanding, between the artful and able Cromwell, and the cunning and cold-blooded Argyle, a sentiment of remorse and shame for the base betrayal of King Charles, fell deeply on the hearts even of that ruling party which sold him; and the other two factions—viz., the moderates and the Scottish cavaliers, united with them in tendering their allegiance, and the crown, to his son, Charles II., who was then at Breda, and who was proclaimed in February, 1649, at the cross of the capital as King of Scotland and the Isles, by the Islay and Snowdon heralds, while the Earls of Cassilis and Lothian were dispatched to Holland to invite him home, on condition of his becoming a presbyterian—subscribing the covenant, relinquishing England and Ireland to Cromwell, and ruling Scotland as his fathers had ruled her of old.

His majesty joyfully accepted the proposals of our ambassadors, and setting sail from Holland, he landed at Leith, with a retinue of two thousand exiled nobles and gentlemen—a few of whom were English—on the 23rd of June, 1650, and rode to the palace of Scone amid the rejoicings of the people.

On the day news came to Glasgow that his majesty had landed on Scottish ground, the city bells rang merrily, enthusiasm lighted every eye, and joy relaxed even the grim visages of those who had never smiled since the signing of the covenant. The cross was decorated with flowers; the fountains ran with wine, the shipping in the Clyde showed all their colours and fired their cannon, while the Black Dragoons rode through the streets with swords drawn, trumpets sounding, and kettledrums beating, and each cornet at the head of his troop, with its standard displayed. Three times we fired all our carbines at the market cross, where many a puncheon of ale and bombarde of wine were set abroach, and thus the night closed in amid mirth and jollity, the blaze of bonfires, and the clangour of bells.

CHAPTER XL.

THE RECRUIT.

On the morning after my enlistment I was brought, with other recruits, before our colonel, who was quartered, as I have said, in the Laird of Silvercraig's house; and I waited in the passage, with a fluttering heart, and not without an emotion of humiliation, till my turn came to appear before him; for I had received the education of a gentleman, and I had associated with gentlemen, and imbibed all their sentiments; thus one night spent at the recruiting rendezvous, among soldiers, tapsters, and coarse companions, had given rather a shock to my chivalry.

At last I heard the intoned voice of Corporal Mac Snaffle, who held the list of recruits, utter my name.

"Harry Ogilvie!"

I started.

"Hold up your head, comrade," said Sergeant Glanders, "and look like a man; the count is a fire-eater; but he'll like you the better for showing a bold front."

In another moment I found myself standing before my colonel in a spacious room, the walls of which were hung with a species of tapestry. Several officers, richly accoutred, stood near us conversing gaily; but for a time I saw only him. He was a very handsome man; his figure was tall and strongly knit; his hair and mustachios were grey and grizzled; his face, naturally dark and swarthy, had an almost diabolical tint imparted to it, by having been scorched with gunpowder at the storming of Munich, where he led the van of six thousand Scots; and where, as I was afterwards told, an illbushed carbine had flashed in the pan as he levelled it at an imperialist. His name and exploits had long been familiar to us, through the medium of the French *Mercury* and *Gallobelgicus*. On this day he wore a white satin doublet, slashed with pink, and over it a military buff coat. A broad and richly embroidered belt sustained his sword, a blade of Toledo with a gorgeous hilt, the gift of Field Marshal Horne, after the capture of Munich. Round his neck he had a falling collar of the Vandyke pattern, and on his head a black calotte cap. On his heels were a pair of large gilt spurs, which had been taken from Gustavus Adolphus, as he lay dead at Lutzen, by his aide-de-camp, Colonel Hugh Somerville, who now commanded the first troop of the Black Dragoons. His plumed helmet lay upon the table, and on his breast sparkled the orders of the empire.

I have been somewhat particular in my description, because

this noble officer bears a place in my narrative nearly as prominent as that he occupies in the military annals of his country.

He gazed at me steadfastly, and saw that I was—may I say
it without being accused of vanity?—a well-looking young
fellow; tall, stout, and strong. My eye told of a firm heart and
a bold ambition, though my boyish brow was somewhat marked
by the lines of care, of thought, and study.

"'Tis the smart young bachelor I spoke of, noble colonel,"
said Serjeant Glanders, making a military salute; "his volun-
teering yesterday brought to the king at least twelve good
recruits."

"And so, young man, your name is Ogilvie?" said the colonel,
gazing upon me with interest.

"Yes, sir."

"And of what line—which family come ye?"

"Alas, my lord count, I know not; nor kith nor kin have I;
being, as I may say, but a poor foundling."

"Then why this name of Ogilvie?"

"It was written on my baby-clothes."

"Good; I will be thy kinsman as well as comrade, for clansmen are all of one stock. Do your duty, fail me not, and I will
never fail you, but shall rather do all in my power to befriend
you. Remember that a soldier should be brave, firm, polite,
honourable, and true, considering all men before himself, gentle
to women, kind to orphans and to the aged, faithful to God, to
his comrade, and his colours. Every soldier should consider
himself a gentleman. Go, sir, and remember my words. Sergeant
Glanders, let him be enrolled in the Laird of Drumstanchel's
troop."

The last-named officer was a veteran who had served in the
Spanish Imperial Guards, and knew well the discipline of war.

As I left the presence of the colonel, my heart beat high with
hope at his promises, and I learned to my joy, that the lieutenant
of my troop was no other than the Master of Oliphant, and the
cornet, young William Linn, of Linn, in Lothian.

"Vivat! my jolly bachelor," said the latter, as they both
recognised me that evening, when we paraded on the Butts of
the Gallowgate (for I was too proud to approach them *first*);
"what, *thou*, in the Black Dragoons, and but a poor trooper?
Alas! Harry, is this the realization of all thy air-built castles?"

"Nay, it realizes the old song of the Spaniard," said the Master
of Oliphant; and he began to sing,—

> "Now a plague on ill luck when the ready's all gone,
>   To the wars poor Pilgarlik must trudge;
> Yet had I but cash, to rake on as I've done,
>   The devil a foot I would budge."

"Nay, Master, and Laird of Linn."

"Tush!" said Linn; "call us Patrick and Willie, as of old."

"You forget, sirs, that I am but a poor trooper."

"Out upon thee, man! Nay! I insist on't. Only three months ago, we were merry brother students. Oliphant and I were to have visited you on the morrow at the Auld Pedagogie, where we were wont to grub o' nights for Greek and Latin roots; where we fought with Sallust, wrestled with Livy, and found Æschylus as bad as a nightmare; but our troop marched in only yesterday."

"But how came you to enlist, Harry?" asked Linn.

"That unhappy brawl which nearly cost you a life each (and for your brave assistance in which I owe you a thousand thanks), occasioned all."

I related everything that had occurred since our separation, and they laughed immoderately, especially at the scene in pretty Margaret's bedchamber, the wrath of the principal, and the confusion of Zachary Boyd.

"And hence," said Oliphant, "thou hast abandoned the cornered cap for the helmet, the red gown for the buff jerkin, and come to fight for the good old cause."

"Nay, don't call it that, Oliphant, I pray thee," said Linn, laughing, as he twirled up his black moustachios.

"Wherefore, cornet of mine?"

"For never since the world began was a *good old cause* a winning one."

"I am come to fight for neither kirk nor king, but for my country, and for her alone."

"Bravely resolved, young birkie," said the captain of my troop, who overheard us; "be animated by this pure sentiment, and auld John Crawford o' Drumstanchel will never fail or forget thee."

This grim and wiry old soldier had been in all the Danish, German, and Scottish wars. He had lost an ear at the storming of Donauwerth, on the Danube; he had received a pike-wound in that terrible sortie made by the Scots from Stralsund; he had his right arm shattered at the battle of Inverlochy, and was actually on the verge of being buried among the dead after the Scots stormed Newcastle, but was resuscitated by something akin to a miracle. He always wore a rusty helmet and an old buff coat, all riddled by pistol-shot and sword-thrusts, and black with grease, blood, and gunpowder.

Altogether unlike him, Linn and Oliphant were noble-looking cavaliers. The first wore his dark hair shorn short, and had a smart and soldierly aspect; the second wore his chesnut locks in long and flowing curls, *à la Montrose,* and both were graceful.

active, and athletic; thus, the dark accoutrements, from which the Black Dragoons derived their title, befitted them well; and they wore their cuirasses, plate-sleeves, gorgets, and tassettes as easily as their white silk scarfs or pipeclayed leather gauntlets.

I supped with them that evening in a private room at the "Cat and Bagpipes," and we spent the night as merrily as of old. Such intercourse between the educated private and his officers was not deemed inimical to discipline, or subversive of it, according to the gentle courtesy of the old Scottish service in my young days, when the sons of many good families served as volunteers in the ranks, and when the Scots Life, and Fusilier Guards—two regiments raised about ten years after the time I write of—were almost entirely composed of young gentlemen of high birth and accomplishments.

Referring to the escape I had made from the snow, "Good Intent," of Glasgow, and the wardship of her worthy skipper, Master Duncan Campbell,—

"To me it seems almost incredible," said Linn, "that Argyle should be your enemy. Harry, be assured it is impossible!"

"The great, the powerful, the terrible Argyle!" said the Master of Oliphant. in a tone of irony; "a privy counsellor, and lately justiciar of all Scotland, chief of the most powerful clan in the realm, and apex of that presbyterian pyramid which is to bear up the Scottish throne. He who is the corner-stone of the kirk, and chief ruler at the court of that young king——"

"Whose father he sold to the English."

"Why should he be a foe to thee, Harry—a poor student?"

"I know not why, unless it be this name of Ogilvie, to which every Campbell bears a natural antipathy."

"Then be assured, good comrade," said Linn, "it will be perilous work to say a word of this in public, for be it false or be it true, a nod from Argyle would crush thee. We cannot have forgotten how the commissary of Dunkeld and the Laird of Fintray both perished on the scaffold at the market cross of Edinburgh, for revealing (what no man ever doubted) that nine years ago, the great Pharisee had a scheme on foot to destroy the king, and divide Scotland into two dictatorships."

"Better will it be, good Ogilvie, that he deems thee gone with yonder snow to the English plantations, than still among us here; for if indeed a foe, he will deem himself well rid of thee; so keep out of his latitude and longitude in future."

"But I never thwarted, never wronged him, to deserve such deadly and undying vengeance!" I exclaimed, bitterly. "I would that the battles of Auldearn and Inverlochy were to be fought again; I would soon be found among the opp ranks."

"Hush, hush, Harry," said Oliphant, somewhat alarmed by my energy, "remember that thou art but a private dragoon—he an earl, first minister of the king, and leader of the covenanted kirk."

"I hate him not the less," I continued, as the wine mounted into my head.

"In that our colonel, the Count Ogilvie, will be your comrade, Harry," said Linn; "have you not marked, Oliphant, his emotion at the bare mention of Argyle's name?"

"Yes, I have seen his eyes flash, his chest heave, and his powder-grimed visage blacken like his corslet with the passion he sought to control."

"It will be a portion of the old feud between the Ogilvies of Airlie and the Campbells of Argyle."

"But time will discover all," said I, with a sigh.

We separated.

They repaired to their comfortable quarters in the house of a wealthy Saltmarket bailie, and I to my humbler billet on a stabler in the Gorbals.

CHAPTER XII.

MARCH FROM GLASGOW.

FOR three months after this time, I was constantly under the care of the rough-rider or of the drill-sergeant, and so much did I profit by the tuition of the latter—a veteran of the Scottish Horse Guard, whose surname of Halkerton had been turned into *Hackiron*—that within the stated period I was dismissed to my troop as a perfect dragoon.

Autumn being the most favourable season for procuring remounts of cavalry horses, our colonel had completed the establishment in the fall of the year, and as none of the new chargers were in a state for service, during the first weeks of spring we gave them gentle walking exercise, increasing its duration as we augmented the feeds of corn. They were all fine chargers, and above fifteen hands in height. Close and compact animals were selected, broad across the loins, short and straight-backed, close coupled and round barrelled, deep at the shoulders, full-chested, clean in the limbs and strong in the thighs. The greatest care was taken to have the whole regiment—riders and horses—in first-rate discipline and condition, as we were in daily expectation of receiving orders from Edinburgh to march either towards Scone, to guard the court during the coronation, or towards Berwick, into which we had thrown a strong garrison to watch the movements of Cromwell and the English puritans.

Avoiding the college, and all my old haunts, I gave myself up with ardour to the study of my new profession.

I found much civility and a great deal of attention among my comrades, and the non-commissioned officers were extremely friendly (while my pay lasted), each one promising to teach me something. or to recommend me "to his friend the colonel for promotion," or to relax the severity of discipline; but with the exception of boisterous Gideon Glanders or rough old sergeant Hackiron, they all left me to shift for myself after my pittance was spent in wine pots and primero.

These fellows were what we technically style "old soldiers," an equivocal term in its regimental sense, and were, of course, exceptions to the general character of his majesty's regiment of Black Horse, the troopers of which were all fine *sabreurs*, brave, generous, and proud of themselves, their colonel, and their corps.

Count Ogilvie, who had been seven times wounded in the German wars, was an admirable cavalry officer, and though the regiment had now been embodied for nearly twelve years, or ever since the enrolment of the first covenanting army, and had fought in all the great battles of that disastrous time, many of the horses were young; thus, he had us daily under arms and in our saddles, teaching them to stand fire, noises, and alarms, and to be steady while we shot off our carbines between their ears, or to cross rough ground when fully accoutred, to leap hedges, ditches, and gates, to swim, and to disregard dead bodies of men and horses. We ruffled the kettledrums, flashed pistols in the pan, and discharged carbines *at feeding-time;* thus the poor nags neighed and pricked up their ears with pleasure, anticipating fresh corn, when we came to be under fire in grim earnest, ere long.

Amid all these new occupations I had almost forgotten the coquettish Margaret Muir; or, if I remembered her, it was with little more than the boyish desire to swagger before her, in the dashing trappings of a royal dragoon; but the old principal I never forgot; and an emotion of shame, for all that had passed, prevented me from acquainting him with the step I had taken, and from going at any time nearer the college than I could well avoid.

One day I was posted as a sentinel at the door of our colonel's billet, armed with my sword and carbine, when I saw old Nehemiah Spreul, the college janitor, with the same blue bonnet, little mantle, high antique ruff, and vinegar expression of visage, I had last seen him wear, approach me. Despite the change made in my appearance by the care of Drill-sergeant Hackiron, and despite the new attire in which I was arrayed—helmet, back

And breast pieces, gorget, pauldrons, plate sleeves, and jack-boots, Nehemiah recognised me, and hastened up, with outstretched hands, and eyes full of moisture and affection.

"My mannie, can this be *you?*" he exclaimed, surveying me again and again, from spur to helmet. "O'd but ye mak' a braw dragoon, and your iron coat becometh you better than a doctor's surplice—my *ain* laddie, for sic ye are!" continued the old man, weeping as he wrung my hand. "Wow, Harry, but ye carry your head like a king! Oh, youth is a loving and a trusting time; but auld age cometh wi' his cauld gurly blast, and the young leaves grow yellow and sear, and the sap in the tree of life drieth up—so preached Maister Zachary yesterday."

After some conversation, I asked him "anent Maggie Muir?"

The old man laughed, winked, and gave me a poke in the ribs.

"She is beyond the reach o' sic wild fellows as you, Harry," said he; "she hath been married by the principal to worthy Maister Zachary, a man esteemit by all as one pure and upright as Dawniel."

With many pressing invitations to visit the college once again, he left me.

It seemed a strange sacrifice for the lively little Margaret, so coquettish and so blooming, to be the spouse of the sombre, clumsy, and ponderous author of the "Battel of the Soule,"—like a rose engrafted on an old gnarled oak. It cost me a pang, and occasioned much reflection that evening, as I lay on the hard guard bed, or stood again in the solitude of my post at night; but Maggie and her marriage were alike forgotten next day, when a King's Life Guardsman, all covered with the dust of a forty-miles ride, dashed in from Edinburgh, with orders for us to march to Stirling; and in one hour after watering our horses, our trumpets blew "Boot-and-saddle" in the streets.

The whole regiment got under arms, and all in their dark iron harness, with sable horses in admirable condition, the Black Dra- goons, six hundred strong, with standards flying, kettle-drums beating, and trumpets sounding, steel scabbards, chain bridles, and accoutrements clanking, rode through the crowded High street of Glasgow, past my former home, the old university; and leaving the city by the Stirling road, took their march towards the north on the 25th day of August, 1650.

Thus I found myself fairly off to see the world, with a sword at my side, and twenty rounds of ball cartridge at my back.

CHAPTER XIII.

APPOINTED CORPORAL.—AN AMBUSH.

On the same day we marched, I was fortunate enough to mount the first step of the long ladder of military promotion. Our colonel, who had found me useful as an amanuensis in his correspondence with the Marshals Leven and Callendar, and with the Lords of the Privy Council, appointed me corporal, and I had two chevrons, the heraldic badge of fidelity, embroidered on the sleeves of my buff coat. Some of the older troopers grumbled at this preference; but, as I knew my duty and feared no man, I stroked my upper lip, on which a black moustache was sprouting, and touched the pommel of my bilbo with the air of one who would think less of running another through the body, than of eating a slice of ration beef; and thus I silenced all objections.

"Praised be Heaven, that we are clear of Glasgow," said the Master of Oliphant, looking back, and shaking his lofty plume, as we traversed the road which dips down towards the Campsie hills; "for another week had perhaps seen me a dyvour in parti-coloured hosen."

I knew that he was deeply indebted to the goldsmiths, who were then our only Scottish bankers; being a generous cavalier, he lavished his money—or *theirs* rather—like handfuls of sand among his friends. Moreover, this handsome and heedless spark was hail-fellow-well-met with all men. He kissed and toyed with every pretty woman who would allow him, rumpling their fardingales and crushing their tuckers, and kissing them again if they pouted. In Glasgow, he was the cause of many a window being grated, and many a door being barred, as checks to his enterprising nature; and, doubtless, the godly held jubilee on his departure.

Towards evening we saw Stirling and the Ochils rising before us; and as we crossed the Bannock, our colonel, who rode near the captain of my troop, made a half turn in his saddle, and said,

"Drumstanchel, send your most intelligent non-commissioned officer in advance, to inform the provost, that quarters and forage are required for six hundred horse."

It pleased the old laird to select me, and charmed with the preference, I put spurs to my horse, and riding at a hand-gallop, soon passed the advanced guard, who rode with their carbines resting on their thighs. Leaving the regiment far in my rear, I passed the village of St. Ninian, and followed the old highway, which penetrated the recesses of the Torwood, the gigantic and sombre oaks of which were in the full foliage of summer. This forest overhung and darkened the roadway for many a mile. I could hear the wild animals, the deer, the fox, the boar, and the fuimart rushing through the thickets, and plashing in occasional pools of water, where the withered reeds, the fallen leaves, and heavy lilies floated.

The path was lonely and wild; but being less impressed by that than by the drowsy solitude of the summer forest, I allowed the reins to drop on my charger's neck, and rode slowly and dreamily on.

The sinking eve was lovely in the extreme, and at one part of the narrow forest path, I dismounted, led my steed aside, and sitting down by the root of a giant oak—one more than ten feet in diameter—forgot all about my mission to the provost, gave myself up to reverie, and under that "greenwood tree," thought of Shakspeare, the forest of Arden, and the song of Amiens in " As You Like It."

In the west were piled a mass of violet-coloured clouds, which seemed to float in an amber sky; and from behind this solid mass a million of rays were radiating. Suddenly this purple bank of vapour burst asunder, and through the golden-edged gap the summer sun shot forth a flood of rosy light on the distant peaks of the beautiful Ochils, on the fertile valley of the Forth that rolled at their feet, and on the sombre forests of Stirlingshire. Steadily this gush of radiance continued to glow; the woods waved and the waters danced in light; while the stupendous peaks of Bencleugh and Dumiat threw their giant shadows far across them to the eastward.

I was roused from my reverie by perceiving four men stealing hastily but cautiously through the glade. Two of them were accoutred in old buff coats and cuirasses; the former stained and cut by many a rent and wound, the latter dinged by many a blade and bullet. These two men seemed to be Lowlanders. The other two appeared to be wild Highlandmen of the Lennox. They were clad in tattered tartan; their kilts were worn to rags; their feet were cased in rough shoes of undressed deerhide; and they wore vests of the same uncouth material. Their legs and arms were alike bare and muscular; their heads were destitute of covering; and their faces were so overgrown by hair, that their red hazel eyes glared from amid it like those of a pole-cat from the heart of a whin-bush; while I can compare the general aspect of their uncovered heads to nothing else than two enormous *burrs*. These two had Doune pistols and two-handed claymores; the others were armed with troopers' swords and carbines.

I knew in a moment that these four broken men were

disbanded soldiers of the late Marquis of Montrose — the great captain-general of the king and the idol of the clans; for since his judicial murder at Edinburgh, many of his veterans had been prowling among the hills and woods, committing every outrage upon those they deemed the enemies of "the Great Cavalier," their late leader in so many pitched battles and brilliant victories.

Now, these four men were evidently in ambush for some dark purpose; and I need scarcely mention, that for ages the vast Torwood had been the haunt of such outlaws.

I was not kept long in a state of indecision, as we soon heard the clink of hoofs, and saw a personage on horseback, wearing a black velvet cloak, and with a white feather in his hat, approach-ing. Two ladies, with broad hats and sad-coloured riding habits, accompanied him; and a few paces behind were four horsemen, two of whom appeared to be gentlemen. All had swords and holster pistols; and beside them bounded a stag-hound.

I saw all this at a glance as they came ambling along the road from St. Ninian's, and knew, by the sobriety of their apparel as well as the starched bands worn by the gentlemen, that they were puritans, or adherents of my *friend*, the godly earl.

As the wind raised the cloak of the first rider, I could perceive that he had on a buff coat, lined with scarlet silk, embroidered, and left unbuttoned to show his cuirass below; for the times were perilous, after twelve years of unexampled civil and religious war.

The four lurkers lifted their shock heads from the grass, and, after exchanging glowing glances of anger and joy, levelled their fire-arms at the party, which came up at an easy trot.

My heart beat quicker, and mounting, I drew my sword.

In another moment the travellers were close by; the gentle-man in the black mantle was laughing, and having a falcon or male hawk seated on his right glove, was coquetting with the tercel carried by one of his fair companions on her slender wrist.

"Beware!" I exclaimed, "beware!" and rushed forth with my sword uplifted; but at that moment four shots rang on the forest-road; the two ladies uttered a piercing shriek, the hawks screamed in concert and flapped their wings, and three of the attendants fell to the ground; one of these was killed; the other two had their horses shot under them; and before they could recover from their consternation, the two Highlandmen and their companion had fallen on with their drawn swords, uttering a shout which corroborated my surmises as to their character—

"A Grahame! a Grahame! *Blar Aultern!*"

Like every coward whose heart is in his mouth at the first

shot, my friend in the black mantle spurred his horse, and turning, prepared to fly; but very shame made him wheel round; and drawing his sword, he pressed forward to the assistance of his companions, who were maintaining an unequal combat of three to four.

My heart beat high! I was young, full of manhood, spirit, and ardour; thus I fell on bravely, and escaping two pistol shots, cut one Celt through the collar-bone, and clove the jaws of the other; and thus, while the stag-hound dragged down a third, and while the knight of the mantle was brandishing his silver-hilted rapier, and calling on "the God of Jacob and Isaac" to aid him, I saved them all; for the whole of the footpads, awed either by my aspect or dexterity, plunged into the Torwood, and disappeared.

We now drew breath, and surveyed the field of battle.

One valet in livery lay dead on the road, with the blood oozing from a wound in his throat, and forming a black pool among the summer dust. One of the other riders, whom I soon perceived to be a gentleman of lofty and somewhat imperious bearing, limped from the effects of his fall and a kick from the dying horses, which in their agony had rolled from the roadway into the adjacent thicket.

"A strange business this, sir," said the gentleman on foot, who was the first to recover his self-possession, and panted as he wiped his rapier with a cambric handkerchief. "Know ye what manner of villains these were?"

"No more than yourself, sir," I replied, displeased by his menacing eye and the curl of his fierce moustache and beard, which belied his puritanical dress of sad-coloured velvet.

"God warn us and deliver us from evil," said his mounted companion, whose better hand trembled so much that he could scarcely pass the point of his sword into its crimson velvet scabbard; "but, verily, we 'nave had a narrow, a miraculous, and perilous escape; and my father, the late justiciar, must decide whether these blows have been given in *chaud-mella*, or by forethought fellonie.'

A new emotion stirred me, for the voices of these men were not unfamiliar to my ear; but I strove in vain to remember where I had heard them before. Of their faces, I had no recollection whatever.

"We owe you a life of gratitude, fair sir," said one of the ladies, approaching me with a courtly smile, and regardless of the bleeding corpse below her horse's hoofs. I bowed to my saddle, though her eye was bold, her manner imperious and unpleasing—the more so, as her fair cheek was coarsely rouged, a fashion unknown among discreet women in Scotland.

"And now, sir," said he of the white feather, resuming his cold presence of mind, "may I ask to whom we are indebted for aid so friendly and so opportune?"

"To a corporal of the Black Dragoons," said I, gathering my reins, for the whole bearing and manner of these people displeased me, and I was animated by some hidden and mysterious principle of repugnance.

"Oh, in the king's service, eh?" queried the other (who seemed but a few years older than myself), with an undisguised sneer on his thin lip.

"Yes, sir, in the service of his majesty, the King of Scotland, whom God long preserve," said I, fixing my eyes sharply upon him.

"Your name, corporal?" he asked, while they all exchanged glances, the meaning of which I could not fathom. "Speak, sir!"

"That shall be only as I please;—but my name is Ogilvie."

"I would it had been any other," said he, with a dark look, as he wheeled round his horse, and rode slowly off without farther parley.

"It serves my purpose," said I, displeased by this ungraciousness; and turning to his companion, "will *you*, sir, please to tell who is this unmannerly person?"

"Archibald Campbell," said the other, with a frigid smile.

"Hah! there is one of that name to whom I owe a heavy debt."

"Indeed;—is it much?"

"Only a few inches of cold iron; and I shall pay them with usurer's interest on the first eligible opportunity."

"Have a care what you say, sir," said the rouged lady, with sparkling eyes, "and do not undo the great kindness of to-night, for the gentleman who addresses you is Dougal, the Laird of Ardmohr; the other is my husband, Archibald, Lord Lorn. You may hear of us at the Argyle lodging, in Stirling; and so we wish you a very good even, sir; come, Ardmohr, we have tarried too long."

I started at her words as if I had trod on a reptile.

A hundred fierce questions occurred to me, and a storm of anger glowed in my heart. I would have ridden after them, and at all hazards forced an explanation from these imperious puritans, but the fixed gaze of two soft female eyes arrested me, and I received a kind and thoughtful glance, and a grateful adieu waved to me by the hand of the other lady, who had hitherto remained aloof, but whom I recognised in a moment, as she turned her horse, and galloped away, followed by her hound.

The memory of that glance from those soft and thankful eyes, dwelt long in my heart.

She was Flora, the kind young maid whom I had seen at Ardmohr. In the short time that had elapsed since then, she had expanded into the full bloom of beauty, and almost of womanhood; but my interest in her was rather subdued, on finding her in company so hostile to me and to the interests of the king I served. Moreover, the proud and imperious manner of her female companion filled me with anger and honest indignation.

"So you are Lady Lorn—Earl Murray's daughter," thought I, gazing after her, as she cantered under the oaks of the Torwood. "Wretch! and I have drawn a sword to save thee, thou painted harlot, who spat in the face of the dying Montrose, when, bound with cords, he was dragged, but last month, through the streets of Edinburgh! Faith, Harry Ogilvie, thou'st little to do, to peril thus thy bones on this fine summer evening."

And in a bitter and angry mood I rode rapidly off towards Stirling, to fulfil my orders, and troubled myself no more on the matter.

I had returned good for evil; that is, I had saved from death the very men who endeavoured to kidnap me; but from the way in which it came to pass, I deserved but little credit for forgiveness, perhaps.

CHAPTER XIV.

THE OLD RED FOX.

THE delay consequent to this affair forced me to spur on; and on reaching Stirling, I inquired for the provost, whom I directed to provide accommodation for six hundred horse.

"Six hundred! The Lord hae a care o' us," said the magistrate, in consternation; "the haill burgh will be dragooned!"

"Aye—six hundred," said I; "all tried soldiers and tall fellows."

"Under whom, sir trooper?"

"Count Ogilvie of Mariburg."

"Ah! then we shall have no outrages or forcible inquartering. Heaven be praised, it is not the Lord Eglinton and his life guards!"

He appeared considerably relieved; for I write of a time when the troops of the Scottish service were somewhat high-handed and short-tempered with citizens. The whole regiment came in soon after, and with trumpets sounding and kettle-drums beating, and drew up in close column of troops in the Broad Wynd, where the civil authorities "told off," as we phrase it, the men and horses to their several billets. Finding that the noble mansion of the Earl of Argyle was the best in Stirling, the quartermaster gave a billet order on it for our commanding officer; but as soon as the latter saw its name in the document, he started, crumpled it up, and changed colour, while his eyes flashed with a lurid gleam, as he said, hurriedly,—

"Not there—not there, quartermaster; the smallest dog-kennel in Stirling rather."

My horse was stabled at a vintner's; Corporal Bezaleel Mac Snaffle and myself were billetted on a house in the Baxter's Wynd. It was built in the Flemish style, with its gables facing the street, and had carved on its front the following remarkable couplet, which may yet be seen there:

> *Heir I forbeir my name or arms to fix,*
> *Lest I, or mine should sell thos stones and stiks.*

This was done to quiz a vainglorious weaver, who had built the adjoining tenement; but falling into difficulties, had to sell it, after carving his coat of arms thereon. The gudewife of the house, the spouse of a substantial burgher, received us with civility and kindness.

"You are the mair welcome," said she, "for my puir husband's sake. He, too, is a soldier, and hath left me, to fight for our kirk and country; and my soul hath gane awa' wi' him, my dear gudeman!"

"In what regiment, mistress?" I asked.

"The king's life guards; and he has left me with eight wee bairns."

"Eight! alas!" said I, "if aught should befall him."

"Then shall my eight sons become soldiers, ilka man of them, to fight for Scotland and for me!" replied this Spartan dame.

"Verily thou art a fruitful vine," drawled the corporal, as he took the best seat by the fire.

"Is your mother alive?" she asked me, seeing that I was but a lad, when my helmet was off.

"No," said I, sadly.

"I thought sae," said she, passing a hand kindly over my head.

"Why so, gudewife?"

"One sae young would not hae been a soldier, had *she* lived, my puir bairn!"

"Perhaps so," said I, thoughtfully, as I kissed her hand; "but I am a stout fellow, gudewife."

She was more than kind to us, and prepared a hearty supper, which we shared with her and the little ones. As soon as it was over, and Corporal Mac Snaffle had mixed a jug of hot punch, he produced a dog-eared Bible, which he always carried in the same bag with his horsepicker, curry-comb, and spare shoe, and proceeded to read a portion thereof. This he did regularly every night and morning, taking the chapters just as they stood in rotation, like files for duty. It mattered not a rush to him whether it were Chronicles, a crack-jaw enumeration of the tribes of Judah, or the dreary lamentations of Jeremiah.

"A chapter *is* a chapter," he would say; "and it is my duty to read it, and *yours* to listen."

The chapter over, the corporal mixed a second and a third stoup of whiskey punch, and finding that with the gudewife, her eight staring children, her two servants, and myself, he had a tolerable congregation, he smoothed down his hair, slipped the side braces of his cuirass, and proceeded to expound in the most approved fashion, on the growing errors and heresies of the time, in that dreary and *intoned* voice which seems to be half the secret of popular preaching; and he boasted that by the strength of his faith he saw all things with such clearness, that he could demonstrate how many angels could rest on the point of the finest cambric needle. Then flying off at a tangent, he lifted up his eyes, and flourished forth the following rhapsody:

"Arianism, that malapert, perfidious, malicious, and vain-glorious heresy, against which Hiliary, the bishop, blew the trumpet in vain; Socinianism, whilk boasteth of making reason alone its guide, and runneth like a mad horse into glaring incon-sistencies and monstrous absurdities; Quakerism, whilk abjureth all ordination and orders of priesthood; Pelagianism, the cheats of whilk were detected by the synod of Diospolis, and whilk, as thou knowest, gudewife, objected that if concupiscence be one effect of sin, and that if men are born in sin, then must marriage itself be a sin; Latitudinarianism, Scepticism, Anabaptism, Deism, Brownism, and many other heresies, are growing among us in these distracted times. Misery to thee, O kirk of the wise Knox and pious Wishart, for unless thy people keep shoulder to shoulder, girding up their loins, as those who are ready to go forth to battle against the Philistines and Amalekites, thou wilt be bruised by the heel of puritanism, and crushed by the cloven-hoof of prelatism, whilk wi' its surplices, copes and four neukit bonnets, will yet prove to Scotland the most damnable ism of them all! But may the Lord give thee victory and repose in Israel. Let us sing to the praise," &c.

But the corporal's psalm, in which he was devoutly joined by the household, was too much for my nerves, so, taking my rapier under my arm, I put on my helmet, and slipped down stairs into the street.

The night was calm and serene, the moon was clear and bright, and the aspect of the Broad Wynd of Stirling, bordered by quaint and fantastic houses, which shot up in sharp and broken outlines, gable, pinnacle, and chimney, with the flakes of moon-light streaming between them, was striking and picturesque, while the façade of that great unfinished edifice, which was built from the ruins of Cambuskemeth, and from which, in the six-teenth century, the soldiers of John of Mar fired on the troopers of Sir William Kirkaldy, when the Regent Lennox was slain, and the lords of the Black Parliament were rescued, was alike gorgeous and grotesque.

I walked thoughtfully on.

The streets were empty, or nearly so, for men went to bed betimes, and double-barred their doors, for save the kirk session, or the burgh courts—each the unflinching tyrant—the petty star-chamber of its district, the voice of law was almost dumb in Scotland; every man protected himself by his sword, by his friends, his vassals, or clansmen, and everywhere the weakest had to bend like a willow to the blast; and thus, like the willow, many escaped, when the strong oaks, like Montrose, were torn up by the roots.

Such were a few of the evil effects of the mad efforts of the king and the English nation to subvert the Church of Scotland, and to dictate to her people; and such were among the many results of that disastrous civil war which had deluged the north with blood, till religion became rancorous fanaticism, patriotism a ferocious spirit of national animosity, and ultimately all order became disorder.

As I wandered on, I found myself beneath the walls of a magnificent edifice, which stands on the eastern side of the castle hill, rich in aspect, with its round and octagonal towers and conical turrets, its carved doorways, and windows surrounded by semi-classic ornaments. Its casements were filled with light, which streamed in flakes of many colours, between silken hangings, and painted glass across the thoroughfare. Near the arched gateway, which gives admittance to the courtyard of this stately hotel, were a group of armed men, principally High-landers in green tartan: and beyond it were many links and torches blazing; while servitors, armed and liveried, stood by the bridles of richly caparisoned horses; and I could see many a grave-visaged divine, with bands and cuffs of spotless white, clad in their black Geneva cloaks and calotte caps, stalking to and fro, or conversing together in the arcades and passages. Not-withstanding the light, the crowd, and bustle, which pervaded this spacious and magnificent mansion, there was a stolid apathy in the aspect of all about it, that somewhat chilled and surprised me.

A cavalier—an officer of the Lord Duffus's regiment, who was coming down from the castle, with one hand in the hilt of his long rapier, which was upheld by one of those voluminous silk scarfs then worn by all Scottish officers, passed me, singing merrily, with his tall plume nodding, and a jaunty devil-may-care air about him, though he had a wooden leg, and was, as I afterwards ascertained, Captain Roy of Aldivalloch.

"May it please you, sir, to inform me to whom this noble mansion belongs?" I asked, with a bow, for a moment forgetting that I was but a private dragoon.

"Prithee, my good fellow, under what mountain have you been buried, since you know not that since Cromwell played the devil in England, we call this the house of the *Old Red Fox?* Once it was the patrimony of the Earls of Stirling, but ten years ago, the *Fox* laid his paw upon it—tore down the arms of the Alexanders, and put up his own;" and, with a loud laugh, the officer resumed his song and his swagger, and stumped away, leaving me as ignorant as before, but much more curious in the matter, and bent on acquiring information.

"Whose mansion is this, reverend sir?" I inquired of a divine, in one of those eternal black cloaks and caps, with bands and jaws of portentous length, who came forth from the gate, and whom I knew to be no other than Mr. Robert Traill, minister of Elie, and a cadet of the house of Blebo.

"Whose mansion, saidst thou? It is the dwelling-place of one whose soul is pure from every spot of sin; yea, clean from all unrighteousness; one who goeth before Israel as a shining pillar of light!"

"Whence, then, is it named the house of the Old Red Fox?"

The brow of the divine grew black, his eyes pale with a baleful light, and he made a half-step towards the armed men at the gate; but checked it, and said in a stern whisper,—

"See ye the stone shaft of yonder market-cross?"

Surprise at all this made me silent.

"Dost thou see it?" he repeated, imperiously.

"Yes, sir—I do."

"Well—let any other ear in Stirling, save mine, hear thee use this ungodly epithet towards one who is the mirror of truth and purity, of wisdom, grace, and virtue—yea, a star to Israel and the covenanted kirk, and thine ears will be affixed to that stone shaft with a pair of spike nails, thou malapert malignant; for he of whom thou speakest with this irreverence is Archibald, Earl of Argyle."

And with a glance in which piety and anger were curiously blended, his reverence left me, his very cloak seeming to become inflated with righteous indignation; for it had become a maxim —almost a point of doctrine—with his party, that he who doubted the piety, purity, and patriotism of Cromwell's coadju-tor, did not believe in God; so I resolved to be more wary in future.

When I surveyed this mansion, of which the family of Argyle had possessed themselves, and saw the number of vassals, nobles, gentlemen, divines, pages, grooms, ladies and their attendants who flitted about the windows, doors, and arcades, "Can it be,' thought I, "that one so great, so rich, and so powerful as the lord of all this, can have an object to serve or a pleasure to gratify in crushing one so weak, so powerless, and so humble as I—.: poor dragoon ?"

Time alone could solve the mystery.

At that moment I turned away, as several of our officers, all gaily dressed in coats richly laced, and beavers plumed, and with shining sword hilts, rode up and dismounted at the gate. As they entered I recognised the Master of Oliphant, the Laird of Linn, the captain of my troop, and others ; but the colonel was *absent ;* and, for the first time, I felt a pang of bitterness in my heart, as I reflected on my own nameless, obscure, and unfriended condition.

CHAPTER XV.

FLORA.

At an open window stood a lady gazing on the flood of moon‹ light which made the magnificent façade of Stirling Castle, with its palace, prison, and parliament hall, rock, rampart and battery, turret, tower, and statues, knop and pinnacle, glitter as if bathed in liquid silver.

The lady was but a few feet from me, and the circumstance of her being attired in a robe of white muslin, which floated like a cloud of gauze about her, as well as her brow and bracelets being gemmed with many a sparkling jewel, led me to linger for a moment, and (while seeming to gaze at the moonlit fortress) to steal many a furtive glance at her. In this age, when all ornaments had been abolished, and gay attire had given place to sad-coloured garments, save among the high-flying cavaliers and their families, her appearance was no less remarkable than her beauty. A circle of little curls fringed her brow and temples—for such were then the fashion—but a heavy volume of dark brown hair, all glossy and shining, was smoothed over the back of her beautiful head, and fell in a shower of ringlets behind.

One white hand rested on the rough head of a shaggy dog, and thus in a moment I recognised in her the lady I had lent the dint of my sword that day to save, and the little maid, whose rough staghound, Corrie, had saved me from the waters of the Clyde at Ardmohr. I would have given the world to address her ; and while I felt some invisible power, with all the strength of a loadstone, chaining me to the spot, prudence and propriety alike dictated that I should withdraw, for the vicinity was dangerous to me.

I gave a parting glance at that pensive, soft, and charming face, and was turning away with a sigh, when I thought the sound of her voice followed me, and I turned. I could scarcely believe my eyes. She was beckoning to me, and with an elated heart I drew near.

"You are the brave trooper to whom my friends and I were so much indebted this afternoon—our adventure—that horrible scene——"

"In the Torwood, madam."

"Yes; I am right then!"

How prettily she spoke. The sound of her voice was charming!

"I would, gentle lady, that the service I performed were a thousand times more dangerous, since it merits your approval," said I, with a profound bow, and then remembering "the soldier," I raised my gauntletted hand to the peak of my helmet. Something in my air or manner made her pause for a moment, and she said, gravely,

"I fear, sir, you must have deemed that service very ungraciously rewarded; and I blush when I remember that a sneer was the only guerdon you received."

"Oh, speak not of guerdon or of boon," said I, while my heart swelled; "to serve a noble lady—even by the sacrifice of a life —and to have that sacrifice remembered even for an hour, by one so brilliant as you, is guerdon more than enough for a poor corporal of dragoons, who risks life and limb every hour for little more than a doit, Lady Flora."

"How—you know my name?"

"I have known it long, lady; and gratitude forbade that I should forget it."

"Very probably. My father is said to do so many acts of kindness. But your courage to-day——"

"Would have been of little avail, but for that valiant staghound, Corrie."

"Ah, you know my dog too!" she added, with surprise, as Corrie cocked his wiry ears, and wagged his tail at the sound of his own name.

I was on the point of calling to her recollection the half drowned youth he had saved at Ardmohr, when the warnings of Oliphant and Linn occurred to me; and remembering that I was yet ignorant of *who* this gentle and condescending lady was, I resolved to preserve my incognito.

"Trooper, I rejoice in having an opportunity of thanking you

for the service of to-day; it had lain heavy at my heart if unrequited," said she, hastily, as she placed a white hand on the
window-sash, as if about to close it, and I saw the gems sparkle
on her wrist and fingers as she did so; " but for *you*, fair sir,
there had been a wail of lamentation here to-night; for the Lord
Lorn, his bride, and I, had assuredly been slain. Those four men
were broken soldiers of Colkittoch and Montrose, sworn to
avenge the defeat of one, and the butchery of the other. (As
she said this, her voice sank into a tremulous whisper.) But
God warn and defend us from evil!"

She drew a ring from her finger, and said,

" Receive this from me, and keep it, soldier, till you find some
bonnie lass, whose finger it will suit; and receive it with the
assurance that I will add thereto a dowry if she lacks it, as a
proof that, of the strangers you served to-day, *one* at least was
grateful, and remembered you."

The ring glittered as it fell at my feet.

I snatched and pressed it to my lips; but when I looked again,
the casement was shut and the lady gone. A ring to me, a gift
from that young, high-born, and dazzling girl; and taken warm
from her beautiful hand! It seemed all a dream, from which I
trembled to awake. But, alas! cold reason came to show that a
charming delicacy alone had made her aware how money *to me,*
even as a trooper, would have been an insult, and thus she rewarded me by a gift, which, from such a hand as hers, an emperor
might receive with pride.

" Lady Flora—but Lady Flora *who?*—has justly appreciated
the character of Harry Ogilvie!" thought I.

With a proud and happy heart I turned away; in this moonlight interview there was much that charmed my fancy and
soothed my pride.

I had traversed too long the thorny paths of poverty and humiliation to believe in love at first sight; enthusiasm had been
nearly crushed out of me; yet the image of this lady (for Flora
is my heroine) filled my whole soul with such emotions of worship,
as that of a divinity might produce in an untutored savage. It
was perhaps the romance and the poetry of youth, united to a
powerful and ardent imagination, and great aptitude for building
those unfortunate edifices known as castles in the air. I felt
that I was fated to worship this new planet of my sphere from a
vast distance, for the gulf between us was impassable to me; but
it would be that worship of the heart which was peculiar to the
old and knightly days, when beauty was all that a lover required;
for in our riper years and colder times a pure and high esteem
for manner, mind, accomplishments, and personal worth, are all
necessary to make a true and lasting passion.

Of Flora's mind or worth I knew nothing, but her beauty and manner were as winning as her voice and eye were seductive; esteem—but where am I galloping to? Alas! at eighteen how the heart runs away with the head!

I was forgetting that she was a lady of high degree, with her brocaded skirt and high-heeled shoes; her broad oxgangs of lands, and perhaps her sixteen quarters of nobility; while I was a poor devil of a trooper, who could scarcely afford his own pipeclay; and I marvelled whether she would feel more anger or more amusement if she had known my aspiring thoughts, and the hopes or emotions her *graceful* present had excited for a moment in my heart.

I returned to my billet in the Baxter's Wynd, and found the gudewife thereof enchanted with my comrade, our sainted corporal, who was only closing his discourse "anent schism" as I entered, and was bestowing upon her rubicund cheek, for the third time to my knowledge, "the pure kiss of peace," while he drained the last dram from the magnum bonum of her absent spouse.

I now descended from the poetry to the prose of life; but Flora's ring was on my finger, and her image in my heart.

CHAPTER XVI.

I RESUME THE GENTLEMAN AGAIN.

WE were quartered in Stirling for some weeks, during which there scarcely passed a day without my contemplating the lady's gift, which was so small that I could scarcely pass the fourth finger of my left hand through it. It was a plain gold hoop, with a single diamond of considerable value set in it. I had seen the fair donor repeatedly in the streets of Stirling; on these occasions she always bowed to me graciously, and made my heart beat happily for many a lonely hour after.

We were kept at hard drill in the King's Park, as vast bodies of troops—horse, foot, and artillery—were being concentrated round the capital, Perth, Stirling, and other places, by the estates of the realm, who were making every exertion to maintain the young king's authority, and be prepared to resist an expected invasion from the English republicans.

It was always my fortune to be billeted, and of all quarters in the world there can be none more obnoxious to a soldier than *his billet;* for the same man who in a foreign country would be considered a quiet and harmless fellow, if billeted in his own, is often viewed as a military ruffian, or is treated as an intruder, with insolence and contempt, by the whiggish landlord and his ungracious, it may be ignorant, wife; the worst bed and the worst room are assigued him with a grudge; even his poor victuals are ill dressed; and though legally billeted and entitled to comfortable quarters, he is treated as a sorner and hamesucker, and creeps to his kennel sighing over the wounds received in defence of such lurdanes as these. I have endured much of this in my time, and have often thought, if my countrymen in Scotland had occasionally a few French mousquetaires or Muscovite horse quartered among them, they would relish all the better the quiet and orderly soldiers of their own country.

One evening I had just returned to Stirling with a party of my troop, having been at Blackness Castle escorting a party of six Englishmen, who had been shipwrecked in the north, and three others, who had been detected buying cavalry horses in Scotland in defiance of an act of our legislature, and all of whom the governor of the fortress was to march to the next military post, so that they might be exchanged at the borders. I had just groomed my horse, had a can of ale at a change house with my old friend Sergeant Glanders, and was slowly—it may be mechanically—sauntering in the gloaming towards the house where I had seen that fair face which had never for a moment been absent from my thoughts, when the unusual crowds of horsemen, and the number of equipages that were pouring up the hill towards the castle of Stirling, attracted my attention; and on inquiring the reason of Glanders, he informed me that the governor of the fortress, the Honourable William Cunninghame, was giving a grand military rere-supper in honour of Lieutenant-General Leslie, and Argyle, who was one of the six lords of the Scottish treasury; "a devilish snug billet," quoth the sergeant, "and one in whilk he feathers the nests of the Campbells to some purpose."

Lumbering old-fashioned coaches, that might have seen the days of Anne of Denmark, covered with plated bosses, chased ornaments, and coats of arms, driven by laced coachmen, and drawn by solemn Flemish mares with long switch tails, were crawling up the steep streets towards the castle. Gaily-painted sedans, borne by liveried footmen and preceded by link boys, were trotted out from wynd and close, towards the same place; while gentlemen, and officers of cavalry with laced cloaks and waving feathers, galloped briskly up the hill; and the gaudy liveries of Buchanan of Arnprior, who was seneschal of Lennox, and of the Stirlings of Carse, the Livingstones of Callendar, and other old baronial families, were glittering in the torches and moonlight, and all their servants and followers were well armed with swords, daggers, Doune pistols, and Lochaber axes.

Surrounded by a strong band of wild-looking Highland gillies, all clad in Tartan, and having drawn swords and lighted torches, the glare of which produced a strange and barbaric effect, I saw the great rumbling coach of Argyle pass me. It was filled with ladies, and on its six panels bore the quarterings of his family with those of the Earls of Findourie, upon whose estates, like those of many others, he had laid forcible or fraudulent hands; and with these badges were the royal crest and crown of Scotland, with a sword, the ensigns of his present office as great master of the household, and his recent one as lord high justiciar of the realm. The drums of Duffus' regiment beat a roll at the gate, and the guard presented arms, as this coach, which resembled a huge catafalque, disappeared under the venerable arch of the fortress.

As I slowly descended the esplanade towards the town, I re-flected with a sigh—almost of bitterness—that *she*, perhaps, was in that gay scene from which I was now excluded. In my reverie, I came roughly against two gentlemen, one of whom laid a hand on his sword, saying,

"'Sdeath! fellow, art blind as a bat or deaf as a post, neither to see nor to hear?"

"I crave your pardon, Master," said I, recognising the fiery young Master of Oliphant, the lieutenant of my troop; "but, on my soul, I was lost in dreaming of what may never be."

"What! comrade Harry, is't thee?" exclaimed this frank young noble, clapping me on the shoulder; "by my faith, I knew you not in that black helmet and buff coat. Right! 'tis I, Oli-phant, and this is Willie Linn—Orestes and Pylades—or Castor and Pollux—which you will."

"I warrant me, you were thinking of our old college days," said Linn, "when we were wont to wrench the risps and snatch the cloaks of the Saltmarket burgesses, and when we rumpled their wives' coifs and daughters' fardingales—eh!"

"Nay, I was looking forward rather than back."

"Forward! a short way, methinks, since you saw us not. But why so dull and lifeless, Harry?"

"Because there are moments when I cannot help repining, and feeling that surely I was born for better things than being a cor-poral of horse."

"Of course, and so you were, as you shall soon find, when blows are struck and saddles emptied. We'll have a war with England before the year is out."

"And many a royal commission, many a coronet and fair estate, will change hands then, believe me," said Linn. "But we tarry, Oliphant, and the rere-supper waits."

"Farewell, comrade; get thee a pint of burnt sack, and drink to the better time in store for thee," said the master, laughing as he waved his long plume.

"Farewell, noble sirs," said I, with a mixture of respect and familiarity; "you are going where I would give the world to go also."

"How?" asked Linn, pausing.

"Why?" added Oliphant.

"Because," I replied, hesitating, while my cheek burned, "there is a lady there whom I am longing much to see."

"Thou shouldst have said *dying*, man—that is the approved phrase," said Linn.

"Well, dying, then."

"'Zounds! thou shalt go with us."

"Alas! Oliphant, I am no longer your jovial brother-student, the bachelor of Glasgow—I am——"

"The corporal of my troop, and as such may be the comrade of a king, and so may well be 'hail! fellow, well met' with Patrick Oliphant, of Aberdalgie. Come, then."

"But in this black morion and buff coat?"

"Tush!" said Linn; "I have a satin coat with slit sleeves, and a cloak, that will fit thee to a hair. Our quarters are close by—the first turnpike above the Lord Mar's lodging; come with us—come. We shall introduce you as a young volunteer from the German wars—a knight of the Eagle, or Malta—colonel of Brandenburgers, and chevalier of the 'Pig and Whistle,' or something equally great, who has returned to trail a pike under the marshal Earl of Callender—ha! ha!" and laughing and pulling me, these two frank and joyous spirits, with whom remonstrance and protestation were alike unavailing, led me to their quarters, and in a few minutes I had exchanged my plain regimental trappings of buff and black iron for a very handsome pink satin doublet, slashed with white silk, having sleeves slit from the wrist to the shoulder, to display those of the vest, which were made of cloth of silver. A vandyked falling collar, of the richest point lace; a short cloak of purple velvet, lined with yellow silk, dangled on my left shoulder; a pair of long breeches, fringed where they met my wide buff boots; a broad-leaved Spanish hat, with a white plume; a toledo hung in a magnificent sword-belt, with a pair of highly-perfumed gloves, completed a costume in which, after my long cavalier locks had been curled, and my moustachios painted with pomatum, I flatter myself that I looked every inch as much a gentleman as either of my friends, who were two of the most showy men in the king's service, and were very active and merry in dressing me.

"But, zounds! what shall I do," said I, "if our grave, solemn colonel, or the burly old laird of Drumstanchel, should recognise me?"

"Oh—pshaw! put this big black patch over one eye,' said Linn.

"A patch!"

"Of course—a wound received at Leipzig or Lutzen in saving the life of the king or Marshal Horne," said Oliphant, plastering the article mentioned on my left cheek-bone; and in a trice I was ready. They each took an arm; and forgetting for the moment that there was any impropriety, or breach of etiquette or of military discipline, in the matter, or that it was aught more than one of our old Trongate frolics, I joined them in a merry chanson as we went arm-in-arm up the steep street towards the castle hill of Stirling.

CHAPTER XVII.

I BECOME A DISTINGUISHED CHARACTER.

GUARDS, pages, and attendants ushered us through the courts of Stirling Castle, the most magnificent of our Scottish palatial fortresses.

The governor, Colonel Cunninghame, a cadet of the house of Glencairn, remained near the door of the hall, receiving his guests, and near him stood Lieutenant-General Sir David Leslie, in whose honour the entertainment was given. Both were plain and rough-looking old soldiers, weather-beaten and grizzle-bearded, wearing silver-laced buff coats over their cuirasses, with the gold shoulder-scarfs then worn by officers of the Scottish cavalry.

The Master of Oliphant introduced me as an old friend of his, just returned from abroad to take military service in Scotland; and on receiving the governor's greeting, with some confusion, I passed into the glittering crowd which filled that stately hall. This noble apartment is one hundred and twenty feet in length, and was gorgeously decorated by portraits of our kings by Vandyke, Hans Holbein, Sir Thomas Galbraith, and others, whose works were mingled with armour, arms, and banners taken in war.

Among those present, I saw the lairds of Lawers and Ardmohr, both Campbells, and colonels of red-coated regiments of musketeers; for our king retained in the Scottish service this bright colour, which the covenanters were the *first* to adopt, and which most of their battalions wore at the battle of Kilsythe.* Count Ogilvie, our colonel, clad in a rich coat of white satin, with a collar of Spanish lace, and a white feather drooping from his fawn-coloured cavalier hat, now entered, and his rich costume

* See " Britanes Distemper."

formed a strange contrast to his dark sun-burnt and powder-grimed face, which was ever so stern, grave, and thoughtful in expression. On his breast was a gold chain, with the silver badge of the White Eagle of Lithuania, won by him under Hepburn, on the banks of the Vistula, for he was not one whose honours were won by the scabbard. He usually said little, but was one of those who by a single glance can convey a whole sentence.

There, too, came the rough old laird of Drumstanchel, and other cavaliers of the Black Dragoons, whom I felt myself constrained to avoid; and there, also, came the smart officers of the Lord Duffus' regiment, wearing tight buff coats, the bright cuirasses, and long flowing locks of the royal service; while gliding among the gay noblesse and beautiful women who were so richly jewelled and attired, were several severe and sombre divines (with hair cropped close, or hanging long and lank), clad in the usual pinched Geneva cloak and sad-coloured small-clothes, always conferring together or glancing stealthily about, and remarking with solemn emphasis on the evils this temporary levity and partial relapse into the sin of gay costume, flowing locks, and a little merriment, would assuredly bring upon Scotland. Among these black crows, I recognised Mr. Robert Traill, the Rev. Robert Douglas (of whom more anon), and, to my no small horror, the Reverend Zachary Boyd, who had been commissioned by the General Assembly to attend upon the army, and had left his young bride, the blooming Margaret Muir, to pine alone in Glasgow, within a month or two after their marriage. Poor Maggie!

In short, one portion of the assembly was extremely gay, perhaps frivolous in dress and manner, while the other was morose and severe.

The smart beau cavaliers and the ladies of their families were all clad in rich stuffs, of brilliant colours, with flashing jewels and glittering chains, stars and ribbons; their faces wreathed with blushes, smiles, and laughter; while the solemn dames of the covenant wore sad-coloured fardingales and plain white collars, edging faces pinched and prim; and their spouses or brothers had plain buff coats, square falling bands, and long and straight, or close-shorn hair, with enormous iron spadas, to contrast with the bowl-hilted rapiers of the ultra-loyalists.

Such were the fashions of my young days!

But notwithstanding their marked difference of dress and religious or political creeds, at present they had happily relinquished all animosity in the growing danger that threatened the nation from without, and, blended into one united mass, were resolved to make common cause against the puritans of England. Such were the views of the covenanters in general; though in these views, Argyle—our Sergius Catiline, who aimed at the destruction of the Scottish throne—had no share in his secret soul.

"Here cometh the king of the west with his daughters, ready for the ring," said Oliphant, laughingly, in my ear.

"How ?——"

"For marriage, as women always are; and see Linn's lady-love, too—the adorable little Dora, the daughter of old Sir Henry Lennox."

"Give room, sirs!" cried the usher; "place for my lord, the Earl of Argyle."

And passing through the crowd, which parted before him like the waves of the sea, Argyle, bowing to his various friends—but particularly to every Geneva cloak—came slowly up the hall. He was dressed entirely in black velvet, and had his long red hair parted on the centre of his head, and hanging in elf-locks on his shoulders. His obliquity of vision, which gained him among his own gallant tribe, the Campbells, the sobriquet of Gillespie Grumach—or Archy the Ill-favoured—was very apparent as he glanced furtively about him on all sides, as if in search of some one. But this was the mere result of that watchfulness which results from an inborn habit of deceit.

On his right arm leaned a lady, and she, like his four daughters—all of whom were beautiful women, with that delicacy of complexion for which the females of his clan are celebrated—was dressed in that vulgar plainness of attire which distinguished the dames of the puritan party, who always wore either hoods or high-crowned hats. My heart filled with new emotions when I perceived among them the fair Flora who gave me the ring!

"Who is that lady now leaning on the earl's arm?" I inquired of Oliphant, as I recognised the well-rouged dame who had spoken to me so imperiously in the Torwood.

"She with the puritan hat and close ruff?"

"Yes."

"'Tis Mary Stuart—Earl Murray's daughter, and wife of the Lord Lorn.

"I now remember that she told me so," said I, gazing with repugnance upon that cruel and hard-hearted Messalina, who spat in the face of the great marquis, when fettered on a hurdle, and dying with the king's commission and the Order of the Garter on his breast; for we always regard heartless cruelty and rancorous hatred with greater horror in a woman, as being unusual in the female heart, and the very opposite of her character.

With this party was her husband, the Lord Lorn, gorgeously dressed and armed, as colonel of the King's Foot Guards, and his brother, Lord Neil Campbell of Ardmaddie, a boy, wearing a

scarlet coat and black cuirass, being an ensign in Lawer's Musketeers.   As they swept past where our colonel was standing with
the captain of my troop,

"Your servant, Count Ogilvie," said Argyle, with a courtier's
bow and a courtier's smile.

"Yours, my lord and noble ladies," said the count, with a cold
and haughty salute.

"Prithee, why so solemn, count?" asked the smiling Lady
Lorn, as she played with her fan; "why so sad in air and eye this
evening, when all seem happy around us?"

"Like old Count Tilly, madam, and like Wallenstein, with
whom and against whom I have served, I have my *dark hour*—
my moments of bitter reflection."

"Alas, count, I fear that few are without them," snuffled
Argyle.   "Life is beautiful—our daily bread is given us—yet we
walk in a vale of tears; yea, with the shadow of death hanging
over us.   Who among us can say with certainty, we shall see
to-morrow?"

"The voice of years long since gone bye, comes back to my ear
at times," replied the count, in a touching accent.   "I have seen
the axe laid to my roof-tree, and the flames of rapine rise from
the paternal tower of my forefathers.   Tongues and fingers that
made music there, are dust now.   I find no hearts so true as
those that lie under the sod—no souls so pure as those that are
now in heaven; and I have seen a face here to-night that calls
back old memories I fain would bury in the tomb of Time."

"A face—whose?"

"*Your own*, lord earl," replied the count, while his eyes shone
with fire, and the strange dark tint of his face increased.   Argyle
had wronged so many, that instead of demanding a reason for a
reply so peculiar, he quailed beneath the keen, steady glare of the
count's eye, and passed on to address the reverend Messrs. Traill
and Boyd, as he always paid his court to clergymen.

"Drumstanchel," hissed the count through his teeth, to the
captain of my troop, "can we ever forget the bearing of this
cowardly earl—the destroyer of Findourie and ' the bonnie house
of Airlie,' as we saw him at Inverlochy, when he fled to his ship
before the fray began, and cut away the warp, which was laden
with his clansmen, drowning in Lochiel?"

"Yet withal, he rode to Edinburgh, with his arm in a sling,
and stood up before the parliament to prate of his services and
wounds!" was the contemptuous response.

"Yea," continued the count, "he is one in whose purse is the
price of a royal and anointed head; and in whose soul is a stain
as dark as Rizzio's blood at Holyrood.   His shame will live for
ever in the songs of Ian Lom; and the work of that black night

at the tower of Drumstanchel cries yet for vengeance on him and all his kindred."

"Hush, for God's sake, count and kinsman," said the veteran laird; "a word of this in other ears would ruin us all for ever."

I had been an involuntary listener or spectator of all this, and saw that some terrible secret was here involved; but it was no matter of mine.

"Harry," said the Master of Oliphant, "dost see honest old Zachary Boyd, gliding about like a huge black shadow in hob-nailed shoes?"

"I have no wish to see him."

"True—he wedded Maggie Muir, whose pretty face drove you from the auld pedagogie, forcing you to fling up the bachelor's cope, and become a Black Dragoon.   A gay damsel, if rumour says true."

"So gay," added Linn, "that before he returns, he may well quote his favourite text."

"The words of King David?"

"Yes, 'Thou hast exalted my horn.'"

And at this the two madcaps laughed merrily.

"Zounds!" cried the master, "I had almost forgotten.   Well, my thoughtful comrade, have you seen your beauty yet?"

"Twice, good Oliphant."

"And you are charmed?"

"More than tongue can tell."

"But who is she?" asked the master.

"I dare not say, lest Linn and you should laugh my presumption down."

"We are here as brother students to-night; and I ever considered impudence a student's peculiar prerogative."

"I dare no more tell you, sirs, than tell her of the admiration she has excited within me."

"I once read, at old St. Mungo's, that there is a fashion in the East for lovers to testify the strength of their passion by ripping and cutting themselves in presence of their mistress."

"I assure you, Master of Oliphant, that I would infinitely prefer to cut some one else."

"Cut, slash, and hew, as Sergeant Hackiron says.   Well, and who would you thus favour here?"

"Yonder spark in the scarlet coat slashed with blue, and wearing a cuirass inlaid with gold."

"Whew! that is the Laird of Ardmohr, colonel of infantry, and the affianced spouse, saith rumour, of Argyle's most beautiful daughter."

An unaccountable chill fell over my heart, as my friend spoke, and passed on, leaving me to shift for myself, among this new crowd of high-born strangers.

Perceiving me standing alone, Colonel Cunninghame kindly—but to my inexpressible confusion—turned suddenly towards me, and said,

"It will afford me extreme gratification, if I can be of service to you, young gentleman. Allow me, my Lord Earl of Argyle, to introduce to your special notice, a young friend who has left the German wars to serve his own country—our dear auld mother Scotland,"—and leading me forward to the noble mentioned, he bowed and left me, blushing to the temples, and overwhelmed by mingled emotions, which the quick, keen eyes of Argle seemed endeavouring to analyse.

Suddenly he started, became pale as a sheet, and almost trembled, as he said,

"I wish you all success, fair sir, in the path you have chosen. May I ask where you have served hitherto?"

"In Germany," said I, blushing deeper at the petty falsehood, though I had no alternative now but to go through the whole affair boldly; besides, I recalled the plot of his son and Ardmohr against my life and liberty, and sought to connect it with that excitement which he strove in vain to control; and his hand and lip trembled so nervously, that I observed,

"My lord, you appear agitated."

These words acted like an opiate, and at once composed him.

"I crave your pardon, young sir, and bless you in the Lord, with my whole heart and soul. Let not my emotion surprise you, for it is occasioned by your wonderful—yea, miraculous resemblance to one—whom—whom I knew in other days."

"A dear friend, perhaps, my lord?"

"Yes—yes, a dear friend, of course."

"And now dead?"

"Yea and alas!" he replied, turning up the white of one eye, and gazing at the buckle of my belt with the other; "for the flesh of man is grass—yea, dead; but, let us hope, asleep in the bosom of Abraham."

While the earl was speaking, the five ladies of his party drew near us, and I felt almost sinking with shame, for I dared not glance towards my fair one, lest she should recognise, and perhaps expose me to ridicule and contempt. After a pause, during which I had been severely scrutinised by the oblique eyes of the earl, he said, with an undisguised sneer,

"By the curling of your locks, I presume you will stand stoutly by king and high kirk?"

"I will stand only by that kirk and that king which the estates of Scotland support, and am ready to resist unto the death all foreign intermeddling on the part of either French papists or English puritans."

" Right, sir ; for it was the meddling of the so-called Archbishop of Canterbury, and other evil mentors, that caused the late King Charles to invade our church with new, uncouth, and malapert costumes, prayers, and music ; and we must never forget that innovations in kirk matters, be they ever so small, are right perilous. St. Augustine, in his 118th Epistle, said so, long ages ago ; so let us stand up for the purity of our faith, and lay to heart the words of Jude—whom some call *saint*—never to yield to an innovating adversary the smallest jot in matters spiritual ; and what sayeth Calvin, in his 128th Epistle——"

Happily for me, a pause in the earl's discourse saved me from being afflicted with what the learned Picard said ; for at that moment he made a hurried excuse, and hastened after a cavalier who wore a voluminous white scarf. It was no other than my friend with the wooden leg—the same who had called him " an old Red Fox," a few nights ago.

" I crave your pardon, gentle sir," said the earl ; " but I must have a word with the Laird of Aldivalloch. I commit you to God, and will leave my daughter Flora to make amends for my rudeness."

He bowed, and hastened away, leaving me with a lady.

I looked upon her with timid eyes and a faltering heart. She was the donor of the ring, and HIS DAUGHTER FLORA !

CHAPTER XVIII.

THE DAUGHTERS OF ARGYLE.

A FULL minute elapsed before I recovered my presence of mind sufficiently to address her with becoming courtesy ; and she, as if pitying my timidity or shame, seemed for the same period of time to be wholly intent on applying a silver pomander ball to her pretty pink nostrils. At last she broke the ice.

" And you mean to take service at home, sir ?"

" Yes, Lady Flora," I stammered, for now she began to observe me with some surprise and interest.

" Have you a brother here, in Stirling ?"

" No, madam ; I have neither brother nor sister—father nor mother."

" How sad to hear you say so ! Now, marry, but this is passing strange, for your face is quite familiar to me."

It might well be so, as she had given me one of her condescending bows when I rode, that afternoon, after the colonel, through the king's park.

" And your voice, too !" she added.

"Singular! perhaps I have a double-ganger — or wraith. Your recognition is the more pleasing, lady, as your pleasant voice and gentle expression of eye, are—are both familiar to me."

My beautiful puritan coloured a little, and becoming somewhat reserved, turned to converse with her sister, the Countess of Caithness.

I now observed her particularly, and saw that she far surpassed the other daughters of Argyle—three proud, starched, and stately puritan women. Lady Jane was Countess of Lothian; Lady Mary was Countess of Caithness; Lady Anne was never married, as her lover had been slain when the Campbells were routed at the battle of Inverlochy.

Lady Flora's eyes, though blue, were very dark, almost black, and full of the most beautiful expression, to which her well-defined eyebrows gave a fuller point. Her dark brown hair rolled in heavy curls round a pale brow and colourless cheek, falling upon a white and delicate neck, almost shrouded by an immense starched collar. Her features were noble, yet soft and feminine; her figure was now considerably above the middle size, but lithe, active, and faultless in proportion; though its graces were hidden by the unbecoming conical hat and black tubfardingale, which the puritanical taste of the Highland saint, her father, rigidly enforced on all the ladies of his household.

To me she was charming, and seemed something between a child and an angel; but I was awed and dazzled by the difference of our positions, and the false one I occupied; yet my eyes and heart followed her everywhere, and borne away by the romantic and absurd passion that grew within me, I forgot, or forgave, my just cause for indignation against her father.

I forgot that terrible outrage in the streets of Glasgow, and the pleasant voyage projected for me in the snow *Good Intent*—in short, I forgot everything but Flora, whose face and person fully realized all my ideas of perfect beauty; for the mind of a lover sees all as it should be. It seemed as if I must have known and loved her long before we met, for she possessed the face, the eye, the voice, and manner, of one whom I had conjured up in many a lonely hour, as embodying the woman I could love—and thus it was, that when first I spoke to Flora, she seemed to me as one I had loved for years. Yet it was neither her divine purity of complexion, or regularity of feature, that won me; for the first is often a sign of coldness, and the second of insipidity; but it was her sweetness of voice, her winning manner, and varying vivacity of eye.

Both of us were so young, it seemed to me, that if possessed of a very little competence, we could be so rich in love—so wealthy in tenderness and joy—that we might well be the envy of all.

But whither in one minute of time was I going, at full speed, into the land of sunny dreams, and oblivious of the splendid crowd around me, and that I was but a daw in borrowed plumes, among them?

Could I forget that I was poor and nameless, and that this girl whom I addressed in a false character was the favourite daughter of the great regicide—the proud, the cruel, and covetous Argyle? If so, I was, ere long, roughly reminded of it.

"Are you indisposed to-night, Flora?" asked Lady Anne Campbell, "or are you displeased with Dougal of Ardmohr?"

"Sister, for what should I be displeased?" inquired Flora, in the same low voice; but a lover has the ears of a lynx, and thus I lost not a word.

"Because he is not by your side."

"Tush—he is never very far off."

"It was at your request that our father made him colonel of the new musketeer regiment—was it not so, dear Flora?"

"Yes; and hence those idle rumours, Annie. But do not *you* fall in love with him, sister," said Flora, with a soft, appealing, and almost waggish smile to her darker but beautiful elder sister, "for he never could resist you, Annie, and I should lose him."

"Dear Flora, how can you think so injuriously of me?" said Lady Anne, with a saddened tone and a swimming eye; "alas! such thoughts have long been buried on the field of Inver-lochy."

"There must they lie, Anne," said Lord Lorn, with a lofty and supercilious smile; "and I trust, sister of mine, that we shall have no more coquetting with Lawers or Ardmohr, for though both are our remote kinsmen, mere lairds cannot be mate or marrow for the daughters of Argyle. And as for *thy* lover, Anne, what was he that ye should regret him so at this gathering of kingsmen—this military *festum asinorum*—eh? A nameless and penniless cavalier, who fought in the ranks of our mortal foe, Montrose!"

Lady Anne's eyes filled with tears at this harsh speech, and Flora blushed scarlet to her usually snowy temples, while their haughty brother strode away with his gold spurs clanking.

In this short conversation I had received, as it were, two pointed shafts; one was the interest, real or affected, expressed by Lady Flora for the Laird of Ardmohr; and the other was the contempt so openly expressed by the proud young lord for a cavalier whose "nameless and penniless" condition made him so much like myself. Cut to the quick, I was turning away, when a flourish of cavalry trumpets pealed along the arched roof, announcing that supper was ready; and a scarlet curtain, emblazoned with the royal arms of Scotland, which crossed the large doorway at the lower end of the hall, was suddenly parted in the centre, and swept up into two large festoons, displaying beyond it another stately apartment, with the long vista of the governor's hospitable board, glittering with crystal, gorgeous with plate and epergnes of flowers, amid which the vapoury steam of the viands was curling.

With Lady Lorn he led the way to table; and I stood a moment irresolute, until a glance from Lady Flora decided me; and feeling conscious that "to hang fire" now would be unpardonable, I drew off my right glove, presented my hand, and leading her to a seat, placed myself beside her!

CHAPTER XIX.

THE RERE-SUPPER AND THE RING.

THE feast to which we sat down was lordly and unlimited, being the best that the ancient royal kitchens in the castle of Stirling could furnish; and it was served up and carved down by yeomen, sewers, and pages in the livery of the governor, with the arms of Glencairn—*argent*, a shakefork *sable*, and an unicorn's head coupéd on their breasts and sleeves.

There was a serviette for every guest, but each, according to the old fashion, brought his or her knife, as forks were less known in Scotland than in South Britain, where they had been partially introduced by the late king. About two hundred persons sat down to table. There were venison pasties, beef boiled, roasted, fried, and in collops; lamb, veal, geese, capons, capercailzies, ptarmigan, plovers, and partridges, hares and pheasants, cooked in every imaginable way; with three castles of pastry, decked with little flags and peacock's plumage, flowers and gilding, while all around were dishes of pudding and pies of quinces, marmalade and rice, coloured with saffron and sugar, while many a brave runlet of canary and Bourdeaux, Hocheim, sack, and claret, with many a bombarde of Lammas ale, were set abroach by the pantlers. The hall blazed with wax lights, and in the centre of the table stood one of those enormous wassail candles which we were wont to light only at great feasts.

To my no small annoyance, Colonel Campbell, of Ardmohr, in the splendidly laced coat and cuirass of the Red Musketeers, was seated on the other side of Lady Flora, and divided her attention with me, on whom he gazed furtively from time to time, with no favourable eye, for he was a proud, a haughty, and withal brave fellow, some twenty years older than myself; and I had every reason to hate him.

Could he have discovered that I was merely a private trooper!

Flora spoke of many things in a manner that charmed me, for she had the peculiar, and to a pretty woman, invaluable, talent of investing every trifle with interest; and I performed all the attentions due from an accomplished cavalier to this beautiful puritan, by assisting her to everything she expressed a wish for, and filling her glasses with hippocras or milk posset for the loyal and patriotic toasts proposed by the governor from his chair at the upper end of that long and magnificent supper-table—toasts which were heartily responded to by all, including the pages and servers at the buffets.

Amid all this, when warmed a little by the wine, and charmed by the beauty and wit of my companion, I had become almost happy or oblivious of my false position, until recalled to it by finding four cold and stern eyes fixed on me from the head of the table. They were those of the Earl of Argyle and his son, the Lord Lorn, who for some time had evidently been observing me It was difficult to endure this cold, steady, and hostile expression of eye with indifference or equanimity; but after a minute or so, I was relieved of it, for unobserved or unremarked by those about them, the earl and his son quitted the table together.

And now occurred a new annoyance.

One of Lady Flora's bracelets—a beautiful string of Scottish topazes, linked together with gold, fell from her wrist; but she quickly recovered it, and both Ardmohr and I proffered our services to replace it on her white and tapered arm.

Pausing, with a half blush and smile, she said,—

" You are an old friend and clansman, Dougal, and can excuse me."

And placing her pretty hand before me, I was permitted to clasp on the ornament, and while doing so, my heart beat joyously even at this petty preference, though I could not mistake the hostile frown that shot across the brow of Colonel Campbell, of Ardmohr. Unfortunate incident! This little act of attention nearly destroyed me!

When in the very act of clasping her bracelet, the merry eye of Flora fell on the ring which I wore on my finger—*the ring* which she had given to me as the guerdon of a simple dragoon; and notwithstanding the splendour of my costume, the whole falsehood of my pretensions and position flashed upon her at once, and confirmed her previous recollection of my voice and features.

Her smile faded away, and an expression of anger replaced it. She became pale and white, and coldly withdrawing her hand, gave me a mortifying bow, and turned to address the unconscious Ardmohr—for he was unconscious at least of this little discovery, which stung me to the soul. I took the first opportunity to rise, and mumbling something—oh! I know not what—by way of apology, left the hall, and passed unseen where Linn and Oliphant, in some measure the thoughtless causes of my present humiliation, were sitting, flushed with wine, and laughing till their corslets strained, at the manner in which "a corporal of their troop" had paid his devoirs to a daughter of that great earl for whom, as cavaliers, they entertained a mortal grudge.

My heart swelled with shame, with passion, and a sense of mortification, that was somewhat unmerited; together with a sharp pang of pain at leaving that proud and stern baron with Flora, and in quiet possession of the field. In my confusion, I mistook the staircase which led to the courtyard of the castle, and lost myself amid a maze of chambers and corridors, through the lofty windows of which I saw the bright moon beaming on the mighty valley of the Forth, and the vast mountain peaks of Clackmannan and Dunblane.

My pulses throbbed, and throwing myself upon a seat, I drew the hangings of a window round me, and strove to compose my thoughts; but the footsteps of two persons coming along the shadowy gallery, direct from the very room in which James II. thrust his dagger in the heart of Douglas, aroused me, and their conversation, though they spoke in low and stifled tones, whetted my curiosity, and riveted all my attention.

The speakers were the Earl of Argyle and his son. the Lord Lorn.

"Is he still at table?" asked the earl.

"No."

"Ha!"

"He has just left Flora's side, and gone no one knows whither."

"And you have not discovered who he is?" asked Argyle, in an agitated voice.

"No—none can say with certainty."

"'Sdeath! who brought him here?"

"The Master of Oliphant."

"Umph! a fool and villain!" said the earl, grinding his sharp teeth; "didst ask *him?*"

"I did, my lord."

"Well—well, and what said he?"

"Oh! that our spark in the pink doublet and velvet cloak is a gentleman, returned from service in Germany to avoid a princess of the House of Hapsburg, who had fallen madly in love with him; that he was colonel-general of the imperial cuirassiers, governor of Vienna, and knight of all the orders in the empire."

"Absurd—absurd! why, he is but a youth."

"Yet the laird of Linn, who is a cornet in Oliphant's troop, confirmed all this, and added, that he is supposed to be privately married to the young Queen of Sweden."

"A couple of insolent knaves—king's-men both, and I shall have their heels in fetter-locks one day!" continued Argyle, rasping his cat-like teeth together again. "We must discover and have him removed by fair means or foul; for, by the wounds of God, I tell thee, son of mine, we must!"

"A fine oath!" said Lorn, with a sneer. "How if the Reverend Messieurs Traill, Boyd, or Douglas were to hear thee ruffling and rapping it out in this fashion—eh, my lord and father?"

"Gibe me not—gibe me not!" continued the earl, in an agitated voice; "his resemblance is miraculous : yet he cannot be the same ill-omened brat whom you placed on board the *Good Intent*. It is impossible!"

"Of course—for did not Duncan Campbell swear by Heaven, and that which he reverences much more, the black stones of Iona, and by all that was dear to him on earth, the boy fell overboard when far out at sea, and was drowned?"

"Oh! yes—yes, Lorn; he cannot be the same."

"Let me but see this gallant once again," said Lorn, "and I will soon force him to tell who he is."

"Force him?"

"Yes, force him!" reiterated Lorn, striking his large sword on the floor, while I loosened my own in the sheath, and threw back my tasselled mantle, preparatory to rushing out and confronting them both.

"But do thou bear in memory, Lorn, that he seems a gentleman of good birth and proper bearing," said the earl, as they reached the end of the gallery.

"Well?"

"And ye would force him, Lorn!—but how?"

"Very simply. I bite my glove, or fling it in his face; he draws, and I draw too; I am ten good years his senior, and his better twenty by experience; one passado at his throat——"

"Your lordship had better take some other means, lest he may overmatch you," replied the earl, quietly; then I heard a door close; and rushing, sword in hand, into the moonlighted ambulatory, found it empty.

My friend the reader may imagine all I felt on hearing this mysterious and remarkable conversation, and how naturally emotions of indignation, curiosity, and surprise were excited within me. What injury had I done this powerful family; or what deadly wrong had *they* done *me*, that thus they had an interest in my life or death?

A thousand times before I had asked myself the same question; and now, when I remembered the friendly warnings of Oliphant and Linn, it seemed better perhaps that I had been unable to fulfil my first and furious impulse to rush upon Lorn, to hurl him to the earth, and to force him, with my sword jarring on his throat, to say unto whom my "resemblance was so miraculous" —to disclose this terrible secret—and to say why I was an object of such hostility to him, and abhorrence to that subtle and snaky politician, his father.

The gust of passion passed away, and now my whole object was to return to my billet, and once more relinquish the cavalier for the trappings of the Black Dragoons.

Reaching the courtyard, I passed slowly through the illuminated fortress, heedless of a confused noise of tongues that rung like Babel in the soldiers' barracks on one side, and from the festal hall on the other; heedless, too, of the appearance of an officer of Lord Cassilis' cuirassiers, who dashed up the steep esplanade and across the swinging drawbridge, splashed with mud, and having the rich housings of his horse, his jack-boots, and gambadoes, flecked with foam.   He was the bearer of important tidings, for I heard him asking in haste for "Lieutenant-General Leslie and Colonel Cunninghame, the governor."

In one minute afterwards, just as I was passing Argyle House, the flash of a cannon gave a red gleam on the walls, and reverberating with a thousand echoes among the spires and towers, the rocks and woods of Stirling, the report rolled away through the clear sky of an August night.

Another and another boomed upon the sky.

"Three guns!" said I, as a clamour of voices arose in the town which clusters on the castled ridge.   It was the signal that the English, our long-expected invaders, had crossed the Tweed; and now, in answer to the beacon that glimmered like a star, thirty miles distant, on the citadel of the metropolis, a broad and lurid flame, from the highest tower of Stirling, shot skyward, to rouse the surrounding country, and to send the cross of fire— the signal for battle—the summons to arms—through the slumbering clachans of the distant north, to the isles of the west, and through the deep dark glens of a thousand warlike tribes in the land of the Gaël.

CHAPTER XX.

BOOT AND SADDLE—TO HORSE!

I RUSHED to the quarters of Linn, to procure the accoutrements I had left there, and hurried to my billet in the Baxter's-wynd;

and Corporal MacSnaffle, who had just started from bed and the comfortable oblivion of his first nap, had no opportunity for expressing astonishment at the change in my appearance, or the splendour of my costume, which I stripped off in the dark and crushed into my vallise. Then, with soldier-like rapidity, I donned my buff coat, jack boots, and iron trappings; slung on my sword and musketoon, and leaving the serious corporal to console our terrified landlady by an assurance that "the host of Baal—the Amorites and Amalekites of Cromwell—would soon be smitten by us, both hip and thigh," I repaired to the stable, procured my horse, accoutred him in the twinkling of an eye, and mounting, galloped to our place-of-arms, where the different troops of the Black Dragoons were already mustering, each under its corporal-major, amid a din that shook the walls of Stirling.

Alarm bells were ringing, drums beating the *générale*, and our trumpets blowing "Boot and saddle," in every thoroughfare, alley, wynd, and cul-de-sac. A thousand persons were at their windows; thousands more were hurrying about the streets, half-dressed, and their clamorous inquiries added to the general uproar; while overhead, the blazing bale-fire shed its lurid gleam on tower and spire, on mountain, rock, and river.

Three mounted cavalry officers of Marshal Leven's regiment, heavily accoutred, and wearing triple-barred helmets, rode in succession furiously past our place-of-arms. The first bore an order for "all troops to close to the front, and march for Edinburgh, without delay;" the second required Lord Lorn to place himself at the head of the Foot Guards at Scone Palace; and the third was the bearer of tidings that "Oliver Cromwell, lieutenant-general of the army of England, had reached Berwick, at the head of 18,000 infantry, and that his advanced guard had actually crossed the Tweed!"

Two battalions of the Lord Duffus' regiment were rapidly mustered in *battaglia*, under their officers, in close column of companies, upon the esplanade of the castle, and all their drums beat the Scottish "point of war" about three o'clock in the clear balmy morning, as their colours were displayed.

Like myself, all the Black Dragoons were gay and excited at the prospect of coming to handy blows with the enemy. Sergeant Glanders was uttering rough jokes; old Sergeant Hackiron sat with a grim aspect on horseback, gnawing his long wiry moustaches; and our colonel, sheathed completely to the boot-tops in a gorgeous suit of plate, with a large white plume in his helmet, to distinguish him from us all, walked his proud, coal-black, and high-stepping horse impatiently to and fro, inspecting us, as the rolls were called by lamplight; and in a few minutes the six troops were wheeled into line, motionless and still, but in heavy marching order, fully accoutred, every man with his charger's nose-bag, watering bridle and log, picker, brush, currycomb, and spare shoe; his cloak, vallise, and holsters strapped securely to the high military saddle.

Sir William Keith, of Ludquhairn, our adjutant, reported to the count that "every man was present."

" 'Tis well; I never knew it otherwise with my Black troopers in time of peril. Prepare to draw—Draw swords!"

All the trumpets sounded a shrill and triumphant flourish, as we drew our swords; and this blast was repeated twice, in honour of Lieutenant-General Sir David Leslie and the Earl of Argyle, who now rode down the street, accompanied by a crowd of mounted friends and followers. Both were accoutred *à la cuirassier;* and two divines, wearing high-crowned hats above their long-eared calotte caps, rode beside them. These were the reverend Messrs. Boyd and Traill, who bestrode sleek and ambling ponies, and their short Geneva cloaks seemed puffed out with the ardour and righteousness that inflated the hearts of the wearers.

"Would it please you, my lord count, if I, or my reverend brother, emitted a small discourse upon our present peril and tribulation?" asked Mr. Traill, in a querulous and quavering voice.

"Please me, reverend sir? Assuredly not!" replied the count, sharply. "We march this instant. Heard ye not that an army of crop-eared English rascals, led by Oliver the brewer, are at the gates of Berwick, and have thrown their vanguard across the Tweed, thereby invading this our ancient kingdom?"

"We have heard so much," was the nasal reply; "but our hearts are strong—yea, shielded as it were by bucklers of triple brass; for the Lord is with us, over us, and among us; and our sharpened swords shall smite the accursed sectaries, even as lightning smiteth the bearded grass."

"A—men," added Corporal MacSnaffle.

"Silence there, fellow; or by my soul thou shalt run the gauntlet!" exclaimed the count, who held all cant to be an abomination. "Let no man presume to speak when under baton."

"Ye say truly, and speak most purely and sweetly, reverend sir," said the intoned voice of Argyle; "but let us pray, Master Traill, that Cromwell may not prove but the rod of God's wrath, to scourge these rebellious and stiff-necked nations."

As the earl spoke, with one eye fixed on the divine and the other on our colonel, I could perceive that stately officer start as if a hot iron had seared him; he gave the noble a brief but furious glance, and gathering up his reins, made his magnificent charger curvet as he uttered the order,—

"Black Dragoons—three's right—forward!"

Then, with all our trumpets sounding and kettle-drums beating a fine old Scottish march, our swords flashing in the twilight, and the standard of each troop displayed at its head, we descended the steep streets of Stirling towards the Falkirk road, and every heart in the regiment beat responsive, while our horses champed their steel bits, and shook their chain bridles, as they tossed their proud heads from time to time.

On descending the Castlehill, I saw the windows of Argyle House filled with anxious faces, and many ladies were there, notwithstanding the untimeous hour. Among them was *one*, whose soft features and timid air, in her charming deshabille, I recognised in a moment, and she, half hidden and half seen, as the morning light fell on her, seemed to have all that beauty of face, and depth of light and shade, we find in the pictures of Holbein and Vandyke. I thought of Romeo in the garden of the Capulets, where he says,

> "What light through yonder window breaks!
> It is the east, and Juliet is the sun!
> It is my lady—O, it is my love!
> *Would that she knew she were!*
> She speaks, yet nothing says: what of that?
> Her eye discourses; I will answer it.
> I am too bold; 'tis not to me she speaks;
> Two of the fairest stars in all the heaven,
> Having some business, do entreat her eyes,
> To twinkle in their spheres till they return."

And distinguishing me—O happiness!—yet I know not how among so many hundred horsemen—she waved her hand to me, in token of forgiveness for the presumption of last night, and of farewell too, for I was marching to battle—she a daughter of Scotland's greatest earl!

Overwhelmed by joy and confusion, I bowed to my holster-flaps, and drawing off my glove kissed the ring, which, like a fairy spell, had bound my heart to her; and again, as of old, I plunged into the realm of fancy, for it seemed a link between us—a bond between that charming being and me—for the idol of a lover is something more than a mere *woman;* and yet what a wild vision was all this to indulge in, when the object of these vague hopes and glowing thoughts was placed at a distance so immeasurably above me!

Six light galloper-guns, or field-pieces, which were to be attached to our brigade of horse, and two of which had been recently taken from Montrose's German artillery at the rout of Invercarron, were limbered up, and their horses traced; and with

all their matrosses, gunners, and fire-casters on their seats or
saddles, we left Stirling with them, just as day began to dawn;
and broke into a hand gallop, as we rode under the long leafy
archway formed by the oak forests of the carse.

"Well, Harry Ogilvie," said the Master of Oliphant, spurring
up to my side, "saw ye at the rere-supper that pretty maid by
whom you were so smitten?"

"Yes," said I, with a little reserve.

"And who may she be?"

"Never my wife, I fear."

"A sly fellow! I ask you her name?"

"I dare not say."

"Well, keep your own secrets, comrade, for a secret is only so
while it is known to *one;* but you left early, and just when I
was putting you on the high road to preferment with Leslie and
Argyle."

"I displeased the lady."

"And you quarrelled; well, this will test the strength and
purity of your passion, even as acid tests the purity of gold."

"Believe me, noble master, I require no such test."

"Well, take courage, Harry—thou art a fine and a handsome
fellow, and will, I doubt not, have some pretty bird ere long in
the jesses; but was it wise of thee to confer so much with Lady
Flora Campbell? In thy fair one's presence, was it not dangerous? Ha! ha! how Linn and I laughed to see thee seated
by *her* side, in the highest place of the synagogue, as her snuf-
fling father would say."

How little could the master conceive that Flora herself was
the object of my passion; but reckless—though leal-hearted—
as he was, I dreaded his ridicule too much to enlighten him on a
subject so near my heart.

"You say it was dangerous, Oliphant; but how?"

"I affirmed to the Lady Lorn that you were a colonel-general
of German reitres, and had left the emperor's service in disgust,
anent an amour with a princess; and dame Lorn will speak of
it, for doubtless she hath a large portion of mother Eve's only
legacy to all her daughters."

"Which is——"

"A most active tongue; so Argyle's curiosity may excite him
to make inquiries."

"Alas! no such whet was needed," said I, as his words caused
a pang within me; and drawing him aside from the ranks, I
briefly related the conversation I had overheard in the ambulatory.
The Master of Oliphant remained silent for a few minutes, and
then said—

"In all this, Harry, there lurketh some strange mystery; but in Heaven's name beware ye of Argyle! Be assured, *he requireth a lang shankit spune wha sups kail wi' the deil.* But attend to your duty, comrade; be brave and leal as we have ever known you, and you may defy the plots and wiles even of such powerful foemen as Lorn and his father."

"To high emprise there can be no nobler stimulus than my present position," said I; "I love a lady whom I dare not address until I obtain a higher rank—and even then a hundred barriers may be raised up between us."

"Storm them all, Harry; for we lightly prize that which is lightly won. A love surrounded by perils, doubts, and difficulties, is the true love of romance."

As the road opened before us, I looked back to the rear, and saw the dusky outline of lofty Stirling reddened in the rising sun. *She* was there who now filled all my thoughts, although perhaps I was by her already forgotten.

Several regiments of horse joined us on the route, but being the oldest regiment in the Scottish service, *we* furnished General Leslie's guard; and for this duty one captain, one lieutenant, one cornet, two sergeants, and fifty Black Troopers were "told off" daily.

CHAPTER XXI.

INVASION OF 1650.

FOR some years previous to these events Scotland had wisely and nobly adopted the maxim, *si vis pacem para bellum*—and to secure peace was ever ready of war; but a foreign war came at last, for the English were nearly as foreign to us in habit and customs as the Turks would have been.

It had long since been known in London that the government of the King of Scotland had levied a military force consisting of twenty-seven thousand infantry and cavalry, exclusive of their other troops in garrison, and that some of the privy council vehemently urged an invasion of England. To anticipate this measure, Cromwell, who had certain and secret intelligence of all our movements and our *most secret* councils, from Argyle and Sir Archibald Johnston, the infamous Laird of Warriston (who were both inimical to the cause of their king and country), left London on the 29th of June. By their means he had a manifesto circulated in Scotland, and its commencement is strongly characterised by the rank fanaticism which disgraced the age.

"To all that are saints and partakers in the faith of God's elect," it was addressed, and boldly it adduced explicit reasons for bringing the late king *to justice;* for hewing off his head on the scaffold; for excluding his family from the thrones of Scotland and England; and for abolishing the parliaments of those countries, and proclaiming a universal commonwealth and community of everything.

The army of the English republicans consisted of eighteen thousand men, with horse and artillery. They were all Independents, burning and boiling with religious fanaticism, as every man among them might assume the clerical office; thus their camp resounded with psalms, exhortations, expoundings, cant, prayer, and groanings of the spirit; and they styled themselves the whips and rods of God, destined to scourge the men of the new covenant.

On halting at Berwick, Cromwell had another manifesto secretly distributed by Argyle and his partisans. It recapitulated the statements of the former, and assured the people of Scotland that no injury would be offered to their persons or property, provided they remained quiet in their habitations; and in this instance I must acknowledge that Cromwell nobly and humanely kept his promise.

Proclamations on both sides preceded the war.

Our parliament issued manifestoes, in which the grounds of the quarrel are stated at full length; but as all the accusations of past bloodshed and old injustice contained in these documents belong rather to history than to my narrative. I hasten to the part played by his majesty's worthy old regiment of Black Dragoons in the sanguinary Scottish campaign.

On the 20th of July we reached Edinburgh.

I shall long remember the joyous ardour that rose within me when, on defiling between the wooded hill and the broad shallow loch of Corstorphine, we came in sight of the city of the gallant James's—the Edina of Buchanan—the queen of the north, as she rose on all her rocky steeps before us. There frowned the old fortress of a thousand memories; there stood the spire under which Knox preached; and far down below, secluded in the vale, lay Scotland's heart of hearts—the old palace where Mary wept, and many a king lies sleeping in his shroud. We raised ourselves in our stirrups, and brandished our swords with a fierce enthusiasm and a glorious joy, on beholding the city we were hastening to defend.

On arriving, most of us were quartered in the Canongate, as there all our nobless had their hotels and lodgings, and there were many chateaux on each side of the palace with gardens and stables. As we rode in by the west porte, under the brow of the stupendous castle rock, and defiled through the quaint and timber-fronted Grassmarket in open column of troops, with standards advanced and trumpets sounding the *cavalquet* (for we imitated our ancient allies the French in all things), seven pieces of cannon were fired from the Half Moon in honour of Lieutenant-General Leslie.

By the judicious management of the lord provost, Sir Andrew Ramsay, the Scottish capital presented the appearance of a well-ordered garrison rather than of a city threatened by an invading army, for her burghers had long been inured to war, and the craftsmen—brave fellows and leal Scots at all times—were all mustered in arms, with buff coats and bandoliers, each trade being led by its deacon, and their three-and-thirty banners, bearing the insignia of the corporations, floated above the town barriers, which were mounted with cannon.

The committee of the three estates had made vigorous preparations for the defence of the capital and of the nation. The castle of Edinburgh was garrisoned by a body of chosen troops, commanded (unfortunately) by a young soldier, Colonel Walter Dundas, of that ilk; seventy pieces of cannon and mortars were mounted on its towers; eight thousand stand of arms, eighty barrels of powder, and a vast store of shot, shell, coal, and provision, were stored up there for the use of the garrison.

Twenty-one thousand well-appointed infantry were intrenched behind a ditch and breastwork which lay parallel with the road that leads to Leith. Their right flank was defended by the Calton-hill, which was covered with redoubts of earth, platforms and fascines bristling with brass field-pieces and iron mortars; their left flank was defended by the cannon on the walls of Leith and the old porte of St. Anthony. A line of trenches and breastworks, where iron morions and steel weapons glittered by day, and the red watchfires glowed by night, was drawn between the Calton and the craigs of Salisbury, from thence to the hill of St. Leonard, and round all the passes and approaches on the south to the foot of the castle rock, were brigades of cavalry, having outposts and advanced videttes. On the north, the city was protected by water. Thus, by the skill and experience brought into our camp and councils by the veteran soldiers of the thirty years' war, the capital of the Stuarts was impregnable, and her citizens quietly followed their daily avocations in shop and booth, but clad the while in buff coat and cuirass, with sword at side and musket close at hand.

Corporal MacSnaffle and I being comrades, were billetted together in a narrow street near the hotel and chapel of the French ambassador. I remember well the long turnpike stair, for over it was the date 1616, and the significant legend, *Tecum Habita*. It was one of those lofty tenements, built in that style of architecture which we borrowed many ages ago from France; and they were indicative of a good old social system, combined with strength and security. The Scottish and French turnpike stair is literally a vertical instead of a horizontal street.

In the tenement on which I was quartered, the sunken vaults were occupied by a dealer who displayed his wares on the pavement by day; the two flats of the first story were occupied, one by the Earl of Lothian, and the other by the Lord Borthwick, whose numerous followers stowed themselves Heaven alone knows where. Our adjutant, Sir William Keith, of Ludquhairn, and the Laird of Merchiston, had the two flats above; two wealthy burgesses held the third; a small fraternity of tailors occupied the garrets, and peeped from the dormer casements into the Cowgate below; while above all were a colony of pigeons, who resided in the oyster-shelled chimnies, and fought with the rooks that located every morning on the corbie-stoned gables.

The doorways of these perpendicular streets were always surmounted by a pious legend, to scare away evil and sorcery; the doors were generally of solid oak, well studded with iron, and furnished with bolts and bars to keep out unwelcome visitors. There was an eyelet for reconnoitring, and frequently a couple of loopholes well splayed out on each flank, to afford ample range for a few muskets, in case the said visitors proved importunate, in which case, the whole turnpike became at once a garrison. Moreover, until fanaticism and new-fangled absurdities from the South or the Continent disturbed the even current of old Scottish social life, all the inmates of these turnpikes were on the best of terms. Thus, the earl with his laced coat and small-sword politely made way for his neighbour, the tailor, in the fustian doublet, and offered him a pinch from his diamond snuff-box, while "spiering for the gudewife and the bairns," and flattered by this good-fellowship, the tailor and the tailor's children would have gone to the cannon's mouth for the earl or his family; for there they all dwelt happy, and content with the same accommodation, the same dwelling, and the same sturdy oak furniture that pleased their fathers in the days of Flodden and Pinkey. But I have lived to see all this sociality swept away, and a chasm opened up between the ranks of men, that death alone can close.

The Scottish peerage and the Scottish people are no longer *one*.

MacSnaffle and I were billetted on one of the burgesses, who proved to be no other than Evan Tyler, printer to the king's most excellent majesty. He made us welcome guests; for the approach of an English army had created some alarm in Edinburgh, and thus most of its citizens, with those of Leith, Falkirk, and Linlithgow, had taken the precaution of securing their most valuable effects in the fortresses and walled towns of Fife.

Rumours of Cromwell's alleged bitterness of spirit and of his vindictive temper (notwithstanding the mildness of his proclamations) had unfortunately preceded his invasion of Scotland; and these reports were certainly strengthened by the undoubted atrocities committed by his troops in Ireland.

CHAPTER XXII.

APPOINTED SERGEANT.

ON the night we marched in, Mr. Tyler gave us a hot carbonado —*i. e.*, a well-broiled steak—for supper, with a jolly stoup of Bourdeaux, over which we talked of Cromwell and the strange sectaries who followed his standard; and we related all the current anecdotes of the butchery and havoc they had made among the poor Irish, especially at the siege of Drogheda.

"It hath been alleged," said our landlord, with anger and horror in his voice and face, "that in Scotland he meaneth to slaughter every man between the ages of sixty and sixteen, and to mutilate all who are under that age."

"Yea, and to burn the breasts of our women with hot irons, as he did in Ireland, lest they suckle bairns," added his wife, pressing her youngest-born closer to her bosom; for these absurd and monstrous aspersions upon the character of Cromwell had been industriously circulated by the cavaliers and one portion of the Presbyterian clergy.

"Fear ye not, gudewife," said Corporal MacSnaffle, who was mixing a hot jug of strong waters, sweetened with sugar—"fear ye not, for the host of Baal shall wither up and shrink before us, as the Assyrians shrunk before the mighty ones of old. We go forth against them wi' our horses, and our footmen, our chariots of war—our lunts blown and bandoliers filled. *Then*," he continued, taking a great gulp from the steaming jug, "shall we shout, 'Hear, O Israel!' and Israel shall hear! We will make a spoil of their women and cattle, their bread and powder-waggons,—yea, we shall utterly destroy Cromwell and his sectaries, those Hittites, Amorites, Perizzites, and Amalekites of England!"

Though frequently amused by the musty piety, fervor, and absurdity of the corporal, I soon tired of it; and often when he was dividing, sub-dividing, and explaining, in his own fashion, some knotty text of Scripture, I was lost in reverie, and thinking of the soft features and winning eyes of Flora Campbell, or sighing to be with Patrick Oliphant and William Linn, as of old; for their gentlemanly manner and easy style of conversation were more congenial to me than the fanatical cant of a saintly trooper like Bezabel MacSnaffle; and yet withal, the poor man was perhaps sincere enough.

We spent a happy evening with Mr. Tyler, though he was full of dire forebodings of the future; as various omens of evil had occurred of late. The weathercock of St. Giles's had lost its tail in a tempest of wind, said to have been raised by Major Weir, the wizard, blowing thrice through a keyhole; a slight shock of an earthquake had been felt in Lothian; a spectral drummer had beaten the Scottish March before the castle gates; and a spring of pure water had burst out near the *summit* of Arthur's seat, on the very day Cromwell arrived at Berwick, and was then—I saw it daily—pouring like a torrent into the Hunting Bog, and forming that long, bare, rocky rift, now known as the Gutted Haddock; and on the same day, so important in our history, the boom of cannon-shot was heard at noon passing over the whole realm of Scotland, from the German to the Atlantic Ocean.

All these were portentous of terrible events, and Mr. Tyler shook his head solemnly as he spoke of them, and lowered his voice when the wind soughed in the large chimney of his dwelling, while his gudewife gazed dreamily into the fire in search of shrouds and coffins. Yet withal, the dining-room, or chamber-of-dais of his majesty's printer, looked very comfortable and easy. On one side of the warm ingle simmered a brilliant coffee-pot; on the other sat a sleek and middle-aged tom-cat, with his tail folded across his fore-feet, his eyes half-closed, and fixed sleepily on the glowing embers; for he—happy puss!—was alike indifferent to Cromwell and his sectaries, and cared not a rush whether prelacie went up, or king and kirk went down!

Before daybreak next morning we were all in our saddles to relieve the king's regiment of Life Guards and the Earl of Cassilis's Red Cuirassiers, who formed the cavalry picquets between the Burghloch and the right flank of the city wall.

That afternoon, in consequence of the skill with which I posted my advanced videttes from a small party which I commanded near the Quarries of Bruntsfield, it pleased our noble colonel, the count, to appoint me sergeant, and as such, with fifty troopers, I mounted guard next day on the general's quarters in Moray House.

I saw some very strange sights while we were quartered in Edinburgh.

One day I met a quaker, named Swinton, all nude, save a shirt, which was wrapped around him; he was passing a gate of the city, crying with a loud voice,

"To prayer—to prayer! lo, the great Day of Doom is at hand!"

Then he stationed himself at the door of St. Giles's Cathedral, which he stigmatised as "a popish and prelatic steeple-house," and there proceeded to expound to the people; but was briskly engaged in polemics by Corporal MacSnaffle, who argued with him for four consecutive hours, until the trumpets sounded for stable duty, for this was a time when every man in Britain mounted his own religious hobby, and rode it to death.

By Mr. Tyler I was shown the skull of the great Marquis of Montrose, bleaching on the west end of the Tolbooth; and I was also shown the stake where his mutilated remains were interred among those of malefactors, by the side of the highway that crosses the Burgh-muir—a terrible instance of the mutability of fortune, and the rancorous hatred of Argyle and his adherents.

I saw a woman burned alive at Broughton-Loanhead, being accused by the minister of St. Cuthbert's of having borne imps to the Devil; though his reverence was currently supposed to be " auld Hornie's rival;" and on the same day I saw a man have both his ears nailed to Canongate cross, for giving one night's shelter to a jesuit, who was next day taken and hung in chains at the Gallowlee—for it was a time when barbarity and fanaticism had made men as mad in Scotland as they were in the sister kingdom.

The duty of our infantry, in their intrenched position before the city was severe and harassing; while that of the cavalry, whose business it was to furnish advanced posts and patrols, was not less so. We were ordered to be ready at a moment's notice, to sleep accoutred, and to have our horses saddled, bridled, and in marching order, with the bits hanging at their chests.

Cromwell was now on the march through Berwickshire and East Lothian, at the head of a veteran and well-appointed army; but he found the whole country abandoned by the people, the terror of his name having everywhere preceded him from Ireland. On all the route he met none, save a few very aged women, who told his officers that the men were all in arms under the barons of the king, or with the lord general of the Covenant.

The English army marched towards us by the eastern coast, and were supplied with provisions from their fleet; the judicious measures of our ministry and Sir David Leslie, under whom the aged Field Marshal Leven was serving, a volunteer, having swept the southern counties of every means of subsistence. Thus, in a few days, biscuits and cold water were the only repast of the English; and this poor fare was often unpleasantly seasoned by bullets from the carbines of Halkett's Dragoons, and other active corps, which hovered near them. But in our army and our councils—too surely *the latter*—were paid spies and titled traitors, who informed the foe of all our measures, means, and intentions.

On the 29th day of July, Cromwell established his camp and head-quarters within seven miles of us, at Mussellburgh, and placed his magazines in the laird of Stonyhill's mansion, near Inveresk. On that day, every musketeer and pikeman of the Scottish army were under colours in the trenches; every horseman by his horse, every cannonier by his cannon, in the castle, on the Calton, on the walls of Leith, and every officer was at his post.

That night, to Drumstanchel's troop was assigned the duty of covering the road which crosses the Figgate-muir right in front of our position; and he sent me forward with twelve dragoons, and with orders "to keep a brisk look-out, as we expected every moment to hear something of the enemy."

CHAPTER XXIII.

JOCK'S LODGE.

THAT night I never closed an eye, as I knew that to me my captain trusted; and that the safety of the camp depended mainly on his troop; for this road led directly to the enemy's quarters.

I formed my little party into three *reliefs*, and every hour replaced the videttes, one of whom, with his carbine slung, sat on horseback in the centre of the roadway, another I posted about fifty yards on his right, and a third as many yards to his left. Around, all the muirland was open, waste, and bare. On one flank lay a little lonely hut, named *Jock's Lodge*, from a poor idiot who lived there; on the other, surrounded by trees, and situated on a knoll among a morass, stood the old manor house of the baronets of Cragintinny. All was still as death around this solitary outpost, save the boom of the sea on the desolate beach, about two miles distant, or the moan of the wind as it swept across the muir, on which a thick haze was settling.

So passed our night, in silence, mist, and watchfulness.

A faint grey light was stealing across the east when I visited my advanced sentinels, one of whom informed me that he had frequently seen a little figure dancing before him in the misty twilight, and had heard a voice singing, he knew not where. Moreover, he feared that the muirland, like the blasted heath of Forres, "was bewitched."

"There it is now!" said he, in an excited voice, and following the direction of his dilated eye, I perceived a little figure dancing and cutting fantastic capers over the moss-covered knolls and roots of trees, at a little distance, leaping from one to another with great agility, while a sound of singing came towards me on the wind. I was on foot, with my cocked carbine in my hand; advancing some twenty paces or so, I cried,

"Stand—stand—or I shall fire! who comes there?"

"Me," replied a shrill voice, and the figure stood still.

"Speak, I tell you, or I shall fire."

"Keep your bullets for a better use," was the reply, as the figure gathered itself up round as a ball, and making a bound from the stump of a tree, stood before me.

It was an aged and frightful-looking dwarf, with wild glaring eyes, long grey hair, a beard hanging over his little bow legs, which terminated in large bare feet. On his head was an enormous round bonnet, and, dancing round me, he began to sing while playing on a very large fiddle,

> " The deil sat supping the auld wife's kail,
>   With a hey sing ho and a tow, row, row!"

"In heaven's name, who are you?" I asked.

"Jock," was the curt reply.

"But, Jock who?"

"Hoot! a' the folk ken Jock. I byde at the lodge on the muir. My mither byded there before me; but she was a witch, and had a hedgehog that slept in her breist; so the kirk session burned her wi' tar-barrels in Duddingstone Loan. Did ye take me for Cromwell?"

"No," said I, laughing; "but I am glad to see you, carle Jock."

"Then did ye take me for his friend in the cloak o' sad-coloured taffety, wi' the lang red hair and squinting eyen, eh? He that is betraying ye a'—he that maketh braw speeches to the parliament and rides in our Scottish ranks by day, while he sits wi' Cromwell a' the lee long night, poring over books and plans and papers, as I saw him only three hours ago? Oh! if I wasna daft, I might do some grand things!"

"Whom mean you?" I asked, almost terrified to define my own suspicions.

"He who grinned in the face o' the half-dead Montrose. Oh! that was a braw cavalier, wi' his long black hair and his grand laced coat, marching like a king to the scaffold! *He* once gave Jock a brave gowden guinea, when the other gied him a text o' scripture and a lash wi' his whip on the hiegate; but Jock has been watching him, and will see the corbies flapping their wings round his empty eyen and bare jaws yet.

> " ' Oh, the deil sat supping the auld wife's kail,
>   With a hey sing ho, and a tow, row, row!
> But she raxed a het coal to the neuk o' his tail,
>   And fu' loudly he screighed at that scouthering low.'

F

Look ye to horse and harnessing, for *they* are coming—down yonder! Look—look!" he continued, pointing into the dusky mist; "and in three minutes they will be here!"

When I turned from the direction indicated to look after my new acquaintance, he was gone from my side, and I saw him bounding from stump to stump (for this muirland was in ancient times a forest), and he soon disappeared near his hut.

In the space of time he mentioned, three figures on horseback appeared near us. In outline they were dusky and indistinct, for the ocean mist lay thick upon the waste; the day was dawning behind them, and they were seen as through a screen of gauze. On perceiving my vidette they halted, and I challenged, being nearest to them. On this, two unslung their carbines, and discharged them at us. How the whistle of the shot made my ears tingle! My vidette fired in return, but missed. I then took deliberate aim, and fired: one man fell from his horse, which galloped off; the other two paused a moment, and then, wheeling round their horses, trotted away, and were soon shrouded in mist. At the noise of this skirmish, my little picquet sprang to their horses, and came spurring to the spot with all their carbines cocked.

Daylight was now fairly in; and impelled by an irrepressible curiosity and dread, while reloading, I walked deliberately up to the man I had shot (my *first* one)! He was an English dragoon —an officer, apparently, by the richness of his red coat, the inlying of his helmet, and the silver spurs on his black jack-boots. I dreaded to meet *his eye*, though it was impossible that he could know me to be the perpetrator of that fatal shot.

I hoped, yet almost feared, to find him dead; and then I mentally implored Heaven that he might recover. My mind was full of vague apprehension and indefinable sorrow; for I was but a young soldier, and such qualms were natural at my years.

MacSnaffle roughly turned him over on his back.

The poor Englishman! He was breathing heavily, and his eyes were glazing; blood was flowing from his mouth and from a frightful wound in his throat. I could have wept over this unfortunate, but not a tear would come; and I trembled like one who had done an awful deed, for which no remorse could atone. I had slain a fellow-creature by a cool and deliberate shot; and in my remorse, I forgot that it was my duty to have shot the other two.

"The ungodly Hizzite is about to depart," said the corporal.

"Gie the puir fellow something to drink," said Carlourie, a trooper.

"Are they safe?" asked the dying man, as MacSnaffle put a flask to his mouth; "are *they* safe?"

" Who ?" we asked.

" They who were with me—Monk and Oliver."

" *Monk and Oliver !*" I repeated.

" By the light of the tabernacle !" exclaimed the corporal, " we have been within an ace o' making our fortunes and ending the war before it be well begun. But, ho ! there; sound the trumpets."

Drumstanchel had ordered a retreat to be blown, and as the mist drew up like a curtain, we saw a body of the enemy's cavalry on the skirts of the plain, and thereupon we fell back upon the main body of our troop; and thus left the wounded sectary, who, unless found by his own comrades, lay there to die alone, with the unclouded sun of July glaring on his bare and pallid brow. Such is war !

On looking back, I saw an elfin figure capering and dancing round him. It was the idiot dwarf, Jock of the lonely lodge on the muir.

CHAPTER XXIV.

PARADE FOR AN ONFALL.

THE communications of this strange being, which seemed to point to the Earl of Argyle as being in correspondence with Cromwell; my recent encounter with that general and his favourite officer, Monk; together with the effect of the first shot I had fired in earnest, and the memory of the dying man's eyes, found me ample subjects for reflection on that morning. Perceiving me thoughtful and silent, the lively Oliphant endeavoured to rally me, saying,

" Come, brother student—comrade Harry—brighten up a little, as of old. Why, thou growest a very moon-calf!"

" What manner of calf is that ?" asked Linn; " we never heard of it in Lothian."

" 'Tis a being that hath a mother, but no father—old Pliny wrote about it — but thou'st long since forgotten Pliny, I warrant."

We were all under arms, half a mile in front of the trenches, and every man stood by his horse's head. The wide sleeves of our buff coats were buttoned up, and the broad skirts hooked back, to afford us every freedom, and thus we awaited the orders of Sir David Leslie. We were now the second regiment of Sir James Halkett's cavalry brigade; and with us were the king' Life Guards, commanded by the Earl of Eglinton, who lately served with our Scottish army in Ireland, and the cuirassier regiment of the Earl of Cassilis; and assuredly we formed the finest of the seven brigades of horse, of which I append a list to my narrative.*

In strong contrast to our black accoutrements and sable chargers, the Life Guards were entirely armed in bright plate trappings, and rode bay horses, chosen from the best remounts for the king's service. Their standards were variously inscribed, by the express desire of the king, from whom they received them at Falkland Palace, on the 22nd of July.

The guidon of their colonel, Alexander, Earl of Eglinton, surnamed " auld Greysteel," was azure, and bore the Scottish regalia with the mottoes—*Nobis hæc invicta miserunt*—*For Covenant, Religion, King, and Kingdom*. The guidon of their lieutenant-colonel, James Viscount Newburgh, whilome Lord Livingstone of Flancraig, bore a crowned thistle with the royal motto of Scotland; the guidon of the major was the national cross of St. Andrew, inscribed *Pro Religione Rege et Patria*. The troopers were all gentlemen, being cadets of the best houses in Scotland, and their spirit and bearing were alike lofty and resolute. The cuirassiers of John, Earl of Cassilis, usually styled " the regiment of the kirk," were a corps of grim, morose, but gallant men, though somewhat addicted to preaching and expounding. They were well disciplined; and altogether Halkett's brigade was second to none in the king's service.

As soon as it was known that Monk and Oliver had been reconnoitring the city on the west and south, where they had also been fired on by the videttes of Marshal Leven's regiment near Bruntisfield, it was resolved by our general, Sir David Leslie, to make an onfall by night into their quarters at Musselburgh, and it was for this purpose that Halkett's brigade paraded in front of the trenches just as darkness was closing.

" Sir James Halkett, my worthy cavalier, will you please to form in open column of troops," said General Leslie to our brigadier, as we mounted.

" To horse, my hard riders—sound, trumpeter!" cried Count Ogilvie.

" The times are changed with us, Harry," said Oliphant, with his merry laugh, as he extinguished his German pipe and drew his sword; "tempora mutantur—*tan-ta-ra-ra*—I never could finish a Latin quotation."

" Fall into your ranks by troops," said Sir William Keith, our adjutant; and the brigade soon formed in open column, with the guidons in rear of the third file from the pivot of each troop.

" Take ye care and time, sirs," said General Leslie, as the last note of the trumpet saw the whole brigade, two thousand four hundred strong, formed in order, boot to boot and holster to holster; "remember that the extremes of hurry and delay are alike to be avoided in all military matters. Now, my lords and gentlemen," continued this fine old soldier, who had led a body of Scottish horse through the great battles of the thirty years' war, and who had vanquished Montrose at Philiphaugh, "you are already aware of the position occupied by Cromwell's troops. His infantry are encamped on the Links of Musselburgh, and his cavalry occupy the kirk of Inveresk, where they have shown their piety by cooking their beef and puddings by the pews and pulpit; his magazine is at Stonyhill, and as he has strong outguards to protect the bridge, we must fall into his quarters from another point."

"True, Sir David," said the Earl of Eglinton; "then we lack but a guide who kens the fords of Esk, for floods have swollen the stream."

"My cuirassiers are strangers to this part of the country," said Cassilis, "and know not a foot of the way."

"The quartermaster-general should find us a guide," observed Count Ogilvie; "but any intelligent peasant must know the fords, I presume."

"Gie puir Jock a penny, and he'll show ye the way, my noble gentlemen," said a strange little figure, starting up so suddenly among them that the horse of the lieutenant-general reared on its haunches; while the count's made a demivolte, by which he nearly lost a stirrup, and all the officers laughed.

"Who the devil are you, my little mannikin?" asked old General Leslie, stooping from his saddle.

"Jock, Sir David—a' the folk ken Jock; I bide at the lodge on the muir, and ken every rash that grows on Esk bank, and ilka stone that shines at the bottom o't. Gie me a penny for snuff, and I'll tak ye a' round by the Howe Mire, a quiet and canny gate—syne through the Loan o' Newbigging, and up to Cromwell's tent door. I was there no an hour gane."

A brief conversation ensued; the Earls of Eglinton and Cassilis ridiculed the idea of entrusting three regiments of horse to such a guide—"a miserable mandrake," as Drumstanchel said; but Leslie and Count Ogilvie were struck by the shrewdness of Jock's plan of attack, as the detour he recommended was exactly the route they had previously decided upon.

"Will any man here vouch for this poor gomeral?" asked the Earl of Eglinton.

"That will I do blythely, my lord," said I, lowering the point of my sword.

"Why so, friend—and whence this confidence?"

"Because, no further gone than this morning, he saved me and a little party from being suddenly surprised in the mist by Oliver and Monk in person."

"Say you so?" said Count Ogilvie; "then let us take Jock into confidence, my Lord Eglinton, for this Harry Ogilvie, I assure you, is one of my sharpest fellows, and a voucher as good as we need have."

"Jock be it then," said Leslie, laughing; "but let an intelligent trooper ride in front with him across his saddle-bow. Come hither, corporal—what is your name?"

"Corporal Bezalel——"

"Zounds!—what?"

"Bezalel MacSnaffle," replied the proprietor of that cognomen, riding to the front, and sitting in his stirrups rigid and upright as a post; "called Duncan in the days of his darkness, after the son of Uri, the son of Hur, of the tribe of Judah."

"Well, Bezalel MacSnaffle," resumed the general, almost imitating his canting tone, "turn thy beast to the right about, and go thy ways back to the ranks; and look a little more alive, my friend, or, by the soul of Gustavus, thou shalt taste the strappado!"

"Yea, I obey," muttered the corporal, as he reined back into his place; "yet will the scourge not disgrace my namefather, Bezalel, who, with Aholiab, was called to do the wark o' the Tabernacle."

"Intolerable!" exclaimed Count Ogilvie; "yet he is a brave fellow, Sir David, natheless his solemn absurdity. Harry Ogilvie, do thou ride forward and take our diminutive guide across your holsters, if he will mount."

"Na, na," said Jock, "mony thanks—I'll tramp it mysel; but Lordsake, general, dinna forget the penny."

"Little one, thou shalt have thy bonnet full if ye fail not—but look well to him, Sergeant Ogilvie," said Lord Eglinton, loftily.

"And look to yourself, my lord," said Jock, making three astounding summersets in the air; "for mind ye, a gowkit captain has often a glaiket guard."

This proverb made the old colonel of the Life Guards very angry; and as the brigade moved off, advancing by threes from the right of troops, I spurred a few paces in front, accompanied by Jock, who talked incessantly either to himself or to me, while by turns he capered, danced, and fiddled to his favourite ditty:—

> "The deil sat supping the auld wife's kail,
>   With a hey sing ho, and a tow, row, row!
> But she raxed a het coal to the neuk o' his tail,
>   And loudly screighed he, at the scouthering low.

> He girned, he growled, he gabberd, and grat,
>   With a hey sing ho, and a tow, row, row!
> And doon on the ingle he shivered the pat,
>   As he flew up the lum wi' his tail in a low."

"Adieu, Sir James," said Leslie, as he parted with Major-General Halkett; "success to you on this outfall."

"Fear not, Sir David," was the confident reply; "for every saddle of ours emptied to-night, ten sectaries shall be struck from Cromwell's muster-roll."

CHAPTER XXV.

THE NIGHT ATTACK.

THE night was dark and cold. Over the flat muirland a chill blast swept from the sea; a lurid streak in the north-east showed where the sun had sunk beyond the black mountains of Fife, and other light there was none, save a red spark that burned in the quaint old manor house of Restalrig, and threw a tremulous ray on the deep loch that washes the rocks below. Around the little village, which lay among its orchards in the hollow, all was still as death, for the people had fled at the approach of the invader; not even a dog barked, or cock crew; and as the brigade advanced, I heard only the clank of accoutrements and the dull tramp of many iron hoofs on the turf.

Jock of the Lodge gambolled beside me with an agility wonderful at his years; for his long floating beard was grey, and his face was lean, wan, and withered, while his little legs were stunted and crooked like the limbs of an old thorn tree. Altogether he was of a strange and supernatural aspect, and resembled the bogles, brownies, warlocks, ghaists, and kelpies, of whom he chattered incessantly. Running by my stirrup, he paused occasionally to point out to me where the corpse-lichts of slain men were shining on the muir, and where the lamps of gambolling spunkies glinted in Craigintinny morass. Passing his dwelling, the lonely hut or lodge upon the waste, we crossed the eastern flank of Arthur Seat, and traversed the pretty village of Duddingstone, secluded among the summer woods, with the great shadow of the steep hill falling upon its placid loch, which border the little peninsula of its venerable church. We defiled through the Loan, in which I have heard, in happier times, the birr of two hundred looms, for the village was populous; but the encroachments of the plague on one hand, and those of an avaricious earl on the other, have swept away the people since then.

"Hush!" said Jock, grasping my bridle; "byde ye, and let me count; ane, twa, three, four."

"What do you see?" I asked, unslinging my carbine, being in front of the advanced guard, which was commanded by Linn.

"I see the lumheids, and can reckon how mony witches are in Duddingstone. Weel do I ken the reek o' a witch's lum, for my mother was one, and they burnt her, just at that auld thorn tree; and see ye, sergeant, there are thirteen lums—a deil's dozen—reeking in the loan. Look at the sparks o' hell, how they glint i' the lift! Sawtan and a' thy works, I defy thee; and Cromwell too! But hush, for if the witches come out o' the well-ee-moss, they'll rive me to ribbons."

"By Mahoud!" said I, "after all, I don't think we are over wise in being led on such an expedition by a demented brownie or hobgoblin like this!"

We crossed the hill of Edmonston, and dipping down towards Dalkeith, forded the Esk below the old castle of the Douglasses, and wheeling to the left, to avoid the English outposts at the Bridge of Musselburgh, and the batteries by which they had strengthened it, we approached Inveresk from the south, and filing by threes, in darkness and silence, along a narrow path, which was known only to the mannikin, our guide, and which led directly through the deep and dangerous morass named the Howe Mire, we found ourselves under the brow of the thickly-wooded ridge, on the western shoulder of which stood the venerable kirk of St. Michael of Inveresk. To the east were a number of new chateaux and handsome mansions, named the New-bigging. These were full of Cromwell's officers. The old kirk was occupied by his cavalry, and the Roman rampart of Agricola beside it was mounted with cannon and howitzers.

The time was an exciting one, for every moment we expected to see the red flash of a field-piece from the wooded eminence, announcing that our approach was discerned; but the blackness and softness of the morass formed by the Esk, and the intense darkness of the night, completely shrouded our movements; and as Jock assured me again and again that he knew the exact position of Cromwell's tent, I began to nourish hopes of killing or capturing that celebrated soldier with my own hand.

"By my faith, Jock, but ye have well earned your guerdon," said Major-General Halkett, as the whole brigade formed to the front by divisions, on the soft turf, in a place where they were concealed by the overhanging wood. This was rapidly done on the march, by the three leading troopers halting, while the remainder moved up into their places on the left, as they defiled from the morass.

"For every plack I promised thee, Jock, thou shalt have a silver pound," said the general.

"Keep it to yoursel, general, for a time may come when you will need it mair than me," replied Jock, who, as he danced about, with his broad overshadowing bonnet, reminded me of an enormous mushroom waving in the wind; "I never tak siller frae sodjers."

"Why, my little man?"

"For fear they might enlist me."

At this reply the troopers laughed.

"Hush," said the brigadier. Again the word "forward" was given, and with drawn swords we ascended the shoulder of the hill, and, as the ground was open, formed into troops at a trot. Making a detour by the woods and manor of Wallyford, we saw before us in the gloom of the night the white tents of Cromwell's camp, which covered all the Links of Musselburgh. In the foreground we could perceive, here and there, a red light like a glowworm. These were the burning matches of his advanced sentinels. I had now taken my place in the ranks, and our little guide had crept near the count, who rode with the brigadier.

"On these Links, thirty years ago, I won the provost's silver arrow," said the count, with a sigh, to Drumstanchel.

"And beat Argyle at archery, I believe?"

"Yes, and gave him one other cause for enmity. We shot three shafts each, and mine——"

"Count," said Sir James Halkett, coming close to him, "our mannikin, who, though half-witted, seems both sharp and cunning, assures me that the tent of Cromwell, the English general, stands on yonder knoll, with the standard of the Commonwealth above it. Those of General Monk and Colonel Sir Arthur Hesilrig are close by. We have not a moment to lose," he added, holding his watch close to his triple-barred helmet; "'tis just eleven o'clock. My lords, you will form squadron, and advance without sound of trumpet. Eglinton, you will hew the way with me. Open your files—dash right through the camp, cutting down all who oppose us; and then, after re-crossing the Esk, we shall muster on its eastern bank."

"From troops, form squadron!" was now the order; it was given in a loud whisper.

"Left troop, to the left incline—trot," cried the Master of Oliphant; all the rear troops of the Black Dragoons formed up to the front, and the moment the squadrons were complete the veteran Earl of Eglinton, without waiting for the command of the brigadier, gave with great rapidity the orders—

"Gentlemen of the Life Guard, march — trot — gallop— charge!"

Count Ogilvie had barely time to repeat the orders, when we, with Cassilis' cuirassiers in our rear all spurring and pressing forward, dashed right at the enemy's camp, with swords uplifted, and a tumultuous cheer ringing along our ranks.

Two or three muskets flashed, as the advanced sentinels fired and retreated on their picquets or out-guards, which poured one irregular volley upon us, and then fled. My left-hand file was shot through the girdle, and on falling from his horse, was trampled to death by the rear squadrons; but *forward* was still the word, and before the guards had time to re-load, we had ridden them down like nine-pins, and broken right into the camp, cutting and slashing at tents, and cords, and men, or whatever came in our way. Our squadrons broke into troops, sections, or files, as they poured like an iron tempest along the streets of tents, hewing to the right and left, and destroying all who attempted to withstand us. We had several men and horses wounded by the scattered discharge of musketry, which opened upon us from all quarters, or by falling over tent-pegs and cords; but while the confusion and consternation lasted, we made a terrible slaughter of the sectaries.

"God and the kirk!" was the cry of Cassilis' Cuirassiers.

"King and covenant!" was the slogan of the Black Dragoons and Life Guards.

Cromwell's tent was cut to ribbands, and at its very door I hewed down an officer, who rushed forth in a black capote, and armed with a half pike. This person proved to be Lieutenant-General Lambert. Of the English protector we saw nothing; and for five minutes there seemed to me only a maze of countless tents before us, and a confused roar of voices, as the startled camp rushed from sleep to arms—an incessant clashing of swords and flashing of musketry, as, like a mighty and irresistible flood, we burst through, sweeping away or bearing down all in our passage. I felt my cheek flushing, my eye dilating, and my breathing thick and difficult, while my heart leaped within me with triumph and tumult; and then I heard the rush of hoofs on the soft turf, as the whole brigade issued from the enemy's camp on its western side, and spurred on to reach the river, after wounding one lieutenant-general, and killing five lieutenant-colonels and five hundred soldiers. Had our attack been followed up by two more such brigades as ours, we had assuredly made a total rout of the whole English army.

"Close in!" cried I to the troop. "Comrades, here is the standard!" I added, as Linn held up his guidon at arm's-length, as a rallying point; but at that moment a musket-shot struck the back of my helmet full upon the cone; otherwise it had pierced my brain. Hurled right over my horse's head, I fell heavily on the ground! I remember hearing the plunging and rush of horses, as the brigade forded the swollen Esk in solid squadrons, and the wild hurrah that was given as they reined up on the opposite bank, to close their files and breathe the horses.

I strove to stagger after them, but again fell to the ground, while a volley of bullets from the English camp swept over me. In another moment, I felt hands laid roughly on me. I was dragged up, and saw around me a crowd of furious and fanatical soldiers, all clad in buff coats and black iron helmets, with swords, muskets, and collars of bandoliers for their powder—unlike our Scots, who carried their cartridges in pouches.

"Oho," said one, "here is one of the lions who came in the night to devour the people of Zion."

"A son of Belial!" said a second, blowing his match.

"An impure Amalekite," said a third, ramming home a bullet; "marry, now, what shall we do with him? Dash him against the stones?" he added, clubbing his musket.

"Nay, nay, take time, I command thee, Hezekiah-accepted-of-Islington—yea, in the name of Cromwell, do."

"Wherefore, brother?" demanded the other furiously, through his nose.

"Because," twanged the first (who was Sergeant Melchisedeck Makepeace, of Monk's regiment), in a strong Somersetshire accent, "lo, you all! on the verge of our camp standeth a ruined chapel of the Pagan times; let us take him there, and hang him from a tree—there groweth many thereabout."

"Nay, brother Melchisedeck, such places are an abomination unto us, even as the place called Gehenna, or the vale of Hinnom, was unto Israel. Yea, my brethren," he continued, raising his voice, and beginning at once to expound, "for there it was their apostate fathers sacrificed their children unto Moloch."

"Yea," interrupted the sergeant, "brother Hezekiah, thou meanest the place defiled and rendered execrable by the man Josiah, who, like Charles Stuart, was falsely named a king."

"Yea—yea," groaned the other, turning up the white of his eyes, as he bit a fresh cartridge.

"What sayest thou, brother Timothy?" asked the sergeant of another soldier.

"My name, brother," he drawled, "is Corporal Fight-the-good-fight-of-Faith—once, in the days of our darkness, called Timothy Twaddle, of Tadcaster."

"Verily, verily; but what sayest thou?" he inquired of another who had groaned mightily in every pause of this strange discourse, which was of such terrible import to me.

"I say unto ye, take this Amorite to yonder Gehenna—yea, unto the walls of Moloch; there fix a lantern to his neck, and sacrifice him unto the Lord of Hosts by shot of musket."

"'Woe unto the nations that rise up against my kindred'—Judith xvi. and xvii.," said the sergeant.

"And hath not the Scot so risen up against us?" asked the corporal with the long name.

"And are not we the kindred of heaven?"

"O yea and verily, brethren," drawled the crowd.

"Then away with him; and I would that yonder gibbering idiot, who dwelleth in the desert place near unto the city of Baal, and who this night led these Assyrians among us, were with him."

By these strange and inflamed fanatics I was roughly dragged along the skirts of the camp to the wall of an old chapel, which stood near it. I was silent; I knew that entreaties would be made in vain, for in direct defiance of Cromwell's orders, the soldiers of Monk had frequently behaved with great barbarity to our people; and one of our troopers who fell into their hands had his eyes torn out, after which, they stripped him nude, and sent him towards the Scottish trenches, with the words, *I am for the king* traced in blood upon his back.

Among men so blinded by barbarity and fanaticism, I knew that no mercy could be expected, and though I had few to love and little to regret, all my past life came before me, while the love of existence grew strong in my heart.

As if in the time I take to write it, every incident of my past years rushed back upon my memory. I thought of my mother's terrible fate, and her yet undiscovered story; I saw myself again the poor *protégé* of kind Nehemiah Spreul and of the grave, stern principal of Glasgow College; I saw my little room that overlooked the gardens, where, when a heedless child, I had chased the bee and butterfly, and when a youth I had conned Nepos, Sallust, and Livy. Years sped on! I was a gallant, a ruffler, a swordsman. Then came my mysterious kidnapping and my enlistment. The faces of my patrons and comrades—the grave, kind colonel, of Linn, Oliphant, and others, came before me, and chief of all, the features of one who in birth and station seemed far above me as the sun above the earth—dear Flora Campbell, the gentle and the generous! All these past faces, scenes, incidents, and years, hopes, fears, and wishes, seemed to rush back upon me with my last breath!

Deprived of my sword, and with my arms pinioned, they dragged. pushed, and struck me; twenty hands or more were upon me, and I had scarcely time to think over my terrible situation, when I found myself thrust against the wall of an old ruin, and then a lighted lantern was tied to my neck.

By its faint glimmering, even at that terrible moment, I could perceive one who, by his laced scarlet coat, broad hat, and white falling bands, I conceived to be a man of rank; but his face was dark, contracted, and forbidding.

"Sergeant—answer me, I implore you," said I; "is that man an officer?"

"Yea, a colonel—he bears the heathenish name of Arthur Hesilrig."

"Save me from this butchery," I exclaimed; "save me, Sir Arthur Hesilrig—I am a prisoner of war!"

"Die, Scot, and be d——d," replied he, turning away; "'tis the bolt of the Lord that hath overtaken thee."

"Hezekiah Accepted—Zerubabbel Meek—Habakuk Killsin," said the sergeant, "and thou, Corporal Twaddle——"

"I tell thee, brother," snivelled the other, in great wrath, "my name is Fight-the-good-fight-of-Faith, so Twaddle me no more."

"Yea and verily—fall in! we will dispatch him by a platoon;" and at the distance of forty yards I could discern these four fanatics through the gloom, by their white falling bands, as they drew up opposite to me, and began to handle their arms, while Sergeant Melchisedeck drawled out the words of command according to the approved fashion of Cromwell's army.

"Poise your muskets—cock your muskets—guard your pans —present—*fire!*"

The four muzzles seemed to flash through the dark into my very eyes.

"God receive me," I sighed, as the four bullets crashed on the stone wall round me, and fell amid lime and dust at my feet, while every pulse and fibre tingled within me, and my startled heart stood still!

"Verily, but the Amorite is shot-proof," cried the crowd of soldiers who were looking on.

"We shall soon prove that—cast about to charge!" resumed the sergeant, as coolly as if upon parade; "handle your chargers —open them with your teeth—draw ramrods——"

I am assured that even had I escaped this second intended platoon, I must have fallen to the earth, from mere over-tension of the heart and brain; but before they could level at me again, the stern voice of one vested with authority exclaimed,

"Recover your arms—shame upon ye, men—fall back, upon your peril fall back! Is it thus my orders are obeyed?"

All shrunk off as this person approached. His presence and bearing were lofty and commanding, but his face was massive and coarse; his nose was large, and his eyes were piercing; he wore a plain black hat with a broad brim, a steel cuirass, buff coat, and starched falling bands. By some intuitive knowledge, I recognised the English lieutenant-general—OLIVER CROMWELL

—and such the speaker proved indeed to be; thus I was at once unbound by many officious hands, and relieved from the lantern.

"Away with him to the court-of-guard," said Cromwell.

And in a few minutes I found myself placed in a tent on the eastern verge of the camp. By a small chain, which was passed round the pole, I was secured within, while a sentinel with a loaded musket walked to and fro without.

Grey morning was stealing across the east, and I seated myself on the turf floor of the tent to think over the sudden changes a single night had made in my position and my fortunes.

I was the only prisoner taken by the enemy in that night's camisado, and my brigade had only ten men and three horses killed.

CHAPTER XXVI.

THE MAN IN THE VELVET MASK.

ON this occasion I had ridden into action full of hope and ardour, and with the expectation of distinguishing myself; and *now*, after narrowly escaping a cold-blooded death, I was a prisoner of war.

The idea has often occurred to me that soldiers, by some mysterious intuition, know when death is near them, having heard many of my comrades say, before going under fire, that they felt assured of being shot, and I have observed that those fatalists invariably *were killed*, yet they ever did their duty bravely.

I was very kindly treated in the English camp; but longed for liberty, and dreaded being sent into England, or off to Cromwell's fleet, which hovered along the coast, supplying the army with provisions, and, after fighting with our armed vessels, had twice insulted the fortifications of Leith and Burntisland.

Cromwell had hitherto been triumphant, when fighting against the only troops he ever had to contend with—viz., undisciplined English cavaliers and wild Irish kerne; thus we confidently believed that he would never be able to withstand the experience of those Scottish generals and marshals who, in the greatest war that ever ravaged Europe, had led to battle the finest armies of France, Denmark, Sweden, and the vainglorious Empire. But I could not fail to be struck by the grave austerity—the almost savage morality which pervaded his camp; no inebriety, no dicing or gambling were seen, and few outrages were as yet committed on the people by his soldiers. From amid their tents I heard the incessant singing of psalms, and the noise of scriptural disputations or expounding, as some cockney pikeman or

Yorkshire musketeer was moved by the spirit to favour his brethren with a savoury discourse. I had deemed our Covenanters gloomy enough; but Cromwell's buff-coated saints were more morose by a thousand degrees, for they buckled on their swords, as they phrased it, to extend the reign of the saints on earth; while *we* fought only for religious freedom, and the integrity of our king and country; thus with their pious fervour the armies of the Covenant mingled a high spirit of Scottish nationality.

Cromwell's gunpowder-saints had all baptised themselves anew, as their old English names were deemed heathenish and ungodly; thus it was, that in Monk's regiment I heard such remarkable cognomens as Sergeant Melchisedeck Makepeace, Corporal Fight-the-good-fight-of-Faith Twaddle, and Privates Hezekiah-accepted-of-Islington, Zerubabbel Meek, and Habakuk Killsin, whose appellations I have good cause to remember; and such was their rage for this style of affairs, that these military religiosos intended to have their court of chancery abolished; the Mosaic law established as the sole system of English jurisprudence; to have Scotland united to and merged in England; with a hundred other projects, equally absurd. But to resume.

I had just finished supper on the evening of the second day of my captivity, and was, as usual, longing very much to stretch my limbs beyond the narrow compass of the bell-tent in which I was confined, when the long and solemn visage of Sergeant Makepeace, with his earthly tabernacle fully accoutred in a coarse red coat, with a collar of bandoliers, sword and belt, appeared at the door, and said,

"Peace be with thee, brother—yea, and verily, the lord general awaits thee."

This was said so abruptly, that nearly a minute elapsed before I could comprehend what he meant; and, on expressing my readiness to accompany him, he unbound the fetter which secured me to the pole, and we issued from the tent, at the door of which were two of Monk's musketeers to guard and accompany me.

Through the quiet, clean, and well-ordered camp, I was conducted towards a tent that was larger than the rest, and over which waved the symbol of the English commonwealth, a simple white standard, having a red cross, and the words, "God with us." Near this tent were several mounds of fresh earth. Therein lay those who had fallen on the night of our attack : five hundred in whom the great republican, Death, had laid his icy hand.

I was at once ushered in, and found myself before several plainly-dressed and coarsely-accoutred officers, all wearing their hair either very long and lank or closely shorn, with shaven chins and square falling bands. They were grouped round a table, on which were several maps and bundles of letters. In one of the group, I recognised the ruffianly Sir Arthur Hesilrig, governor of Newcastle; in another, who was a mean-looking little man, with curly locks but forbidding features, I discovered General George Monk; he was conversing in whispers with a red-haired man, who wore *a black velvet mask;* but in the tallest person present—he whose eyes were grave, keen, and quick, and whose coarse visage was disfigured by two or three unsightly warts—I recognised the greatest man that ever trod on English ground—the Lord General Cromwell; he who had so opportunely saved me from the second fusilade of Sergeant Melchisedeck Makepeace.

While I made a respectful salute, he gazed at me sternly for a moment, as if he would read my inmost thoughts, and said,

"So—so, you are the prisoner whom we took the other night?"

"I have the misfortune to be so."

"Your rank?" he asked briefly, making a note.

"A sergeant in the Black Horse—Count Ogilvie's dragoons."

"Your name?"

"Harry Ogilvie, my lord."

"I am no lord. Ogilvie—umph! A high-flying and ungodly name among you Scots, I believe."

Here the man in the velvet mask turned and scrutinized me keenly, and I saw his breast heave, as if with some sudden emotion.

"I presume you are anxious to be released from captivity, that you may rejoin those sons of Cain who are now in arms against the kindred of God, in the cause of Charles Stuart the younger, the son of Agag—yea, the son of the God-abandoned!"

"I am naturally anxious for liberty, my lord; but if any information I am to yield be its price——"

"Ye would withhold it: spare me the blunt avowal, young man, for in thine eye I can read the very soul of a Philistine—yea, a worthy follower of the younger man Charles, whose heart God hath hardened, even as he hardened Pharaoh's of old."

"Then Pharaoh was not to blame," said I.

Here all present adjusted their bands, and prepared to plunge at once into polemics.

"It matters not: his heart was hard, and his punishment——"

"Was death," said I.

"And such shall be the punishment of the crowned man, Charles Stuart. I seek no tidings from you, boy. Thanks be unto the Lord, we have numbered your host to a man; we know every cannon you have, and the weight thereof; we know all your footmen and horsemen, and knew them well before we crossed the Tweed at Berwick."

Here his eye fell involuntarily on the red-haired man in *the velvet mask,* and at once I divined him to be a colluder with the foe; for although ladies and gentlemen in Scotland frequently wore masks as a disguise, the puritans would never tolerate such an accessory to intrigue.

"'Tis a spy—a traitor," thought I; " else why this mask? Were *you* the source of all this information?" I demanded, turning suddenly upon him.

A cold smile flitted over Cromwell's face. The mask started: his sinister eyes sparkled, and then he bent them in silence on a map that lay before him.

"Speak," said I, while a glow kindled in my heart; " speak! for if you are a Scot, I shall strangle you where you stand, even in this presence!"

"Silence, fellow!" he hissed through his teeth, while he trembled with rage; " silence! or, by the God of my kindred, ye shall die!"

"Silence!" repeated all present, with tones of anger and authority; but *his* voice went through me like a sword, and I knew in a moment that he was—who?

A man to whom the government of Scotland and the management of her inmost affairs, civil, military, and ecclesiastical, were committed; he who occupied the chief place in her senate and treasury, at her councils of peace and war, and who co-operated with her generals and officers of state—the leader of the Scottish covenanting peers—*Archibald, Earl of Argyle!*

Still following the *ignes fatui* of a Scottish dictatorship in conjunction with an English protectorate, he was true to his class and false to his country. I was frozen—awed into silence by this terrible discovery; and the strange words of the poor maniac, Jock of the lodge, flashed upon me.

Before I could speak, I heard again the sonorous and impressive voice of Cromwell.

"Sergeant," said he, " we war not with individuals, and least of all with the humble in place, like thee. We have come to wage a christian strife; to extend the reign of God's chosen people upon the earth; to abolish for ever all the false demigods, saints, images, oracles, altars, priests, and their worshippers; and while, with the carnal weapons of war, we oppose such as gird up their loins for battle against us, we have also spiritual weapons for those who meet us in the fair field of open argument."

" Yea," growled General Monk; " but if your people fail to be convinced, they shall number more dead than living in their tents and dwelling-places."

"It is our intention to set you free, trooper," said Cromwell; " free, with liberty to return to the host of Agag the younger, provided you will bear unto the Reverend Messieurs Hamilton, Gowan, Low, Traill, Bogle, and Boyd (particularly to the last, who brooketh the Lord's inheritance in a city called Glasgow), these our separate letters, which we are vain enough to believe will convince them that *we*, the army of England, are the favoured, the chosen, and the consecrated host of Heaven before whom their warriors shall lie prostrate in the dust, like the bands of the Assyrian. Like Genseric, I war against all 'who have provoked the anger of God;' and, like Atila, I say, 'the star falls and the sea is moved, for I am the hammer of the earth;' and so shall I hammer the Scots, who are in darkness and the shadow of death! Promise me, on the gospels, that you will deliver these six packets, each unto the minister for whom it is addressed, and the next moment beholds you free."

"I dare not become the bearer of secret messages from an enemy's camp," said I, without a moment of hesitation; "nor would I stoop to an act so base, even though your gallows waited me."

"Beware of your words, sirrah," said Cromwell, while his brow darkened; "for I have been recommended (and here his eye fell again on *the mask*) to ship off to our English plantations in Virginia all Scottish prisoners taken in this godly war against the godless—so beware that I begin not with *thee!*"

"It would not be the first time I have found myself under sail for the same distant shore," said I, with a fierce glance at the mask; "but kind Heaven favoured me, and I have still a heart and hand at the disposal of my king and country."

As I said this, the disguised earl seemed convulsed by some inward emotion: he darted at me another furious and scrutinizing glance, and drew back. As he did so, the map that lay before him fell at my feet, and by one glance I divined its whole contents; and though General Monk hastened to snatch it up, *they were graven on my memory.*

"Then you will not obey my wishes?"

"My lord, I will rather die!"

"Then away with him," said Cromwell; "Sir Arthur Hesilrig, you will send him off with the first boat that leaves this for the fleet of Blake, and have him kept in the bilboes until despatched to London with any others we may take—see to it; and now let us to supper;" and he added, in that canting fashion which did not sit easily upon him, as it was entirely assumed to suit the time and temper of his followers, "Scot, thou mayest go—the Lord hath done with thee."

I was marched back to my tent, and left to my own reflections. They were many and bitter. Amid them all, I saw ever before me the thin spare figure, the flaming locks, the black mask, and the fierce gleaming eyes of Argyle, with the sinister smile that filled them, when I was conducted from the tent of him whose tool and plaything he was, and for being the coadjutor of whom he paid the penalty of his head in years to come.

CHAPTER XXVII.

PRIVATE ZERUBABBEL MEEK.

THE evening had darkened into night; the drums had been beaten, prayers had been said and psalms sung; the English camp had sunk into repose, with all their guards and sentinels doubled and extended, and strong patrols of horse upon all the adjacent roads; as our late attack *à la Cossacque*—a tactique learned by Leslie and Halkett in their campaigns on the Vistula—made Cromwell and his generals more wary.

Silence sank over everything; I soon heard only the monotonous tread of my sentinel outside the tent, and at times even that ceased, when he paused, and, leaning on his musket, gave himself up to pious and abstracted reverie.

My reflections were of a gloomy cast; I thought of the ring that was on my finger, of the beauty of the donor, and the wild and presumptuous hopes her gift had awakened. I thought of her father with sorrow, anger, and contempt; for though it was nothing new to find a Scottish peer selling himself, body and soul, to the enemies of his country, and to the government of England, it *was* assuredly something rare to find one who pretended to be a Highland chief so servile and so base—trafficking thus with a man who was but a private gentleman of Huntingdon, and who in 1642 was only a major of cavalry in his own country (though his headlong valour, matchless ability, and subtle hypocrisy, had nearly set him on its throne); and with the treacherous and brutal George Monk, who was a private soldier, when Scotland and England sent an allied force on the disastrous expedition to Rochelle and the Isle Rhé. Such things were new to us in Scotland, where birth and station were viewed as something divine; though it is a lamentable fact that Scotland's patriots never sprang, like her traitors, from the loins of her aristocracy. But this is as well known as the fall of Adam.

However great my repugnance to the deep and double game Argyle—he who was always "thanking God that he was not as other men are"—was assuredly playing with Cromwell, it was secondary to the concern I felt for myself. I contemplated, with emotions amounting almost to agony, my chance of being banished from Scotland at a time so perilous to her, so exciting to myself;

and being sent on shipboard, and, in flagrant violation of international law, transported I knew not whither; for I remembered the early and mysterious cause of enmity evinced towards me by the potent earl and Campbell of Ardmohr; and now I had no doubt that their influence with Cromwell would warp or blind the natural sense of justice and humanity, which were leading features in that great soldier's character, and that he would really send me as a slave to the English plantations.

In the excitement and aversion such a prospect roused within me, even the soft image of Flora faded, or was forgotten. I saw only the cool, calculating visage of her father, the *ci-devant* dictator! I abhorred him in my soul, and longed to be free that I might avenge myself upon him and baffle his dangerous plots. I remembered the map that had fallen at my feet, and every feature of which I had seized at a glance and committed to memory.

An attack upon the Scottish redoubts and trenches which covered the eastern flank of the capital was evidently on the tapis, for that map contained a diagram of the city, with the hills which overhang it, the outworks of Leslie, his camp and fortifications. The lines of attack had been traced in *red ink;* and I perceived that, while a brisk assault was to threaten our front towards the east, a flank movement of horse and artillery was to be made on the south side of Edinburgh near the suburb of St. Leonard, our weakest point—and who could have informed Cromwell of *that?* who but a traitor!

This very night perhaps the columns of attack were leaving the camp! Oh, how I longed to inform the general of their intention! but a prisoner, in the heart of the English tents, within their guards and picquets, who formed a wakeful zone around it, what hope had I of escape? I bit my lips and groaned in very agony of spirit as I threw myself upon the cold turf, and wrapping my head in a capote which a soldier had lent me, strove to forget my sorrows in slumber. Vain effort and futile wish!

About midnight my sleepless and bitter reflections were interrupted by a hand giving my hair a violent pull, and on starting up, by the light of a lantern that hung on the tent pole I saw the strange and grotesque visage of Jock the idiot, peeping in beneath the low wall of the tent, with his red ferret-like eyes overshadowed by the circumference of his enormous bonnet, through various fractures of which his grey hair hung in tangled elflocks.

"Hush!" said he, in a whisper close to my ear; "dinna speak —it is the price o' my life to be found here—they've turned my puir lodge on the muir; but I'll be even wi' them yet.'

"They—who?"

"The English. They put a lunt into the thatch and burned it owre my very head last night; I was weel nigh smoored in the reek, but I'll be even wi' them yet, like the auld wife wi' the deil that supped her kail, wi' a hey-sing-ho, and a tow-row-row."

"And what brought thee here, my poor gomeral?"

"Your affairs, sir."

"Mine?"

"The Master o' Oliphant and Sergeant Glanders are waiting for you on the causeway, at the east end o' the Howe Mire. I ken the place weel, for there Pinkey's hirsel was elfshot by my mother, and there she sowed the knot grass to spite the laird, so the spot has been barren and bare sinsyne."

"At the Howe Mire, say'st thou? Oh, hasten to them, my poor imbecile, and bid them beware of the English patrols, for heavy squadrons cover all the roads."

"They wouldna thank me for coming back wi' that advice alone—na, na, though he *is* a fule, Jock didna come here on a fule's errand. But hush, for a limb o' Sawtan is at the tent-door."

"How did you pass so many sentinels?"

"By creeping on my wame like a muckle partan; now hear me, for wisdom may at times come out o' a fule's mouth, as weel as out o' the mouths of babes and sucklings, as Corporal Mac Snaffle says. Listen," he continued, putting his hideous mouth close to my ear. "There is at the tent door a sentinel, whose duty it is to guard you alone; he has a musket, but when I wet the match wi' this can o' water," he added, taking up the vessel which contained my usual beverage, "that musket will be nae better than an auld besom."

"But he has a sword—I have none, and the guards are close by."

"A sword—bah! I'll fight him myself."

I could not forbear smiling, when I saw this confident little mannikin, whose stature was about two feet and a half, with his enormous head and bearded face, bowed legs, and shapeless hands, speak of encountering the English musketeer.

"The guard occupy the opposite tent."

"I'll find wark for them."

"I had long since cut a hole in this one, and escaped—but had not a knife."

"I'll find wark, too, for that strong sectary, Zerubabbel—he wi' the nose like a priming horn, and eyen like the spots on a peacock's tail. He'll think that he has auld Michael or Mahoun himsel' to deal wi'! When you hear him cry out, rush frae the tent, and make straight awa—the nicht is mirk, and the mist thick as a witch's reek."

"But you, my poor fellow—how shall I leave you?"

"Fearna for me—it's long or the deil dies; and as my mother was burned for suckling imps, who kens but I am ane? Fearna for me, I'll sune follow ye."

And with my flagon of water in his long lean hand, he withdrew himself, heels foremost, from under the walls of the tent. With no great hope of his success, I waited in breathless suspense for the next movement of this strange little man. Though the idea of rushing out and attempting to surprise or disarm the English sentinel had often occurred to me, I had deemed it madness to risk the certainty of being shot down by his comrades of the guard close by; but just as the solemn and godly Zerubabbel Meek untied the ropes which secured the tent door, and inserted his long visage between the canvas folds, to inquire "with whom I held converse, or if the spirit was moving me," he suddenly staggered backward with a cry of terror, and I heard the crash of the water flagon as his eyes were deluged by its contents —while the imbecile, now frenzied with excitement, exerting his wonderful agility, sprang like a wild cat on his back, where he sat perched and immoveable.

In great tribulation, the broad-shouldered Saxon kicked, wriggled, and plunged, making vain efforts to cast off this incubus, this strange animal, this—he knew not what—which had so suddenly sprung upon him.

"Lo, the evil one—gramercy!" he cried, in a stifled voice.

"Sma' mercy will ye get," shrieked Jock, winding his crooked legs round Zerubabbel's waist, while his long, bony, and misshapen fingers encircled his neck; "sma' mercy will ye get; it was you, or such loons as you, that burned my puir lodge on the muir, but I'll be even wi' ye yet, ye psalm-singing tyke!"

"Off, off, I tell thee—get thee behind me, Satan."

"Weel, so I am behint ye," laughed Jock, who kicked on Zerubabbel's ribs as if he was spurring a restive horse.

> "The deil sat supping the auld wife's kail,
>   With a hey sing ho, and a tow, row, row:"

"Help, good brethren in the Lord," yelled the musketeer, in a half-strangled voice; "help, for lo and verily, the evil one hath beset me!"

"Wheesht," hissed Jock in his ear; "wheesht—or I'll rive the soul out o' ye, even as I wad blob a bumbee."

"Ho, the guard—guard ho! a Scot's devil!"

A crowd of soldiers hastened in a moment to the spot; but the mannikin gave Zerubabbel a last squeeze of the throat, which brought him prone to the earth, almost dead and breathless. He then glided from among them, and vanished with a shout of elfin merriment.

In great alarm and astonishment, the quarter-guard and inmates of the adjacent tents crowded in the dark round Zerubabbel Meek. He lay at full length on the ground, with his face buried in the grass, muttering prayers and pious invocations, in great tribulation of mind and body. Favoured by their preoccupation, and finding the tent door open, I slipped out, and passing in rear of a row of tents, glided through the camp unnoticed by all, save two of the advanced sentinels, who were posted on the verge of Pinkey Wood, and who both challenged. Receiving no answer, they fired at me, but their bullets fell wide of the mark, and plunging into the black coppice, I escaped their sight; and without delay proceeded towards the eastern end of the Howe Mire, which I reached with great difficulty, as the locality was strange to me, and I could only judge of its position by keeping in view the little conical spire of Inveresk, which stood upon high ground, and overlooked the morass.

I could hear the reiterated cry of "All's well" passed from man to man, and dying away on the night wind along the chain of cavalry videttes, who were posted round the mount of Inveresk, and from thence to the Roman bridge which spans the river; and at one time I was so near that I could distinctly perceive a trooper, muffled in a long and dark capote, sitting motionless on his horse, with a carbine resting on his thigh, as the partial gleams of a waning moon beamed for a few seconds over the wooded ridge of Carberry Hill, and then sank in clouds, leaving the landscape in total darkness. Then the bell of St. Michael tolled two, as I floundered down the steep bank into the soft and shifting moss of the black Howe Mire, and luckily struck upon the old and half-hidden Roman causeway, which traversed it towards the south.

Pausing a moment to look around me, I could perceive, in dark outline, at its eastern end, the figures of two mounted men, one of whom led a spare horse; and I was hastening towards them, when the sound of steps made me turn and, with clenched hands and a throbbing heart, look back. It was no pursuer, but only poor Jock, who sprang to my side, panting and breathless, with his mouth agape, his round eyes staring, and his wild grey hair floating in elflocks on the wind; yet he capered and danced in the morass from one tuft of heath to another, flourishing about him his long arms and flexible little legs, while singing his absurd ditty, and never pausing for an instant, save to urge me onward, as Cromwell's sectaries were on our track.

"It is he!" exclaimed a familiar voice; "and Jock, too—O thou incomparable natural! welcome, little fellow—my familiar —my Mephistophiles!"

"Oliphant," said I, "my faithful friend and comrade, how am I to thank you for this; and honest Gideon Glanders, too?"

"By using your spurs, if they are still on your heels, Harry. Here is a stout nag which we brought with us on chance, for I had but little hope of rescuing you."

"I had much hope, comrade Harry," said our bluff sergeant; "I knew that diabolical imp, Jock, of old, and believed he might essay and achieve much, where a troop of horse would fail."

"And the sequel proves you were right."

A rush of galloping hoofs, as a party of troopers came over the hill of Inveresk, and descended by the causeway towards the Howe Mire, cut short all further parley. Jock sprang on the crupper of my horse, where he sat perched like a huge marmoset, while we rode furiously towards the west, to reach that long chain of outposts, which formed a girdle round the city of the James's.

"There was a traitor in yonder camp last night," said Jock, putting his mouth closer to my ear than proved quite pleasant.

"Know *you* that?" I asked.

"Right weel do I, for I tracked him from Leslie's door to Cromwell's tent."

"But you must never mention his name to living man until I tell thee, Jock," said I, anxiously, as I thought of Flora.

"That is unco' queer; but why?"

"Promise me, Jock," said I, with increasing anxiety, for at that moment the gentle Flora dwelt more in my mind than the danger accruing to Scotland; and I urged the imbecile with such importunity, that he said emphatically,—

"By my mother soul, I winna mention his name, though I ken it well;—it begins wi' an A. Had *she* been alive, puir body, she had soon settled him, I warrant."

"How?"

"When she had a spite at any ane, she caught a toad at the waning o' the moon, and dipped it thrice in the broo o' three boiled adders; then she stuck seven pins in it, and after going thrice round the lodge widershins, between the night and morning, buried it alive in a jar on the muir; and so as that bewitched toad pined and dee'd, so did her enemy. She was a braw carlin, my mother, and had she no been brankit and burnt on a pile o' dry sticks, had soon settled Arg——"

"Hush! I tell thee hush!" said I, furiously.

"That was the way she slew the Laird o' Dolphinton in his tower yonder, for he dee'd mad and phrenzied wi' pain; sax men couldna hauld him in his death agony; but noo he lies quiet enough in Seaton kirk, under a ton o' marble, wi' his sword and helmet owre him.

"But what had the laird done to provoke such vengeance?"

"He shot her urchin—a hedgehog that folk called her *familiar*. It slept in a cozy neuk o' her bed at night; but I thocht it weel awa, for it was a sair rival to me, and aye got a share o' my sowans and kail."

While this strange being talked away in this fashion, my two brave companions rode in silence beside us, and were wholly intent on putting as great a distance as possible between themselves and the enemy; but we had soon to rein up, as we drew near the eastern shoulder of Arthur's seat, for on the pathway there was a piquet of the Life Guards, under Sir William Livingstone, of Westquarter, whose mounted videttes challenged us, but on exchanging the parole and countersign, we passed onward, and reached the camp or bivouac, as our troops remained in the trenches night and day—each trooper by his horse, each gunner by his gun; for we knew not the moment an attack might be made. Tidings that a prisoner had escaped from the enemy's camp spread like wildfire, and I was soon summoned to the presence of the general, Sir David Leslie, who with a number of officers commanding regiments and brigades, occupied a comfortable old house, which belonged to the Moultrays of that ilk, and stood upon a high knoll westward of the Calton hill, and situated midway between the city and the right flank of our main position.

These officers were all sleeping in their harness, and muffled in their mantles, with swords and pistols beside them, on chairs and benches in the large dining hall, on the table of which stood many a flagon, bottle, and flask; but lights were brought, and all sprang to their feet to question me as to the strength, number, and probable movements of the enemy.

I answered the queries on these points to the best of my knowledge, and the old general seemed well pleased with my information; but when I mentioned the plan I had seen, and the strong probability of our being attacked on the southern quarter of the city,

"Hah!" said he, striking his heel on the floor, "you're right, sergeant—that point is indeed our weakest; but it shall be looked to! Oliphant, ride to the quarters of Lieutenant-General Lumsdaine; desire him to move his brigade a little more to the right, and to take with him the horse of Adjutant-General Bickerton. See to it, sir."

The Master of Oliphant hurried away to obey this order.

"You have done well, young man," said the veteran general, surveying me with a kind and approving eye.

"And the first cornetcy that is vacant——" began our colonel, with a glow on his dark face.

"Shall be *his*," said Leslie, "for I doubt not, Count, but he has been the saving of our position."

" By whom can Cromwell have been informed that the post at St. Leonard was our weakest ?" said a voice that made me start; and there, divested of mask and mantle, I saw the calm, cold features, the long red hair and squinting eyes of Argyle, turned placidly towards me. " Can there be a servant of Agag among them ?—a spy—a traitor ?"

" *Your lordship* knoweth best," said I, unwarily, as I gave the general a profound salute, and withdrew. But oh, my heart was beating wildly! I felt pleasure at the general's notice, gratitude for his promise, and pride for the praise he had bestowed upon me, struggling with anger at that false and plotting noble, though this emotion was rather subdued by the memory of his gentle daughter Flora, and somewhat of terror, lest his vengeance would one day overtake me! How could I, a poor sergeant of dragoons, hope to escape the deep-laid snares and long-devised toils of him, before whom the great Montrose, the captain-general of King Charles, had gone down to a felon's grave from a common scaffold ?

As I left the apartment, I saw him exchange a smile of deep and terrible import with Colonel Campbell, of Ardmohr.

I dared not tell all I knew concerning him, for who in Scotland would believe one so humble in rank as I ? I felt myself hovering, as it were, on the brink of a precipice, or like one above whose head hung the sword of the Sicilian flatterer.

" Let me be wary and silent," thought I; " watchful and true to myself, for a little time may yet unravel all this mystery."

CHAPTER XXVIII.

REPULSE OF THE PURITANS.

I was glad to find that my horse had returned to head-quarters with the regiment. The attachment between a soldier and his charger is natural; thus I have seen many a brave fellow lamenting its loss in battle, as if his best friend had fallen. I remember Charley Carlonrie, one of our troopers, being ordered to despatch his horse, which was wounded in a skirmish, and declared unfit for service. He loaded and cocked his carbine and walking thrice up to the poor charger, thrice withdrew At last he dashed his weapon on the ground, and burst into tears.

Thou art a brave fellow, Carlourie," said Count Ogilvie, and deserve well to be spared this trial." So the poor charger was put out of pain by old Hackikon, who had fewer scruples, or perhaps less humanity.

"The first duty of a dragoon, in peace or war," continued the Count, addressing us, "is to devote himself to his horse. and to the study and anticipation of all its little wants, for in time of war it is subjected to many new privations and severities, especially when on outpost duty, for then the rider may occupy the saddle for two hours as a vidette, and then it may be accoutred with holsters, carbine, and valise, forage, spare shoes, &c. &c., for twenty-four consecutive hours, exposed the while to every kind of weather. I have ever found that the humane and kind-hearted troopers were the best-mounted men in the regiment. The horse and his rider are one! Both must know alike the flash of a carbine and the twang of a trumpet, and both must be ready for action at a moment's notice."

My heart yearned to my horse, and the poor animal licked my hand, rubbed his nose against my cheek, and neighed, when I groomed him again, for he knew well my whistle and my voice when I caressed him, and we shared together the contents of *a jug of ale*, over which Glanders, MacSnaffle, and I were discussing our late adventures.

I had to rehearse my strange story twenty times to the officers and men of the Black Dragoons, whose bivouac was in rear of the infantry lines.

These rang the livelong day with the varied noises of clinking cans, prayers and psalms, foreign oaths, camp songs, and the scraps of such ditties as cheered the quarters of the Scots brigades who won the fields of Lütter, Leipzig, and the Vistula. Though nearly 30,000 men were intrenched in front of Edinburgh, our camp was well supplied, and provisions were cheap; the price of a whole lamb was only one shilling and ninepence; of an entire sheep, five shillings; of a salmon, fourpence; of a dozen eggs, twopence; and we had the finest of canary and Muscadel for one-and sixpence per quart, French wines at sevenpence, while a stone of hay for a trooper cost our quartermaster only fivepence. Soon after my return, my troop had the pleasant duty of escorting from Leith the stores of three English ships, taken by ours: viz., beer, biscuits, powder, shot, and three thousand ells of red cloth for clothing.

On Monday, the 24th of July, by order of the general, the whole troops were under arms an hour before daylight; we fed our horses with the bits hanging at their chests; the infantry were all in the intrenched lines; the cavalry formed in brigades, and the artillerymen stood by their guns, with rammer, match, and sponge. Tidings had been received that Cromwell meant to attack us. During the whole of the past night there had been signs of preparation in his camp, and the plan of his movements proved the accuracy of my suspicions and suggestions on the night of my escape.

The morning dawned in unusual splendour; a gentle shower had fallen over-night, and now every shrub, flower, and tree was gleaming with dew, while a light and silvery mist rolled along the mountain slopes. I have already described the position of the Scottish army, which surrounded the city by lines of horse and foot, strengthened by redoubts, overlooked by the fortifications of the town and the garrison of the castle, on the walls of which were now seventy pieces of ordnance. Our main body was intrenched along Leith Loan, and thanks to the skill of our officers, who had fought the armies of the Empire, our position was impregnable.

At noon, when the brilliant sun was at its height, an excited muttering ran along our lines; the gleam of arms became visible to the eastward, and we saw the enemy advancing in heavy, close columns, which slowly and laboriously, with a solemnity of movement peculiar to the Puritans, deployed into line, with their ranks three deep, as they cleared the rocky eminence and broomy knolls of Restalrig, marching with their left resting (as Cromwell names it in his despatch) "on the place called *Jock's-lodge*." Their long lines of shouldered muskets, their helmets, cuirasses, and swords, shone in the meridian sun, and we saw their white standards with the red cross of better times waving in the wind. As every English company carried one, their aspect was alike showy and formidable. Some of the brigades were clothed in coarse red coats, not a few had white, while others were attired in plain buff, with black casques and leather boots.

As they advanced steadily and rapidly over the open waste, a tremendous cannonade was opened upon them by forty pieces of cannon from the brow of the Calton, from the ramparts of Leith, and a brigade of field-pieces and *canon à Suédois*, under General Wemyss, who occupied the quarries above the abbey hill, thus enfilading their approach on both flanks. At the same time, twelve English ships of war, anchored stem and stern, poured their broadsides on the northern walls of Leith.

A storm of grape and round-shot, shells, and grenades, fell among the advancing columns, and long before they came within range of musketry, we saw them wavering, pausing, and filling up their gaps, as many a man and many a standard fell, dotting all the green-sward with killed and wounded.

We (the cavalry) sat in our saddles, mere spectators of this carnage; but steadily and bravely the English came on, entering this *mouth of fire*, as old Leslie named it, by a rapid march; and the bad generalship of Cromwell, in assailing such a position, and in open day, too, drew exclamations of astonishment from all; but excited by the slaughter made by our brigade in the recent night attack, the Puritans came on with great ardour.

A gleam passed along the serried lines of the Scottish infantry, as nearly twenty thousand muskets were suddenly levelled; and the roar of their first volley, when it ran along from flank to flank, drowned for a moment the din of the rapid cannonade, while the sunny air seemed to tremble and stand still under the terrible concussion.

For a time, all in our front was shrouded in rolling smoke; but amid it we could see the flashing of steel ramrods, as our men re-loaded and cast about their muskets, maintaining their running fire with spirit and rapidity, while pipes yelled, drums were rolled, and standards waved in defiance, as our regiments, both lowland and highland, emulated each other in their energy.

Our artillerists had received particular orders to fire upon the English general; but as that notable person was in no way distinguishable from the rest of his officers, unfortunately the desire of Leslie could not be fulfilled. On the smoke clearing partially away, a cheer rose from Halkett's brigade, and we brandished our swords; the whole of Cromwell's troops were seen in full and precipitate retreat, double quick, leaving the ground strewed with dead and writhing wounded. Among these lay several drums, colours, and cannon. At that moment Sir David Leslie dashed up to our brigade at full gallop, with his silver hair waving from under his steel cap, and his keen grey eyes sparkling with fire and animation.

" Sir James Halkett," said he, " a column of the foe, stronger than I anticipated, with a brigade of horse and several pieces of cannon, have made a detour by the flank of Arthur's Seat, and now menace the city by the southern road, which approaches the Pleasance. Draw off your brigade, take with you the regiments of Lawers and Ardmohr, and see to the defence of that Fauxbourg. Away, without a moment of delay. Our honour, the safety of the city and our position, depend upon your bravery, sirs !"

The two Highland regiments of musketeers went off double-quick, with their arms at the trail.

Our brigade was in close column of squadrons, with the Life Guards in front under the Earl of Eglington.

" Three's right," was the order; " trot—gallop !" and away we went at full speed, leaving all our forage and other incumbrances in the bivouac behind us. As we passed the head of the trenches we were cheered by the king's Foot Guards; but I was struck by the pallor of their colonel, the Lord Lorn.

CHAPTER XXIX.

DEFENCE OF ST. LEONARD'S HILL.

WE rode through St. Mary's Wynd, up St. John's hill, and, leaving the two Highland regiments to follow as fast as they could, issued out by the Pleasance Porte, and debouched upon the roadway, which lies through open fields, unencumbered by hedges, walls, or other enclosures, save near the Royal Park; but while we were in the act of forming up to the front, from threes into open columns of squadrons, the two battalions of Celts—all gallant Campbells—rushed through the valley which lies between the Craigs of Salisbury and St. Leonard's Hill, and swarming up the steep brow of the latter, like a herd of mountain cats, lined the walls of the King's Park, and some hedgerows close by, and manned the ruined chapel of St. Leonard, from whence, with great skill, they opened a fire upon the enemy.

"The brigade will advance—forward, trot, my gallants!" cried Sir James Halkett, and forward we went, full of ardour and emulation, the loud blare of the trumpet ringing on the flank of every troop, as we came in view of the foe.

A column of infantry in line, with colours flying, two pieces of cannon in front, and cavalry moving on both flanks, advanced over the open pasture ground which lies between the overhanging and columnar basalt known as Samson's Ribs, and the ancient highway which leads direct to the Pleasance Porte. In this column were the foot regiments of Monk, Pride, and Goff, commanded by Sir Arthur Hesilrig, whose own Horse covered one flank, while Alured's dragoons were on the other.

As we came on the trooper who rode next me suddenly threw up his sword, crying, "My God, I am shot!" and fell under his horse's feet. At that moment a ridge of smoke streaked with fire rose before the line of English infantry; I heard the balls whistling past, and the clatter of accoutrements as many of our troopers fell heavily from their saddles on the turf; and while our infantry from the walls and hedges poured a furious musquetade in reply, Sir James Halkett gave the order to charge, and the three regiments advanced in open column of squadrons at a rapid trot, to get our horses well in hand. Under old Greysteel, the Life Guards were on our right, and the Cuirassiers of Cassilis on our left. I was the extreme left file of the leading troop, and my breast filled with furious ardour as we rushed at the cloud of smoke in which the enemy had enveloped themselves; and from amid which there came two successive volleys of grape shot, that plunged through our ranks with terrible effect, tearing the horses to pieces, ploughing up the grass, and raising those little puffs of dust that always rise when grape or canister fall on a roadway in summer. Meanwhile, the report of the firing rang with a thousand reverberations among the hills.

"Gentlemen and brother soldiers," cried Count Ogilvie, turning round as he cantered in front of the Black Dragoons, and towered above us all, for he was a noble specimen of a cavalier; "remember, that tide what may, this *white plume* of mine will be your rallying point, and the beacon that shall guide you to honour and victory!"

These words, which were nearly similar to those used by Henri of France in one of his battles, drew a loud hurrah from the regiment; and, though men were falling fast on every hand, we still pressed on. The word of command went through me like electricity.

"Gallop—charge!" was the cry; and with the shrill twang of the trumpet again ringing in our ears, on we swept like a whirlwind, boot to boot and bridle to bridle, while the very earth seemed to roll away beneath the rush of our squadrons; and such was the fury of our advance, that Sir Arthur Hesilrig had barely time to throw back the flanks of his infantry with a stand of pikes in front, and draw the artillery rearward, when we were among them.

A glow of heroism—a fierce tumultuous joy, swelled up within me, and goring my horse with the spurs until he was more than twice his length in front of the squadron, I forgot that I was only a sergeant, and *not* a paladin of romance. I forgot that my officers were all cadets of noble families: men who on the line of battle would stoop their crests to none; and, brandishing my sword, I cried,

"Come on, come on! an Ogilvie! an Ogilvie! *follow me!*"

"To it, my brave lad; thou shouldst be a chieftain of our name, and not a poor dragoon!" exclaimed our colonel, as his dark face glowed, and his eyes flashed fire. "To it, my stout Ogilvie, and God bless thee!"

There was a momentary check; a frightful crashing of wood as we came thundering upon the levelled pikes; a rasping of steel blades and whirling of clubbed muskets; now, I only remember seeing all at once before me a triple line of grim and determined visages, in black helmets, with square cut collars, as we fell on sword in hand, and broke through the ranks of the puritan infantry, making a terrible slaughter among them, hewing all down, on the right and left, by our long straight broadswords.

The English cavalry stood better. Alured's dragoons drove back the leading squadrons of the Life Guards, and forced them to recoil in confusion on the rear; but the grim, black, and determined Cuirassiers of Lord Cassilis, with loud shouts of "God and the Kirk!" bore down Hesilrig's troopers, and hurled them among the disordered infantry; and, save for the noble bravery of Colonel Alured and his regiment, we had assuredly destroyed them all.

For some minutes the wild *melée* was general; horse and foot were combating together, and amid them I saw Sir Arthur Hesilrig fighting valiantly; with a glow of rage I rode forward, and after making three futile efforts, reached him. He was armed to the knees in tempered steel, over which he wore a loose scarlet coat. He made an inside cut at me below the wrist; but dropping the point of my sword outwards, I parried it by a half-circular guard, and ran him right through the left ribs; then, without waiting to see whether I had killed him, I turned to seek another adversary.

I am certain that every man of my squadron slew at least three on that day; and when Viscount Newburgh, who was major of the Life Guards, brought up the three rear squadrons of the brigade, the rout of the enemy became total and irretrievable. They fled under Samson's Ribs down into the hollow near the Wells of Wearie, and round the Loch of Duddingstone, to escape. The infantry threw away their pikes, muskets, and bandoliers, to accelerate their speed, but were all killed or taken; while the cavalry and artillery retired at full speed, closely pursued by us.

"A hundred crowns to the man who first reaches the cannon!" cried Count Ogilvie, and I found the advantage of being well mounted. My horse carried me far beyond my comrades, and I was soon within a pike's length of the enemy's rear rank; but Linn, our cornet, Sergeant Glanders, MacSnaffle, Carlourie, and others were pressing close behind me. Dashing at the nearest piece of cannon, and escaping the balls of more than twenty pistols, I shot the riding-wheel horse by my carbine; it fell in the traces; the second gun came crash against the first, and the stoppage caused confusion; there was a fresh discharge of pistols and flashing of swords, but the guns were taken. This occurred among some sauch trees that grew in a swamp at the western end of the loch.

"Well done, Harry Ogilvie," said the count, with ardour; "I will never forget thee, my brave lad!"

As a new brigade of the enemy was approaching, we slashed away the traces of the dead horses, wheeled round the cannon, and with these and our prisoners we rode back towards the city.

"Ah, this affair has been a devil of an echauffourée!" said our colonel, laughing, as he wiped his fine rapier in his silk scarf.

"Aye, and a bonnie flash in the pan, too!" added Drumstanchel, curling his obstinate moustaches.

"Forty-four men and thirty-two horses killed and wounded," said our adjutant, Sir William Keith.

For this service our brigade was publicly thanked by the general, and we cut a great figure before the fair ones of the capital, as we rode through with our prisoners and cannon, with kettle-drums beating and trumpets sounding. We left the dead to the peasantry, placed the wounded in Heriot's Hospital, and in half an hour afterwards were dining quietly at the bivoua. in rear of the trenches, and thinking no more about the affair.

CHAPTER XXX.

THE KING.

AFTER this lesson, Cromwell, finding the Scottish position in front of the capital impregnable, and that he had already lost six thousand men by the sword, desertion, and disease, fell back upon his camp at Musselburgh, and, save a little picqueering in the fields between the cavalry patrols, all remaiued quiet for a few days.

At this time his majesty was in Leith, and on the 29th of July the whole army was reviewed by him on the Links, where I had a good opportunity of seeing our gay young king, who was very dark-complexioned, with a black curly wig, merry roguish eyes, and moustaches well pointed up. He was attired in plain buff, with a broad blue riband over his breast, and the collar of the thistle hanging at his neck. A crowd of officers rode near him all in full harness, and several ministers, who were alike his mentors and tormentors; for if the poor young monarch did but wink at a bonnie lass, he was straightway rebuked with the severity due to so atrocious a crime. He expressed himself "highly delighted with the efficiency of the troops, but chiefly with the regiment of Black Dragoons."

On the 2nd of August he passed along the line of trenches from Leith to the capital; and all the drums were beating, and every standard was lowered in salute, while the batteries fired their salvoes. He was surrounded by the Life Guards under Eglinton, all riding in divisions of troops, with swords gleaming, plumes waving, trumpets sounding, and banners advanced. About him were the chief of the nobles and great officers of state, whose names were kindly told me by the Master of Oliphant. Here I saw Lord Chancellor the Earl of Loudon, who was also President of the Privy Council and a Commissioner of

the Treasury; the Earl of Sutherland, the Lord Privy Seal; the
Earl of Balcarris, who was Secretary of State; Sir Archibald
Johnston of Warriston, the Lord Clerk Register, a servile and
truckling lawyer, who rode beside Argyle, and, conferring together, they looked as like two conspirators as men might be;
Charles Duke of Lennox, the Lord Great Chamberlain; Lord
Lorn, Colonel of the Foot Guards; a crowd of nobles, and with
them a mob of ministers, all spurring and prancing on shaggy
ponies and Galloway cobs, clad in their black Geneva cloaks and
conical hats—black, black, all black! They looked like a flight
of rooks or other birds of ill-omen; and by their presumption,
mismanagement, false prophecies, and pretended revelations, such
indeed the clergy proved to be before the bloody campaign of the
English invasion was ended.

While the king was passing, a skirmish took place at Restalrig
between Cassilis' cuirassiers and some of the enemy, when an
English major and several of his men were killed.

After being banquetted by the municipality in the parliament
house, the king returned with his brilliant escort to Leith, where
he occupied the noble mansion of the Lord Balmerino in the
Kirkgate. There he remained for some days, and then he went
to the palace of Dunfermline to hunt, until arrangements were
made for his coronation. After this we became impatient for
action, and longed to take the field.

At midnight on the 5th of August, Cromwell broke up from
his camp, and marched eastward to Dunbar, where he received
supplies from his fleet; but these were so trifling, that finding
subsistence impossible in a district which our active cavalry had
swept alike of fodder and provant, after a three days' halt he
returned towards the capital, which he menaced again upon the
south and west; but we were all under arms to oppose him.

On the 10th we saw the enemy hovering along the northern
slopes of the Braid Hills; but Leslie, whose supplies and retreat
were alike secured to the westward, remained quietly watching
them through his telescope. At the head of Monk's regiment—
now the Coldstream Guards—Cromwell stormed the Tower of
Redhall and Colinton House, using the defenders with great
severity. Thus encouraged, he approached Edinburgh again;
but so ably did we hold our new position, which covered the
city on the westward, with redoubts and fieldworks, having our
musketeers entrenched behind the drains and mill-leads at Sauchton and Coltbridge, that after an ineffectual cannonade, and the
exchange of a few bombs, he drew off, *and, completely baffled,*
began his retreat once more to the east under cloud of night.

Till dawn we passed the chill and comfortless hours on the
ground in our capotes, and when day broke not a vestige of th.

foe was visible, save a few columns of smoke that rose from burning homesteads into the clear and sunny sky. The morning was beautiful; the deep green of the old woods that waved on the crest of Craig Lockhart, and those of the old manor of Meggetland, was becoming tinged by crimson and yellow tints; a russet brown was stealing over the slopes of the Pentlands, the lofty peaks of which were mellowed afar off in sunny haze, and deep shadows lay along their western sides. The water was gleaming and blue in many a loch and trouting stream, and the autumn wind sighed along the ploughed fields, the furrows of which were marked by the passage of cavalry, by the cannon shot that had rolled across them, or by the deep holes torn and dug by exploded shells.

Our regiment occupied a piece of swampy pasture between Coltbridge and a curious old vaulted house named Roseburn, in which tradition points to a chamber occupied for a time by Bothwell and Queen Mary, when on their way to Linlithgow. Herein the count, Drumstanchel, and several of our officers, had passed the night merrily enough.

After watering my horse in the Leith, I was in the act of sharing some bruised biscuit with him at breakfast-time, when, just as our adjutant galloped from Roseburn, crying, " Bit your horses, my lads—look to spur-leathers, and prepare to mount!" Cornet Linn rode from the courtyard towards me, and reining up, said,

" The general has directed the count to send an officer to learn the damage done overnight by the Roundheads at Redhall and Colinton. The colonel selected me, desiring me to take a trusty trooper—so I have chosen *you*. Are you ready, Harry ?"

" Ready for anything," said I, shortening my reins and mounting; " which way go we ?"

" Right across the country to the front, and round by these hills."

" I am at your service."

While riding off, we heard the drums and merry fifes of more than thirty regiments of infantry, waking the echoes of hill and wood, as they broke up from their position to follow the retreating enemy; and then rang the blare of brass trumpets, with a proud flourish, when the cavalry standards were unfurled and swords were drawn, previous to moving on the same glorious errand; and we spurred on furiously, in hope to execute our duty and rejoin before blows were struck or shots again exchanged.

CHAPTER XXXI.

CONSTANTIA DE CEZLI.

I HAVE said the morning was beautiful; the dew lay on every herb and tree; the leaves glittered in light; the lark and the crow hung over us in mid-air, and the sky was without a cloud. We passed the manor of Meggetland, crossed the Leith at Slate-ford, and entered into what was then a wild and uncultivated tract, through which the river runs between well-wooded banks, on which revolve the wheels of innumerable water-mills. We found the ancient place of Sauchton, the patrimony of the Elphin-stones, gutted and rifled, with its stackyard in flames; and everywhere else we saw sad traces of Cromwell's ravagers.

As we approached the tower of Colinton, which Monk's mus-keteers had stormed, we found it roofless and windowless, for volumes of smoke and flame had rolled together through every aperture. Iu some places the walls were rent by fire; in others, breached by cannon-shot. The yetlan-gate of the barbican lay flat in the yard; and the old ancestral lime-trees of the avenue were sawn down, and lay across the way to form an abbatis. The court was strewn with scorched hangings, furniture, and books. Among the latter, I picked up a handsome volume of Shakspeare. Ruin and desolation had fallen on this fine old baronial house, which Sir James Foulis, of that ilk, defended valiantly.

At the fortress of Redhall the same scene awaited us; but there, as the attack was more recent, we saw the dead bodies of several of Monk's musketeers lying among the rich grass which covered the slope crowned by the tower. A poor old peasant, who was mourning over the body of his son, a fine sturdy lad who lay at the barbican gate, shot right through the heart, told us that, at both mansions, "the English gained admittance at night by a foreknowledge of the watchword."

"Treason again!" said Linn, biting his nether lip. "By my soul, Hamilton, we seem to live in an atmosphere full of it."

"You have but a gloomy tale to tell the general."

"So, Cromwell's fellows went no further this way?"

"No, sir," sighed the old man, drawing a grey plaid over the face of his dead son; "and for some o' us, they came far enough. Of my house they have left but the ground-stone, and my cattle are a' driven off. Thank God, they gaed nae farther up the glen!"

"So say I," said Linn, throwing his purse to the man; "so say I, with all my soul, for I have some dear friends near this."

The beautiful little hamlet of Colinton, or Hales, as it was often named, was destroyed. Far down in the wooded vale, which is so leafy, dark, and secluded, we found but a crowd of sad and heart-broken women, weeping over the terrible fortune of war. All their thatched cottages had first been rifled, the doors and furniture carried off to the English bivouac, and then fire had been applied to consume everything. Thus, calcined walls, empty windows, and an occasional rafter, all black and scorched, alone remained. The aspect of these burned homesteads and hearths made desolate kindled our ire, and roused in our hearts a greater longing for vengeance than a lost battle-field had done.

Several women and children were sitting in the old kirk-yard, among the grassy graves, on which the sunlight, as it pierced the dense foliage of the deep glen, fell at times in glittering rays. These poor people were gathered in little family groups round certain humble tombs, where the grey-stone, green with moss, and spotted with lichens, or half sunk amid the long rank weeds, marked where some beloved head was lying; and there they clustered as if, in their fear and sorrow, to seek a fellowship with the dead.

Bare-headed, with his silver hair glistening in the sunlight, an old man, attired in black, was addressing them; and as we stopped our horses by the low bordering wall for a moment to listen, we knew at once he was their aged pastor, exhorting them to be comforted, and to be patient in ill.

Heaven knows, I am no bigot; yet when I heard this old man speak, and saw close by the old village kirk, every stone of which had been cemented in the blood of our forefathers, I asked myself how it was that the great ones of our land were choosing another and more showy faith, because it was deemed the more *gentlemanly* of the two.

"It matters not, Harry, this sack and havoc," said Linn, as we trotted up the glen; "our time for vengeance will come."

"Which way now?" I asked, on reaching the crest of the hill; "let us keep the road by the burghmuir, lest we fall in with English stragglers."

"Nay, Harry, I mean to ride further eastward yet."

"On what errand?"

"To see a fair dame, jolly sergeant o' mine—and a fairer we never toasted in our wild student days. She is the bonniest and the blythest lass in all the Lothians; and believe me, Harry, I know the country hereabout well."

"True, your house of Linn——"

"Lies near Kirkliston, on the Almond side. Some day thou shalt see the place, Harry, and taste my old wine, too! But 'tis

for Lennox Tower I am bound just now—and you shall see Dora
Lennox.   But 'tis a pity, you must sit below the salt."

"True—true; why did you bring me?" I asked, with a sigh
of bitterness and pride.

"Heed it not.   But her father is full of odd fancies and old
fashions; thus all his servants dine at table, as his father's did
in the time of the sixth James; so, were you the king's son, as
a sergeant of dragoons you must sit below *his* salt-vat.   You
wince.   Tush! the first battle may give you my silk scarf and
gilt gorget, and send me to rot in a ditch.   Meantime, I shall
like to have your opinion of Dora."

"Doubtless it will be the same as your own."

"She has a beautiful friend——"

"Ah! now I shall find myself the trooper again."

"My dear fellow," said Linn, laughing, "were you even a
colonel of dragoons, there would be but small chance of *her*
falling in love with you."

"Is she so cold and impregnable?"

"Neither—but proud as Lucifer; and I detest all her family."

"Her name?"

"Lady Flora Campbell.   You have seen her."

My heart leaped!   I was so piqued by Linn's confidence in
her pride, that he nearly tempted me to draw off my glove and
display her ring; but I checked at once the unfortunate impulse.

We passed the tower of the Skenes, at Curriehill, and descended
into the hollow, through which the Leith was brawling, crossed
the ancient bridge of Currie, and leaving on the left the old kirk
of the Templars, shaded by its venerable sycamores, we rode
along the ridge which leads to Lennox Tower, the battlement
and chimneys of which were visible above the coppice about a
mile distant.

"Dora is charming!" resumed Linn.   "Her mother was
French, and thus she is full of the most delightful *espiéglerie.*"

"French, say you?"

"Yes; a daughter of the famous Constantia de Cezli, whom
all the world knows about."

"Nay, I crave pardon, and assure you that I never heard of
her ladyship till this moment."

"Never heard of—is it possible?   Why, man, she is a heroine;
and her adventure is quite a story," said Linn, checking his horse
a little, for the animal was impatient, and knew well *where* a feed
awaited him.   "Sir Henry Lennox——"

"Was he a hero?"

"He was a brave fellow, at all events, and fought valiantly at
the head of the Scottish Gendarmerie at the siege of Dreux; and
was one of the twenty Scottish gentlemen who, led by the Master

of Wemyss, made that most glorious charge at the battle of Contras. During the wars of the League, Du Barri de St. Aunea, Governor of Leucate, an old town of France, about twenty miles from Perpignan, left his garrison, to hold a conference with the Duc de Montmorencie, who commanded the troops in Languedoc. He had no arms with him but his sword and pistols, and only one companion, Sir Henry Lennox, then a very young man, but a host in himself, as he was hardy, brave, and strong as a lion. On the way they fell into an ambush which was laid for them by the Lord of Laupian; their horses were shot under them, and, after a desperate resistance, both chevaliers were made prisoners by the Leaguers, who now formed a junction with the Spaniards, and marched exultingly towards Leucate, where the wife of Du Barri, Madame Constantia de Cezli, had put herself at the head of the troops and inhabitants to defend the town. The Leaguers commanded the unfortunate Du Barri to *insist* upon his wife surrendering the place, threatening both him and Lennox with a barbarous death in case of non-compliance; but he heard their threat with the indifference of a brave man; and in a last message, which Lennox was permitted to deliver to Constantia, he exhorted her to set an example to the citizens and the soldiers, and to defend the city, whatever might be the fate of himself and his friend.

"'Go back to the Leaguers, Sir Henry Lennox,' said the beautiful Madame Du Barri, clasping her youngest born to her bosom, 'and say unto them, that if they are determined to perpetrate so barbarous a crime as the murder of my gallant husband, I do not think it conducive to his honour to prevent it by an act of cowardice; nor will I purchase his safety by the ignoble surrender of a fortress, in defence of which he would gladly lay down his life.'

"'Madame,' replied Lennox, 'those words are indeed noble, and the sentiment is worthy of you; but it is our sentence of death!'

"And retiring from the presence of Constantia and her two daughters, leaving them, natheless this proud reply, overwhelmed by sorrow and consternation, this devoted soldier rode back to the army of the League, full of no ordinary emotions, for he was going back to *die!*

"To die with a secret in his heart; for the beautiful Dorotée Du Barri, who was the image of her mother, had made a deep impression upon him. People still fell in love at first sight in those primitive days, Harry; as neither men nor women had educated or very cultivated minds—beauty of person and a gentle or loveable manner were the sole causes of passion; and their loves, if we may judge from history and tradition, were deep and sincere enough.

" The generals of the League, with unyielding barbarity, brought the noble Du Barri de St. Aunea before the walls of the city, unarmed, bareheaded, bound with cords, and there slew him, in presence of his wife and children! Led on by the Lord of Laupian, the Leaguers, with all their united forces, made a furious assault, but the exasperated garrison resisted so vigorously, that the siege was raised, and they retired, leaving in the hands of Madame du Barri the Lord Laupian, who had been taken prisoner in the breach by the gallant Master of Wemyss.

" The soldiers of Leucate were about to take summary vengeance on their captive by putting him to a cruel death, but the generous Constantia opposed it, and set him at liberty; and Henry the Great, who knew well how to appreciate deeds of chivalry and acts so graceful, presented to the heroic Constantia the government of Leucate, making the office hereditary in the person of her son, the infant. Now, was not her conduct worthy of a Spartan dame?"

" It was indeed; but not being M. du Barri, I am perhaps weak enough to wish for a wife a little less heroic. But what of Sir Henry Lennox?"

" I had quite forgotten. His life was spared by a Scottish Marechal de Logis, who served the Leaguers. He became Constantia's lieutenant, and married Dorotée, her youngest daughter, one of the most lovely women in Languedoc. Now, she lies in yonder burial-ground; but her charms are renewed in those of her daughter Dora, as you shall judge for yourself—for see, the end of my story has brought me to the gate of the tower."

The mansion we now approached was a small but strongly-built fortlet, which stands on an elevated plateau on the right bank of the Leith; and from its battlements a beautiful panorama of the Forth of Fife and the adjacent country can be commanded. Its windows were all grated; the walls were more than eight feet thick, and the outer one, which encircled the brow of the hill, was more than fourteen hundred feet in length, and perforated by loopholes for arrows; moreover, it has a subterraneous outlet to the river. In remote times, it had been a residence of the old Earls of Lennox; and on the outer wall I discerned a time-worn shield, bearing the saltier engrailed, cantoned with four roses, being the arms of Earl Malcolm, who fell in battle for his country at Halidonhill. It was an interesting old place, for there Queen Mary had resided in her youth, and with Darnley afterwards, in the flush of her early love; and there, too, in after years, dwelt the grim and tyrant earl, James of Morton, Regent of Scotland.

The barbican gate was shut, and many armed men scanned us warily from the summit of the wall, or from the loopholes that flanked the approach; for the time was full of peril, and every Scotsman was a soldier.

Linn was soon recognised, and on the barrier being opened, we entered the spacious court, rode round to the low-arched door on the northern side of the tower, and dismounted. Here we found ourselves surrounded by armed servants in livery. Some of these wore the Lennox colours; but others had the well-known badge of the Campbells embroidered on their sleeves. The tower was evidently full of visitors, and had been prepared for resistance; pikes and muskets stood against the wall, and shot were piled beside four old brass cannon which peered above the entrance, and overlooked the highway.

Just as I gave the bridle of my horse to a groom, a brilliant-looking girl, sans all ceremony, rushed forth to greet the young Laird of Linn with an affectionate, warm, and glad-hearted manner, that was very striking in this age of starched composure and morose discreetness of bearing.

"Are we in time for dinner, Dora?" asked Linn, as he drew off his long leather gauntlet, and kissed her pretty hands.

"It is just about to be served up. I verily believe you scented it far down the glen, for you began to spur furiously when within a certain distance of the gate."

"We are in good time, Harry," said Linn; "gloriat! Evoe Bacche! as we used to cry at college; 'tis the sergeant of my troop, Dora—Harry Ogilvie—the boldest rider in the Black Dragoons," he added, on seeing her large eyes fixed inquiringly upon me. "In former days he was my brother student: and now he is my brother soldier."

"I have heard of you before, and how poor Willie was run through by your side," said she, bowing and smiling; "sir, you are welcome."

"Were you afraid of Cromwell, Dora?" said Linn.

"No—we were all ready for him, as you may see; and my father was quite joyful at the prospect of a siege."

"So were they at Redhall and Colinton; but the Foulis have been routed, and their strongholds taken."

"We had no fear," continued the lively girl; "the tower is full of armed men, and the Lord Argyle is here. *He* had been visiting Sir James Foulis only an hour before the attack, and narrowly escaped being taken."

"Argyle?" I whispered in my heart. Oh, now I knew how Cromwell had obtained that *watchword* which cost the brave little garrisons of Colinton and Redhall so dear!

"Argyle here, Dora?" said Linn, with an air of displeasure.

"Yes—but Cromwell never came near us."

"'Tis strange," said Linn.

I did not think so.

"The ladies Anne and Flora are with him, and the Lord Lorn is coming anon, to ride back with him to the Committee of Safety, which accompanies the army," she continued, tripping gaily before us up the circular stair of the tower.

"Did not my duty force me to attend you, Linn," said I, hastily, "I would this instant mount and return to the regiment."

"Wherefore, Harry; what gnat stings thee now?"

"Those are here whom I have no wish to meet."

"I know that well—but come on—face this cunning earl like an honest man, and dread nought."

My heart contradicted my words, for the longing to behold Flora was strong within me.

In the manner of Linn and Dora Lennox to each other, I could easily perceive that in the former the gallantry of the lover was blended with the kindness and familiarity of the betrothed, for such they were. His little estate of Linn lay in the neighbourhood, their marriage had been all adjusted, and but for the invasion and consequent strife, old Sir Henry Lennox would ere this have bestowed his only daughter on this gay cornet of the Black Dragoons.

CHAPTER XXXII.

LENNOX TOWER.

> "Thou art a carle of low degree,
> *The salt* doth stand 'tween thou and me,
> But if thou hadst been of gentle strain,
> I wolde have bitten my glove again!"

THIS verse of the old ballad came into my mind as we sat down to dinner in the hall of that ancient tower; and from my place, alas! below *the salt*, I scarcely dared to raise my eyes to those of Flora Campbell, who sat above it; for I remembered with unmitigated shame the false character and splendid attire in which she had last seen me.

Yet she gave me a quiet and gentle bow as we took our seats, when the earl, her father, who affected somewhat the character of a preacher, asked a long and dreary blessing on the repast; and as the steward of the house, a respectable old personage, clad in black velvet, with a silver chain, waved thrice his wand, as a signal to begin. Argyle, on lowering his eyes again to the victuals and other sublunary things, recognised me in an instant, as I knew well by his glance of keen surprise, and by the paleness that for a moment overspread his face.

Sir Henry Lennox, an old fashioned gentleman, who wore steel hooks to his small clothes, and whose memory went back to the wars of the League, in which he had served; and who, when a youth, had seen the Maxwells and Johnstones slaughtering each other with great zest at the battle of the Dryfe-sands, was somewhat antiquated in his habits and ideas. He wore a bonnet of King James VI.'s time, and had his grey hair curled in long locks; these, with his pointed mustachios, his rich ruffled lace, gold snuff-box, diamond ring, and jewelled rapier, all declared him an undoubted cavalier and perfect gentleman in attire, as he was in bearing. But he maintained all the old customs and domestic rules of his youth; hence this fashion of making all his household dine together—a fashion, which, in imitation of the English, we had already abolished; and which, notwithstanding its hospitality and kindliness, I banned in my heart, for I would rather have dined with his servants in the kitchen of the tower, than with them in the hall, where I was seated at that part of the long table which was destitute of cloth, where wooden trenchers were found in place of delft-ware, tin cups in place of crystal, horn spoons instead of plate; where ale was drunk instead of wine, and where a great silver saltvat—a cup with two handles—placed in the centre of the long table, formed the line of demarcation. This cup was the work of George Heriot, long, long ago; and amid its chasings were the engrailed saltier and four roses of the house of Lennox; and this was the time-honoured barrier between the gentle-blooded and the *canaille,* of whom I had the misfortune to be considered one.

Here I was made to feel that, though a gentleman by education and conduct, I was only a trooper; and the petty sting was increased by the knowledge that I could not demand in right of blood a loftier place, for I was the poor foundling of the college gate, the offspring of a murdered outcast—one who knew not whence or from whom he sprung. However, appetised by my long ride, and having had no other breakfast than the ration biscuit, which I shared with my horse, I sliced down a chine of beef, and chatted with the old steward and the venerable housekeeper, who, she told me, was the mother of Tom, the trumpeter of our troop; and we drank our brown ale together, I to the hope that better times were before me, and she to a speedy peace.

Sir Henry, whose whole soul had been fixed on the anticipated glory of being besieged in his little tower, and of obtaining the thanks of parliament (as he never doubted his ability, with his four small cannon, to rout the whole English army), was much mortified and discomposed by Monk's regiment retiring without molesting him. This was the more galling to the worthy

baronet, because his rival neighbours, the Laird of Redhall,
and Sir James of Colinton—the Bluidy Foulis of the Covenanters—had their towers attacked and stormed.   It was a sore
subject with old Sir Harry, and he spoke of little else during
dinner, having put aside his antique panoply with the greatest
reluctance on Cromwell's retreat.

Some relief was afforded to me by the circumstance of a
gigantic *epergne* of flowers standing between me and Lady
Flora; and though I heard her conversing in low tones with
Dora Lennox and Linn, we did not see each other; but I had an
oppressive consciousness of her presence.   There was an enchant-
ment in the knowledge that she was near me, yet I would have
given the world to have been many miles away.

I envied Linn, he looked so happy in his place above that
infernal saltvat.

He was remarkably handsome and noble in bearing; his black
hair waved in thick cavalier locks round a forehead pale and
high; his eyes were of the darkest and keenest grey; his nose
was somewhat aquiline; and his mouth expressed merriment,
firmness, and hauteur more than any other I had seen; and at
times, when excited, in severity of expression, it resembled the
sternly compressed lips of our colonel; and everyway the lively
Dora seemed worthy of him; yet I can scarcely describe *her*
beauty.

It was of a peculiar kind, and consisted more in variety,
piquancy, and brilliance of expression, than in perfection of features; her dark eyes were alternately full of eloquence, wonder,
sadness, and drollery, while the most charming dimples came
and went with every sunny smile.   The steward of the tower,
an old grey-headed carle, plucked my sleeve, saying, "that they
were indeed a winsome couple, and ilk just the marrow o' the
other."   She so gentle and playful, and Linn so manly, tall, and
soldierlike, with his lofty bearing and well-knit figure, his face
so expressive of firmness of purpose, of courage, intellect, and
resolute will.

The frank old cavalier Sir Henry Lennox, whose military
bluntness and farmer-like roughness had been considerably
smoothed over by the many years he had served among the
Scottish troops in France, with his open brow and clear blue eye,
that beamed with honesty and kindness, formed a strong contrast
to the narrow-headed and cold-hearted Earl of Argyle, who sat
upon his right hand.   While every pulse beat high, I scrutinised
this celebrated kirkman and politician—he who had sold his king
like a cask of his Campbelton whiskey, and who had quietly
proposed to split Europe's oldest monarchy into two Scottish
dictatorships—and I was struck by the expression of duplicity

that flitted over his face at times, giving strong evidence of the consummate hypocrisy, the cruelty, and malice which he strove to veil under the bland and meek exterior of a lank-haired and long-visaged puritan—a character totally incompatible with the nature of a Highland chief.   His hair, which was red, as we see that of Judas Iscariot represented in old tapestries, was all knotted at the ends in elflocks, as if the fairies had been weaving it over-night; and I detected a strange smile curling his thin wicked lips as old Sir Harry filled up a foaming cup of Rhenish, and standing erect with a hand in the hilt of his sword, made the old roof ring "to the health and glory of his sacred majesty, the King of Scotland and the Isles—to the eternal broiling of Cromwell, and all other enemies, with a hip, hip, hip, hurrah!" and the whole Rhenish went down Sir Harry's loyal throat at one capacious gulp.   Argyle found himself constrained to follow his example, which we all imitated with hearty goodwill.

"Another bumper, my lord earl," cried the hearty old laird; "fill the cups, ye loons," he added to the servants; "may all who would circumscribe the ancient monarchy of this land, may all kirk commissioners, quakers, puritans, and such like, swallow the devil with a red hot harrow at his tail; owre wi' your wine, my lord—and God bless the king, the country, and the lawful monarchy!"

Again the goblets, cups, and luggies were drained, and our loyalty began to warm apace.

"Alas! Sir Harry," said the earl, in his most whining voice, "I fear that our sentiments, like our toasts, are somewhat old-fashioned now."

"Auld-fashioned, eh? what mean ye, my lord?"

"Under favour, Sir Harry, we cannot close our ears and eyes to certain facts which indicate the tendency of the times."

"Eh—how?"

"Monarchy, to wit—kings, emperors, and princes; aristocracy, to wit—dukes, earls, and lords; priesthood, to wit—bishops, deans, and rectors; had all their origin in the dark, barbarous, and unlettered ages of the world; and hence it is that respect for them is passing away as time rolls on; so verily it is that an age will come when all such distinctions of men shall cease to exist; or it may be that *other* privileged orders shall take their places."

Now, to Sir Harry, who but a few years before had been created a baronet of Nova Scotia, when the late king was crowned in Holyrood, and who had been duly infeft in a certain imaginary barony in our Scoto-American colony, with the earth and stone at Edinburgh castle gate, this new doctrine was very unpalatable, if not incomprehensible; and though it was an Argyle who spoke, I could not but feel there was truth in what he advanced, though it was a perilous time to say such things in high monarchical Scotland.

"What think you of this maxim, Harry?" asked Linn; "we were wont to have some such discussions at old St. Mungo."

"I know not," said I; "such matters, Linn, are overdeep for me."

"You are right, sir," said the old baronet, with an approving glance; "and owredeep will they ever be for those who, like you and I, are soldiers. My service to you, trooper—your health; I have smelt powder and heard bullets whistle in my time, so every man who rides under the flag of the king is my friend and comrade. Oh, if that blasphemous limmer Cromwell had only come doon by Currie-brig!"

"It would seem, my lord earl," said I modestly, in the desperate—perhaps pitiful hope to win a little favour from Flora's cold and artful father, "that if the purging of the third order you named—to wit, the priesthood, from all dignities be perfection, our Scottish kirk has attained it, for these were swept away a hundred years and more ago."

"Yea," said the earl, bending his cold grey swivel eyes upon me, "by Knox and Wishart, those master builders of a kirk that is indeed the church of God!"

Here all the old women who sat below the salt groaned, beat their breasts, and swayed themselves to and fro, saying, "hear to him—hear to my lord!"

"I have not the presumption to go this length," said I (unfortunately for myself); "whether it may be the kirk of God, as your lordship says, I know not; but one fact is undeniable—it is at least the kirk of Scotland."

Old Sir Harry burst into a fit of laughter.

"Thou speakest like a doubter," said Argyle, knitting his brows; "art thou a malignant, or a prelatist?"

"None of these, my lord, am I, but only a Black Dragoon."

He gave a sour smile at this simple answer.

"Be assured, young man," said he, "that our kirk of Scotland is free from all taint of unscriptural prelacy, and is the church to which St. Augustine refers in his first book, chapter thirty and three, wherein he saith, 'whosoever doth apprehend to be deceived through the obscurity of the question, let him ask council of *the church*, which the holy Scriptures doth demonstrate, without any ambiguity or doubting.'"

"But, my Lord, was not St. Augustine, who wrote in the fifth century, considered a papist?"

The earl frowned, and Linn laughed.

"Yet Calvin says," I continued, being bitten by an irresistible desire for argument, "that he—St. Augustine—is the best and most faithful witness of all antiquity."

"Where do you find all this?"

"In the fourth book of his institutes, chapter fourteen."

"Ye are right, young man," said old Sir Harry, "though it is devilish little I ken or care either about Calvin; but it seemeth to me that if either St. Paul or St. Augustine were to come back again to earth, it wouldna be to hear Zachary Boyd or Mr. Zephaniah Bogle preach they would gang to the kirk."

"With my right hand, yea, with all I possess, save my poor soul, would I defend and redeem from trouble our covenanted kirk," said Argyle, haughtily, as he rose from table; "but enough of this," he added, with a dark look; "thou art somewhat prelatic, Sir Harry; and it was not to discuss such points with a bursar fresh from Glasgow College I came here."

"Traitor!" thought I; "Heaven only knows on what errand you came hither; but the visit has cost our brave outposts at Redhall and Colinton dear enough."

"This is a strange place for *you* to be, sir," he added, pausing as he turned to retire; "are not all our troops advancing in pursuit of the enemy?"

My cheek flushed crimson at the taunt; but Linn came to my rescue.

"I was sent on duty to visit the strongholds of the Foulis and Otterburns," said he, "and I chose Harry Ogilvie as my companion, for he is one of the bravest lads in the Black Dragoons; and is it more strange for him to be here than your son the Lord Lorn, who is now approaching?"

As he spoke, from the great east window of the hall we saw Lord Lorn, attired in the gorgeous trappings of the Foot Guards, ride into the barbican of the tower, and at that moment we all rose from table to disperse. I made a low bow to the earl as I passed him.

"My young friend," said he, sternly, "tremble! for your immortal soul is in danger of perdition!"

"Tremble for your own, my lord," said I, haughtily.

CHAPTER XXXIII.

THE ARBOUR.

WITH a mingled sense of pleasure and mortification I withdrew, and descending the turnpike stair of the tower, sought the garden, which extended down the wooded bank to the rocky bed of the river.

I reflected on my parting words with the great earl, and my heart smote me, for I ought to have remembered that he was by several years my senior, and that he was the father of Flora; but an emotion of auger came to my aid, and I hastily passed Lorn, who in reply to my dutiful military salute, merely accorded a keen, fierce glance, while very undisguised scorn and bitterness curved his thin and livid lips.

This young lord was the son of Margaret Douglas, of the house of Morton, a lady who, after she became Countess of Argyle, by a master-stroke of villany furthered to a vast extent the grasping spirit which for ages has characterized the potent chiefs of the race of Diarmed. On pretence of forming a great family chartulary, she got into her possession all the charters granted to various proprietors in the West Highlands, but particularly in the province of Cantyre; and these documents she basely committed to the flames at Campbeltown. Thus did the house of Argyle revoke all its ancient grants and charters—those of Campbell of Kildalloig alone escaping by the shrewdness of a gilly, who concealed them, while all the other *gudemen*, whose documents were unrecorded in the office of the great seal, lost every ancestral acre they possessed. But this was only one of a thousand unscrupulous measures resorted to by the family of Argyle to aggrandize themselves at the expense of others.

But to resume. I passed into the garden, and seeking a bower of hawthorn, near the brink of the stream, the steep and rocky banks of which are overhung by heavy copsewood, gave myself up to reverie.

It was evening now. The sinking sun was shining on the dun peaks of the Pentlands, the rocky brow of Kinleith was bathed in purple light, the leaves drooped in dewy silence over the rushing water, the flowers that grew in the clefts of the rocks were opening their chalices, while the drowsy bees buried themselves in their petals; the gnats swarmed in the lingering sunshine, and the spider spun his fragile net from one dewy spray to another. The leaves of the giant waterdocks, which grow in such rank luxuriance along the banks of every Scottish stream, were becoming laden with dew; the time and the place were alike calculated to encourage reverie; and I had much to ponder over.

When reviewed, the strange history of my short life, the obscurity or mystery that involved my origin, the terrible fate of my mother, and the ill-concealed hostility of the potent noble on whose obnoxious presence and on whose crooked paths and subtle purposes a perverse fate for ever thrust me;—yes, even in the camp of the enemy—my conviction grew stronger, that all the terrible secrets I longed so much to unravel were known to

him and to Lord Lorn. I recalled the fragmentary conversation
overheard in the Castle of Stirling, and an emotion of hostility
swelled up within me that made me pant with passion! Then
I reflected, that in this secluded tower, crowded as it was with
his armed, fanatical, and unscrupulous followers, my personal
safety was very far from secure; and then I thought of his
daughter, and my poor heart grew sick within me.

When I had mused or nursed myself into this pleasant frame
of mind, a large hound bounded past the arbour, and then
returned with many a curvet and gambol. I recognised the dog,
and my breast filled with undefinable emotions, when I heard a
step on the gravel walk, and, with a book in her hand, Flora
Campbell approached, and coming straight towards me, entered
the arbour!

She was still attired in sober black satin, with her hair in
ringlets, a little row of which were curled across her forehead.
She had a large fan of feathers in her hand, but other ornament my beautiful Puritan had none. She started and grew
deadly pale on seeing me; other women might have blushed.
I arose, and was retiring with a profound bow, when she arrested
me by observing,—

"We seem fated to meet often, sir."

"In that alone is fortune kind to me, lady; but I have never
forgotten the last time, for the shame with which it filled my
heart."

"Shame?"

"Yes, lady—shame; for I feared that in remembering me,
you would only do so with the contempt due to one who played
a double part, or acted a false character. But believe me, kind
Lady Flora, that in being present at the entertainment given in
the castle of Stirling, I was actuated more by a love of rash
frolic, spurred on by the Master of Oliphant and by the Laird of
Linn, than a spirit of presumption or effrontery. Alas! poverty,
obscurity, and neglect have cured me of pride, if I ever possessed it."

"Pardon me," said she, while her fine eyes drooped, and
assumed a kind and dove-like expression; "but say, how comes it
that a young noble like Oliphant and a landed laird like William of
the Linn, are so familiar with you—for you all seem like old
friends?"

"And such we are, Lady Flora, because we were fellow-
students at Glasgow, and comrades in many a brawl and wild
adventure; but times have changed with me sorely; and believe
me," I continued, with a swelling heart, "there was a day
when I never thought to tread path like this—so humble and
obscure."

L

"Nay, call it honourable and glorious!" said she, while her fine eyes sparkled with such a glow of *amor patria* as never filled that empty husk, her father's heart; "you fight for our country—for dear old Scotland's kirk and king—her liberty and honour."

"True—true, Lady Flora."

"And Linn has told us how valiantly and well you bore yourself in your first battle."

"He is indeed most kind and generous; but when I speak with you, I can only ponder sadly on what I was, or rather what I wished to be."

She coloured slightly, as she read my too apparent emotion; but she was calm and quiet, and without the least outward timidity, being too well-bred, too highly schooled to exhibit any sign of being moved.

"Are all sergeants raised from the ranks?" she asked.

"Yes, madam."

"And have *you* been a private trooper?" she continued, with an emphasis which I could not feel otherwise than flattering.

"Madam, I once had the honour."

"It is passing strange—a trooper?"

"I was such, or little more, when I first had the joy of meeting you."

"In the Torwood — I remember that terrible meeting well!"

There was now a brief pause, and I could perceive that she had imbibed for me the natural interest one usually feels for an unfortunate gentleman; but, unluckily, Scotland has been very prolific of that class.

"Was your birth above your present fortune?" she asked, timidly.

"My birth!" I dared not tell her that I was a poor unknown; but she was so beautiful and gentle in aspect, that all my heart rushed to my head, and, sinking on one knee, I took her hand in mine.

"Ah, madam," said I, "pardon me; I am an unfortunate man, reduced by an untoward and mysterious fate to serve as a trooper, and it is the greatest of my sorrows, that by this very circumstance my lips are sealed, and I am forced to lock in my breast a secret which, if told, would only fill you with ridicule and banish me for ever from your presence, by exciting your irony and contempt."

"A secret!" she faltered.

"Yes, a secret that, if told, would reveal hopes of unexampled presumption; which, if told, would deprive me of your esteem, the only joy of an otherwise joyless life; and which, under the rude contempt of a selfish world, would crush me to the dust—and yet this ring——"

"Oh! heavens, what are you about to say?" she asked, becoming very pale, as I pressed her gift to my lips; and she continued, with a trembling voice—"That ring was a mere gift to reward your bravery in the Torwood. To give it was a foolish and a heedless act; yet I trust that you have never——"

"Oh! no," said I, clasping my hands and anticipating all she would say; "can you suspect me of a vanity so unworthy? Ah! Lady Flora——"

"Rise," said she, trembling violently, while the blood that mantled from her neck to her temples declared that her heart divined the secret I referred to; "rise, sir, for Heaven's sake, and do not let us—do not let yourself be seen thus; we must each remember only who we are, and recal this most unpleasant scene no more."

And withdrawing her hand, she walked hastily away towards the entrance of the tower, leaving me in an agony of doubt whether she was offended with me or not. Offended! How could I hope that she would be aught else, when I reflected on the absurd and colossal ideas of birth and ancestral pride in which the Scottish noblesse are reared.

In Flora seemed the poetical realization of the face, and form, and manner I had dreamed over a thousand times, as being perfection in a woman. I had found them all now, but what availed they me? She was the daughter of him who hung like a cloud on the horizon of my fortunes.

I hurried from the vicinity of the bower, conscious that two persons were walking on the other side of a privet hedge close by. One was attired in sad colours, but the other wore a coat that sparkled with lace and gold spangles. I could not discover who they were, but a terrible suspicion occurred to me—were those eavesdroppers the earl and his son? If so, could they have overheard all that passed?

I sprang up the staircase of the tower, inquired for my apartment, and an old servant in the Lennox livery ushered me into a small wainscotted chamber, and saying that it was the identical one in which Henry Stuart, Lord of Darnley and King of Scotland, was born, left me.

I was too full of my own affairs to care much for his archæology then. As the atmosphere seemed stifling, I threw open the window which overlooked the garden, and sat down to cool my hot and throbbing brow.

CHAPTER XXXIV.

FLORA'S LOVER.

"HAVE they overheard us?" such was the question I asked myself again and again; "if so, poor Lady Flora! to what insult and contumely may I not have exposed you, and to what dangers myself!"

This petty mystery was soon solved; for I perceived the earl and his son ascending the steep walk between the privet hedges, conversing earnestly, and lingering as they drew near the tower wall, immediately under my window. My first impulse was to draw back, and not *again* to overhear their conversation; but with the foreknowledge that it too surely concerned myself, perhaps the secret of my origin and the fate of my ultimate life, how could I resist the inclination to overhear, or the necessity of listening, when the conference of these subtle enemies might be of such terrible import to myself?

With this mental apology to my own scruples, I drew close to the grated window, and heard the earl say,

"Lorn, speak out, I command you; on matters such as this, you were not wont to play the fool with *me!*"

"Nay, Heaven forefend, my lord; but your favourite daughter has another lover."

"My daughter! which? Your sister Anna?"

"Flora. The simple Anna never was your favourite."

"A lover! She, so quiet, so modest, and gentle!"

"Yea," replied the other, with one of his deep smiles.

"And who may he be that so honours us?"

"You will never guess 'tween this and Pentecost."

"It cannot be—let me think! who have been about us of late?—it cannot be the Earl of Melrose: he is too old."

"And wived already."

"It cannot be the Earl of Airth, for he is a Grahame, and dare not aspire to the hand of a Campbell; nor the Lord Balvaird, for he is a man of yesterday, who but nine years ago was plain Sir Andrew Murray. You laugh! say not so—is it he? I would rather see her in her shroud at Kilmun than the bride of a holiday peer!"

"But Ardmohr, for whom you have so long destined her——"

"In default of finding some one better——"

"Well, he is neither wealthy nor titled."

"But he is a Campbell—one of our own blood and sirname. The estates of the forfeited Earl of Findourie, which shall be Flora's dower, will make them rich enough, and bind this

Dougal unto us. He hath been inclined of late to hunt, and host, and ally himself overmuch with that overweening Laird of Breadalbane. But enough of this! our Flora's lover——"

"Is a sergeant of the Black Dragoons—ha! ha!"

"God's death! you dare not say so in earnest."

"I do," responded Lorn, in a voice hoarse with shame and passion.

"Not *he*—he—who is here?" asked the earl, infected by the same fierce emotion.

"The same, my lord."

"May this day of the year be for ever cursed! How know you this?"

"I was walking near yonder bower, and saw the interview. Oh, the devil! I soon discovered my fine gentleman to be a lover."

"But how?"

"Oh! by the old symptoms—blushes, tenderness, attention, and respect."

"And she?" asked the earl, panting, while he bit his nether lip and crushed the gravel under his heel—"and she——"

"Was diffident and coy," continued the sneering Lorn; "casting down her eyes—with modesty, no doubt. I tell you, my lord and father, that sister though she be of mine, I could have smote her to the earth!"

"Well, they who sow the wind must expect to reap the whirlwind," said the sinister-eyed earl.

"It tortures me that we owe this fellow, worthless lozel that he is, a favour."

"A favour—how?"

"That rescue from Montrose's broken ruffians in the Torwood."

"True. By what accursed fatality is he thrown for ever thus across our path?"

How often had I asked this question of myself!

"Had that blundering blockhead, Duncan, the skipper, done his duty, our lover had now been hoeing sugar-canes in Virginia. He is a bold and resolute fellow."

"Yes, Lorn. 'Tis strange how his banished father's spirit" (my father's spirit!—*he* knew him then!) "swells up within him, and he feels himself at least a gentleman."

"But he is a beggar, and must be taught to bear himself as becomes one."

"Her lover—this boy—of all others in Scotland—the son of him we crushed and hated—the——"

The voice of Argyle sank low; I strained my ears to hearken, and the perspiration, wrung by anxiety and shame for the act of which I was guilty, oozed over my brow.　My heart throbbed, and, regardless of all hazard, I snatched up my sword and rushed down-stairs to confront them, when, at the lower door of the tower, I met Linn, who said, hurriedly,

"We must mount and begone, comrade Harry; the gloaming draws on apace, and we have far to ride before we overtake the troops.　The Black Dragoons must not fight Cromwell without us."

My breast was torn by many contending emotions, and Linn appeared just in time to prevent some desperate catastrophe.

"In Heaven's name, let us begone, then," said I.　"Our horses are in the yard; I have ordered them out."

After a delay caused by Linn giving the steward's little son a ride on his high charger, we mounted and rode from the tower.

"Adieu, dear heart," cried Linn, waving his hand to a window where *two* ladies were observing us, as we rode eastward along the narrow bridle path.　Linn was in high spirits.　"Now, what think you of Dora, Harry?" said he.

"She seems a lively little fairy."

"She *is* little," said he, laughing; "but dame Nature could not afford to make a large person half so good as my dear Dora. How lively she is!　If you had heard her rallying me on the growing curl of my mustachios."

"The deuce she did!　I would have considered that a very broad hint just to——"

"Well, so I did; for the next instant saw them pressed to her pretty little mouth.　It is dangerous in such as Dora to throw out hints so broad—though I don't think she meant it.　How shy and cold Flora Campbell was to-day.　All the women of the Campbells have such exquisite skins, though, one can pardon anything in them."

I made no response, but spurred on.　The night was darkening fast.　We soon crossed the narrow bridge of Currie, ascended the opposite bank, and dashed eastward by the same road we had pursued that morning.

"I am no longer," thought I, "the mere lover or the dreaming student; I am a man—a leader of men!　I have been mad to indulge in the hopes and thoughts that have possessed me.　Flora, Flora, farewell; of thee I'll think no more!"

It was a valiant resolution, but very hard to keep!　Alas, that, instead of the mere story of the Scottish Campaigns, these pages should contain the history of a heart—*the journal of a destiny!*

CHAPTER XXXV.

A CORNETCY.

A WHOLE day's march lay between us and the army, to overtake which we rode at a rapid pace; and as the gloaming deepened around us, and the long shadows of the hills fell over the hollow, through which the wind whirled the russet spoil of the autumnal woods, and when the bat, or "the short-horn beetle," the dragon moth, and other strange insects alone were abroad, in this calamitous time of war and invasion, we crossed the southern shoulder of Craiglockhart, and skirting the wild waste of the Burghmuir, passed eastward by the narrow bridle-path which traverses the barren and furzy hills of Braid, amid which we lost it, and narrowly escaped a fall over certain rocks into the swollen mountain burn that roared through the glen below the Black Ford.

Near an old tower and homestead, which bore marks of recent sack and fire, we found a poor woman lamenting over a cow which, she asserted, had been *elf-shotten*, because it had suddenly fallen down dead. This person very intelligently and readily put us on the right route to overtake the Scottish rear guard.

After wantonly demolishing the chapel and well of St. Catharine, which had been built by James V.; after plundering the tower of the Winrams of Liberton, and demolishing other places, Cromwell had retreated to his old camp at Musselburgh, where he embarked five hundred sick and wounded for Berwick, and then fell back on Haddington, doing incalculable damage by fire and foray among the villages, castles, and farm-houses, until Sunday, the 1st of September, when he arrived at Dunbar, off which his fleet rode at anchor; and *now* he hoped to achieve something great; for this bold Anglo-Saxon was weak enough to indulge in the belief, that the month of *September* was fortunate for his undertakings. But it must be remembered to his honour, that on finding the poor people of Dunbar suffering from famine, he distributed two hundred and forty pounds worth of bread among them.

On the Lammermuir, about midnight, we came up with our rear guard, which consisted of the three Dragoon regiments of the Master of Forbess, the Lords Mauchline and Brechin, commanded by Colonel Sir William Douglas, of Kirkness, who informed us that our brigade was far in front; thus the next day had dawned before we rejoined. I remember being struck by the red glow of the matches, in the dark morning, as we passed

our columns of infantry, all of whom marched with colours un-
cased and matches lighted, as they closed up to the front.

During these operations, a strange correspondence had taken
place between Cromwell and the leading Scottish divines, nearly
four hundred of whom hovered about our line of march. This
correspondence, in which each party laboured hard to convince
the other, that they were " the true sons of Jacob, and the chosen
of the Lord," was conducted by a constant interchange of flags
of truce. It was a source of great annoyance to our generals,
and had ultimately a most fatal effect upon the conduct of the
army, over which these divines, in public and in secret, possessed
unparalleled influence.

We had hung upon the right flank of the English, while their
left rested on the sea; and when hemmed in at Dunbar, all
hope of escaping into their own country faded away, and they
conferred among themselves *anent* a capitulation as prisoners of
war.

The comfortless morning of the 1st of September—St. Giles'
Day—dawned on the dreary headlands, on the barren shore and
bleak old burgh of Dunbar; there were alternate gusts of wind,
with gleams of lightning, and during the whole of the past night
the rain had fallen in torrents. Halkett's brigade had halted on
a piece of waste muirland; and just as grey dawn began to steal
along the watery horizon, the order was given, " Link horses,
Black Dragoons—Prepare to dismount!"

It was obeyed with alacrity, and was performed thus:

Each trooper dismounted and stepped one pace in front of his
charger, fronted its head, and then linked the chain bridle under
the reins to the collar-ring of the next file—each troop or squadron linking towards its centre. Thus we rested our horses for a
time, while fires were lighted in front of the line, and our men
prepared their breakfasts.

The last horse of Drumstanchel's troop had just been linked,
when my old mentor, sergeant Hackiron, came to me, saying that
" the colonel required me;" and with some curiosity, I followed
him, stumbling over the wet muir to where I saw the count's
tall and stately figure, on foot, near the head of the regiment,
with the bridle of his beautiful horse hanging over his arm.
Linn of that Ilk, the Master of Oliphant, the Laird of Drumstanchel, Colonel Hugh Somerville, and other officers were grouped
about him, and to these I accorded the usual military salute.

" I sent for you, my worthy clansman and comrade," said the
count, in his usual grave but kind manner, " to announce to you
a piece of very good news. I mentioned your name again to the
general, Sir David Leslie, yesterday, and he has bestowed upon
you the cornetcy in Somerville's troop vacant by the death of

Pitblado of that Ilk, who was shot in a little piqueer we had yesterday near Haddington. This is the reward of your bravery at the Hill of St. Leonard."

"Good morrow, Cornet Ogilvie," said Colonel Somerville, the brave aide-de-camp of the great Gustavus, shaking my hand, before I had time to recover from the flutter into which this announcement threw me. "I give you joy of your promotion, fair sir. Your commission will assuredly be wetted to-night, but *not* with wine."

I know not now in what terms I thanked our gallant leader, for the friendly welcome and warm congratulations of my brother officers were crowded so thick upon me; and I was so full of joyous, fiery, and suffocating thoughts.

And Flora Campbell! I was one step nearer to her now— nearer and more worthy of her. I thought of Lorn; *now* even he dared not insult me with impunity; but he was *her* brother, and at that happy moment I could forgive—aye, even him.

The instant that breakfast was over, Sir William Keith, our adjutant, gave the order to "stand by our horses, and prepare to mount!" Every man sprang to his horse's head, and grasped the bridoon rein near the ring. In less than a minute, the whole regiment was mounted, and formed in hollow square, when, amid drawn swords and sounding trumpets, my commission was read aloud by our major, and I was formally conducted to my new troop with the kettle-drums beaten before me, while every sword was lowered.

Keen indeed were the emotions of pride, of joy, and satisfaction that thrilled through me at this moment. Many a year has passed since then, but in memory I feel them still! This was the first salute I had received. It was accorded by the whole regiment in honour of the king's commission, but to me it then seemed a recognition of my manliness and courage, and my new rank in my profession.

In one short hour, the mighty chasm which separated me from Flora and from the upper class of society had been completely bridged over!

This induction, so interesting to me, had scarcely been concluded, when an aide-de-camp of the general, a plain-looking, weather-beaten old cavalier, splashed, muddy, and with his heavy steel trappings all rusty and dim, dashed up to Sir James Halkett, with an order "to get his brigade into marching order, and move a few miles to the right, as effectual measures were being taken to hem in the English at Dunbar."

"There," as Corporal MacSnaffle said, "were the host of Pharaoh encamped, as over against Baal Zephan; but sore afraid, natheless their horsemen, musketeers, and chariots of war."

That plain-looking old man who brought the order for us to march, was no other than Field-Marshal the Earl of Leven— the venerable—aye, the immortal Leslie of the Swedish and covenanting armies, who now finding himself too old to assume the great responsibility of leading our Scottish forces in the field, had relinquished the high prerogatives of his military rank and experience; and now it was with pride and reverence we saw this glorious old soldier, the greatest general in Scottish history, and in the Thirty Years' War, he who had been the conqueror of the Poles at Dantzig and the Austrians at Francfort, commander of Westphalia, and "governor of all the cities on the Baltic shores," riding as a simple volunteer, on the staff of our commander-in-chief at Dunbar.

I took my place in the supernumerary rank of my troop, carrying its standard for the first time, though I was still attired in my plain trooper trappings; but Linn gave me a plume of most cavalier-like dimensions for my helmet, and Oliphant presented me with a gold scarf to spread over my shoulder; and now the long-treasured and enthusiastic aspirations of my boyish heart seemed on the eve of being fulfilled. I felt perfectly happy!

CHAPTER XXXVI.

THE CAMP-NIGHT OF THE 1ST SEPTEMBER.

HALF a mile eastward of Dunbar, Cromwell and his chief officers occupied Broxmouth Park, the residence of Henry Kerr, Earl of Roxburgh, who died in this year; and the most of their troops were bivouacked in swampy places, where no tents could be pitched. Cutting off their retreat into England, the Scottish army was encamped on the Doonhill, a portion of the Lammermuir range, about five hundred feet above the level of the sea. We were well supplied in all the provision and munition of war, while the English were destitute of both; and no hope of escape remained to them, save a disastrous flight through the Peas Den, a deep and savage gorge near Colbrands-path; and even that was already occupied by the two battalions of Lord Duffus' regiment, General Bickerton's brigade, and a battery of cannon; thus, when Cromwell sent nine regiments of infantry to force the passage, they signally failed; and never was an army more completely out-generalled than his, and never did an army seem more assured of an easy and bloodless victory than ours; but, alas! the treason and absurdity of the clergy ruined all.

The rain was falling heavily on the 1st of September, as we took up our position on the Doonhill, above Dunbar.

"Lo ye now," said MacSnaffle, as Halkett's brigade took possession of the ground assigned it by the quarter-master general: "is it not sinful, Mr. Ogilvie, and an abomination in the sight of the Lord, to have so many banners with red lions rampant, and Andrew's crosses, uplifted against the Philistine?"

"How?" said I, briefly, holding my capote in my teeth, to keep the drenching rain from my corslet.

"I mean those regimental flags, with their varied and ungodly devices, the offspring of heraldic waggery, and chief of all, that which waveth over the Quartier General, the cross of Andrew, the saint—so called in heathenish times."

"The devil! 'Tis the flag of our country. What would you have, corporal?"

"I would have the camp divided into four quarters, with banners conform thereto, like unto those of the four divisions of the twelve tribes; Reuben, the man; Judah, the lion; Joseph, the bull; Dan, the eagle. Thus it should have been, for verily the scripture provideth us with potent examples for all things."

This wretched cant may be taken as a specimen of the fanaticism which ruined our affairs, though my comrade, the serious corporal, was brave as a lion and true as steel.

Some of our men had strange superstitions. They believed in carbines being at times spell-bound, so that an enemy could never be shot by them, let the aim be ever so true; and the blame of these spells was invariably laid to the charge of some luckless old woman on whom they had been billetted, and whose meal-ark or almrie they had too closely investigated. Others, who had served with the Scottish horse in the German wars, believed in bullet-proof men, and put in a silver coin with their bullets, when aiming at any particular officer; hence it was said that our men shot as many good Scottish sixpences at Cromwell as would have filled that cunning individual's broad-brimmed beaver.

With the grim accompaniments of thunder pealing among the hills, lightning flashing over the storm-flecked sea, wind sweeping through the hollows, and rain drenching the mountain sides, we rode towards our appointed ground, and there, just as we halted, occurred a terrible episode!

A sergeant named Cavesson, a brave fellow, who had fought at Newburnford, and been wounded at Philiphaugh, rode out for a point, and was holding his long sword aloft, when its blade attracted the electric fluid, which struck down horse and man, killing them both on the spot. The regiment formed close column of troops over the place where they lay, and when I reined up, I was close beside the remains, which presented a terrible spectacle!

Caresson's helmet, corslet, dress, and accoutrements were torn off his body, and lay strewed around him; his sword was melted to the hilt, his face was swollen and black, and his whole body, which was almost stripped, was marked by the lightning. His steed was also dead. Its eyes glared, its nostrils were distended, and its legs were twisted up under its belly.

We buried the dead man immediately, linked our horses, covered them by our capotes, and proceeded to pitch our tents. Colonel Somerville, Linn, Oliphant, and I, sat by a camp fire drinking whiskey-and-water, and broiling on wooden skewers the tough slices of a patriarchal ram, while the cold wind that swept up from the German sea was enough to "make each particular hair stand on end, like quills on the fretful porcupine;" but we laughed not the less, nor were we a whit the less merry because we knew that before long our game with the foe must *come to the musket;* nor amid the discomfort of a wet tent flapping in the wind and rain, with its low wall lifted by every gust of the tempest, did we sleep the less sound, because we knew that on the morrow some among us would assuredly exchange their beds for those that are made, not by the kind hands of women—God bless them—but by the hasty shovels of the bearded pioneers.

Such is the life of a soldier!

I lay long that night musing on Flora, and wondering whether her thoughts were of me. In my brief and exciting interview at Lennox, I had betrayed too clearly my love for her; and was she thinking of it, and how? I asked these questions of myself a thousand times, and longed to make her aware that I was now an officer. I endeavoured to recal the words I had spoken, the tenour of her answer, and the expression of her face; but, alas! all was like a hazy dream to me, then; and thus it was, I kept my valiant resolution to "think of her no more."

At this time Cromwell was holding his famous council of war in Broxmouth House; and, full of desperation, he thought only of embarking his infantry and artillery on board of his storm-tossed fleet, and attempting to cut a passage at the head of his cavalry across the Scottish frontier. This proposal, as we understood afterwards, was vehemently opposed by Lieutenant-General Lambert, who was still suffering severely from the sword cut 1 had given him at Musselburgh; and who advised his leader boldly and energetically to trust to the fortune of war, rather than expose the English army to disgrace and destruction.

"The position of the Scots," he is reported to have said, "is not so strong as we have supposed; being confined between a ravine in front and a hill in their rear, they cannot deploy their regiments and bring them all into action; consequently, if we can attack their right wing with success, victory is certain!"

The result of this council was, that we should be attacked in the morning; but it was discovered about dusk, that Leslie had moved a body of heavy cavalry—among which was our brigade—and several batteries of cannon, to strengthen his right wing. Thus the gallant Lambert's suggestion was abandoned, and Cromwell ordered his army to prepare for any emergency on the morrow; but chiefly *to seek the Lord*—his expression for prayer; and, after a long devotional exercise with his principal officers at Broxmouth, he said,

"I feel my heart enlarged, sirs, so take ye courage; for be assured that God hath heard us, and will appear unto us on the morrow."

On that night there was also a meeting of brigadiers and colonels in the tent of Sir David Leslie, and Count Ogilvie, who was present, favoured me with a relation of it.

"The only question debated," said he, "was whether we should fall upon the enemy, and utterly destroy him by the edge of the sword; or allow him to languish in Dunbar, and yield when the last of his horses had been shot and *fricasséed*. My Lord Argyle (and at *that* name the count ground his teeth), with his son Lorn, Sir Archibald Johnston of Wariston, and all those clergy who crowd our camp with sword and pistol in their girdles, urged furiously that no time should be lost in smiting the accursed sectaries; that we should leave the Doon Hill, and descend against the Philistines at Gilgal, and so forth. We—the officers of the army—are sure there is a great hazard in attacking a host of determined Englishmen under such desperate circumstances; and advised that a trumpet should be sent with permission for them to march quietly home, with all they possess, save their cannon and colours. Even this the frantic zealots have overruled. God, they say, speaks out of their mouths — they urge on attack, and promise victory. Four hundred of these black-coats, most of them armed to the teeth, were around Leslie's pavilion; and I vow to you, Mr. Ogilvie, we were almost torn to pieces! But as for Argyle," said the count, pausing, as he turned from the camp fire to seek his own tent, "that man's soul is a very abyss, and I cannot fathom his purposes."

The great ability and skill of Sir David Leslie inspired us with every confidence. He was the soul of the Scottish army, and his courage, confidence, and resolution, were communicated to his brigadiers, from them to the colonels, and thence to the troops. We had no fear of gaining a most decisive triumph, if

our position was maintained.   Leslie's orders were always laconic
and imperative.   Had the general votes of the army been taken,
he would have been chosen for the post assigned him by the
government, as a brave army always confers its suffrage with
justice and impartiality.   It was indeed no bloodless sword that
knighted Leslie, as he received his spurs from Gustavus on the
field of Leipzig.

But these tidings of divided council filled me with anxiety
for the issue of the morrow.

The stormy night passed away; the rain and the wind lulled;
the clouds dispersed in heaven; and slowly and grey the wished-
for morrow came at last.

The morning of the second of September dawned heavily and
louringly on the misty Lammermuirs and the russet woods of
Broxmouth Park; the smoke of the night fires that dotted the
brow of the Doonhill, and which during the stormy night had
marked the Scottish position to the watchful English outposts,
rolled away with the shadows of the dawn; and as the thick
veil of dun clouds, which formed a solid bank across the eastern
quarter of the sky, burst slowly asunder, the brilliant sun came
forth in his morning splendour, and the sparkling sea and the
dew-dripping land glistened in light and radiance.

It was autumn now.   Notwithstanding the invasion by Cromwell, and the moisture of the season, the land was cleared of its
crops; and the stackyards, barns, and granaries in the snug
homesteads and thatched farmtouns were filled.   The great
fields of East Lothian were covered by brown stubble, and in
some places this was disappearing as the plough turned up the
shining furrows.   In the woodland districts, the cutters were
stowing away their faggots and trimmings for the coming winter,
and heavily their laden carts were drawn over the newly-ploughed
fields or the rain-soaked meadows.

It was autumn indeed, that melancholy season of the year
when the earth seems so naked and bare; and when the red or
yellow leaves are swept by the blustering wind through the
hollow valley, and when the little patches of green are covered
by the whirling spoil of the withered coppice.   But uninfluenced
by the decay of the year, our spirits rose on this auspicious
morning as the sunshine brightened, and gladly we stood to
arms, as the long notes of the trumpet pealed along the Doonhill side; for it was no mere animal courage or confidence in
brute strength that inspired us!   With many, no doubt, it was
the glow of fanaticism and hatred of the sectaries, as they
named the English; but with many more it was pure love of
our native country, the land of our forefathers—that glorious
sentiment which God has implanted in the heart of every honest

man, whatever be his race or clime; and without which no man will prove either a dutiful son, a kind parent, a tender husband, a brave soldier, or a good citizen.

Our infantry, 20,000 strong, stood to arms; the artillery were in their front, or on the flanks, with matches smoking; the cavalry, 7000 strong, were on the wings; all, save the reserve under Major General Holbourne. Halkett's brigade was on the extreme right, and as the English artillery began to play upon our lines at six in the morning, and ours replied, the excitement and the longing for close conflict grew every moment stronger.

Lieutenant-General Sir James Lumsden, of Invergellie, commanded our right wing, on which Leslie mainly depended for cutting off any attempt of Cromwell to force a passage through us.

"Invergellie," I heard him say, checking his grey charger for a moment as he galloped past us, "to you I look for good service to-day. If the enemy moves, your first line of cavalry will attack; the second will support it; while the musketeer battalions of the Laird of Gleneagles, my Lord Kirkcudbright, and the Master of Lovat, will form your reserve. The artillery will cover your advance, and if the gunners flinch, by the soul of Gustavus I will chain them to their guns! When you charge, let it be in the name of the God of battle and of storms; but our slogan to-day is THE COVENANT."

The dispositions of our general were admirable, and ensured an almost bloodless capitulation of the invaders; and longing for the order to advance, we sat on horseback, checking our impatient chargers, and listening to the sharp ringing shots of the artillery as they rang between the Lammermuirs and the woods of Broxmouth, where the English general was watching us through his telescope from a knoll which is yet named " Cromwell's Mount;" but, alas! our clergy blighted everything.

Despite the prudent remonstrances of Generals Leslie and Lumsden, of Count Ogilvie, and others, these reverend meddlers insisted that our troops should leave their strong position, " and assail the troublers of Israel in the plain, that God's judgment might be more fully manifested." Aware of the ruinous influence they possessed among our soldiers, they spared neither tongue nor trouble to achieve this, by such harangues as the following:

" Trust not in carnal weapons, but commit yourselves, O ye faithful, to the invincible protection of the Lord of Hosts!" cried Zachary Boyd, halting his rough Galloway cob in front of our brigade, and raising his bony hands above his head, while his long, lank hair fell in tangled masses on his Geneva cloak; " for lo ye, the God of Jacob is fighting in your ranks, and your cause *must* prosper. On, on, and spare not! Hough and hamstring their horses! Cut and hew ! Smite them both hip and thigh —smite and spare not, lest ye be not spared ! Descend, O Israel, and crush the Egyptians, the brood of Pharaoh, in their camp——"

"You urge a mutiny, reverend sir," cried Count Ogilvie; "'tis ruin and madness, this ! In the king's name I command you to be silent and begone !"

"Speak, my Lord Argyle," said General Lumsden, in great wrath; "speak, that this babbling may cease. What say you ?"

"Verily, I say," snuffled his lordship, who came up at that moment with several preachers, all clad like himself, in the ever-lasting Geneva cloak—"I say, beloved brethren, that we should rush down and charge; and, verily, ye shall see that the name of this place, now called the Doonhill, shall be changed unto Bethel or Jehovah-jirah, where the Divine power shall be signally mani-fested through our humble hands."

"March down, march down !" cried another personage, with a voice like a screaming hawk; "and your swords shall bear terrible testimony to our new covenant, even as the terrors of Sinai bore a testimony unto the sanctity of the old law."

"Upon them !" resumed Zachary, "and I prophesy that they shall fall before you, even as the haughty Philistine fell before Samson; and the sun shall not go down until, like Joshua, ye have exterminated the last fugitive !"

"Behold the legions of Goliath—this boasting giant, this blasphemous brewer ! who came to scowl upon the children of the covenant," cried a furious specimen of the kirk-militant, lantern-jawed, wild-eyed, long-locked, with a brace of brass-barrelled pistols in his girdle, a Bible in one hand, and a broad-sword in the other; stern, inflexible, and, in his conscious rec-titude, fearing nothing on earth; "out of my mouth, O troopers, I promise ye victory; and your brows shall be bound with blessed laurels, even as the shields of the Maccabees were with olives after their wars with the insulting Antiochus."

No less than four-hundred trumpet-tongued pastors were spur-ring their shaggy ponies from regiment to regiment, with ha-rangues such as these; and many there were who blasphemously affirmed "that God would *no longer be their God* if he delivered them not from the sectaries."* The effect of this was soon evident. Shouts began to ring along the lines; colours were waved, and weapons brandished. The troops would no longer be restrained; and yielding to the torrent of fanaticism which dis-concerted all his measures, General Leslie was compelled to order the whole line to advance; and thus we began to descend into

* See Whitelock, p. 419.

the plain, accompanied by those sable-coated prophets of victory.
On seeing this rash movement,

"*God hath delivered them into our hands!*" cried Cromwell,
with joy, as he sharply closed his telescope, leaped on horseback,
and galloping from Broxmouth Park, ordered his troops to close
to the front.

CHAPTER XXXVII.

THE BATTLE OF DUNBAR.

BEFORE we moved, the English artillery had been bowling shot
through us, tearing and furrowing up the green hill-side in long
lines.   Our grave, dark colonel was cool as if on parade in Falkland palace-yard.   We were in open column, with our flanks to
the foe—a dangerous formation at such a time—when Major-
General Halkett ordered the brigade to form line.

"Gentlemen and cavaliers," said he, "the cavalry are to begin
the battle."

"The regiment will wheel into line," cried Count Ogilvie.
"March! Steady, my comrades, steady. Front ranks dress to
the centre; rear ranks and serre-files look to the wheeling flank,
and cover their front leaders."

"Halt! Dress by the standard!" cried Somerville, Drumstanchel, and every other captain of a troop, as the long line of
steel helmets and cuirasses was formed with beautiful exactness.

"Forward!" was now the order, and we began to descend the
hill at a walk; but on passing the flank of our infantry, the brigades of cavalry broke into a swinging trot.   Every heart beat
high, and every cheek was flushed.   We soon attained the level
ground; and clearing the broom, whins, and furze, saw right
before us, and advancing leisurely in line, a great column of
cavalry which covered the English left wing, all well mounted,
and attired by entire regiments in white or red coats.   A shout
rang along our line: it was our united war-cry—"SCOTLAND
AND THE COVENANT!"

On, on we poured, a long line of at least two thousand cavalry;
steel bridles and bits, stirrups and scabbards, clanking; horses
champing, and tossing the foam from their nostrils; uplifted
swords flashing, and plumes waving.   The aspect of the Life
Guards was brilliant, being all glitter and splendour; but the
iron front of the Black Dragoons was dark and sombre, with
Ogilvie, Somerville, old Drumstanchel, Oliphant, Linn, and other
noble spirits leading them on, as, goring and spurring, till the
mass of troopers, wedged boot to boot and holster to holster,

rushing at full speed like a tornado of men and horses, they fell furiously and blade in hand upon the heavy masses of the foe.

There was a dreadful shock as we met six regiments of English cavalry hand to hand; hundreds of men and horses went down on both sides as we came dashing furiously against each other. There was a clashing of swords, a storm of voices, a confused discharge of pistols; and after an obstinate contest for about fifteen minutes, we bore all down before us, though our ranks were considerably broken. The enemy's cavalry were led by Lieutenant-General Fleetwood, Colonel Twiselton, and Commissary-General Whalley—a brave fellow, who had two horses shot under him and his sword-hand nearly hewn off by the Master of Oliphant, as we pressed after the fugitives. One powerful sectary clove the centre-bar of my helmet by a back-handed stroke that made a thousand stars dance before me; but before he could withdraw his sword, Sergeant Glanders ran him right through the body, and he was dragged off the field with a foot in his stirrup. Then a dainty gallant, wearing a lady's glove in his hat, checked his horse, and thinking perhaps to capture my standard, let fly his pistols at me. Exasperated by my double danger, I couched the standard-pole like a spear, and exclaiming, "Come on, sir, you'll find this other work than flaunting your feather in the military garden at London." He turned upon me, but I drove a foot of the pike and the black silk banner through his body together, and spurred over him.

"Yonder seems one in high authority," said Linn.

"'Tis Cromwell!" I exclaimed, recognising the broad hat, the black corslet, the plain buff coat, and immoveable visage, with its large nose and unseemly warts; "'tis Cromwell, and my carbine is empty!"

"The regicide—now Heaven aid my aim!" cried Linn, who fired a pistol, the ball of which grazed the Englishman's hat.

"Out on thee, fellow," cried Cromwell, with remarkable coolness; "wert thou officer of mine, I would cashier thee for a shot so bad as that."

But our career was now stopped by the red-coated infantry regiments of Lieutenant-General Goff. Cromwell had hurried these forward to replace his routed cavalry, who fled round their flanks; and then a sheet of lead tore through our line, heaping men and horses over each other, dead or dying. A captain-lieutenant and two corporal-majors were killed beside me; it was perilous hot work!

"Close in, close in," cried our colonel, galloping along the line of fire and carnage without his helmet, which had been struck off in the first melée; "close your files, and forward! Down upon these God-forgettors! hack and hew! stab and slash! forward, my Black Dragoons! forward—charge!"

"The covenant! the covenant!" we cried, and, like the waves of an iron sea, dashed ourselves against the squares of Goff's infantry; but, like waves from a headland, we were forced to recoil from the wall of English pikes; though we were so close, that above the rush of our horses, the cries of the wounded, and the roar of the musketry, I could hear Cromwell crying—

"Bring up the cannon—let God arise, and his enemies be scattered!"

Loaded with grape, the cannon belched forth upon us, through openings in the infantry; and whole ranks of ours went down beneath that iron tempest. Death menaced us on every side; the Life Guards had given way; Cassilis' cuirassiers had nearly all their officers killed; and being only mortal men, the Black Dragoons could do nothing more. Wheeling round, we retired at full speed, leaving our lieutenant-general and all his brigadiers wounded in the enemy's hands; while nearly three hundred of our men lay on the ground killed or wounded; among the latter was poor young Oliphant. Thus was the Scottish right wing left wholly unprotected.

By this time all the infantry on both sides were engaged, and all the low ground about Broxmouth was veiled in smoke, amid which we saw standards waving and weapons glittering; flashes glared from the brass cannon and black-mouthed mortars; while each square of foot was zoned by fire and steel.

Our infantry fought bravely, and every battalion charged with its drums beating; but some of them unfortunately were raw troops and fired ill, their ramrods having become wood-bound by the rain overnight. And then the brigades of Monk, Lambert, and Hesilrig, on one side, and those of Pitscottie, Hepburn, Innes, and Ardmohr, on the other, fought bravely foot to foot and breast to breast; but our rout—a rout caused solely by the loss of so many officers—left their right flank exposed, and proved our second cause of ruin; for the able Cromwell lost not a moment in reforming and leading on his discomfited cavalry; so bearing down upon our infantry, before some of the regiments could form square, a frightful scene of death and havoc ensued. Some of our foot made a noble resistance; and one entire brigade of Highlanders perished on the spot, for not a man would *turn his heel* to save his life. The regiment of Kirkness lost thirty officers, and Sir William Douglas, its colonel, was slain as he lay wounded in a thicket.*

While the gallant Count Ogilvie was endeavouring to reform Lumsden's shattered horse into something like order, Sir David

* Where his tomb is yet to be seen.

Leslie, attended only by old Marshal Leven, dashed furiously up to us. As I happened to be next him,

"Cornet," said he, "ride for death and life to Major-General Holbourn of Menstrie, and desire him to bring up his reserves without a moment of delay, or the day is lost!"

Now there were two ways of reaching the reserve: one by encompassing a hill in our rear; another by riding straight through the hollow, which was swept by a tempest of balls of every sort and size; but I did not hesitate an instant in taking the latter, as it was the shortest, though I had to cross the front of our Foot Guards, who were firing in line from the summit of a knoll.

As I galloped along the hollow, a shower of musketry from the enemy greeted my appearance; but our Guards suspended firing, and for a few seconds recovered their firelocks. I was still riding on, when they opened again from the flank which *I had passed*, but at that moment a ball struck my holsters. It was a *pistol* shot. I turned with the speed of thought, and saw the lieutenant-colonel of the Foot Guards—to wit, the Lord Lorn —in the act of deliberately returning to his holsters a pistol, from the barrel of which the smoke of its recent discharge was yet curling.

"Wretch! one day I hope to return this shot elsewhere!" I exclaimed; and with breast swollen with rage, I rode on my perilous mission. It was but too evident that Lorn had hoped that his shot, if it hit me, would pass for one from the enemy; but of this more anon.

To Holbourn, a slow and inactive officer, I delivered my orders, but he was so long in bringing up the reserves, that before the head of his column reached the scene of operations the whole Scottish line had given way, and was in full retreat from that bloody and disastrous field, which they had maintained for two hot and hazardous hours, the losses of which I may sum up in one brief but sorrowful paragraph.

On the narrow plain between the Doonhill and Lord Roxburgh's house lay the wreck of that gallant army, which the treason of some and the fanaticism of others had destroyed. Colonel Louis Home of Wedderburn, the elder, and Lieutenant-Colonel Louis Home the younger, father and son, lay side by side; Colonels Sir William Douglas, Lord Liberton, Sir John Haldane of Gleneagles, Maxwell of Calderwood, Montgomery of Craigbuey, Kerr, Wemyss, Scott, Gray, and Stuart; Major Cockburn, Rittmasters, Collesse, and Lidington of Saltcoates, with more than three thousand of our soldiers, lay dead upon the field; and there were many among us who thought it better to have died like them for our dear mother Scotland, than to live with the knowledge of defeat. Of the wounded I can give no computation, but a thousand were sent in carts next day as a present to Elizabeth of Herries, Countess Dowager of Winton. There were taken ten thousand prisoners, among whom were eighteen field officers, thirty-seven captains, two hundred and four subalterns, and fifteen sergeants; two hundred stand of colours; fifteen thousand stand of arms, thirty-two pieces of cannon, with all our tents, ammunition, and baggage.

Amid all this *débris* of war and its attendant horrors, for in some places the dead lay in piles, in others they lay in long lines like swathes of grass cut down by a mower, all with their white faces and glaring eyes turned to the blue sky, and all trampled by the charging cavalry, or torn by round shot, grape, and shells, or half sunk in pools of curdled blood, in which the flies and gnats were floating—amid all this, I say, the English sectaries, flushed with victory and sated with slaughter, sang the 117th psalm; and as they sang, the cries and groans of the wounded, and the sighs of the dying, mingled with their voices and went up to heaven.

To many a heart and home in Scotland did the carnage of that morning carry woe and desolation!

CHAPTER XXXVIII.

THE RETREAT.

HAD it not been for the able manner in which Count Ogilvie, with the Black Dragoons, the remnant of Cassilis' Cuirassiers, and the Life Guards, covered the rear of our army, and checked Cromwell's advance, our retreat had infallibly proved more bloody and disastrous. We fell back on Haddington, and just as darkness was closing, had a sharp skirmish with our carbines, and one brisk camisade with the sword, near the old chapel of St. Martin at the Nun-raw, where we routed Hobson's Horse, and secured the retreat of the whole army, which marched leisurely towards Stirling.

The clergy, the chief promoters of that day's mischief, had been the first to fly; and I saw many of our soldiers, in their rage at the issue of the field, empty their carbines at the stray black-coats, who, like fugitive crows, came careering along the highway towards the west. General Leslie, who, with old Marshal Leven, rode beside Count Ogilvie, reviled them with great bitterness, as "false prophets and colluders with Cromwell."

"Bigots and traitors," said the count, sternly, to two who rode near him, "where now is your promised victory?"

"Alas," whined one, who was no other than the famous minister of Elie, "the Gideons, the Samsons, and the Maccabees are no more; and captivity is before and wrath behind us!"

"With the gallows, too, I hope, for the disgrace that you and such as you have thus brought on Scotland."

"Hush; had ye faith, even as a grain of mustard seed, ye must have prevailed this day in Gilgal; but it was not in ye."

"No faith in such canting fellows as thee, at all events," said Linn, whose head was bound up, having received a severe sword-cut. "But *now* we may see the result of all the correspondence between Cromwell and our clergy; so, d—n me, if I don't turn prelatist from this time forward. My poor friend, Patrick Oliphant is wounded, and taken prisoner with the rest."

"Did you see him unhorsed?" asked the count.

"Yes; cut down by a stroke that may cost him his bridle arm, I fear."

"Severe, that," said I; "think of requiring another to cut one's food every day."

"That mattered little when we served in Alsace, my dear fellow; for when there, we had no food to cut," said old Drumstanchel, whose visage, brown as mahogany by campaigning and hard drinking, was now flushed by excitement.

"A black day's work this has been. I have lost two hundred of my Life Guardsmen," said Greysteel, the Earl of Eglinton, joining the group at a hand gallop. He was a brave old fellow, seamed by sword-cuts and riddled by musket-shot.

"My Lord Eglinton," replied Count Ogilvie, through his clenched teeth, "Scotland has always had a few nobles who, like yourself, have stood boldly forward to vindicate her rights and national honour; but subtle villains have betrayed, and servile slaves like Arg——tush! have sold them."

To this bitter speech no one replied; but the count's meaning must be plain to every Scotsman who knows the history of his country, and is consequently aware, that since the removal of the court to London, the interests of the Scottish people and their alienated aristocracy are completely rent asunder. The Earl of Argyle was nowhere to be seen, though the parliamentary committee, who accompanied the army, made numerous inquiries for him; and I must own to having suspicions, that he was perhaps sipping the Protector's wine at Broxmouth Park.

At every halt, I enquired for the Lord Lorn; but could nowhere discover him, greatly to my chagrin, as I longed to bring him to account for his late cruel attempt to murder me, when exposed to an enemy's fire. The revenge of his father I knew to belike flaming heather, which consumes all within its circle; and though ever on my guard against *him*, I was ready to bring matters to a crisis by defying his son and heir to mortal combat,

albeit such trials of skill and courage were strictly forbidden by
General Leslie. And as for Flora, my mind was so excited by
the terrible issue of the battle, that believing our Scottish affairs
on the brink of ruin, and my love for her more than ever hopeless, I cared the less for giving full swing to my hearty hatred
for her brother. I knew the earl to be steeped to the beard in
treason—that treason which afterwards cost him so dear—that
treason which I might denounce; but for what end, in a country
governed almost by himself, and when he, by a word, could crush
me to the dust?

While we continued retreating, the English captured all the
strengths in Lothian. Colonel Monk, with a column of horse
and foot, four guns and a mortar, stormed Dirleton House, and
barbarously put Major Hamilton and his garrison to the sword;
Colonel Thomlinson cannonaded and took the great castle of
Borthwick; and soon after, Tantallon, on being bombarded by
cannon and mortars for forty-eight hours, was also taken. Blackness was besieged, and the strong castle of Edinburgh, which
was manned by a brave garrison, whose energies were cramped
and encumbered by a horde of fugitive ministers, was next in-
vested closely by Cromwell in person. On being strongly rein-
forced from England, he rigidly commanded his soldiers to abstain
from all violence and plunder in and around the capital; and it
is to the honour of the English army that he was implicitly
obeyed. The only place he did *not* attack—doubtless to the
great disgust of its warlike occupant—was the little tower of
Lennox, in the secluded glen of Currie.

Enraged by the defeat of his army through the interference
of the zealots and clergy, Leslie resigned his baton; but being
prevailed upon to resume the command, he made Stirling his
headquarters, and soon remodelled the army, which was reduced
to the number of 16,000 Infantry, 7000 Horse and Dragoons,
with fourteen pieces of cannon; but these were all trained soldiers, " and well accomplished," as Linn said, " in the noble science
of manslaughter."

The young king rode daily among our parades and tents, clad
in a laced buff coat, with a well-plumed beaver, and a black flowing periwig, and wearing the green ribband of the Thistle over
his shoulder. Round him were ever a number of gay cavaliers,
handsome women, and sombre preachers; but the latter were
thick as blackberries in Scotland, and intruded themselves everywhere.

In Stirling Park, we shot a corporal and three of the Life
Guards for alleged misconduct at Dunbar.

In the same park there was a grand review before the young
king, who was attended by Marshal Leven, by the Earl of Argyle,

and his compatriot, Sir Archibald Johnstone of Warriston, Lord Clerk Register, who was afterwards executed for his enormities; by Charles Duke of Lennox, the Lord Great Chamberlain; by Hamilton of Orbieston, the Lord Justice Clerk, and other officers of the crown, together with the Countesses of Winton, Roxburgh, Eglinton, Cassilis, and a brilliant assemblage of ladies, all on horseback.

Among them was one whose figure I recognised. She was clad in a blue habit trimmed with silver, and wore a broad hat with a drooping feather, while long white gauntlet gloves encased her little hands. This fair rider was Lady Flora, and she was laughing and talking with the greatest animation to a gentleman who rode beside her.

" 'Tis Argyle's daughter, whom we saw at Lennox Tower," said Linn, on perceiving that my eyes followed her.

" And the gentleman?"

" Is her affianced—Colonel Campbell of Ardmohr. Dora Lennox—ah, there is Dora just behind her, in the pink riding-habit —Dora told me, they are to be married after the coronation takes place, when it is believed that the colonel, for his services at the Hill of St. Leonard, will be raised to the peerage by the title of Lord Campbell of Ardmohr. I do not like him," continued Linn, without perceiving how I writhed under his court gossip; " and I believe that poor Flora will never be happy with him. Dora says that he is dark, intriguing, fierce, and unscrupulous; and like all the westland whig lairds, has committed many cruel and atrocious acts to further the schemes of the Argyle family."

I was about to remind Linn of the attempted kidnapping; but could only bite my lips to impose silence on myself, as the order to wheel back from line into open column of troops, cut short the conversation. After this, I saw no more of Flora for a time, but was informed that she was residing at the Palace of Scone, which was guarded by Ardmohr's musketeers, and Lorn's Foot Guards.

The committees of the kirk and state, and all the great officers of the crown, were in Stirling, which now became the centre of all our operations, while our parliament sat in Perth, where the heedless monarch, it was averred, with his tongue in his cheek, boasted that he was " the first covenanted king of the Scottish nation."

Cromwell had possessed himself of Linlithgow, and garrisoned the palace, on which, it is said, the royal swans disappeared mysteriously from the loch, and returned no more until the Restoration. He had thrown his advanced posts into the castles of Almond and Hayning, while we marched our entire forces from Stirling to Falkirk, and encamped on strong ground, having the Carron in front and the whole country in our rear, open for supplies or for retreat. Cromwell was unable to pass us; every avenue was secured, and a brave garrison occupied Callander House—a point on which the general mainly depended for the strength of his new position.

Now comes my own part of this adventurous game, after Linn and I were appointed lieutenants, in consequence of the recent slaughter.

The old castle of Callander, the walls of which were defended by a moat, and surrounded by the most beautiful copsewood, was the ancestral seat of Field-Marshal James, Earl of Callander, one of our best Scottish generals in the former war against England. Its ramparts were of great strength, its outworks were mounted by cannon, and the garrison consisted of one hundred musketeers, under a Lieutenant Galbraith, of Duffus' regiment, and a chosen body of the burghers of Falkirk, all of whom were the Lord Callander's vassals. To prevent Cromwell from approaching this place, a narrow and important pass between Callander wood and a deep and dangerous moss was always occupied by a picquet or outguard of cavalry; and on a dark night in December, this duty fell to me.

When ordered to march, the general in person saw the picquet ride off. An officer accompanied him. I recognised the Lord Lorn; and deep and fiery were the glances we exchanged; but in Leslie's presence I was forced to conceal my just anger, and add it to the general amount of vengeance I was scoring up against this young noble, whose deep and peculiar *smile* portended something, but I knew not what; and I pondered over it as we marched to our post.

There had been storms of wind, sleet, and snow, with an occasional deluge of rain, which swelled the Carron and all the streams in our vicinity. The skies were dreary and grey, the forests red or leafless, and mountains bare and bleak.

With twenty of the Black Dragoons, I occupied the defile, and posted my two videttes (an old soldier and a young one) about the eighth of a mile in front of it, on horseback, and in such a way as to enable them to observe every avenue by which an enemy could approach us. As they unslung their carbines, I reiterated the orders of our adjutant, the Knight of Ludquhairn, "to shoot dead all who approached, be they kindly Scots or English thieves;" and I reminded them that the honour and safety of the garrison in Callander, and of the whole army, depended on their vigilance.

The rest of the detachment lay on the ground, or reclined against stumps of trees or fragments of rock, each man with his charger's bridle on his arm; some were smoking, some were sleeping, others told stories, and all were muffled in their rough capotes, for the night was chill, and the place peculiarly desolate.

As midnight approached, every sound ceased; but the solemn darkness of the rugged defile was lessened by the half-waned moon that rose slowly and palely behind the oak woods of Callander, to shed upon the savage landscape its cold but mellow light, casting black and mysterious shadows far along the ground. The dew was glittering on the blades of grass, on the silent leaves, and on the manes of our motionless horses, while from the low grounds through which the Carron flowed, a thin white vapour ascended into the chill, clear atmosphere.

Though weary and benumbed, I was wakeful and restless, as I knew the importance of the post we occupied, the enemy's advanced guard being within three miles of us—but a mile Scots contains three hundred paces more than a mile English.

Drowsiness was stealing over me, when—*bang! bang!* the double report of two carbines in the gorge, gave me a shock as if a shot had struck me, and I sprang on horseback.

"Up, up,—to horse, my lads! Sergeant Hackiron, get the men mounted—unsling carbines, and ride to the front," said I, goring my horse's flanks, and galloping towards my videttes, whom I found in the act of quietly reloading.

"How now, Carlourie—what is the matter?"

"There was something stirring in the bushes yonder, sir; we challenged, but got nae answer—so we fired, and a' is quiet enough now."

"I wish this quietness may continue," said I, as the whole picquet came up at a hand-gallop, with their carbines unslung.

The moon had now sunk behind the black mountains, and a solemn gloom and darkness enveloped everything. I was anxious and restless. I dismounted, took a pistol in one hand, my drawn sword in the other, and, accompanied by old Corporal MacSnaffle, advanced softly to the front for about a hundred paces, and then we paused to listen, but heard only a loud and continual barking of dogs; and this I have found to be an *invariable sign* of troops being in motion, especially in a pastoral district.

"There is something astir in the carse to-night, MacSnaffle," said I, "though all seems quiet in our own vicinity."

"Yea and verily—but what hath Carlourie heard?"

"A stray sheep, perhaps."

"Yea—or a ram caught in the thicket; but lo ye, sir," said the corporal, grasping my arm—"look yonder!"

Close by us lay two figures stretched on the ground, but quite motionless and still. In fact, they were both dead. We approached cautiously, and on examining them by the light of a stable lantern, found them to be two Englishmen, partly disguised by bonnets and plaids; but under their rough frieze gaberdines we found the coarse red coats of Monk's regiment. One was shot through the breast, the other through the head, and I could not but express surprise that two balls fired almost at random should prove so fatal. Each of these men had suspended at his neck the oval silver medal, given at Cromwell's suggestion, by the English parliament for their recent victory. On one side was a droll representation of the regicides sitting in Westminster-hall, with their broad beavers on; the other bore an admirable profile of Cromwell, warts and all, with the legend — THE LORD OF HOSTS — WORD AT DUNBAR — SEPT. 2ND, 1650.

I was about to give some instructions concerning their burial at daybreak, when we heard the galloping of a horse. It was in our rear, and approached rapidly.

"Stand — on your life, halt! Who comes there?" I demanded.

"A friend," replied a half-stifled voice.

"The parole?"

"*Montrose*," cried the other, riding up boldly.

"Have you come to ascertain what the firing meant?"

"No, but with an order from the general," said this personage, who was muffled up to the eyes in a great cloak of drab de Berri, and who wore a hat flapped over his eyes, so that no part of him was visible between his brow and his military boots.

"And this order?——"

"Is, that you instantly retire—fall back and rejoin your brigade at Camelon village, without delay," said he, wheeling round his horse.

"I should like this order in writing, fair sir," said I; "this pass is so important—Callander House is in our rear, and——"

"Let Callander House look to itself," said he, imperiously, as he drew himself up; "I am as unused to be doubted as the lieutenant-general is to be trifled with; I gave you the parole— a sufficient guarantee. You have now your orders, my beau coq —and so, your servant."

Turning his horse, this haughty personage, whose voice seemed somewhat familiar to me, galloped westward, in the direction from whence he had come. I was surprised and offended by the lofty bearing of this officer, whom I endeavoured to remember; and certain suspicions convinced me that he was no other than Colonel

Campbell of Ardmohr—the friend of Lorn and Flora's lover, however, obedience is a soldier's first duty. I called in my videttes, and at the head of my little party rode leisurely past Callander House, the lights of which were twinkling amid the copse wood; past the town of Falkirk, then sunk in darkness and in sleep; and reached the village of Camelon, where I rejoined the regiment, to the astonishment of all, but of none more than Count Ogilvie.

Long before daybreak the sound of firing had brought the whole brigade to horse; and the first tidings we heard were, that Cromwell's whole army had passed in silence through *the defile* between the wood and morass, and that his infantry had crossed the beautiful lawn in front of Callander House. Though taken by surprise, its garrison had fired briskly from every window, loop, and aperture; but the place was stormed by Monk's regiment, by whom the young and gallant Lieutenant Galbraith, after fighting for an hour with a half-pike, was slain, with sixty-two of his soldiers; while the brave men of Falkirk, to whom the cannon, gate, and outwork were entrusted, after combatting as men can only combat when defending the honour of their wives, and the lives of their children, all perished to a man, for *no quarter* was given them!

These tidings, which were brought by the Baron-baillie of Falkirk, filled me with horror and consternation; and I was in the act of explaining to Count Ogilvie, for the twentieth time, my *rencontre* with the strange officer at midnight, when General Leslie, accompanied by the Earls of Eglinton and Cassilis, came furiously up to the brigade, on horses covered with foam.

"In God's name," cried he, "where is the officer who over-night commanded the outguard?"

I rode forward, and lowered my sword in salute.

"Wretched traitor," he exclaimed, "you have betrayed us—the king, the army, and your country! Our flank is turned—the position lost—oh, woe betide thee for this black deed!"

"I retired in obedience to your own orders, Sir David Leslie," said I, firmly.

"*My* own orders?" he reiterated.

"Your express commands, delivered to me at midnight by a mounted officer, not ten minutes after we had an alerte, and shot two of the enemy's spies."

"Young fellow, thou ravest!" said the general, gnawing his gauntlet.

"The order was given to me in presence of Sergeant Hackiron, the corporal, and twenty troopers."

"I sent no one—I gave no orders—by the life of the king, I did not."

"Ogilvie, some false traitor has outwitted thee," said the count.

"A traitor who must have possessed himself of the parole."

"Now, by my father's soul, I would give ten thousand crowns to know who this villain is!" said the old general; "describe him, sir—what manner of man was he?"

"Stout and dark, muffled in a black cloak, and hat that was flapped over his face; he wore jack boots, and rode with long holsters."

"This description will suit any thousand men in the king's army," said the Earl of Eglinton.

"His voice——"

"Hah!"

"Was not unfamiliar to me."

"Indeed!"

"But it might be rash and unjust to say where I think 1 heard it," said I, evasively; to accuse the colonel of one of Argyle's prime regiments, on mere suspicion, would have been a dangerous experiment for me; and but for the united testimony of my troopers, the affair might have gone very hard with me.

"Sergeant Hackiron," said Leslie, "how was it that an old trooper like thee was also foiled or fooled? 'Sdeath, sirrah, I have known better things of thee in Low Germanie?"

The trooper grumbled out his excuses; but the irate general turned away without listening.

"My poor veteran," said I; "'tis I who have brought this severity upon you from the general."

"I heed it not, lieutenant," said he; "old Leslie and I were the best of friends in Saxony; and more especially at Philiphaugh, where I saved him from the sword of Montrose; but he forgets all that now."

I was deeply stung and humiliated; and, perceiving that I was cast down, the grim count, our colonel, touched me kindly on the shoulder, and bade me "take courage."

"'Tis useless," said I, in the bitterness of my heart; "for I have a potent and secret enemy, against whom it is in vain to struggle."

"An enemy?"

"'Tis Argyle!" said I, striking my clenched hands upon my corsiet.

"Hah!" whispered the count, while his eyes flashed fire, his dark face glowed, and he grasped my arm with fierce energy; "what! is this gorefed Argyle—unglutted yet with Scottish blood, and withal so sparing of his own—is *he* thine enemy?"

"Alas! I have but too much reason to think so," I replied, startled by the sudden energy and fire of the usually placid count; "my humble rank and obscurity should have been my best protection against a distinction so fatal as his hostility; but there is some dark mystery in it, which I cannot fathom or unravel."

"Argyle your enemy? 'tis well; when was he other than the foe of an Ogilvie? Thou, and I, Harry, shall be the firmer friends from thenceforward. 'Tis no protection, your being poor —I have heard you were so—having had, perhaps, like too many of our Scots' cavaliers, a grandfather who spent all *your* money as well as his own. Was it so?"

I coloured deeply, being too proud to acknowledge, even to the kind count, that I was a foundling; but I was surprised by his abrupt manner, and the sudden emotion excited within him; though I had frequently before this, observed his ill-suppressed animosity to the Earl of Argyle.

"Oh, colonel," I exclaimed, "could I but discover the villain who betrayed me, that I might hurl death and defiance in his teeth—that I might slit his nose with my sword as a mark——"

"Nay, nay, such doings are unknown here in kindly Scotland; let us bide our time, and we shall unmask those traitors one day."

What more might have passed I know not; but while our troopers were grooming their chargers, making as much noise as a brood of serpents, by hissing through their teeth, our brigade suddenly received orders to decamp from Camelon towards Stirling; and in ten minutes after we retired, without breakfasting, in heavy marching order, every trooper having his nosebag filled with corn, and a supply of hay, sufficient for twenty-four hours, trussed up on his crupper. Over my shoulder I had a havresack, containing a pound of beef, four barley-meal bannocks, and a flask of whiskey, the parting gift of the gudewife of my billet. Everywhere the people had the greatest love and admiration for their native troops, who were struggling, under such treasonable and adverse circumstances, to defend the kirk and liberty of Scotland; and everywhere we met with welcome and kindness.

CHAPTER XXXIX.

THE MOSS LAIRD.

WE marched to Dunmore, on the right bank of the Forth. Our headquarters were established in the old tower of that name, and the regiment was cantoned in all the little cottages and farmtouns of the thirty tenants of Dunmore, who were denominated Moss Lairds, in the immediate vicinity of the fortress;

we kept a strong outpost on the road to Airth, while a chain of communication was maintained with other forces on our right, and our flank and rear were protected by the river and the deep mosses of Letham and Dunmore. But since the capture of Callander, Cromwell remained pretty quiet, and contented himself with mining and bombarding Colonel Dundas and his gallant garrison in the Castle of Edinburgh.

Colonel Hugh Somerville, Linn, and myself were quartered on a Bonnet-laird, whose farm stood on the verge of the Moss. He was a strange old fellow, and his oddities were a source of amusement to us. One day he lost a sixpence in the moss, and employed six of our dragoons for a week, at a shilling each per day, to search for it; on another occasion, he insisted on shaving the head of his Grieve, and then piling several pounds of butter on his bare scalp, that he might laugh at him while it melted; and he kept a horse-bucket filled with whiskey and water constantly in his stables, a domestic institution which made him decidedly popular with the Black Dragoons, till the utensil gave one of them the glanders. Our moss laird was superstitious too, and had suspended in his stable the lid of an ancient quern, a horseshoe, and rowan-branch, to protect his cattle from witchcraft. Yet he was sorely troubled by the presence of certain fairies and spunkies, who dwelt in the adjacent moss; as well as by a brownie, a quaint little hairy man, who after nightfall was wont to slide down the kitchen chimney, and sit on the kailpot link, the chain of which he grasped, and there swung himself the livelong night over the glowing peats, an amusement which no one dared to interrupt.

At the head of his box-bed hung a perforated stone; this he named a *hagstane*, as it prevented the nightmare in the form of a neighbouring witch from perching on his stomach; and at his neck he wore a piece of a coffin, to prevent ague from assailing him, as he dwelt so near a moss. His whim-whams served to amuse me during the first day or two I was quartered there; but the memory of the late affair at Callander Wood still rankled keenly in my breast.

"Oh, if that traitor really *was* Ardmohr!" I repeated a thousand times, while the demon of jealousy added stings to my just hatred. Hitherto I had been successful in acquiring and retaining the friendship and esteem of my comrades, and in working my way from the rank of private to lieutenant easily and rapidly; but this late attempt to ruin me filled my heart with rage and passion. There is a culminating point in the career of every man, after which fate or fortune seldom befriend him more. I began to fear that my star had passed through its meridian But I comforted myself by the recollection that " there is a divi nity doth shape our ends, rough hew them how we will;" and so I hoped for better things, and better auguries.

One evening I was sitting alone on a turf seat at the door of our billet. Somerville, Drumstanchel, and Linn were smoking and drinking hot punch with the laird. I had been loitering about the stable looking after my horse, and now sat watching the winter sunset, as it lingered redly on the wooded hills of Airth and Dunmore. The pious Corporal MacSnaffle sat near me at the stable door, reading aloud a chapter of the Bible, which, as I have already mentioned, he did daily and nightly, taking them in regular rotation without regard to the subject; and as his intoned reading was interrupted by occasional orders to the troopers near us, the effect was absurd, if not a little profane.

"Of the tribes of the children of Judah and of Simeon Josue gave cities, whose names are these. To the sons of Aaron of the families of Caath of the race of Levi he gave (a feed of corn to that bay mare, Jock Sourock) the city of Arbe, the father of Enac, which is called Hebron (Carlourie, show that infernal gomeral how to bridle his horse), in the mountain of Judah, and the suburbs thereof roundabout (headstall parallel to the cheek-bone, I say)! But the fields and villages thereof, the Lobnam with the suburbs thereof, and Jether, and Estmo, and Hebron, and Debir—put your nose-band beneath the bridoon headstall, or, all the devils! I'll hae ye weel scabbarded!" cried the corporal, losing all patience, for he had kept one eye to his duty and another to the Book of Deuteronomy.

Undisturbed by this, and unmoved by the grave absurdity of the seriously-disposed corporal, I was musing on that base cozening which had drawn on me the anger of my general, the suspicion of some, and the ridicule of others; for the name of "Lieutenant Ogilvie" was, I believed, in the mouth of every man in the Scottish service. I remembered the words of the Spartan, who, on being asked if his sword was sharp, answered, "Yes, sharper even than calumny;" and was revolving how mine could probe the affair of Callander Wood, and unmask the perfidious traitor who deceived me there, when I perceived a poor wanderer clad in rags approaching me. He leaned on a knotted staff; his figure was tall, but rather graceful and familiar to my eye. He came straight up and accosted me, on which I sprang to my feet.

"Heavens! can this be possible!" was my exclamation.

This mendicant, so miserable in aspect, was Patrick Master of Oliphant, the most gallant of our cavalier officers.

"Praised be God, I am again among the Black Dragoons," said he. "What, Harry Ogilvie, is it thee?"

"Welcome," said I, taking both his hands in mine; "welcome, dear Oliphant—this is indeed an unexpected joy!"

"An unexpected meeting you mean, Harry; I cannot vouch much for the *joy* of it."

"But whence this woeful plight? Why, man, thou art a veritable gaberlunzie, and lack but a wallet, ' with spindles and whorles for they wha neid,' to be complete. Poor Patrick, I saw thee cloven down close by me——"

"By yonder burly sectary——"

"Aye, on that black day at Dunbar."

"The blow cost him dear, for I dragged him from his horse, and thrice plunged my shortened sword through his body."

"And your wounded arm?"

"Has troubled me sorely, though now it is almost well; but such a tale I have to tell of suffering and of misery—yes, more than enough to call God's lasting vengeance down on yonder canting regicides who slew King Charles."

He was deathly pale; his cheeks were wan and hollow; his locks, his beard, and moustaches were all grown long and woven together into one black tangled mass; sans shirt and stockings, his attire consisted of a pair of tattered breeches, which had once been velvet, and over all a frock of coarse linen, such as I have seen the peasants of France and England wear.

I conducted him into the house, where Colonel Somerville (we always gave him the Swedish rank, though he was but a captain in Scotland), old Drumstanchel, and Linn, with the gudeman and gudewife, spared no pains to make him comfortable. Fresh logs were heaped on the warm winter hearth; the candles were trimmed anew, a smoking jorum of whiskey toddy was brewed by the colonel, and a steaming dish of hot and savoury collops placed before him; and after a time we heard his story, which he told briefly and in a few words; but though few, they sufficed to inflame our national animosity against the invaders of our realm; and albeit the horrors he related are incorporated with the histories of the war and of the time, I cannot forbear rehearsing them shortly here.

CHAPTER XL.

PATRICK, MASTER OF OLIPHANT.

"ABOUT five thousand of the prisoners who were taken at Dunbar" (began this young noble), " being found able to march, were ordered towards England by General Cromwell, and I was thrust among them, being an officer and the son of a Scottish peer; for it is a maxim with these sectaries, to level all ranks and to acknowledge none.

"We were stripped of almost every article of clothing by Sir Arthur Hesilrig's soldiers, who guarded us. Our purses, rings, watches, sleeve buttons, and every ornament and article of value, however trifling, was torn from us. We received blows from the butt-ends of muskets, cuts from swords, and an incessant torrent of abuse mingled with hard scriptural names, pious objurgations, and long harangues. But as we obtained neither pay nor provisions, we were soon reduced to starvation and despair. I was marched on foot among some privates of Marshal Leven's regiment; the poor fellows did all in their power to alleviate my sufferings, which, as my wounded arm was undressed, were excruciating, till I reached Berwick, where I found a man of pills and potions, who applied a bandage and other remedies, in mere christian charity.

"From Berwick, Hesilrig marched us under a guard of horse to Morpeth; and as our miserable men had not received a morsel of food since they breakfasted on the Doonhill of Dunbar, the morning before the battle, they were now weak, fainting, and raving with hunger, amid the boasted plenty of England; and their sole relief consisted in reviling the Scottish clergy, Argyle, Warriston, and others, who had taught them to despise the orders of their officers, and assumed the gift of prophecy to lure them from their strong position. I repeatedly complained to Hesilrig, but he mocked me as 'a pitiful patch—a Scots zany,' and so forth. Zounds! how my blood boils up at the recollection of these things!

"At Morpeth we broke through all restraint, and neither swords nor carbines could restrain us. We devoured a field of raw cabbages amid the laughter of the military saints who guarded us; we ate the very leaves—ay, the half-withered leaves off the hedges and trees that bordered the roadway. It was an awful scene, sirs, to behold five thousand men, fashioned in the image of God, devouring, like wild animals, this swinish repast, and this was in a so-called Christian land! But *march* again was the word; and then the ever-infamous Hesilrig—doubtless a worthy descendant of that Hesilrig who murdered the wife and little ones of Wallace—when he had tired of laughing at the scene, drove us like a herd of wild animals to Newcastle. The distance was only nine English miles; but such was the effect of the raw leaves upon us, that, in this short distance, *two thousand* men died by the wayside, and only three thousand entered Newcastle, cold, naked, weary, footsore, sick, and sinking!

"So much for the ferocious fanaticism and sham piety of the Puritans!

"There, without other food or refreshment, we were thrust into the church of St. Nicholas, where many died in the night; and I counted seventy-three almost expiring in the great aisle when the trumpet blew for the march next morning. Many more perished on the road to Durham, and most of these were shot dead because their excessive weariness incommoded and delayed the progress of the rest. Major Hobson's troopers alone pistolled thirty-two.

"Only a few hundreds survived to reach the city of Durham, where we were crowded into the bishop's castle; and there our sorrows partly ended, as we were no longer under the control of Sir Arthur Hesilrig, and as the citizens had mercy upon us, and supplied us with food, fuel, and even with clothing."

"Prisoners starved!" said Drumstanchel, with a mighty oath. "Well, when I served the Duke Muscovy, I saw prisoners impaled by the Turks and roasted alive by the barbarous Kurds; but I never thought we should hear of more than four thousand Scottish men being murdered thus on English ground."*

"Go on, Oliphant," said Linn, biting his glove, while the gudewife wept, and the laird gnawed his nether lip, at the narrative; "*our* day of retribution will come."

"Now, at Durham a deadly fever broke out among us, and every morning a few of my miserable companions were found dead, stark and stiff, on their beds of straw, and were borne away on hand-barrows by the English soldiers, to be buried coffinless in deep pits that lay beyond the castle-wall; for no one cared to be at the expense or trouble of decently interring the wretched captives. Weak, faint, and ill, I hourly expected that *my* turn was coming next; but the loss of blood I had suffered from my wound probably saved me; and though many perished who seemed stronger than I, yet by the mercy of Heaven I escaped; and the marshal of the castle, on discovering that I was son and heir of the Lord Oliphant, and, moreover, an officer of cavalry, allowed me the liberty of traversing the whole castle; but none could go a yard beyond its walls without the risk of being instantly shot.

"A month slipped away, wearily and drearily, and no tidings ever reached us in our prison of what was occurring at home.

"One evening I sat moodily at the castle gate. The sunset, though a winter one, was clear and bright, and a red glow shone on the square towers of that grand cathedral church which was built by Malcolm III., of Scotland, when all the northern counties of England were ours, on the broad waters of the Wear, and the russet woods that clothed its banks. I was thinking sadly of you all, and of my own home among the Perthshire hills,

<hr>

* All fact. See Notes.

N 2

where my mother and sisters were, perhaps, sitting mournfully by the stone fireplace in the old hall of Aberdalgie, while the winter blast strewed the spoil of Dupplin woods along the banks of the pastoral Earn, and I knew they would be lamenting me as one who was with the dead. While my mind was full of these thoughts, the sound of hoofs made me look up, and rising hastily, I saluted a lady who rode in, attended by an armed servant.

"She was young and handsome, with bright blue English eyes, and a profusion of chesnut hair. She gave me a glance of pity as she passed, for I was pale and wan as a spectre, with a long beard, and attire that was not very select, as it consisted only of my breeches and shirt, with a beard that had never been shaved since the morning of Dunbar. Opening the purse at her girdle, she very cleverly threw a guinea *into* my hat, and whipping up her horse, cantered into the court, to visit the marshal's wife.

"'Sdeath! low as I had been brought, this was neither to be accepted nor borne.

"'Here, fellow,' I cried to the servant, 'a thousand thanks to your fair mistress for her kindness, but say that I am unaccustomed to receive it in this fashion. Pocket this gold piece and begone. But stay one moment—*who* is your lady?'

"'Mistress Harriet Morton, daughter of my lord, the Bishop of Durham.'

"'Thank you; pray tell her that I am Patrick, Master of Oliphant, an officer of Scottish cavalry, and am unused to charity.'

"The fellow pocketed the guinea, and followed his pretty mistress. Whether he repeated all I said, whether the bishop's daughter inquired about me, or whether the marshal's garrulous wife informed her who I was, I know not; but before leaving the castle, about an hour after, she walked her horse straight up to me, and said, in the most charming accent in the world,

"'I crave your pardon, gentle sir, for when I offered you my mite, it was done in ignorance that I was addressing a gentleman of rank. I feel for you deeply, sir, and for all who fight for the king. My father is Thomas Morton, Bishop of Durham, formerly of Coventry and Lichfield; but now, ejected from his palace by the puritans, he dare neither preach to the people nor appear in his canonicals, which they style the garments of Babylou. My heart feels the greatest sorrow, believe me, when I see a Scottish cavalier-noble reduced so low; and again I beg you to pardon me for offering you money, and to be assured that I will lose no time in endeavouring to alleviate your situation; and so, sir, fare you well.'

" ' Sweet madam, fare you well,' said I; and like a notable blockhead, allowed her to go without saying more.

" She whipped up her horse, scampered through the castle gate, and was gone in a minute; but the kind expression of her gentle face, and the soft, modulated tones of her voice, yet lingered in my memory, and that night, on my truss of straw, I dreamed more than once of this blooming English face, shaded by its broad hat, its chesnut curls, and waving feather, and was glad that at last I had found something English that might be thought of without anger and impatience.

" It was now the 8th of November, and there were only *six hundred* Scotsmen alive in Durham.

" The bishop's servant, a witless, but honest Saxon boor, whose hair resembled a bunch of flax, and whose mouth gaped like a mussel-shell, came repeatedly to the castle after this inter-view, and always brought me a basket containing wine, cold fowls, bread, &c.; and these I shared to the last drop and crumb, so far as they would go, among my poor comrades.

" One day, when loitering about the castle gate, I again saw the fair daughter of the bishop ride in. On this occasion, she was accompanied by a gentleman, and I felt piqued to find her thus attended; but dropped my tattered hat (oh, what a beaver it was for a cavalier!) and thanked her for the many kindnesses I had received; but beckoning me a little way within the gate, and beyond earshot of the watchful Puritans (two of Hobson's dismounted troopers being always there as sentinels), she said, while the colour heightened in her cheek,—

" ' Have you the courage to attempt an escape, if the means are afforded you ?'

" ' Madam, I have the courage to attempt anything you may do me the honour of suggesting; moreover, the native rashness of my heart is sharpened by desperation; but in escaping, I leave my poor comrades behind.'

" ' That cannot be helped,' she replied, sorrowfully; " you have not a day—not an hour to lose, as all the prisoners here, without distinction of rank or person, are ordered by our lawless English parliament to embark for Virginia, to become the slaves of our planters.'

" ' Dare your parliament of England so violate the law of nations and the customs of war ?'

" ' You forget, sir,' replied this cavalier dame, ' that this parliament of England brought its king to a scaffold, and there slew him in the face of the people.'

" ' Should this be their mode of making war, the estates of Scotland will wage an eternal strife, that shall ruin all the isle of Britain; and vengeance will be the whole task of our lives.'

" ' But about your escape, sir——'

" ' Lady, alas, I see no way, and can think of none. These fierce and uncompromising Puritans, with loaded carbines, guard every part of the walls by day, and by night, too, even when gates are securely locked, and all the prisoners have been numbered; though death is thinning fast their roll.'

" ' My brother; this gentleman is my brother (thank heaven! thought I), Mr. Anthony Morton; he has a suggestion to make.'

" As she spoke, this person, a sallow-visaged, but handsome young man, of a bold bearing, a *roué* and debauched aspect, approached, with a jaunty air.

" ' Zounds, sir !' said he; ' I do not half like being involved in this piece of work; but women are infernally wilful, and my sister Harriet has her full share of this disposition; moreover, my father, the bishop, is inclined to serve you, having heard that you are the son of a Scottish noble; but say not a word of all this, sir, as it would cause our destruction—our irreparable ruin.'

" ' If you mistrust my honour, sir, leave me to my miserable fate.'

" ' The truth is, sir, your fate is a matter I care very little about; but my father and sister are the prime movers in this projected escape; for myself, I beg to inform you that I am an officer in the service of the English parliament.'

" ' You—*her* brother ?'

" ' He needs must whom the devil drives; and my devil is poverty. The parliament pays well; and we have no king now. But to return; you cannot come out of Durham Castle as a living man, so what say you to leave it as a dead one ?'

" ' Sir, if you come but to jest with my misery——'

" ' Nay, nay,' said he, laughing, ' I came on quite another errand.'

" ' Then you speak in enigmas.'

" ' Listen; 'tis an idea I have, though it shocks poor Harriet sadly, and my father, the old bishop, calls it sacrilege, and worthy the invention of one so lost as I, for he who serves the Parliament is doubly damned, according to orthodox views of all nighflying churchmen.'

" ' To the point, sir ;—your proposal ?'

" ' It is this. A day seldom passes without three or four dead prisoners being borne out in the parish shells to the charnel-house, near the cathedral, for interment.'

" ' True, sir; and two poor soldiers of our Royal Life Guard are now lying dead on their beds of straw.'

" ' So much the better. My idea is this. Endeavour to assume

the place of one of those dead men to-night, when the porters
come to bear away the shells. You will thus be carried out of
the fortress, and I will meet you at the dead-house, near the
cathedral. Then leave the rest to fortune and to me. Dost
understand?'

"'I do fully,' said I, 'and thank you with all my soul.'

"'Then think of it, and I will not forget. So now, as we
have spoken long enough together, we had better part; and so
fare you well, sir.'

"'Sir, fare you well,' added the pretty girl who accompanied
this facile republican; and smiling a kind adieu, they cantered
from the castle, and left me.

"I had ample matter for reflection; and though there was something to me repugnant in feigning death, and assuming a dead
man's place, as it could do *him* no harm, and I had been so
accustomed to horrors ever since that fatal day at Dunbar, I
soon cared in reality less for the act than at other times I might
have done, in adopting a quaint costume or disguise, and
felt pleased that I would probably be enabled to steal a
march upon the cruel Major Hobson and the canting castle
marshal.

"The dreary November day lagged slowly on; evening came
at last; and as darkness stole over the old cathedral city and
the waters of the Wear which sweep around it, my heart swelled
with anxiety; and just as the dusk closed in, and before the
barrier gates of the old fortress were secured, I saw the porters
or bearers of the dead arrive; for they generally came under
cloud of night to convey our deceased comrades to the charnel-
house. The deaths being fewer now, because there were fewer
of us to die, our dead were no longer interred in pits, but in
regularly dug graves, which contained two, three, or four, according to the casualties of the day.

"After responding to my name when the list of the prisoners
was called over by Noah Shufflebotham, one of Major Hobson's
sergeants, instead of lying down as usual on my wretched pallet
of straw, I slipped away, and reached the outhouse where the
dead men lay, and entering by a window which stood constantly
open, found myself in a gloomy, little vaulted den, where three
rough shells of common deal, shaped coffinwise, painted black,
and having spoke handles, lay upon the pavement. A momentary
chill came over me, as I saw these grim objects in the gloom of
the descending night; but my ears began to tingle and my
pulses to beat like lightning, when I heard voices in the yard
and footsteps on the gravel. They were approaching, and not a
moment was to be lost, if I would be free!

"I raised the lid of one of those uncouth biers, and saw the tall form of a dead soldier in the tattered finery of the Scottish Life Guards, and coldly the wan moonlight streamed through the open window on his pale features, shrunken and emaciated by famine and disease. My conscience smote me, and that strange chill returned as I threw my arms around the body, and endeavoured to drag it out of the temporary coffin, intending to deposit it in that part of the chamber which was shrouded in darkness. But I was too weak, or the dead corpse was too heavy for me. The guardsman was of gigantic stature ; I could scarcely raise him, and with a sigh of bitterness let fall the lid.

"The voices were nearer now! A perspiration broke over me, and clenching my teeth, I rushed to the bier of the next dead soldier. Whether he was more wasted by disease, and hence was lighter ; or whether desperation had endued me with fresh vigour, I know not ; but I soon dragged the body into the dark corner, threw myself breathlessly into the noisome shell, and had only time to close the lid, which was hinged, when a key was inserted in the chamber door ; the lock was turned, and the sergeant, who had so lately called the roll, entered with the bearers, six in number.

"'Brother Shufflebotham,' asked one through his nose, 'how many are there to-night?'

"'Two,' snuffled the sergeant, in the same intoned voice, and pausing in a hymn which he had been singing ; in quick succession he opened and again banged down the lids of the shells ; 'just two, and a plaguy tall fellow this Amorite hath been.'

"'Two!' growled one of the bearers ; 'then what the devil do you call this here?' he added, stumbling over the body in the corner ; and now deeming discovery certain, I felt my heart stand still, for any prisoner caught in the act of escaping was pistolled without mercy.

"'Verily, there were but two this morning ; look into the shells again, brother,' said Sergeant Shufflebotham.

"'All right, I tell thee ; there are two in the shells still enough,' said one of the bearers.

"'Then this must be one we have missed last night,' said another, 'so tumble him into that empty shell, and let us begone ere the gates close. A Scot more or less will not be missed by the marshal—eh, Sergeant Shufflebotham?'

"'Verily and truly no ; for these Amorites perish as if all the plagues of Egypt were among them.'

"In another minute my two grim companions and I were lifted and borne out, and I soon heard the heavy clank of the castle gates (a welcome sound) as they were barred behind us, and the cracked voice of Sergeant Noah Shufflebotham dying away in dismal quavers as he resumed his hymn, the burden of which

was something to this purpose, as we may find it in ' Fig-leaves,
by a God-fearing Fifer'—

> " I like a bottle am become,
>   With holy spirit fill—ed ;
>   Lord ! let me not by wickedness,
>   Be overthrown and spill—ed."

" I became more and more excited as the distance increased
between us and the castle, and consequently lessened between me
and the cathedral, where the grand discovery must take place ;
but even six unarmed porters were less dangerous antagonists
than *one* of Cromwell's armed puritans.   Strange thoughts came
into my mind.   What would be my fate if I should fall into a
fit by weakness and excitement, or mere over-tension of the ner-
vous system ?

" I should be buried alive !

" I breathed hard, and endeavoured to control my wild fancies,
as I had no wish to perish like Acilius Aviola, the Roman citizen,
or the Prætor Lamiæ, of whom we used to read at old St. Mungo.
Being almost suffocated in that hideous and unwholesome box, I
frequently raised the lid a little for breath and air, and was glad
to perceive that the streets were silent and empty, and as dark
and foggy as a chill November eve could make them.   At last
we reached the cathedral, and the deep full sonorous notes of its
bell clock striking eight seemed to ring out just above me, as
the three shells were flung carelessly on the pavement, and the
door of the charnel-house jarred as it was pushed open.

" The moment for decisive action had come ; so raising the lid
of my shell, I looked warily round me.   Two of the porters had
borne one of the bodies into the vault where the dead usually
lay, till the sextons were at leisure to inter them ; most fortunately for me, the other four had slipped aside into an alehouse
near the cathedral, or built between two buttresses of it.

" I leaped out and hurried away, without looking once behind
me.

" Running round the great church, animated only by the vague
craving to find a place of concealment, I suddenly found myself
grasped by a man.

" ' 'Sdeath and fury ! let me go, or I will strangle you !' I exclaimed, full of rage, and believing that I had been discovered ;
' I will never be taken alive—your English puritans shall no
longer play the cur with me !'

" ' Hush—how, sir—have you forgotten—is this acting like a
discreet gentleman ?   Zounds, sir, 'tis I—Anthony Morton, who
promised to meet you here.'

" ' Alas, sir,' said I, having altogether forgotten him in the
confusion of my thoughts ; ' can you pardon me, for my fatal
outcry may have ruined all '

"'Hush, I say, and no excuses—this way, this way. You have managed this admirably; there will soon be a devil of a hue and cry, for those fellows who carried the shells were scared out of their seven senses on finding that one of their dead men had evaporated; but old Hobson, whom I know well, will at once suspect the trick you have played him, and have the whole country scoured. Can you swim?'

"'Like a fish.'

"'All the better.'

"'But why?'

"'Because the Wear is before us yet, and Hobson has a guard at the bridge.'

"I cursed Hobson with all my heart, and longed for the time when I might punish the barbarities to which he had subjected us. We hurried along a dark and narrow street, overhung by quaint old gables and galleries of wood, and reached a place known to Morton, where the old and ruinous wall of the city was so low that we could drop from it. On doing so we found ourselves in a garden, through which we sprang, making sad havoc among some worthy gammer's winter worts; and notwithstanding the coldness of the season, we plunged boldly and without a moment's hesitation into the Wear, at a place where its waters being deep were unguarded, and there we swam steadily across.

"'How shall I thank you for all this trouble, care, and risk on my account?' said I to Morton.

"'Thank me by doing so much for me if I by evil chance should be similarly situated in Scotland. Now I might have had horses waiting; but it is wiser to walk than to ride after a cold dip like that, in a November night—so let us push on for my father's house.'

"'Is it possible that you are an officer of the English Commonwealth?'

"'Quite—and it is equally possible that I might have been an officer of the king had he been alive to pay me; for we Englishmen must feed ourselves well, and cannot serve sans pay, like those Scots cavaliers who fought the eight battles of Montrose. No, no; we must have our well-roasted beef and our nut-brown beer; and as old Noll pays his privates eightpence per day of good English money, his officers have always enough and to spare. I am a lieutenant in the regiment of Overton. But say no more of this,' he added, with something of irritation, 'for I hear enough about it from my father the bishop.'

"He guided me for three or four miles through a beautifully-wooded district, where the old and narrow paths were all bordered by hedges and shaded by trees. The moon was up now, and I saw the square towers of King Malcolm's cathedral reddened by her dun and hazy light. Turning off by a narrow and grassy footway through the fallow fields, he conducted me to a picturesque mansion, which had steep gables of carved oak, a rustic porch, and little latticed windows, having brick mullions and clustered chimneys, over which the leafless woodbine and honeysuckle clambered in masses with the dark green ivy, and where many a swallow and pigeon had their nests.

"Lieutenant Morton conducted me to an apartment on the ground floor, where a large fire of logs and coal was blazing and sparkling on the spacious hearth ; and where he gave me from a buffet a silver cup full of brandy and water, saying,

"'Drain that at a draught, my bonny Scot, to keep the cold out.'

"The aspect of this mansion, with its high-backed chairs, all richly carved, cushioned, and surmounted by gilded crests ; its soft straw mats upon the polished floor ; its family portraits panelled into the oak wainscoting ; its mullioned windows full of painted lozenges ; and its carved doors screened by heavy drapery or rich arras, all indicative of old English comfort, and of long years of peace, of ease and pleasure ; in everything so unlike the garrisoned manors and moated towers of Scotland, seemed strange and new to me, who for such a long period had known no other home than the wet flapping tents of Leslie's camp ; and latterly, the straw couches, the starvation and horrors of Hobson's prison-house.

"In the recess of an oriel window were a bird's cage, some flowers, needlework, a book, a cythara, a flageolet, and a pretty little glove, all indicative of fair inmates that were not far off.

"In a few minutes an old gentleman of a most benign and prepossessing aspect appeared, and bade me welcome, with great kindness of manner. He wore a black cassock and callote cap, for he was the Lord Bishop of Durham.

"'May God bless you (though a Scot), Master of Oliphant,' said he, 'and all who fight for his sacred majesty, the king.'

"At this his son whistled, and the pale face of the bishop reddened as he pointed to a chair, and bade me 'be seated;' for the defection of this youth from the royal cause—or his utter indifference thereto, was a source of great grief to this right reverend prelate, whom I could not treat otherwise than with profound respect, although we know of no such dignitaries within the kingdom of Scotland. But Master Anthony was one who had wasted his private means in gambling, tavern-brawling, horse-racing, and every manner of ribaldry ; thus, for subsistence, and to be independent of his father, whose fortune was somewhat impaired by the late civil war in England, he had joined the army to fight against the king in Scotland ; though the old bishop would rather have seen him in his coffin, than armed 'against Heaven's anointed.'

"When the Scottish army under Marshal Leven, then General Sir Alexander Leslie, captured the Palatinate of Durham, ten years before, Bishop Morton and his clergy deserted the cathedral, and from that time the see had been dissolved. He was thus not overwell disposed towards the Scots in general; yet, during the week I remained with him, nothing could equal his kindness to me."

"But how is it that we have heard nothing about the bishop's pretty daughter?" said Linn; "nothing, at least, save that her glove was lying on the table."

"You perhaps anticipate that I have a charming love-story to tell, but be assured that never were you more mistaken. Harriet Morton was every way attractive, and I beseech you to imagine her thick soft hair, her sunny smiling eyes, her delicate eyebrows traced as it were by the pencil of Vandyke, her dainty nose with its proud little nostrils, her perfect mouth and chin, her plump little figure, her buoyancy and a certain *espiéglerie*, which make her the exact counterpart of Dora Lennox, whom everyone in Edinburgh knows as well as St. Giles's steeple."

"Well," said Linn, colouring in turn; "this *does* look somewhat like the beginning of a love-story."

"While her brother (whose rough, boisterous, and swaggering manner I disliked quite as much as many strange points I detected in his loose, reckless, and desperate character) was making arrangements for my transmission or escape across the borders, all my time was spent either with the old bishop or his daughter—generally with the latter; as to avoid the risk of betrayal, my presence was concealed from all the servants, save one, an old and faithful adherent of the family. Thus, for several hours daily I had an opportunity for cultivating the friendship of this beautiful girl. We read the same books; we sang the same songs; we sketched the same old gnarled tree at the same time, and then compared the result of our labours. Immersed in correspondence with the fugitive Rupert and the English cavaliers, the dreamy old bishop left us to ourselves; and for seven short and happy days this delightful intercourse continued almost without interruption, and unknown to all, save the aged servant, with whom I was a great favourite, for he had been a soldier in his youth in Captain Morton's company, under Sir Horace Vere, Lord of Tilbury; and his life had been saved from the Croats by some of Sir Audrew Gray's Scots at the great Bohemian battle of Fleura.

"Conceive the charm of my situation, after the horrors of the past two months, to be thrown constantly into the society of a bright, beautiful, and witty English girl! She incited me to build a thousand airy castles, and in the ardour of my esteem for her character and admiration of her loveliness, I gave myself up, unheeded and unchecked, to dreams as dear as they were delusive. The war waged between our countries; the rebellious invasion of Cromwell against our king, and the barbarities to which our prisoners had been subjected, were all forgotten now, and I thought only of how this blooming English flower should be transplanted to the banks of the Earn, and pictured in fancy how the old castle hall at Aberdalgie would ring, when with brimming cups my people hailed her as Harriet, Mistress of Oliphant.

"In the midst of these dreams her brother announced to me that horses were prepared, and that on *this* very night, after dusk, disguised as an English yeoman in a large canvas gaberdine, I must depart towards the Scottish frontier.

"This brought matters to a crisis, and I ventured to make that declaration which I am vain enough to believe she expected; but, judge of my consternation on being informed, by two very pale and quivering lips, that she was betrothed, plighted, and pledged to her brother's most particular friend, Captain John Thurlow, of Colonel Overton's regiment.

"Her eyes were cast down, and she trembled excessively, on telling me this, and dropped a few tears, murmuring something about 'not daring to displease her brother Anthony.' I perceived that some mystery lurked under her conduct in this engagement, which I could not, or dared not, venture to fathom; but I pressed both her hands to my lips, and at that moment her brother appeared with a riding whip in his hand. He delivered it to me, and this was the appointed signal for my departure.

"'And now,' said he, 'what money have you got?'

"'I have not had a tester in my possession since I was wounded and taken at Dunbar.'

"'Chut! 'tis infernally unlucky, this; you cannot travel without money, and I have lost my last Carlisle sixpence at primero with old Hobson. What the devil shall we do? Run, sister Harriet, like a good girl, and tell the bishop about this.'

"The old bishop came with hands uplifted to bid me farewell, and said with great kindness, that if ever these fatal wars were ended, and a peace re-established between Scotland and England, nothing would afford him greater joy than to welcome again, as a friendly visitor, the son of the Lord Oliphant, whom he remembered to have met at Edinburgh during the coronation of King Charles I. at Holyrood. He begged me to beware of a highwayman who haunted Lanchester heath; on this his son laughed boisterously. He then spoke of his reduced circumstances; of the dilapidation of his cathedral, and the shorn splendour of the English church; and, craving pardon for the slender assistance he could offer me, placed a purse of twenty spur-rials in my hand.

"To have declined would have mortified the good old man, who was sensitive as he was generous; moreover, the current of my thoughts was arrested by the singular expression which I detected in t' eyes of his son.

"'Twenty spur-rials—and I don't own a doit in the world!' I heard him mutter, while his eyes seemed to glare for an instant as they gloated on the wretched twenty pieces of gold. I saw it all in a moment. The spendthrift and ruined gamester grudged or coveted the sum his generous father had given me; but there was no time for parley. Our horses stood at the private door, and the night was dark and moonless. I pressed the old bishop's hand, kissed his daughter's brow, and, with a bursting heart, set forth at a rapid trot, with Master Anthony Morton, who was to guide me for a few miles on the road towards Scotland, the nearest town of which, Cannobie, was seventy English miles distant.

"One circumstance particularly impressed me as we left the bridle path which led from the bishop's gate. The old valet who held it open, as I was passing out, shook my hand, and whispered,

"'For God's love, sir, beware of Master Anthony, and examine your pistols after he leaves you!'

"The pallor of the old man's face, and the earnestness of his voice, deeply impressed me; and both lingered long in my memory after I had left the poor fellow for ever.

"After riding in silence together for some time, until the last of the lights of Durham had disappeared in our rear, I drew up, and giving many thanks to Mr. Morton, begged him to return, to which he made no objections. Then remembering the expression of his face, I said, that the kind and reverend lord, his father, had given me twenty spur-rials to carry me to Scotland, but that five were quite sufficient; would he now do me the favour of accepting the remaining fifteen.

"'Grant me mercy,' said he, 'Master of Oliphant; for what manner of man do you take me? Nay, nay, sir; I give you many thanks. The road lies straight before you to Whitefield, at the little change-house beyond which you will find a relay of horses; but when you cross the moor near Lanchester, three miles from this, be wary, as it is haunted by a dangerous foot-pad. Farewell!'

"He wheeled round his horse and galloped off."

"By my soul," said Drumstauchel, "he should have escorted you over the moor."

"So thought I then; but remembering the words of the valet, I examined my holster pistols—a pair which the bishop had given me. Though I had loaded them that morning with care, the balls had been *drawn;* by whom, Heaven only knew; but I carefully charged them again, and rode briskly on at a trot. After passing several villages, churches, and manor houses, the path became more sequestered; and now, unlit by moon or star, the flat moor of Lanchester spread before me, and I had some diffi- culty in keeping the right track.

"All was still as death, and I heard only my own hard breathing and the clank of my horse's hoofs, till suddenly, on the soft moor, I detected a sound, and lo! close to me, on my right hand, towered the dark figure of a horseman. He was approaching swiftly, but all in black outline, for he wore a cloak, a mask, and broad Spanish beaver flapped over his face. Oho! the highway- man! thought I.

"'Soho, sir,' said he, in a gruff voice; 'what's o'clock?'

"'Twelve, past so long, that you'll have a hard ride to overtake it,' said I, quietly drawing a pistol from my holsters.

"'Stop, sir—a word with you,' he cried, with an oath.

"'Well, sir,' I replied; 'your business?'

"'Simply your purse or your brains,' cried this ruffler or bully, coming fearlessly up with a pistol levelled straight at my teeth. 'Which am I to take?'

"'Neither, thou scurvy rascal,' said I, and shot him right through the shoulder. His pistol exploded; the ball grazed my ear, and his horse swerved furiously round, hurling him heavily to the earth, and then it stood still like a well-trained charger.

"I dismounted, and found him groaning and bleeding. On tearing the mask of black taffeta from his face, judge of my horror and astonishment to find this assailant to be Anthony Morton—the brother of the beloved Harriet—the son of the amiable old bishop!

"For some time I stood like one who had been turned to stone, and heard him addressing me, as he staggered to his feet; but though I scarcely knew what he said, it was somewhat to this purpose:—he was crushed by shame and remorse that I had discovered him to be the son of the Bishop of Durham—the very man whose hospitality I had so recently been sharing, and one of the social companions of my residence there for the last week; but ruined by wanton gypsies and bold-pated wittolds, and by gambling rendered desperate and penniless, he had for some months haunted the heath, and resorted to this infamous and nefarious mode of recruiting his finances. He had thus be- come a robber of his father's guest; for the sight of the twenty golden spur-rials had excited his cupidity beyond all control.

"I was grieved and mortified by this humiliating revelation, and pitied him more than he deserved. I bound up his wound as well as circumstances would permit; remounted him; and placing in his pocket, whether he would have it so or not, the fifteen rials proffered before, bade him adieu, and, with a sad-dened heart, I watched him riding slowly back along the path I could never again pursue.

"Whether or not he had intended to shoot me, I cannot say; but at Whitefield there was *no* fresh horse awaiting me; and on my reaching the little change-house early in the morning, and in-quiring for another nag, the rosy mistress, whom I had just roused from bed, stared, and feeling somewhat suspicious about me, bade me begone—adding, that though she was a lone widow, she had a large dog and plenty of help at hand. But I was resolved to spare no pains to conciliate her, and procure a fresh horse; so assuming something of my old dragoon swagger, I threw down a rial, and called for a cup of wine, of which I in-sisted she should first take the half.

"'Your health, my pretty one,' said I, 'and the health of the happy fellow whom you accept for a husband.'

"'I don't know,' said she, pouting, 'whether you be yeoman or gentleman; but I am sure, sir, that when I first saw you in that coarse gaberdine, I took you for some paltry cockrel assum-ing the air of a gallant which did not become him. But here is your health, sir; and a safe journey to you.'

"'What, my pretty one! without a fresh horse?'

"In three minutes it was saddled and at the door; this was the effect of judicious management, and a little innocent flattery. I slipped another rial into her hand, for which she gave me a torrent of thanks; but I soon stopped her mouth.'

"How?" asked Linn.

"By the only mode of stopping a woman's mouth—kissing it; and mounting, I rode off in time to escape a tap on the head from a pair of steel poking-sticks, which were heating in the fire to plait her ruffs.

"Without accident I got clear of England, crossed the borders, and reached Cannobie, among the woods in Dumfries-shire, where I found shelter for a time in the old Tower of the Hollows. After that, I fell among the mosstroopers—some wild Johnstones, who were lurking in that huge serbonian bog, the moss of Tarras. They sacked a farmhouse where I was sleeping one night; shot the gudeman, houghed his cattle, and took away my horse, saddle, and holsters, my boots and my last rial, reducing me to the state in which you found me. Edinburgh, and all the roads leading to it, are covered by Cromwell's patrols; thus I had great diffi-culty in making my way towards Leslie's headquarters; and it is by the most slender chance in the world that I have fallen to-night so happily among my old comrades of the Black Dra-goons."

The night was far advanced before Oliphant concluded; but our landlord, the Moss Laird, brewed a fresh bowl, while we renewed our congratulations on the many escapes of our comrade, and rehearsed to him all that had taken place since our retreat from Dunbar.

"And so you really fell in love with this little Englishwoman?" said Linn, as the hot punch went round for the tenth or twelfth time.

"Yes, and would have married her; but have *you* not married Dora Lennox yet?"

"'Pon my faith, Oliphant, I was beginning to think of it."

"Long may you continue only to *think* of it," grumbled old Drumstanchel, who, it was averred, had one wife in Russia and another in the Low Countries.

"You would then be laird of Lennox Tower," said I.

"Not exactly; Sir Henry is a hearty old fellow, and likely to live for the next hundred years; and I wish he may do so, with all my heart."

"Before any of us think of marrying, sirs," said Colonel Somerville, "we must clear Scotland of these English puritans."

"Right," said Linn; "and meanwhile, I'll feed myself on love."

"Deevilish puir provant you will find it," added old Drumstanchel, with a cynical smile.

"Besides, I fear little Dora may think me too wedded to soldiering——"

"To *wed* her, eh?" said I; and thus, amid banter and fun, interspersed with songs, the night slipped into the morning, and the winter sun began to gild the hills of Airth and Dunmore before we separated. I need scarcely remind my readers, that all the horrors related by the gallant Master of Oliphant are fully corroborated by the reports of Major Hobson and the proceedings of the English parliament; and while it is undeniable that, when fighting in Scotland, the bearing of Cromwell was gentle, charitable, honourable, and conciliatory, the conduct of the servile Monk, of Hesilrig, and some others who commanded his troops, was base, butcherly, infamous, and cruel.

CHAPTER XLI.

CAPTAIN AUGUSTINE.

ALL continued quiet for some time, and nothing occurred save one desperate piece of service, in which I had the honour to bear a part.

The month of December had now arrived. The woods were

leafless, stripped, and naked; the spoil of the past summer rustled in every passing breeze; the hills were bleak and barren in aspect, or heavily mantled with snow. The linns and lochs were frozen, the air intensely cold, and all the marshes and mosses about Dunmore were reduced to the consistency of flint. From the farm-houses, the old baronial towers, and the thatched villages which nestled near them, the broad black smoke of the winter fires curled into the clear air in heavy columns, and everything announced the close of the year, the decay of nature, and the repose of labour; but there was no rest for us.

Cromwell remained at Edinburgh in very bad health, and superintending the siege of the castle, which he closely blockaded, daily cannonading it, and endeavouring to breach the Half Moon by mining; but so bravely was it defended, that he despaired of capturing it by ordinary means. Yet our gallant soldiers contended in vain; for their leaders, Colonel Dundas, of that ilk, and Major Abernethy, with certain divines who had taken shelter there, were as thorough-paced traitors as any that ever fought against the king.

In these wars, there was a certain soldier of fortune, named Captain Augustine, by birth a high German, who had followed Marshal Leven from the campaign in Westphalia, and who had served gallantly as an officer in the Scottish Cavalry; but being somewhat of a roisterer, who loved his glass of Rhenish, a pipe of tobacco, and occasionally did *not* dislike pretty girls, he made himself obnoxious to the Earl of Argyle and the Commission of the Kirk; and being deprived of his rank on the night before the battle of Dunbar, he collected about twenty mounted men, with whom he daily and nightly harassed the English, making his retreat at one time among the Pentland hills, at another to the Lammermuir or Soltra.

A week seldom passed without something gallant being done by the discarded Captain Augustine. Once he broke into Cromwell's quarters, and slew three officers and thirty men; and everywhere he cut off his patrols. Thus our soldiers extolled his bravery, while the peasantry idolised him. "The noble Captain Augustine—the gallant High German!" was in the mouths of all. At last he discovered that the garrison in the castle of Edinburgh was in great straits by the want of bread and wine; and he immediately communicated his information to General Leslie, offering, if two hundred dragoons were placed at his disposal, to cut a passage through Cromwell's guards, and supply the fortress.

This offer from the poor cashiered German officer charmed General Leslie, raised the ardour of us all, and on two hundred volunteers from the cavalry being required to follow him on this desperate and hazardous expedition, nearly all the officers of the seven brigades of horse sent in their names; but Leslie said,

"This will never do, sirs, for if my officers are killed, who will remain to lead their men?"

The number of officers was restricted to one hundred, and of these Halkett's brigade furnished a fair proportion. The hundred private troopers were mostly taken from the Black Dragoons and Life Guards; and although I was one of that party, I may be pardoned in saying that two hundred better mounted, better equipped, or braver cavaliers did not exist in Christendom. On the evening of Wednesday, the 16th of December, we were to rendezvous at Wallace's Oak, in the Torwood, in full marching order; and the quartermaster-general was to supply us with two hundred small runlets of whiskey and two hundred bags of bread, which we were to carry with us for the garrison of Edinburgh Castle. On the 12th they had been summoned in the name of the English parliament, and had replied by a storm of shot and shell.

The expedition was kept secret; and for some days before we thought of nothing and spoke of nothing else but Augustine and his enterprise, and daily we superintended the grooming of our horses, to have them in prime condition on the night of the 16th.

The count, our colonel, had his quarters, as I have said, in the old tower of Dunmore, a mile or two distant from us; and on Tuesday evening I was returning from thence after having dined with him by his own invitation. As I rode home in the dark, over the fields and muirland wastes coated with snow, I was reflecting on his peculiar gravity of manner in general when contrasted with his animation, fire, and energy in action; his coldness to some when compared with the flattering regard with which he distinguished me; then I thought over the strange and wild stories he had told me of his adventures in the war between the Swedes and Imperialists, for the civil and religious liberties of Germany—a contest in which he had commanded a division of three thousand Scottish cuirassiers, when I was roused by a voice calling on me to stop, and reining up my horse, I looked round. A rough, weather-beaten man, buttoned up to the throat, and wearing a broad Lowland bonnet, pulled well over his shaggy eyebrows, rode up to me, mounted on a stout pony. He wore rough boots and spurs, had holsters at his saddle, and a broadsword at his left thigh. The reflected light of the snow made everything distinct, so I could perceive all this well enough.

"So ho! sir; ye are, I believe, Mr. Harry Ogilvie, a lieutenant of the Black Dragoons?" said he, gruffly.

"Yes, sir—but who are you?" I demanded, feeling rather displeased by his abruptness.

"I am one who has been in search of you—that is, I have been waiting until you left the count's residence."

"For what purpose?" I queried, briefly, as this man's face and voice came back to my memory like the fragments of an old and unpleasant dream. "For what purpose?" I reiterated.

"To deliver a message from my lord the Earl of Argyle," he replied, touching his bonnet respectfully at *the* name.

"To me?"

"To you, sir."

"Impossible!"

"Not in the least."

"Well—and this message?"

"Is simply that he wishes to speak with you at the House of Scaithmuir, where he abides at present."

"Well, tell your lord the Earl of Argyle, that I beg to decline the honour of this conference," said I, shortening my reins.

"How," said he, furiously, while his hand went involuntarily towards the basket hilt at his side; "you will not speak to Argyle?"

"No; and who in the name of all the devils are you, that question me in this fashion? You are a seaman, I think?"

"I have been; I commanded the snow *Good Intent*, a trader between Virginia and Glasgow."

"So—so; woe betide you, fellow; you are that Duncan Campbell who, like a wretch as you are, left a poor boy to drown in the waters of the Clyde! But God aided him whom man had abandoned, and in my person he is spared to express his contempt for you to-day."

For some time the man was silenced and confounded by this attack. After several efforts at articulation, and seeming to suffer with emotion, he said,—

"As heaven is my judge, sir, I was in no way to blame for that untoward business. I am but a puir man, whose bread has been earned by the patronage of the Lord Argyle; and if you are indeed that young callant, whom I was ordered by him—my lord, chief, and master—to take to Virginia, I give all praise unto heaven that you escaped the death we thought you had dreéd, and that you are a hale and sound man to-day. There is my thumb on it, sir; I crave your pardon in all gude earnest and amity."

We pressed our thumbs in the old fashion, and then shook hands, after which I touched my horse with the spur.

"Then are you still resolved to decline a meeting with the earl?" said he.

"After the discovery I have just made, how can you expect
it?"

"But he cannot know you to be the callant with whom I
sailed from the Broomielaw."

"He does know it, and his son the Lord Lorn knows it too.
And now, Mr. Campbell, as you have given me your hand in
amity, tell me honestly and truly, as a Scottish seaman and an
honourable man, know you the reason of that most infamous
project to kidnap me in my boyhood?"

"As God hears me, Mr. Ogilvie, I do not! I was told by the
Laird of Ardmohr that such was the desire of our chief, the
earl, and I obeyed, as was my duty, without questioning. Why,
sir, I'd have shipped off the half of Glasgow, if he had ordered
me! But what answer shall I take to Scaithmuir?"

"That I decline."

"I dare not say so to Argyle? Remember, there may be those
who will say you are afraid—you, a soldier."

"Lord Lorn—bah!" said I, with rising anger.

"The Lord Lorn is guarding the king at Scone; but other
men have tongues as well as he."

"Afraid, eh? Nay, no man shall ever say such a word was
even whispered to a Black Dragoon. Lead on, sir; I follow you.
But beware, Duncan Campbell! I have my sword and pistols;
and the first sign of treachery shall cost thee dear; and dearly,
too, shall I sell my life if it is invaded. Had I known that I
was to close the evening by a visit to your Earl, I should certainly have doffed the trappings of a dragoon, as I dislike doing
dirty work in the attire of a soldier."

And taking from their holsters my loaded pistols, I stuck
them in my girdle, and rode after the great Maccallum Mohr's
strange envoy, who whipped his pony into motion, and galloped
along the road, half the length of his barrel-bellied charger
before me.

CHAPTER XLII.

SCAITHMUIR.

AFTER riding on in sullen silence for some time, we found the
road dip down among some naked coppice, where the dry frozen
leaves and snow lay thick together on the ground. Several
lights now began to twinkle before us, casting long white lines
across the snow; and my friend said,—

"This is the Place-house, where my lord the earl bides."

"The great devil spit him!" muttered I, between my teeth;

'ut Flora's upbraiding eyes came before me, and I felt some compunction for my animosity.

The venerable mansion of Scaithmuir reared its fantastic outline against the winter sky.   It presented many styles of architecture; but in the centre rose the square, grim tower of the
first proprietor, Sir Reginald de Moreham, Lord of Abercorn and
Dean (whose father, Sir Herbert, was murdered by Edward I.
of England), and Lord Great Chamberlain of Scotland in 1329,
under David II.   Built in the days of King Alexander the
Fierce, it had been added to in the time of James I., and
demolished by the revolutionists who slew James III.; repaired
in the reign of Mary, it had been partly blown up by the Bandes
Francaises of General d'Esse;   burned down by the Regent
Lennox, it had been rebuilt in the days of James VI.; hence,
after all its vicissitudes and hard service, it was a picturesque
mass of architectural patches, covered with dates and encrusted
with legends, and armorial bearings of the Lindsays, into whose
family it had passed; and hence it had been so often changed,
that had any of its ancient lords arisen from their vaults in the
neighbouring kirk, where they slept each beside his dame, crosslegged, with shield on arm and sword at side, as we may see
them in effigy, not one would have known his old residence.
Around it was a thicket of giant oaks, with gnarled stems, past
which, perhaps, the armies of the Bruces and Plantagenets had
marched; and dark Scottish pines and drooping silver birches, amid
which old rooks cawed in lazy and complacent tones, that declared
they felt themselves quite at home.

How happy, thought I, must those be who possess such old
ancestral dwellings, with the names and achievements of their
fathers carved in stone upon the walls! then I thought of my
own nameless and obscure origin—a paltry regret, and the
emotion of a moment only, for I reflected proudly on the name
and fame I would yet hew out for *myself*, and fence around by
gallant deeds, each of which should be worth a thousand performed by a departed ancestry; for he must indeed possess
small merit in himself, who has to borrow a lustre from the dry
bones of the mouldering dead.

After considerable scrutiny and ceremony by servants who
were either well armed or had weapons at hand, we were
ushered into a chamber of dais; the walls were lofty, and
panelled with oak, hung with portraits of the Mores of Abercorn, the Grahames of Eskdale, and the Lindsays of the Byres.
to whom in other times this princely house belonged, and who
looked grimly from their panels in their steel doublets, high
ruffs, or long fardingales.   The chairs were high-backed and
cumbrous, the cabinets were richly carved, ponderous silver

candlesticks stood upon the table, which was massive and old, for the Chevaliers d'Esse, the Marquise d'Elbœuff, and Gaspare Strozzi, had held wassail round it, in the wars of other years. Now it was littered by papers, letters, pens, and ink, while wine-glasses and a large china jug of claret showed that business had proved but dry work.

The hearth was wide, and in the centre of it stood a basket-grate on four feet, full of blazing coals. Corrie, the stag-hound, was basking before the fire, and snorted as we entered.

Was *she* here?

Near the fire stood a chair, as if some one had just retired, but a man's glove and a sword lay upon it. Opposite to this chair stood another, in which the Earl of Argyle was seated with his legs stretched out before the fire; his elbows rested on the cushioned arms, his hands were folded before him, and he was in deep reverie.

"Malediction on that fellow Duncan—he loiters yet—and the other too! It is impossible she can love him," he muttered, as he gazed into the fire; "is she not my daughter, and proud as she is beautiful? Yet Lorn will have it so—absurd!"

My heart told me who was "the other" referred to; but here my conductor stumbled against a tabourette—the dog growled, and the earl started from his seat.

"Oh, 'tis you, sir—so Duncan has found you at last—welcome to Scaithmuir," said he, with a bow of lofty condescension; "welcome even in this spring time of Zion's trouble and affliction; but let our feet not slide in the hour of temptation, for the kirk shall yet be triumphant."

This noble, who never omitted an opportunity of interlarding his discourse with clumsy fragments of piety, now filled up a glass of claret for me—claret in that winter night, cold as his own heart—and I drank it in silence, while he made a signal to my conductor to withdraw, and pushed a chair towards me; but I was resolved not to sit, and asked in a very reserved manner,

"To what am I indebted for the unexpected honour of this interview, my lord?"

"I will tell you, sir, in a few words—but meantime, take another glass of wine."

I gazed steadily at this red-haired peer, and his demeanour recalled what I had read during my student days of Catiline, in Sallust; for his eyes, like those of that arch conspirator against his country, had a disagreeable glare; his face was pale, and his manner was alternately quick and slow; but I gazed upon him with emotions of very mingled cast. I felt contempt for his reckless treason, of which I was so fully cognisant, with a just anger for the wanton wrongs he had done myself, and an anxiety to draw from him those secrets which he certainly knew concerning my parentage; and above all, with these bitternesses, there struggled my love for his daughter—that passion which nothing could extinguish, for it had now become a portion of my own existence. All this ran through my heart and brain together, and I became almost giddy with the whirl of thought.

"My lord," said I, "will you have the kindness to say quickly what your pleasure is, for the night is cold; I am heavily accoutred as you see, and have far to ride—moreover, my horse stands at the gate in the snow."

"I have a duty for you to perform."

"A duty for me, my lord?"

"I have said so."

"Of what nature?"

"To become the bearer of a packet——"

"Nay, nay, by the soul of the king, but this is too barefaced, Lord Earl of Argyle!" said I, with a sudden gust of anger; "it is some infamous snare, and I would rather die than touch any packet of yours. It is enough, my lord—we know each other."

"Cavalier, that knowledge should make thee wary," said the earl, making a violent effort to control his rising passion, and veil it under a bland exterior; "but—you start as if a wasp had stung you!"

"Say a snake, my lord, and you will be nearer truth."

At this rash speech he grew pale, and stretched his hand towards a bell that stood on the table, but immediately withdrew it. Diplomacy, not violence, was now his object.

"My lord, my lord," said I, "the snares you prepare for me are cruel and base, and——"

"Snares, sir! dare you accuse me of this, before you have heard me to an end?"

"I do, earl," I replied, boldly; "for why select *me* to bear your precious packet—addressed to General Cromwell, I suppose?"

"It is *not*," said the earl, trembling with suppressed anger; "it is for the officer commanding one of the king's strongest garrisons."

"Then find some fitter messenger, I pray you, my lord, and leave me to my own duties, to my own secrets, and my own sorrows."

"To your own secrets undoubtedly, but not to your sorrows if I can help it," responded the earl, mildly.

His momentary kindness touched me. "Oh, that I could love this man," thought I; "is he not the father of Flora?"

"Let me remind you," said he, "of what the blessed Psalmist says—those who sow in tears shall reap in joy; those who go

wn to Babel and weep by her stream shall also return in joy
d mirth."

" Cursed crocodile—canting again !" was my next thought.

" Verily this is a valley of tears ; but blessed are the peace-
makers, and blessed are all soothers of affliction," continued the
pious lord, folding his hands and closing his eyes ; " I have heard
that, Mr. Ogilvie, that—excuse me speaking of such things—
that you were in love ?"

" You, my lord ?" I stammered, remembering his conversation
with Lorn in the garden, every word of which was engraved
indelibly on my heart.

" I have heard so, and a soldier in love——"

" Enough, my lord—do not trifle with me ; you have been
rightly informed, but by *whom* I know not, as the deadly secret
has never passed my own lips, even to the object of it."

" Deadly ! a strange phrase verily ; but this is neither a time
for marrying nor giving in marriage, when all the land is in
mourning and sorrow, like Haded-rimmon in the valley of Me-
giddon ; but are you utterly without hope, or does the lady love
you in return ?"

" I dare not hope that she will stoop so low. But what has
all this gossip to do with our conference, my lord ?" I asked,
perceiving his thin lip to curl scornfully.

" Then you have no hope of wedding her ?"

" Alas, none !" I replied, with the honesty of intense sadness.

" Take courage—this is just what the Laird of Ardmohr said,
when asking permission to address my daughter Flora ; he then
was hopeless ; yet they will be married as soon as these broils
are over."

Great was my internal agitation on hearing this, but I struggled to conceal it ; for I could not fail to perceive the keen, cold,
sarcastic manner of the querist, who made this direct stab merely
to discover if Lorn's surmises were correct ; but I baffled him,
saying—

" My lord, you honour me by this confidence, but 'tis a matter
with which I have nothing to do."

" Take courage, I say, and be of good cheer, for we know not
what a day may bring forth ; strive thou to please the Lord, and
he will make thine enemies at peace with thee."

I sighed with anger and contempt at these words, from which
I could gather no encouragement—and it was Flora's father who
spoke.

" You march to-morrow night to relieve the Castle of Edinburgh ?"

" I deemed this matter a secret."

"But not from a lord of the council. You march then?"

"Yes, my lord, with two hundred dragoons, under Captain Augustine, lately of Bickerton's regiment."

"Then I ask you for the last time to deliver this packet from me to the governor."

"My lord, I will give it to Captain Augustine to deliver—may Heaven forgive me if my evil genius should embroil that gallant spirit. Lord earl, *once and for ever*, I beg respectfully to decline the honour of being your messenger."

Placing my sword under my arm, I was about to retire, when the earl grew pallid with rage, and saying, "Stay, sir, yet one moment," cried aloud to some one in an inner apartment—

"Sir Archibald—Warriston!"

The arras covering the door was drawn back, and a personage, whom I too shrewdly suspected had overheard the whole conversation, entered with a sealed packet in his hand.

This was Sir Archibald Johnstone of Warriston, a lean and sallow-visaged, but acute and hollow-hearted man, whose crimes brought him justly to the gallows in after years, without even the formality of a trial, and who, from commencing life as a penniless advocate, by taking a prominent part in the disputes of the time, and being at first an active confidant of the patriotic and covenanting party in Scotland, distinguished himself as a commissioner for the Treaty of Berwick, which secured a brief peace between Scotland and England on the 11th June, 1640. By fawning, cringing, and that complication of meanness and ability which form the usual ladder at the Scottish bar, he clambered into office as Lord Advocate and M.P for Ayrshire, and next he became Lord Clerk Register. Like too many of these Scottish officials in later times, this man proved a sordid traitor to his country, and intrigued deeply with Cromwell for the subversion of her liberties, till the axe of the Maiden cut short his career of political wickedness.

His temples and cheeks were hollow; his eyebrows were shaggy, and his jawbones prominent; his eyes were stealthy and snake-like in expression, and his beard was well peaked forward. He wore a black coat buttoned up to the throat, with lace collar and cuffs, a black calotte cap and Geneva cloak.

"Sir," said he, sternly, "do you decline to deliver this packet, addressed to Colonel Dundas, of that Ilk, Governor of the Castle of Edinburgh?"

"I do, sir—perceiving no reason why I should be selected as its bearer."

"Some one must be selected. So you decline? Are you not, sir, an officer in the king's service?"

"Yes," I replied, haughtily, offended by his categorical queries; "I am Lieutenant Ogilvie, of the Black Dragoons."

" And who am I, pray ?"

" Sir Archibald Johnston, of Warriston Tower—the Lord Clerk Register."

" Then at your peril refuse to convey this packet; for I shall immediately report your conduct to the Earl of Balcarris, our secretary of state, to Marshal Leven, and to General Leslie, as you have no legal right to decline obedience."

" Then I shall obey," said I, feeling my resolution waver

" And remember that you must show it to *no man*, but the Governor Dundas."

" I have once already been deceived," said I, " by false instructions, when on out-post duty at Callander Wood. If again I am deceived, tremble, Sir Archibald Johnstone, for, by the grave of my mother, I will pistol you with my own hand!"

Warriston started as I said this; but Argyle gave me a cold smile as I took the packet.

" Recollect, sir," said he, " to whom you speak."

" I do recollect; and moreover I recollect the *masked man* whom I met in the tent of Cromwell, and who gave to Colonel Monk a plan of the hill of St. Leonard," said I, with sombre fury, as I retired abruptly, and in one minute more was galloping along the avenue from Scaithmuir.

" 'Tis a snare—an infamous snare, formed, perhaps, for my ruin; but God help me, what can I do, but obey?" said I, aloud, on leaving the avenue behind, and spurring along the hard frozen road, at a gallop, towards the Moss of Dunmore.

On reaching my billet, my first thought was to consult Linn or old Drumstanchel, but I remembered the injunction of Warriston, that I was to let "no man" see it. Even that was suspicious! On dismounting, the trooper Carlourie, who acted as my servant, startled me by the announcement that a letter awaited me; I say *startled*, for, being without relations, and having no friends beyond the circle of the regiment, I had never received a letter in my life. From whence came it—from whom could it be?

The seal was without a device, I hastily broke it, and saw but a few lines.

" A friend begs leave to warn Mr. Ogilvie that he is about to be deluded into an act equally repugnant to his honour and dangerous to his safety. He will act wisely by declining to become the bearer of any letters which may be pressed upon him; and, above all, he is warned to beware of the hatred borne him by the Lord Lorn and the Laird of Ardmohr."

It was in a lady's hand, and undated; but I had no doubt from whom it came. My heart beat lightly—almost joyously, and my head grew giddy; but the kind warning of that gentle spirit had come too late; for already this accursed packet—a pretty heavy one too—was in my possession, and I had pledged my word to deliver it."

I kissed the letter like a lover in a romance. I read it over twenty times, and imagined myself raised above all the evils of this sublunary sphere, by the consciousness that Flora Campbell really had an interest in my safety, and was the guardian of my fate. Then I tortured myself (but what lover does not torture himself?) by fears that the letter had come from some other quarter, for it was without signature, and the writing of Flora was unknown to me.

"Who brought it, Charlie?" I asked.

"Jock, sir; the old daft mannie that bided on the Figgate muir."

"The idiot whom we saw rambling about Edinburgh?"

"The same, sir, and a long way he seemed to hae come, wi' his bare feet among the snow; but the moment he placed it in my hand, and got a whang of bannock and cheese frae the gudewife, off he set again, as if the de'il was after him."

"When was this—think well?"

"Just about the gloaming."

"Would that I had been here! Said he from whence he had come?"

"No—for he would answer nane o' our questions, and seemed to be under a promise o' secrecy, though he laughed, and carolled his auld rant, about the de'il that sat supping the auld wife's kail."

"And you think he had travelled a long way?"

"I am sure he looked weary enough, sir; and he spoke o' being at Kirknewton and Midcalder yesterday."

Kirknewton is not far from Lennox Tower; thus, if Flora was there, and he had been her messenger, this plot of the packet for Dundas (if plot indeed it was) must have been devised some days, or perhaps weeks, ago. I had thus more than enough to think of that night, and it was far advanced—aye, the cocks were crowing in the dark winter morning, before I fell asleep.

CHAPTER XLIII.

THE PACKET AND ITS RESULTS.

THE evening of Wednesday, the 16th of December, was cold and clear. A haze, through which the red winter sun, shorn of his rays, shone louringly as he rose above the leafless woods and frozen marshes of Stirlingshire, floated in mid air; but the ground was firm and though a slight sprinkling of snow had fallen, the roads were in a good state for our night march; and just about the gloaming we mustered at our place of tryst, the *Wallace Oak*, in the Torwood, that ancient forest, so famed in the annals of war and the chase.

This gigantic tree, where Scotland's greatest hero halted, or, as tradition says, found shelter after his defeat at the fatal battle of Falkirk, spread over us its mighty branches, like the Toaba of Eastern fable, all gnarled, knotty, old, and riven by the storms of centuries. They were leafless and silent, for not a breath of wind passed through this vast forest; but the stirring memoirs that haunted the spot raised pure and daring emotions within us, and even the lightest spirits there—those who had laughed and sung as we rode to this sequestered place of arms, became silent as they surveyed that lordly tree, and turned to gaze on each other, and to think of him who had once stood there. Four hundred years had passed away since then; and still the Scottish cross was unfurled, and the Scottish steel was drawn, to resist the aggressive spirit of the South.

All the volunteers came rapidly in, well accoutred in back, breast, and head-pieces, steel gloves, and buff coats, with their swords, pistols, and carbines, and all splendidly mounted, with their horses in prime condition; a hundred officers, and a hundred troopers, all true hearted men, all tried and brave soldiers as ever drew a sword; and each without distinction had a little barrel of spirits and a bag of biscuits slung across his saddle, where the valise is usually strapped.

Among the volunteers from our Black Dragoons were Colonel Hugh Somerville, Captain Drumstanchel, Lieutenants Linn and the Master of Oliphant, Sir William of Ludquhairn, our adjutant, and myself; with Sergeants Glanders and Hackiron, Corporal MacSnaffle, and some thirty troopers or so—a fair proportion. And here for the first time I saw Captain Augustine, to whom we accorded the honour of leading the expedition he had devised. He was tall, strong, and weather-beaten; his hair was fair, and it was becoming grizzled, like his closely shorn mustachios, which, however, were dark, indicating a life of toil and hard campaigning. His right cheek was seamed by a sword cut, and his voice was rendered somewhat hoarse by a pistol-ball having pierced his throat, at the battle of Invercarron in Ross-shire; but he was a noble specimen of a soldier, whose nerves had been hardened by countless perils and toils. He was well-known to the Scottish officers who had served in the German wars.

"We might have had our tryst at a place of better augury sir," observed Sir William Livingstone, of Westquarter, a lieutenant of the Life Guards, whom we afterwards made Governor of Carlisle.

"True," added Linn; "it is associated with a disastrous defeat in the olden time; but let us not think of that to-night."

"Puir Willie Wallace," said Drumstanchel; "'twas a black time for thee, that St. Magdalene's eve in the year 1298."

"God rest his gallant soul," exclaimed the Master of Oliphant; "but if it can return to earth, be assured it will be with us to-night."

"We are all present—two hundred in number, Captain Augustine, and await your pleasure," said the Baronet of Ludquhairn.

"Brave gentlemen, and noble comrades," said Augustine, with a strong foreign accent, "accept my warmest thanks for the high honour you do me, in placing yourselves under my orders in this expedition—so many officers my superiors in rank and birth—so many soldiers my superiors in worth and bravery; for I am but a poor cavalier of fortune, who feed myself with my sword; but I am a staunch lover of the old Scottish nation, and I think, comrades, we know each other well, for I served ten years and more under old Ramsay, with the Scots Brigades in Germany."

"Bravo, noble Augustine," said the Baronet of Westquarter; "I remember you in Sir John Banier's Pistoleers at Lützen."

"And I, at the sack of Magdeburg, and the storming of Rostock," said Drumstanchel.

"And I, at Gueben, when the noble Marquis of Hamilton stormed it with his five thousand Scottish foot," said some one else.

"Hurrah for the Cavalier Augustine!" exclaimed the Master of Oliphant, and a cheer rang through the vast solitude, as we all brandished our swords and closed in line, irrespective of rank; for we were all simple cavaliers to-night, each with his bag and barrel of whiskey, a good horse under him, and a brave heart below his cuirass.

After a few preliminaries, the command was given to file off at a trot, and away we went, just as the broad and yellow moon rose above the leafless woods; avoiding the old Roman way, we made a detour by Castlecary and St. Lawrence (or as it is now named, Slamannan), and fording the Avon, rode through the woods of Torphichen, keeping well to the southward, to avoid any patrols or parties of Cromwell's troops, a strong garrison of whom still occupied the quaint old tower and magnificent palace of Linlithgow. Much of the ground we passed over was so rough, that we marched for some miles in our jack-boots, leading our horses by their bridles.

We rode at an easy pace all night, and towards daybreak, after passing the hills of Dalmahoy and Kaimes, halted in the secluded village of Ratho, eight miles westward of our destination, entering it by the *eastend*, to deceive any spies who might be thereabout, as to our route.

The sudden entry of two hundred horse spread consternation through the village; but Augustine threw a chain of videttes around it, and, during the whole succeeding day, allowed none who were in the place to leave it. Linn was longing to visit Lennox Tower, which was only a mile or two distant; but was compelled to stifle the desire, though death perhaps was before him.

We groomed our horses in the little street of Ratho, and as the evening of Thursday drew on, we had a most careful inspection of straps, buckles, spur-leathers, pistols, and ammunition; but amid all this, with sore misgivings, I bethought me of the infernal packet with which I was entrusted.

All grew silent in the hamlet and on the wintry hills, as the darkness deepened over them; and a few stars began to sparkle about the snowy peaks of the Pentlands, when we formed line without sound of trumpet, one hour after dusk, and once more began our march towards the east.

Wheeling round by the Buckstone on the western flank of the Braid Hills, we crossed the Burghmuir, and approached the city from the south. At a wild and solitary place called the Links of Bruntsfield, within a cannon shot of the city walls, Augustine called a halt, and wheeling us round him in a circle, spoke thus, so nearly as I can remember.

"Comrades, you all know the position of the Castle of Edinburgh, on the summit of a steep rock, inaccessible on all sides save one, towards the east. On every path and approach to it, Cromwell has posted his brigades of musketeers and pikemen, flanked and defended by trenches of earth, cannon, and abattis of trees; for the fortress is blocked up most completely and skilfully. I have been frequently in the city, disguised as a seller of peats and coal, so I know well every feature of the leaguer. His breaching batteries are cast up on the south near Heriot's Hospital, which is full of wounded soldiers; he has another on the north bank of the North-loch; and a third on the stone bartizan of a house on the Castlehill—the Laird of Ardmohr's town residence. He lives in Sellars'-close, and holds his levees there; but neither he nor his batteries can interfere with us to-night. We shall cut a passage *in*, sword in hand, through his outposts on the south; and cut another *out* through the guards on the north. Once in the city, our passage to the castle gate is clear. Fortunately he has removed the gates from all the barriers of ramparts; thus we shall skirt the Burgh-loch, and rush straight through the Bristo Porte. My orders are simple: keep together

—cut, slash, and hew! take no prisoners, if possible; so ride forward, gentlemen, and follow me, in the name of God and the King of *Schottland!*"

Two hundred cavalry swords flashed at once as they were unsheathed in the twilight, and, four abreast, we rode on, our hearts beating higher as our speed increased, and we drew nearer the long line of ramparted wall which girdled the city on the south, getting our horses well up in heat and hand for the final rush.

Fortunately the moon was veiled in masses of black and impenetrable clouds; the air was cold; a shower of sleet had fallen, and the white shroud of the departing year lay upon the mountain and the plain. The northern quarter of the sky was clear; there a thousand stars and constellations glanced; the crisped snow crackled under the hoofs of our horses, and relinquishing our capotes and rocqueleures, to give our sword arms fuller swing, we rode rapidly on.

"Now, now, we are almost upon them!" whispered Linn, as the voice of an English advanced sentinel, who was evidently alarmed by the rush of horses he could not see, challenged; but ere he could repeat the summons, or even fire his musket, Augustine shot him dead with his pistol.

"Gott in Himmel!" he cried, resuming his native German, in the excitement of the moment; "forward at full speed—spur and close up—hurrah!"

"Hurrah," cried we all; "God and the Covenant! The Covenant and the King!"

"*Vorwarts! vorwarts!*" continued Augustine, his sword and his eyes flashing together. "*Gott und St. Andrew fur Schottland!*"

At this moment, some thirty muskets or more flashed right in front of us. I heard the shrill hiss as the balls swept past; one lodged in my bag of bread, and another fractured Linn's keg of aqua-vitæ, which only excited laughter. Several of our men were wounded, but none fell before this fire, which was from the advanced picquet; and before they could reload, we had ridden over them, poured past the long re-entering angle of the town-wall, which there turns north, and rushed on to reach the open barrier, where a whole brigade of infantry were now under arms, and formed in line, in rear of a barricade of carts, baggage-wains, and other incumbrances, over which we could never leap our horses, and from behind which a fire was opened to sweep the street. As Heaven willed it, most luckily for us, the sleet had wetted their matches; thus, two muskets out of every three hung fire, otherwise we had perished here, horse and man, upon the causeway.

We reined up, firing our pistols and carbines, and the reports rang with a thousand reverberations in the narrow streets, while, undeterred by the clubbed muskets, the levelled pikes, and the random bullets of the brigade, which proved to be commanded by Colonel Overton, six troopers sprang from their horses, and dragged away a baggage wain. Every one of these devoted men was shot, save Carlourie, who sprang to his horse, as we dashed through six or eight abreast, cutting down the musketeers right and left, hewing, slashing, and trampling them under foot. We galloped at a breakneck pace down the Candlemaker-row, and swept up the bends of the Bow, killing every Cromwellian we met. With a wild cheer, we wheeled up the street to the left, passed the ruins of the Weigh House, which had been demolished by the English, past the muzzles of their battery, and spreading over the castle hill with a triumphant hurrah, halted, while Captain Augustine, who had previously made his project known, rode forward to give the parole agreed upon. In one minute more, we all reined up breathless within the strong barriers of that impregnable fortress, after losing only five men; and dismounting to examine our girths and breathe our cattle, we gladly flung down our burdens: viz., one hundred and ninety-five little casks of spirits, and the same number of bags of bread—a welcome sight to the half-famished garrison, who crowded about us with warm congratulations, with outstretched hands, and with water for our foam-covered horses.

Colonel Walter Dundas, of Dundas, a cold but courtly personage, applauded Augustine briefly, and, as I thought, rather bluntly, for his courage; and various fugitive divines—the same black coats who had played the devil with us at Dunbar—groaned and sighed forth their admiration in very spiritual terms, telling us we were worthy sons of Jacob, and thrice-favoured children of Judah—no great compliment as Christians take it.

"You have done well and bravely, noble comrades!" said Captain Augustine, in his hoarse and peculiar voice; "to me, this night is the most glorious of twenty years of war! Christi Kreutz! I have not words to thank you. But the worst is yet to follow, for we have to cut our passage out, and the whole blockading force will now be under arms to oppose us. To horse, gentlemen, to horse again, and let us be gone!"

I now approached Colonel Dundas, and presented my packet.

"From whom?" he inquired, bluntly.

"Sir Archibald Johnstone, the Lord Clerk Register."

He changed colour.

"Hold up a lantern," said he to a musketeer, as he tore open the envelope, and five letters fell out. These were addressed severally to the Reverend Messieurs Hamilton, Smith, Low, Gowan, and Robert Traill, the five fugitive ministers who opened them; and every one of *these missives was signed by Oliver Cromwell!*

Their contents, when first read, appeared to be mere rhapsodical exhortations to be assured that the result of the late battle proved "the Lord was against the covenant;" but I was afterwards informed that something deeper was concealed under this scriptural language. I stood as one transfixed, on finding that I was the bearer of a packet from the enemy to inmates of the king's most valuable fortress! A soldier's honour should be clear and bright as the blade of his sword; yet *a breath* will dim the lustre of that!

I felt all eyes turned upon me with suspicion. What would protestations avail me now, after the affair of Callander wood, and the manner in which I had been deceived there? I covered my face with my hands, and while my heart was swollen almost to bursting, exclaimed,—

"O, accursed be the cozening of these traitors who betrayed me! Gentlemen, hear me. I take God to witness that this packet was thrust upon me by the Lord Clerk Register, in presence of the Earl of Argyle, under threat, that if I refused to be its bearer, I should be reported to Marshal Lord Leven and the King's Lieutenant-General. I am a poor officer, who have only my honour and my commission—what could I do?"

"For your faith, Harry," said Linn, "I will gage my honour and estate."

"And I, Patrick Oliphant, blythely," exclaimed the Master.

"Enough, gentlemen," said Captain Augustine; "hereafter, the sword shall probe this matter. Fare you well, Colonel Dundas; and now, sirs, let us hence—forward, and follow me!"

We filed down from the castle, riding at a furious pace in divisions of troops through the deserted High-street, many of he lofty mansions of which were shattered by cannon-shot, we passed the Market-cross, where, *on a gallows*, hung the stone crown of the unicorn, to show the English hatred of monarchy; after which we found a whole regiment of horse, with cuirasses and triple-barred pot-helmets, drawn up near the Netherbow Porte, to oppose our egress.

"Close your files, comrades," cried Augustine, "and at them with sword and pistol!"

Elated by our success hitherto, and rendered desperate by the chance of being all taken or cut to pieces, we gored our horses with the spur, and rode on with frightful speed, and all wedged together, boot to boot, like a living avalanche, we came down the steep street upon them. There was a momentary shout—a momentary shock—a swaying of swords downward, and deadly thrusts given straight to the front! A lieutenant of the Life Guards was pistolled beside me; but with the loss of him alone we broke through, bearing down horses and men as completely as we had borne down the same cavalry at Dunbar and filed through the Porte with a wild shout of triumph.

The last cry of the young guardsman was still in my ear, for like many a strong and many a brave fellow, when the death struck him, he shrieked like a boy his *mother's* name. Strange it is, that in its last moment, the soul seems to go back as it were, to its first starting-point!

"To your left, gentlemen—to your left! Gott in himmel—wheel by threes!" cried Augustine. And at a breakneck trot we rode down one of the steepest streets in the town—Leith Wynd; but there a fresh obstacle occurred, for we met three squadrons of English dragoons hastening up to aid their comrades; but with uplifted swords we rode right through them with ease, for at first they knew not whether we were friends or foes. My mind was in such a chaos of rage and shame at the manner in which I had been outwitted by the snaky politicians at Scaithmuir, that I was in a very fit mood for manslaughter; yet such was the pressure around me, that I could not strike a single blow; and it was not until after we had hewed our way out of the town, and were galloping westward, among silent and snow-covered fields, that I became aware, that by the bravery and energy of Augustine, Colonel Somerville, old Sergeant Hackiron, and others, we had brought off five English cavalry officers and thirty-five of their horses, with the loss of eight only of our own number; and I afterwards read in the *Diurnal* that eighty of the enemy had been killed by us in the streets.

Towards the close of the next day, we were all in our old quarters again, as quietly as if nothing had happened; but the expedition furnished us with something to talk about over our pipes and punch in the cold nights of winter. Captain Augustine received the thanks of the Parliament,* which was then sitting at Perth; and Count Ogilvie was so charmed by his conduct in the affair, that he obtained for him the commission of captain-lieutenant of the Black Dragoons, in place of the Laird of Aiket, who died of the plague, which was again beginning to desolate Scotland. I heard no more of the letters which I had been trepanned to deliver; but *this* we all heard— that in lieu of cannon-shot, a wordy correspondence had ensued between Cromwell and the five divines in Edinburgh Castle, and the issue was an act of the most infamous treason on the part of

* See Note.

Dundas of that ilk. He pulled down St. Andrew's cross, and his unwilling soldiers, after a three months' siege, marched out with the honours of war, drums beating and colours flying, yielding up our greatest fortress to the enemy, with ten thousand stand of muskets, seventy brass and iron guns, and a vast store of all the munitions of war.

All Scotland proclaimed Dundas " a villain."

The parliament arraigned him, but the influence of Argyle alone saved his head from feeding the crows on the walls of Perth.

Such was the result of Warriston's pretty packet of letters.

CHAPTER XLIV.

GLASGOW AGAIN.

LINN often spoke to me enthusiastically of Dora Lennox, of her gaiety, her beauty and *espiéglerie,* as he was fond of terming her French vivacity; and in one of these moments of mutual confidence, I ventured to confide to him the secret of my regard for her friend—for Flora Campbell, the daughter of the great, the terrible, the master plotter, Argyle!

Never shall I forget his stare of blank astonishment and perplexity, or how deeply his earnest warning, " for Heaven's sake, to beware of such frenzy," sank into my heart.

" Harry," said he, " be wise; act at least with prudence, and do not permit a crazy passion to make a fool of you."

" I shall not be the first wise man who, since Solomon's time, has been fooled by a pretty woman."

" Flora is Argyle's daughter, and, like a beautiful apple, may be rotten at the core."

" I hold her to be gentle as a dove. Bethink you, Willie," said I, " she is the friend of Dora."

" True—to me, her best recommendation for purity and truth; but beware, Harry, beware, or this love will but lure you to ruin and regret."

With his kind but gloomy warnings rankling in my mind, I left my troop about this time on a very peculiar duty, for which I had no particular desire; but for which, as being well acquainted with Glasgow, I was selected by the lieutenant-general, on the recommendation of Count Ogilvie. This duty was nothing less than to hasten after Cromwell, to the great city of the west, in disguise, and to observe what he was about in that quarter.

Attired as a civilian, in a plain and unpretending coat of brown broad cloth, destitute of lace and finery, my hair cut short to a medium length, so as to steer midway between the puritan crop and the cavalier profusion ; a broad hat without a feather, a black roquelaure, and black boots with gambadoes, I rode from the moss of Dunmore in a keen frosty December morning, mounted on a sturdy mare, which I had purchased from a moss laird, leaving my troop horse behind me, in care of Charlie Carlourie, with orders to be as careful of him as he would be of his own father. Under my vest I wore my cuirass, and took with me, of course, my sword and pistols ; as at that time no man ventured abroad un-armed.

My object was simply to ascertain, if possible, what purpose had taken Cromwell to Glasgow, where the king had no troops quartered ; and I also wished to obtain from the reverend prin-cipal of the college the reliques which had been found on the dead body of my mother, on that eventful morning which con-signed them to his care some twenty years ago.

The sky was of the deepest blue ; hill and plain were covered by snow ; the leafless woods alone looked black, and the smoke rose in straight columns into the pure atmosphere. My nag trotted rapidly on, being a good-going mare, that threw her feet well out, as she covered the frozen roadway ; and my spirits be-came buoyant, on reflecting that I was going back to Glasgow in a position so very different from the humble and friendless condition in which I left the college, without a coin wherewith to procure a meal ; and my heart beat the more proudly when I pronounced myself the master of my own fortune—the maker of my own destiny. I thought of Flora, and the warnings of Linn yet sounded in my ears ; I thought of her father, and that syste-matic enmity which, from my boyhood, had made him plot against me, and seek my downfall and disgrace. I endeavoured, but in vain, to analyse that mysterious and instinctive antipathy which filled my breast when near the earl or his son ; for it seemed that I was thus instinctively warned of the presence of a nature antagonistic to my own.

Whence came this strange emotion, and how came it to pass, that it flourished and grew side by side with a love for the inno-cent and generous Flora? Why did not the love soothe the hatred, or the hatred crush the gentler passion? How was it, that in my first meeting with Flora, my heart at once expanded with confidence and admiration ; and that in my first meeting with her father, it seemed to shrink up within me, by a myste-rious intuition of suspicion and hostility?

I was no casuist, and knew better about flanks and pivots than philosophy, so I grew weary of thinking, and on once more look-ing about me, found that I had passed the ruins of Sir John the

Grahame's castle, that I had crossed the Carron, and was approaching the village of Monaeburgh, at the market cross of which I saw a little old woman, wrapped in a black mantle, with a red curchie on her head, exposed to the view of the people by the chamberlain of Lord Livingstone, as a dealer in witchcraft and diablerie against the word of God, by divining with a riddle. For this offence, by order of the Kirk Session, her right ear was affixed by a nail to the market cross, into the stone shaft of which a wooden plug was permanently inserted for such purposes.

So intent were the populace in tormenting and hooting this old woman, whose chief crime was dwelling *alone* in a sequestered cot on the banks of the Garvel, that it was with difficulty, and not without dragooning, I obtained some refreshment; after which I again set forth; but before I passed Barhill, a storm of snow and wind came on, and I was compelled to spur on in search of shelter. Galloping through the cold and whirling drift, at Auchindavie I passed the remains of five enormous Roman arches, built for the purpose of carrying the rampart of Antoninus across the morasses which once lay there. Notwithstanding the storm, I paused to gaze at them with interest, for I could not, without a sigh, reflect on how mighty were the works and how *futile* the wars of that great people in a land where now their name is scarcely remembered.

Shrill blew the wind and heavy fell the snow; cold, wet, and weary, I gladly saw the tower of the Laird of Wester Lenzie, and his old burgh-town before me; but without pausing to look about for an inn, knowing well that all such, in these times of war and invasion, were but ill supplied, I galloped straight to the ancient castle of the barony. It was full of armed men, though the proprietor was absent with the army, being a captain of artillery; but his bailie admitted me without much difficulty as a stranger and traveller, for I did not give my name at the gate, having resolved to preserve my incognito.

The bailie and I supped heartily together. The repast over, he produced some of the absent laird's oldest wine for my entertainment.

This castellan was a hospitable and thickset old man, whose sturdy figure was shown to advantage in his tight-fitting cloth cassock, knee breeches, and ribbed galligaskins. He wore a silver chain round his neck, and had a dirk at his right side. Clay pipes were brought, and we smoked for hours, with a complacence that would have thrown his majesty James VI. into fits. The battle of Dunbar, the incidents of our retreat, the affair of Callander House, and more particularly the recent onfall at Edinburgh, were all rehearsed with new zest, for the old cas-

tellan had been a soldier in '28, and served in the Laird of Mac-
Naughten's archers in Sweden.   Fired by my stories, he gave me
his experiences in the noble art of war, and we mulled fresh
jorums of claret and sack, heedless of the winter blast that howled
round the old walls, and made the candles sputter in the wind as
the night wore on—merrily within, and drearily without.

My head was none of the clearest when at dawn I rode forth
from the old castle of Wester Lenzie and took the road to Calder,
and I had such dreamy recollections of yesterday as that cloudy
old fellow Pythagoras had of being at the siege of Troy, when
in a former state of existence.

The country was covered with soft and new-fallen snow, so
that the horse path I traversed was scarcely to be distinguished.
Once I lost it, and was only put in the right direction by the
parish beadle, whom I met marching at the head of a rustic
funeral, ringing a loud bell, in the old fashion, now fallen into
disuse.   The sky was a clear cold blue; and the atmosphere
proved very refreshing and bracing to one who had passed the
last seven hours as the castellan and I had done.   My head swam
occasionally, but I soon saw the dun winter smoke and magnificent cathedral spire of old Glasgow rise before me; and I spurred
on, all anxiety to traverse its streets once more, and again to see the
old college which had been my home, and the vinegar visage of
Nehemiah Spreul the porter.   I thought sadly of the venerable
principal, and the sunny-eyed Maggie Muir, and of the night I
was found in her chamber; and now I heard the familiar ding-
dong of the cathedral bells ringing on the clear winter air, like
the voices of old friends in welcome; and now the solid causeway
of the Trongate rang beneath my horse's hoofs, and all its buzz
and bustle were around me.

I was again in Glasgow, and then the orphan, the foundling,
the poor soldier-boy, found himself at home!

The signboards, the faces of the people, and their intoned
patois, were all familiar to me; and I remembered the day when,
without a testoon in my pocket, I had sauntered with a bursting
heart along that very Trongate, homeless, and, it might be,
hungry; when I heard the blare of the trumpets, and saw the
glancing of burnished steel, as Gideon Glanders and his gallant
recruiting party summoned the able and willing to fight for Scotland's king and covenant.

I rode straight to the " Cat and Bagpipes," my former " howff,"
and the scene of many a night of junketting and high-jinks in
old college days, but resolving to preserve my incognito, spoke
as little as possible to the garrulous gudeman Adam Wilson, and
to his inquisitive gudewife.   I ordered a luncheon in a private
room, and sat long over a stoup of Rochelle, laying out my plans

for discovering Cromwell's errand to Glasgow, where he had cantoned a body of troops, several of whom I saw quietly mingling
with the people in the Trongate, and gazing into the shop windows and open booths, seeming as much at home as they might
have been in London or York.

I resolved to visit first my old friend the principal (surely he
must have forgiven me by this time), and to obtain from him the
reliques of my mother, and such information as he might have
gleaned up concerning the motions of Cromwell in his vicinity.

The winter eve was darkening on the picturesque façade and
square quadrangle of the old college, when I knocked at the
arched gate. It was slowly and deliberately unbarred, and Nehemiah Spreul suspiciously inquired for "wham I speered?"

"The principal—can I see him?"

"Maybe ye can, and maybe ye canna; but—eh—the Lord
preserve us! it's mine ain laddie—Harry, Master Harry! Come
in, sir—come in, lad; oh, but I am glad to see thee!" And the
old man in his kindness of heart almost wept as he dragged me
through the wicket, and from the porch into his little lodge,
muttering aud talking incoherently about my being "his ain
laddie, that he had carried in his arms and on his back; but I was
a braw man now—a gentleman every inch, and a soldier too!
for I was weather-beaten, and carried my head erect." And
twenty times he shook my hand and stroked my hair, as if I was
still the boy he remembered me to have been.

"And Hannah the gudewife," said I, looking round, "I do
not see her."

"Nor shall ye ever see her mair, my bairn—my puir Hannah
is at rest in the auld kirkyaird," said he, applying his broad
bonnet to his eyes; "she hath gane to the place of her reward,
and lieth where the wicked cease frae troubling and the weary
are at rest. For forty years and mair she was a kind and a
carefu' wife to me; and, oh lad, I miss her sairly; but I'll soon
follow, for I stumbled at her burial, a sure sign that I canna
bide long here. But sit doon, sit doon—there's your creepie by
the fire—the first ye ever set your doupie on—the creepie, no,
the fire I mean. Oh, sir, to think of these days, when you were
as fond o' mischief as the bairns o' Falkirk. Welcome, welcome;
I never thocht God would spare me to see thee again."

"Nehemiah, I have been absent but a few months only,"
said I.

"Months—but months, laddie, are like unto years at my time
o' life."

After he had again praised his "anld gudewife," whose face
and figure were familiar to me as the Tron steeple; and after he
had made me imbibe a sip from *his* bottle before I visited the

principal, I laid him under the most solemn injunctions of secresy
as to my presence in Glasgow; adding that if Cromwell or any
of his people discovered me—an officer of the Scottish army—
there, I would be hanged at the cross without mercy or remedy.
Poor Nehemiah quite won me by his friendship, for kindness is
the surest way to reach and to win the human heart.

Muttering, sighing, and shaking his head, which was full of
reminiscences of other times, when Oliphant, Linn, and I were
the three plagues of his life, he conducted me to the door of the
principal's house. Dr. Zephaniah Bogle was at home, so I was
ushered at once into his presence.

He sat in the same little apartment, the windows of which
overlooked the shady quadrangle, in the same high-backed elbow
chair, entrenched among dusty books, in the same corner, and
wearing apparently the same threadbare coat and old periwig
(sorely singed by candles) in which I had been wont to see
him before. He lifted his eyes slowly from a large volume,
and after surveying me under, over, and through his horn spectacles, recognised me. Suddenly he sprang up, and flinging
away a pinch of snuff, opened his arms and gave me a warm and
affectionate embrace.

"Welcome again, Harry—welcome back, son of mine, for
such indeed you are, laddie," said he, "for never kent ye other
sire than me, or other mother than this auld college, your alma
mater! Welcome again, for thou returnest I doubt not like the
prodigal in the beautiful parable of old. Sit down, sit down—
thou hast much to tell me, and I have much to ask. Where
have you been a' this time? What have you been doing? Have
you been well and able, or sick and ailing? Dost want money
that you have come back to old Zephaniah Bogle? Or come
you back to resume that auld red gown whilk you bequeathed so
irefully and irreverently to the devil when last you were here,
and departed from college by a window instead of the door?"

As he closed this string of questions he pointed to a tattered
red gown, which I recognised to be my old academic garment,
and which in memory of me this kind good soul had preserved
and hung upon a peg in his study.

"I ever said ye would return again, Harry," resumed the
old man, patting me on the shoulder, while his eyes filled, "and
back thou art come to fulfil the fair promise thou gavest us of
old."

"I am indeed come back, dear sir, as you may see, but for a
very different purpose. You are aware that I am an officer in
Count Ogilvie's regiment of horse?"

"I have heard as much, and read in the *Diurnal* that ye did
brave things at St. Leonard's Hill; yet I thought such a lover

of Sallust and Livy might do something still better; though I wore a buff coat and bandoliers myself at Dunselaw in '39, and am ready to do so again—auld as I am—if the covenanted kirk require me.   Aweel, Harry?"

"I have been sent to Glasgow by Lieutenant General Sir David Leslie, to ascertain what Cromwell is about here; and generally to reconnoitre his movements—to watch and report."

"The Lord who searcheth our hearts alone knoweth what he wants here, Harry; for natheless a letter which he wrote the Lord Provost from Kilsythe, promising protection, most of the citizens fled at his approach; and, after entering the city with 9000 horse, foot, and artillery, he desecrated our kirks and burying places, by stabling his horses therein, as he had done in the half-popish cathedrals of his own country.   He first occupied the old archiepiscopal palace of Glasgow; but conceiving, perhaps, that the name had a vainglorious sound, he removed to the Laird o' Sillercraig's, on the east ride of the Sautmarket, and there he holds his levees, his prayer-meetings, and love-feasts.   He is a finished hypocrite, this brewer of Huntingdon; a wretch, verily, in whose mouth are seven abominations; a roaring lion, who goeth about seeking whom he may devour; a bull of Bashan, whom we must take by the horns and bring to divine justice! We must teach him that our swords are on the grindstone, and that we are not the men to hang our harps on the willow-tree, and weep by the waters of Babel."

While the principal was running on in this defiant strain, old Nehemiah Spreul appeared at the door in great tribulation, to announce that au Euglishman wished to speak with him.

"An Englishman?" reiterated the principal, testily; "I ken nae Englishman, nor have I ever seen ane since we were at Dunselaw in '39."

"Very true, sir; but this ane is an officer o' the vile blasphemer, and he'll no be forbidden."

"Can he be in quest of *me?*" thought I, grasping one of the pistols in my belt.

"Conduct him hither, then—we will confront this soldier of Pharaoh," said the principal, wiping his huge circular barnacles, adjusting his singed wig, and assuming a face of stern gravity.

A heavy step was heard approaching, and a man of a square, strongly-built, tall, and not ungraceful figure, entered.   He had a rosy and good-humoured, but rather coarse, face, the result of drinking and good living; and he had the air of a blustering *bon vivant,* with the eye of a devil-may-care fellow.   In short, ne seemed a blunt jolly Englishman, turned into somewhat of a ruffian by war and its necessities.   He wore a large skirted coat of fine scarlet cloth, faced with white, large boots and gloves, a cuirass and helmet of polished steel,

"Your servant, gentlemen—save you, my old buck," said he, nodding to the astounded principal; "I think I met your saintship this morning in dalliance with a brace of turtles in the Trongate."

"Heaven keep me, sirrah; dare ye say sic a thing to me?"

"I do—heyday, and what then? My name is Thurlow—John Thurlow, captain in Overton's musketeers."

"Well, sir?"

"*Well*—you're a blunt old fellow! I've come on a message from the Lord General."

"And this message?" quoth the principal, who was fast swelling with indignation.

"Is merely this," responded the other, bluntly, as he tumbled a heap of Sallust, Cicero, Livy, and Lucan off a chair, and scated himself, brushed a speck off his well-polished jack-boots, and placed his long sword between his legs; "it concerns that which I consider a damnable waste of money. The Lord General——"

"Who's he?"

"You'll soon find that out, my old brigadier, if you cross his flank! The Lord General *Cromwell* understands that the late man, Charles Stuart——"

"Mean ye his sacred majesty, the king!"

"Damn it, old gentleman, don't interrupt me. King? stuff! Well, sir—Charles Stuart, when last in Scotland, thirteen years ago, by a document indited with his own hand (royal, you'll call it, of course?) at Seton, subscribed 200*l.* sterling towards the completion of your college here in Glasgow. This sum Oliver is resolved to pay—and here is the money, every tester, so give me a receipt."

Drawing from his pocket a little canvas bag, which seemed filled with gold, he gave it a thwack on the table, which made old Zephaniah's barnacles jump on his nose.

"There it is—200*l.*—by the Lord, whose presence is about us, that sum would go a long way on tobacco, strong waters, and women," said Captain Thurlow, who appeared to have very little of the military saint about him; yet he was one of Cromwell's favourite officers.

Zephaniah Bogle counted the money with grave deliberation, and proceeded to write a receipt; while the Englishman, after staring at me, and surveying all the apartment with elevated eyebrows, began to whistle "Jumping Joan," and beat the pipeclay out of his gauntlets.

"Thank you, old gentleman," said he, pocketing the receipt; "you haven't a drop of something stiff about you, I suppose, eh?"

"No, sir," was the gruff reply.

"I'm grown rather fastidious since I drank some of the king

of Scotland's tokay at Holyrood and Linlithgow palace—ha, ha, ha!"

Muttering something about "an old Scots screw and sulky bear," Captain Thurlow swaggered out of the room, and passed through the quadrangle whistling, as much at his ease as if he had been at home in England; and now I remembered that he must be the officer mentioned by Oliphant as being the accepted lover of Harriet Morton, the daughter of the Bishop of Durham.

"Well, friend Harry," said Mr. Bogle; "what think you of this unexpected present to *alma mater ?*"

"I know not, sir, and am confounded; but a snare must be concealed under it—more, at least, than we can see."

"'Tis just a sprat to catch a whale, my man—a sly way of currying favour with the clergy—for this Cromwell is a deep-witted loon, and thinketh to bribe the men o' the covenant with his illgotten gold; to place the wages of the devil before us; and to put Heaven in the balance against the *other* place; and though I can see through a millstone as well as he, I'll e'en take the gudes the gods send us, in whatever fashion they come. But supper is on the table, Harry; a bravely roasted capon, a hash o' mutton, and a bowl of Glasgow punch await us! Step awa, ben, and I'll hae a' your adventures by the fire in the chalmer o' dais. I might have rebuked yonder Cromwellian bully; but the puir man is *fey*, and I am weel assured, that the bullet of some godly Scottish musket will 'ere long cut short his career o' sectarianism and wickedness."

We had a comfortable supper, and in that cold winter night right welcome it was, with its rear-guard of steaming Glasgow punch, under the effects of which the old principal warmed and wept, as he shook my hand, and waxed pathetic, patriotic, and polemical by turns, as the spirit moved him.

I inquired after many of my old brother students; most of them were in the ranks of our army; some had gone to Germany to fight against the Imperialists; some had married; others had come to a still more tragic end, and been shot or run through the body in duels, and not a few had died of the plague which was then hovering about.

"A short time has made a sad change here, sir," said I; "who could have believed that so many young hearts would so soon grow cold. But happy are those dead ones whose virtues are chronicled in marble and brass."

"Far happier are they, Harry, whose virtues are treasured in the hearts they leave behind them."

I now begged that he would consign to me the reliques which had been found upon the person of my mother, or that unfortunate whom I had every reason to believe was such; and unlocking an old Scots cabinet of drawers, having a sloping top for a desk and pigeon-holes for papers, he placed in my hands the marriage ring, having two hearts surmounted by a little coronet, which was on her spousal finger; and the gold medal, having a crowned lion, passant, the cognisance of the Ogilvies, and the letters "H. O. E. F.," which was attached to my neck by a riband; with a lock of her black hair, and some fragments of my baby clothes, on which was written the name of "*Harry Ogilvie.*"

These reliques were my inheritance.

The sight of them raised some deep and painful thoughts within me. The conversations of Lorn and Argyle rushed vividly upon my memory, and the certainty that they alone knew the secret that otherwise was buried in the grave of that poor murdered wanderer, came bitterly before me.

"But for Flora's love," thought I, "I would wrench the secret at the sword's point from the throat of Lorn!"

"Preserve them, Harry, and I would they had a tongue! Ye may be the heir of some auld and honourable patrimony, if we could but ken o't—yea, a patrimony won of old, like the heritage of Jacob, by the sword and by the bow."

I placed the ring upon my smallest finger, and resolved to chain the medal to my neck, so that it should never leave me while life remained.

As the hour was waxing late, and the effects of my last night's topering at Wester Lenzie were beginning to appear, after sincerely thanking the good old principal for his kindness to such a scapegrace *protégé*, and receiving a blessing that would have brought tears to my eyes if the keen frosty air had not done so already, I muffled myself in my capote, and made my way through the snow to the inn in the Trongate.

CHAPTER XLV.

THE HIGH KIRK OF GLASGOW.

NOTWITHSTANDING my last night's potations with the hospitable bailie of Wester Lenzie, I sat long in my chamber at the "Cat and Bagpipes," gazing on the reliques I had received from the principal; and I lay long in bed awake, listening to the old familiar sound of the clocks and bells of Glasgow. At last I dropped into a sound sleep; and from dreams of my student days, of the Black Dragoons, and of Flora Campbell, I was roused about the winter daybreak by hearing the *English* reveille (which is quite different from the Scottish) beaten by

Cromwell's drums in the long-echoing thoroughfare of the Trongate. Though, like honest Jack Falstaff, I wished " to take mine ease in mine inn," I was up betimes. In those days, to be absent from church subjected one to the suspicion of being a malignant, and to the disagreeable ordeal of an examination before the nearest kirk-session, with imprisonment in any convenient tolbooth or tower. Thus I roused me early, breakfasted on beef and ale, and accompanied my landlord, Master Adam Wilson, to church. Adam, who was bottle-nosed and big-bellied, as hostellers should be, and who knew me well of old, had not yet recognised me ; for I still preserved an incognito, though he was a vehement loyalist, because his father had been a liveryman in the household of James VI.

We went to the High Kirk, as the great cathedral church of the defunct archbishopric is named.

I wore the plain dress in which I had left the regiment, with a cuirass under my coat, and brace of loaded pistols in my girdle, concealed by my roquelaure. In addition to these I had a sword, which no man in Scotland is ever without.

On entering the spacious burying ground, which slopes down to that deep hollow where the Molendinar burn flows towards the Clyde, and which is almost paved with venerable gravestones I turned first to the well-remembered corner where Nehemiah Spreul was wont to take me so often of old, where she lay—*she*, the nameless and unknown, who left me with her life at Glasgow College gate, and whose relics I bore now in my breast ; but that humble resting-place had been violated ; and now the tomb of some full-fed burgess or Hammerman of renown reared its aspiring front, gorgeous with ghostly carving, amid which the skull and cross-bones, the hour-glass, the crowned hammer, and all his virtues were graven on the stone ! I gave a sigh of anger, and turned away with disgust and mortification.

I gazed on the glorious façade of the ancient cathedral, one side of which was bathed in warm light as the winter sun shone through a yellow haze, and gilded each grey knosp and lofty pinnacle ; the belfry tower, the stupendous spire, round which the cawing rooks, diminished to the size of flies, were revolving ; and that long line of grotesque gurgoyles, which were ever a source of wonder to me when a boy, for through their monster mouths the gutters of the clerestory have disgorged themselves for ages.

I remember once, when a child, being filled with horror on a dark winter night when beholding a number of lambent flames dancing above the tombs that rise, tier over tier, on the sloping bank. I screamed with boyish terror, for these dense and vapoury flames were the *corpse-lichts* of the vulgar—that luminous exhalation (emitted by the chemical decomposition of the dead) which the sensitive or the sickly alone perceive, and even they only at times. These lights have ever been a source of terror to the superstitious in Scotland, where it is confidently believed they are the spirits of the departed hovering near their graves; but my after-studies under our old professor of chemistry taught me to assign another origin for the corpse-licht and solved the problem of many a ghost story.

While these recollections occurred to me, the people were thronging fast to church, as the bells were now "jowing in." The congregation were the same as when I had last seen them. Here came an old farmer clad in his Sunday doublet of Galloway frieze, with his gudewife behind him on a pillion, he seeming to take more care of his grey mare than his better half, who took care of herself; there was an old country laird in laced broadcloth and Spanish beaver, with basket-hilted spada and holster pistols, dismounting at the louping-on stone, and tethering his nag to an ancient tomb; and there were old weavers who remembered the regency of Morton, and old wives of the Drygate and Gorbals in the cloaks and curchies of Anne of Denmark's days, and pot-bellied baillies of the Saltmarket, with laced hats and gold-headed canes, walking pompously in by the great door, leading by the hand their dames in Florence silks and crammasic, each as he passed scattering among the poor a handful of *hardies*, as we named the copper coin of Philip le Hardi, which were still current among us in Scotland.

In the iron jougs at the western door stood a woman accused of casting a spell upon an elder to win his love. She had secretly burned a lock of her hair, and given him the ashes in a cup of canary—a heinous crime in the eyes of the kirk session, who doomed her to the iron collar; and on the cutty stool in the central aisle sat another unfortunate, clad in sackcloth—one who, as the song says, had

> Dearly loved her husband,
> But another man quite as well.

We walked softly down the aisle, and took our places among the silent congregation. The pulpit was yet empty, and nothing was heard but the rustling of bible-leaves, or the clank of swords, for all men had come well armed " to preaching," although nine thousand foreign soldiers were in the city.

The long flakes of hazy light fell through the painted windows on reverendly bowed heads, on white-haired men, and those grave, acute, and thoughtful faces which mark a Scottish congregation; on the darker pews of the choir fell those streams of radiance, lighting faintly the dim recesses of the galleries, where glinted the golden locks of many a fair-haired girl, and the polished hilt of many a sword that had been drawn in the cause

of kirk and covenant; for there were few men in Scotland in that
year of our Lord who had not seen the flash of steel and heard
the whizz of musket-shot.

As I took my place beside the innkeeper, I felt that holy awe
and religious reverence which are inseparable from such old
temples, fill my breast; a sanctity seemed to pervade the whole
church, from the tombstones beneath our feet to the groined
Gothic roof that towered above us.

Raising my eyes, I suddenly became aware that Mr. Zachary
Boyd, my old rival for the love of Maggie Muir, had noiselessly
mounted into the pulpit; and there he sat with a great bible
open before him, his black cloak and smooth white Geneva bands,
his lank hair, and square double-jointed figure, filling up the
space; but, pious, earnest, and resolute as *he* " who never
feared the face of man," in all things the raw-boned author of
" The Last Battel of the Soule," and with all his oddity, a worthy
and noble specimen of the old Presbyterian pastor—unflinching
and uncompromising as adamant.

Just as the psalm was about to be given out by the precentor,
Nehemiah Spreul, we heard the rolling of wheels, the clatter of
hoofs, swords, and muskets, and then red-coats appeared at the
western door.   Every eye was turned in that direction, and lo!
there walked gently down the aisle, clad in his buff coat,
corslet and starched bands, his wide calfskin boots and broadsword, with a broad-brimmed hat under his left arm, and a
horn-headed cane in his right hand, the English general—
Oliver Cromwell! His massive, closely-shaven face, with its
large nose, his keen and piercing eye, caused a thrill to run
through every heart; but he leaned on his cane, and looked sickly
and pale, as his health was so much impaired, that Lord Fairfax
had sent his own coach from London for his use; and he was
now accompanied by Doctors Wright and Bates, two eminent
English physicians.

Sir Arthur Hesilrig, the swaggering Captain Thurlow, and
several other officers, accompanied him.

The obsequious pew-opener hastened to find places for them;
and bowing to the people, the Protector of the English Commonwealth sat down and laid his prayer-book before him, not a pike's
length distant from where I was seated; and now the service
began. A psalm was sung. Cromwell and all his suite joined
in it—all, at least, save Captain Thurlow, who employed his
mind and his hands in polishing the butt of a pistol which he
wore at his girdle.

I felt rather uneasy, and frequently thought that Cromwell
turned his keen eyes on *me;* but very probably every person in
the church had the same idea, and believed that he had looked

at *them ;* but my sensation of security was no way increased on my perceiving among the infantry escort at the door my old acquaintances of Monk's regiment — Sergeant Melchisedeck Makepeace, Corporal Fight-the-good-fight-of-Faith Twaddle, Privates Zerubabbel Mcek and Habakuk Killsin, with many other pipeclayed saints of the same holy calibre, all seated with muskets cocked, and mouths and Bibles open.

Now ensued one of the most remarkable episodes of the English campaign in Scotland.

Though the conduct of Cromwell's troops while in the kingdom generally, and in Glasgow particularly, was quiet and orderly, Mr. Boyd, in his sermon, was rash enough or unwise enough to rail at them with great bitterness; he reproached them as sectarians in terms of unmeasured severity, denounced them as republicans, and inveighed against Cromwell as an enemy to God and man—a foe to all truth and faith, and a vile blasphemer!

Oliver Cromwell listened to this tirade with admirable composure; he winced once or twice, as if stung by Mr. Boyd's remarks, but continued quietly to smooth the nap of his beaver hat or suck the head of his cane, till Captain Thurlow, starting up, drew his pistol (now thoroughly polished) from his belt, and cocking it, said in a loud voice,—

"Say but the word, General Cromwell, and I will pistol this scoundrel in the face of the people!"

The congregation were petrified, and though many grasped their swords, all sat motionless; but the voice of Boyd never quavered, and while he continued boldly to preach, Cromwell said,—

"John Thurlow, sit ye down—thou art a fool, and he is another."

"Allow me, at least," urged the captain, "to scabbard him well —within an inch of death."

"Nay, I will manage him my own way."

Before Thurlow could have achieved either of these acts of sacrilege, I would assuredly have shot him, had no other person anticipated me. When he spoke, I also had started up, and my kindling eye, my flushed cheek, and forward stride, as well as the pistol which I grasped, could not fail to attract the falcon eye of Cromwell. He gazed at me; a light shot across his solid visage, and while resuming my psalm-book I felt all my danger!

He whispered a few words to Captain Thurlow, who in turn gave an order to the soldiers at the door; I saw him distinctly indicate *me,* on which the portly Sergeant Melchisedeck Make-peace grasped his halbert, and marched his military person to

the centre of the passage, barring all escape, and resolved, **doubtless**, to seize me as I went out.

Every pulse throbbed like lightning, and my heart bounded,
for I knew that if I was taken, there remained no prospect before
me but a sudden and violent death.   It chanced that my friend
the innkeeper had also perceived these preparations, and conceiving they were made for him—being a captain of the trained
bands, and about as valiant as these captains usually are—he was
put in great tribulation of spirit.

"I ken it is me they seek," he whispered; "he has recognised
me as a royalist—my father was principal valet to James VI.,
and mairowre my dochter Annie is a servant lass at the palace
o' Scone—wae's me."

The elder Wilson had accompanied James VI., and bound his
son apprentice to a shoemaker in Huntingdon; and now, after
the lapse of so many years, the keen-eyed Cromwell *had* recognised his townsman.   His reverence had now come to the end
of his ammunition; and the moment the sermon was over, Cromwell touched the terrified Wilson with his cane, saying—

"Come hither, my good man."

Trembling in every limb, the innkeeper obeyed.

"Dost thou remember me ?" asked Oliver.

"I do indeed—that is, my lord," replied Wilson, relinquishing
at once his national idiom; "but ah, Master Cromwell, do not
forget the days when I was a 'prentice lad in old Huntingdon,
where your worship's father Sir Oliver lived, when we sat on
the same form, and conned the alphabet and the Lord's Prayer
off the same hornbook, at the grammar school.   Remember how
often I made balls and tops and other playthings for you; how
twice I pulled you out of the Ouse; how we were wont to fish
over the old bridge; how often we fought the boys of Godman-
chester, and beat them with club and bat to their own side of
the river."

"I have forgotten none of these things, Wilson," said Cromwell, giving him his hand; "so wherefore dost thou fly me ?"

"Because—because my father was a faithful servant to the
royal family, and I deemed you might harbour an ill will——"

Cromwell's brow knit, and Wilson paused.

"Thou wrongest me, Adam," said he; "since those days the
Lord hath raised me up to do great things in his cause, so blessed
be the name of the Lord."

"Amen !" snuffled his followers.

"Thou shalt dine with me to-day, Wilson, and this clergyman
too—this Mr. Boyd; I have some points to query with him——"

I know not what more followed, for here I slipped aside.   I
could perceive that with all his loyalty Wilson felt immensely

flattered by the friendly notice of the terrible Cromwell, who with great tact left nothing undone to conciliate the Scots in every way. My safety was now my first thought. The centre aisle was filled by a dense mass of people. Many surrounded Cromwell with wonder and interest; but many more were making their exit with hatred and alarm in their faces. As I stood for a moment irresolute which way to turn, I was plucked by the cloak, and turning, encountered the hard features of old Nehemiah Spreul, who acted as janitor of the college and precentor of the high kirk.

"This way—come this way, before it is owre late," said he, in a whisper; " I suspeckit something was agee."

Following him under some low-browed and gloomy arches on the right side of the western doorway, where Cromwell's guard was stationed, we descended to the crypt of the cathedral—one of the grandest sepulchres in Europe—by the stair which was built by the first Archbishop Blackadder, who died on a pilgrimage to the Holy Land in 1508.

Rushing down this steep flight of steps, we threaded the aisles of the crypt, the shafted columns of which stood thickly set as the stems of a stone forest, and between them the sunlight struggled in dim and misty streaks. Passing St. Mungo's shrine, we reached a little door which opened near his well in a dark corner. Pressing the hand of old Nehemiah, I sprang down the sloping bank of the burial ground, crossed the Molendinar burn, and ascended the opposite bank, where I sought the shelter of a thicket of fir trees, in which I had often bird-nested and played the truant of old.

———

CHAPTER XLVI.

MISTRESS ZACHARY BOYD.

How Captain Thurlow and his worthy halberdier, Sergeant Melchisedeck, accounted for my sudden evaporation I know not; but until the dusky winter eve closed over Glasgow, mingling its dun haze with the thick smoke that darkened every thoroughfare, I loitered on the skirts of the city, nor ventured through its gates till perfect obscurity shrouded its snow-covered streets. I now distrusted mine host of the " Cat and Bagpipes," and instead of returning to that hostel, or to the college, as both might be beset, I sought the mansion of Zachary Boyd, which stood in a close of the Trongate. A servant admitted me, after a long reconnaisauce through the eyelet-hole of the door; for these sharp times made people inhospitably cautious; but I was ushered into a snug, warm, and wainscoted room, where a large fire blazed between jambs covered with the whole book of Genesis in blue delft, and where everything bespoke comfort.

A table spread with a clean white cloth, and on which stood a round of beef, a tankard of spiced ale, a loaf of white bread, and other good things, announced supper in preparation; a silver pot of hot coffee simmered on the hearth, and after my long ramble in the frosty air a glow spread through me at the prospect of a meal.

Above the mantelpiece hung a portrait of Zachary, painted by Jamieson, with a volume in his hands, labelled "Last Battel of the Soule." In one corner of the room stood a carved cupboard of dark walnut; in another a beauffet, having a basin of those golden fish which were first brought from China to Scotland in 1621; beside it stood an antique clock surmounted by a dome of metal, on which the hours were struck sonorously; a set of chess-men carved from the tusks of the walrus, and a handbell, the ringing of which was supposed to scare away evil spirits. I had just taken all these things in at a glance, and deposited my pistols and roquelaure on one of the massive chairs, when Mrs. Boyd—my old love, Maggie Muir—entered, all dimples and rosy smiles, to welcome me with outstretched hands.

I was almost piqued to see her so merry, though I had forgotten all about my passing admiration for her until this casual return to Glasgow.

"And so you still remember me kindly, Maggie?" said I, kissing her hands.

"Oh yes, though your escape down that pear tree nearly ruined me for ever. Such a fury you were! Do you recollect bequeathing your red gown to the devil?"

"Ah, you still remember that?"

"Yes, and your very words."

"Indeed!"

"Yea, in sooth do I," said she, smiling, "for the last words of those we love and those who leave us are seldom forgotten."

"True, dear Maggie."

"The last words and the last glance of the dead and absent are ever remembered, and hard must be the heart and stubborn the soul that are moved by neither."

"By my faith, Maggie," said I, kissing her pretty white hands again, "you are become quite a little preacher."

"I am a preacher's wife," she replied coyly, and withdrew a little; "and so remember you must 'Maggie' me no more. I am Mistress Zachary Boyd, and our old follies must be forgotten now."

"Your husband——"

"Is dining with the English general in Sillercraig's house,

and I wish he were safe home again, for he is bold in speech, and fears no man."

"Dining with Cromwell!" I reiterated, while a vague sensation of uneasiness came over me.

"Yes, and I expect him home every moment—and meantime you must see my bonnie wee bairn."

Nothing was wanting but the production of this clerical bantling of a month old to dispel my little romance; and in its pug features I traced the square massive jaw and thick nostrils of the lean, bony Zachary, who had taken the blooming Maggie of my student days to his heart and home: and yet Heaven knows that for the mother's sake my soul yearned with new and undefined emotions towards this youngling.

I had just recounted the peril I had escaped that day, and expressed a hope that I might be allowed to pass the night in her house, as I meant to decamp from Glasgow to-morrow, when a sharp application of the *risp* at the outer door made me turn involuntarily towards my pistols, while poor Mrs. Boyd grew quite pale.

"Oh, 'tis my husband," she said, joyfully, on its being repeated twice, and in a moment more the Reverend Mr. Boyd appeared, with his face expressive of great things, though we could not define what they were; his voice, his eye, his towering forehead, and his manner, were full of importance; and no sooner had he welcomed, and assumed his elbow chair by the fire, than he proceeded to relieve himself of his leathern spats, and a lengthy praise of Cromwell together. He detailed, with dreary minuteness, the dinner, the attentions, flatteries, speeches, and opinions of the English general, who had completely won his heart and esteem by the piety of his discourse, and the fervour of his devotions; for when the repast was over, it seemed that they had prayed together for *four* consecutive hours, while Thurlow and Hesilrig drank their wine. I was piqued on hearing all this, and said,

"I am sorry, reverend sir, that you mistook the excellent qualities of this foreign republican so greatly this morning. Your devilish sermon nearly cost us both our lives! I presume you are aware of Captain Thurlow's kind intentions regarding you at that time?"

"Yea, my gude sir, and how *your* pistol was as ready as his —but to preserve me. I shall never forget that brave resolution, and the nobler it was in you, Harry, because we parted in bad blude, and I remember me that I reviled you sorely."

"I forgot all that, reverend sir, and in proof thereof behold me here to seek but one night's shelter, for my life is not safe if once in English hands. That Captain Thurlow——"

"Is a fool, and we a' ken that a fool's arrow is soon shot. You are welcome to my hearth and roof, Harry Ogilvie, for a year, if you like, with God's blessing; and for the generous intent of to-day I owe thee many an hour of thankful thought and prayer. To-morrow——"

"I must rejoin my regiment, though gladly would I tarry with you a week; for here is such comfort as we soldiers seldom know—and, moreover, the charm of perfect happiness."

"Happiness," said Zachary, turning up his melancholy eyes; "alas! did not the patriarchs live to the term of eight ages, and yet found it not?"

"Because none o' them had a dear wee Maggie, like me," said his pretty wife, smoothing his hands, and playfully kissing his large square mouth.

"True, true, my sweet gudewife," said Zachary, as he thawed under the sunny influence of her playful manner. "Verily. Maggie, thou art a crown of glory to me," he continued, caressing her soft hair with his huge bony hands; "in thee I find much comfort — yea, as David the father of Solomon found in the society of Abishag, the Shunamite. But now let us to supper, for I doubt not that poor Harry Ogilvie is well nigh famished."

We were now joined by Maggie's uncle, the Laird of Glanderston, an old lieutenant of horse, who had lost an arm at the battle of Tippermuir, and wore the fatal bullet at his neck by a silver chain. He was a fine specimen of a weatherbeaten soldier, and had a great fund of stories, with a predilection for Glasgow punch, for singing rough old cavalier songs, and swearing a round oath or two, to the great discomposure of the reverend Zachary.

"Glad to meet thee, brother trooper," said he, shaking my hand; "I served with Leslie and Ruthven in the Low Countries, and learned to stand fire before I was sixteen years old—and to swear in high Dutch, and conjugate *Ich liebe* with equal success."

Supper over, and a long prayer given, during which the one-armed lieutenant enveloped himself in a cloud of tobacco smoke, I prepared to retire.

"The night is cold, and a soughing wind blows keen down the Trongate," said Zachary, as he took up a candle to light me to my room; "but our box-beds are of snug oak, and you'll sleep sound enough. Yet what think you Captain Thurlow said at dinner to-day? There is a bed at Ware, in Hertfordshire, that will hold forty men."

"Tush, Zachary," said the old lieutenant; "I have seen a bed that held a thousand men or more."

"Ye laugh at us, Glanderston."

"I mean a trench that held a thousand slain on the field of Kilsyth—there were five such, and there we flung them in——"

"God rest them—to await the day of resurrection and of judgment—dear, dear! we live in awfu' times, sirs!" said Mr. Boyd, shaking his head sorrowfully, as he led me upstairs to my bedroom; and, presenting me with a copy of one of his works, bade me adieu with great kindness, and left me.

CHAPTER XLVII.

CAPTAIN THURLOW.

THE volume he had given me proved to be, of course, "The Last Battel of the Soule;" but my mind was running more on Maggie Muir's playful manner, her laughing eyes and winning way, than "the comfort of sicke soules," contained in the tome of Zachary, which did not exactly suit my train of thought. I threw it aside, and finding a volume of the poems of that good and loyal cavalier, William Drummond of Hawthornden, whose sonnets, though tinged with the quaint conceits of the Italian school, are so full of harmony, sweetness, and delicacy, I soon became immersed in them, as better adapted to my wayward thoughts. Instead of undressing, I sat long by the warm fire, and continued to dip into the volume here and there—to think of Flora and of Maggie, the present and the past—to pause and to ponder, and to build castles among the glowing embers, until my eyes closed, and I sank into a profound sleep.

This dreamless slumber must have lasted for some hours, for midnight was long past, when a loud knocking and noise aroused me. I started and awoke. The peculiar sensation of waking in a *strange* place is seldom felt by a soldier, as he is wont to make his bed wherever he halts, or the night finds him; so I started up just as my expiring candle sank down into its socket, and the last glow of the embers died away in the grate. I was in darkness.

There was a loud and angry knocking on the strong outer door, which closed the turnpike stair of the tenement; the sound of voices, and the trampling of many feet, rang in the narrow close, and the faint light of a few lanterns flickered upon the snow which covered the Trongate.

I raised my window, and saw—what?

An armed crowd of English soldiers in the street. I saw their dark capotes powdered with snow, their black morions and their lighted matches, which gleamed like glow worms in the dark; and by the lantern light I could perceive that one fellow carried in his hands *a coil of rope*. This terrible symbol was not to be misunderstood!

The house was surrounded—it was assailed, and doubtless I was the object of their search.

Resolving to die rather than be taken—and to die resolutely too—I tried the charges of my pistols, and stuck them in my belt; I girt my sword tighter about me, and rolled my roque-laure round my left arm. In one moment I seemed to live all my life over again, and bitter and agonising thoughts of Flora and my comrades rushed upon my mind—yet these served to nerve me for bold and desperate things.

I groped my way through the lobby, past the Laird of Glan-derston, who had armed himself with a red-hot poker; past the kitchen wench, who had armed herself with a choppin bottle and rolling pin; and past poor Maggie, who was all in tears and terror, until I reached the door at the foot of the turnpike stair, where I heard Mr. Boyd remonstrating firmly with those who battered at his door.

"Open," cried Captain Thurlow, without; "open, in the name of the Lord General Cromwell, or it may prove the worse for you, old cropear."

"Away, sir; begone, in the name of the Lord, whose unworthy servant I am. Away, and peace be with you."

"Deliver up the spy who is lodged here, that we may hang him at the cross, and we shall leave you to your Scots prayers and your Glasgow punch, my old cock o' the game!"

"There is no spy here."

"'Sblood! I tell thee thou liest, old man, despite thy Geneva cloak," cried Thurlow, imitating the voice of Boyd; "come hither a file of musketeers, and blow me this d—ned lock to flinders!"

The turnpike stair ascended within a round tower which pro-jected into a close, which was dark and narrow; yet from a loop-hole I was able to perceive Captain Thurlow standing near the door, wearing a broad hat and dark mantle, with his sword drawn in one hand, and the other leaning on the mane of his horse.

In a moment the report of two muskets shook the mansion, and a couple of bullets shattered the door; but without opening it, as it was secured by a strong oak bar which crossed it trans-versely behind—the usual mode in Scotland. I saw that nothing but a bold stroke would save me, and remembering that there was a recess behind the door, I rushed down, with a pistol in each hand, and drew back the bar.

At once the door was dashed open, and I was pressed into the recess behind it, as a band of more than twenty musketeers, led by Sergeant Melchisedeck, rushed with a shout up stairs, making a terrible din with their cocked muskets, drawn swords, and heavily-heeled boots; and now ensued a complete investigation of Mr. Boyd's premises; bullets and sword-blades being sent into every bed, bolster, panel, and press in which they thought concealment might be afforded.

I had now only Thurlow to cope with, and one man seemed nothing after escaping from twenty; so, with a vengeful heart, I issued from my lurking place against him.

Still leaning on the pommel of his saddle, this gallant was whistling, and very leisurely surveying the high towering mansions and dark-grated windows of the close, when I sprang upon him, and grasping his throat, by twisting my left hand in his cravat, I pressed the muzzle of a pistol against his face.

"Captain Thurlow," I gasped, for I was much excited.

"Well, sir," he said, calmly, but with a ferocious glance.

"Make one motion—utter one sound, and I will blow your brains against that wall!"

Uttering an oath, he endeavoured to wrench my hand from his throat, and drew back the hilt of his sword to give me a home-thrust. There was now no time to lose. Lowering my pistol, I fired, and the bullet shattered his shoulder; and, with a curse, he sank heavily under his horse, the bridle of which I dragged from his hand, as I sprang on its back with the speed of a goblin, stooped my head to clear the arch of the close-head, and dashed at full gallop, pricking the flanks with my sword, along the silent and empty Trongate, past the cross, past the English cantonments in the Gallowgate, and in five minutes more I had left old Glasgow far behind, and, heedless whither I went, if I only placed distance and security between me and the foe, crossed over the snow-covered country. But for my own presence of mind, I had assuredly swung before dawn at Glasgow cross, and these pages had never been penned to enlighten or amuse my reader.

Infuriated and crest-fallen, but perceiving no sign of pursuit, I slackened the speed of my newly-acquired horse, and after adjusting the stirrups to the greater length of my own legs, rode more leisurely, and began to congratulate myself on the success of my escape. There was no moon, but the sky was a clear and starry blue; and the sheet of white, spotless snow which shrouded the whole country, rendered distant objects visible, while it gave them quaint shapes and quainter shadows.

The dead hour of night had passed; save the hoofs of my horse which rung on the crisp and frosty roadway, not a sound woke the echoes of the country, unless when a watch-dog barked in some remote farm-house or sheiling far among the hills. On my right rolled the waters of the Clyde, dusky and black between its snow-covered banks. At a cross-road swung the corpse of a man in chains, giving additional dreariness to the way, and I was glad when the long-drawn crowing of a cock in some adjacent roost gave token of approaching dawn—the dull, dim winter dawn that was yet a long way off. By this time I had become conscious of pursuing the wrong route; but the snow had so altered the features of the country, that without some one to direct me, I knew not how to reach the Stirling road.

The grey hazy light of morning stole across the sky, and, shrouded in dim vapours, which gradually drew aside like veils of gauze, the sun arose, and the poor robins began to chirrup and twitter on the frozen branches of the leafless trees, and everything in the landscape glittered and shone, while field and cottage-roof gleamed with dazzling whiteness under their snowy winter mantling. The brooks hung half-frozen from the rocks with icicles long enough to make one's teeth chatter, and the wayside rivulets distilled their cold waters between frozen reeds and docks and the dripping winter grass, from which their exhalations curled in the dim and distant sunshine; and afar off, like the huge billows of a frozen sea, the Cathkin hills looked down on the valley of the Clyde.

I felt cold and benumbed; my nag, which proved to be a fine English charger, with a broad chest, small ears, square nose, and full and fiery eyes, began to droop a little, as the foam hung in icicles from bit and bridle, and I looked wistfully at the dun columns of smoke rising into the clear sky from the huge inglelums of the farm-houses, and where, doubtless, many a hot and smoking breakfast was being prepared. After spending some hours in needless detours and perambulations, I found myself close upon the venerable burgh of Rutherglen, with its old church, wherein the infamous Menteith betrayed the guardian of the nation, and its half-ruined castle, where the Lairds of Shawfield resided.

Meeting a bandy-legged little man on the road, with a shovel on his shoulder, I asked him if there was an inn in the town. He gave me a scrutinising glance, and perceiving that my attire was perhaps somewhat disordered, said, with impudent caution,

"Wha may you be, sir, that seek one?"

"An officer of the Black Dragoons, sirrah," said I; "and who the devil are you?"

"Hab Howker, the sexton o' Ruglen—at your honour's service," he added, touching his bonnet slyly.

"Thank you, Carle Hab; I would rather find you *at the service* of some one else."

"Left ye Glasgow last, sir?"

"Yes, after narrowly escaping the English; and now seek the nearest road to Stirling."

"Preserve me, sir! you are far frae that. But tak tent o' the gate you gang; for a troop of the blasphemers' dragoons are quartered in the town."

"Zounds! do you say so?"

"Troth do I, sir; and there have they been for three days, eating and drinking the best that the provost, the bailies, and Shawfield can furnish, and settling their debts wi' a screed o' a psalm or a roll on the drum. My cottage is close-bye, and if a cup o' milk, a mouthfu' o' sour cake, or a coguefu' o' gude porridge wi' the bairns will satisfy your honour," added the old sexton, touching his bonnet, " you are right welcome. 'Od, sir, I wish I was as young as you, that I might buckle on my bandoliers to fight for auld Scotland. But, God be thanked, I have five braw sons, that will soon be men.''

I breakfasted with this loyal Scot, gave each of his "five braw sons" a silver bonnet-piece, he put me on the right road, and thanking my stars for a second escape, I struck across the country to reach the Stirling road.

As I ascended a rising ground near the old Roman way, I was astonished to see, almost at my feet, the whole of Cromwell's force from Glasgow, on the march towards the east; and I remained on the ridge observing them pass, with their drums beating and sharp fifes ringing in the clear frosty air; and so far as a military eye can reckon, there were fully (as the principal had said) 9000 Horse, Foot, and Artillery. This array looked very imposing as it wound round the base of the snow-clad eminence, with pikes, muskets, and helmets shining in the sun, and the white standards of every company of Foot and troop of Horse waving in the wind. A large and lumbering coach, attended by several mounted men, and followed by a led saddle-horse, indicated where and how the general travelled; and a party of soldiers, relieving each other by turns in the conveyance of a sedan chair, suggested that my friend Captain Thurlow, of Overtons, perhaps found this mode of locomotion conducive to the ease of his wounded shoulder. I watched them with interest and anxiety, and as soon as the rear-guard of buff-coated and steelcapped cavalry rode past with carbine on thigh, I crossed the road, and pursued my way with increased speed towards the place of my destination.

Cromwell was only three days altogether in Glasgow. I afterwards ascertained that he was retreating towards Edinburgh, and that he nearly lost, when marching through the middle ward of Lanarkshire, his train of cannon in a half-frozen swamp at Bertam-shotts. We had no more encounters with the English during the winter, save a cavalry affair at Kilsyth, where Colonel Montgomery beat up Hobson's quarters, and killed a number of his men.

On reaching Stirling, where we had about 14,000 infantry cantoned, I was informed by old Sir Henry Lennox, whom I met in the Broad Wynd, that my regiment had marched through that very morning *en route* for Perth, where the Life and Foot Guards, and the artillery, were to remain until after the coronation of the king. I thanked the baronet, who was more than ever enraged at Cromwell for not deeming his paternal tower worth powder and shot. I was glad of his tidings, being heartily tired of my monotonous billet on the old Moss laird; and pushed on for Perth, at the cross of which I found Mosse, the English spy, hung by order of the Estates.

About nine o'clock next morning I sought the quarter-general, to report unto Leslie all I knew of Cromwell's futile expedition to Glasgow. I found Sir David at breakfast in the Gowrie Palace with the famous Sir Ewen Cameron, of Lochiel; old Sir John Macleod, of Duairt (colonel of a regiment of Highland musketeers, raised among his own clan, the six companies of which were commanded by six sons, all tall and stalwart Duine-wassels); Colonel Sir James Lumsden, of Invergellie; Count Ogilvie; and other old soldiers, who laughed at our battles as frolics compared with those of their young days.

"My brave young namesake," said the count, shaking me by the hand, "you have always the fortune to be engaged in something desperate."

"It may be so, count," I replied, laughing, "if danger is fortune; but I was as near death as on that night of our onfall at Musselburgh."

I breakfasted with the general, and, flattered by my reception, hastened to rejoin my troop, which was quartered in the Skinner-gate. That night I had a joyous carouse with my comrades; and Oliphant was so pleased to hear that I had punished Captain Thurlow, his rival for the love of Harriet Morton, that he set abroach a prime bombarde of Rochelle; and we drank in the sluggish winter morning amid songs, glees, and hearty military merriment.

Linn told me that Flora was with Dora Lennox at the palace of Scone; and again I began to build my airy castles and bowers, of which the dark-eyed Flora was the chief inhabitant.

While some of the border counties of Scotland were overawed by the presence of Cromwell's army, the parliament and the king's troops kept all the country beyond the Forth, and the government now resolved on celebrating the long-deferred coronation as a pledge of their intention to uphold the constitution. Fanaticism was likely to shed such a gloom over this solemnity, that the heart of the poor young king quite failed him as the day drew near; for all the evils of the nation and the success of the

enemy were attributed by the clergy to the looseness of his life
and they "worried" him almost to death by daily sermons six
hours in length, prayers, fasts, and love-feasts; besetting his
palace, his meals, and his sleeping-chamber; and it was hourly
thundered in his ears that, " even although his own heart were
pure as that of King David, God would no more pardon the sins
of the house of Stuart for *his* sake, than He did the sins of the
house of Judah because of the holiness of Isaiah;" and he was
openly told every Sunday in Scone kirk, that if his prospects were
bad in this world, they would be considerably worse in the next.

For the little peccadilloes of royalty, the commissioners of the
Universal Kirk had no mercy; and on divers occasions when his
sacred majesty had ventured to put his arm round a pretty girl's
waist, or to pinch her dimpled chin, or kiss her cheek, a just and
righteous storm of indignation burst about his ears, and much
presbyterian pulpit eloquence was uselessly displayed, for in these
propensities the royal culprit seemed incorrigible.

Now, his sacred majesty was not exactly of a temperament
sufficiently holy to endure this priestly tutelage; thus, sick of
prayer, preaching, and rebuke, he galloped away from Scone late
one night, and, attended only by a kind spirit, the reckless and
jovial Master of Oliphant, rode to the village of Clova, on the
Grampians, and thus literally fled with no other desire than to
leave the sour features and black gowns of the General Assembly
behind him.

A few devil-may-care cavaliers, of the loyal clan Ogilvie, and a
band of ranting, rieving Highlanders, received him with open
arms; but his tormentors were resolved not to let him slip so
easily. A troop of the Lord Cassilis' Cuirassiers, the regiment
of the holy kirk, was despatched on the spur, and discovered him
holding wassail in the hall of Cortachy, and in the act of singing
" Deil stick the minister;" he was with difficulty prevailed upon
to return; and though the influence of the officers of state forced
the meddling divines to relax some of their iron rules, and relinquish their intolerable interference, still they had power to cast
considerable gloom over the coronation, which was fixed by parliament to take place at Scone on the first day of the new year,
1651, lest his majesty might levant again; and thereafter a
national fast was to be held for his royal peccadilloes.

CHAPTER XLVIII.

A HAPPY NEW YEAR.

THE winter of 1650 was a gloomy one. The old lightness of
spirit and joyousness of heart which we shared in common with

"our ancient enemies of England," and still more ancient allies of France, had been crushed out of us by war, by pestilence, and religious fanaticism. Blood had drenched the land. Sixteen thousand covenanters had been slain in battle by the cavaliers of Montrose alone; thus many a hearth was desolate, and many a chair and many a place were vacant; and the disastrous result of the battle of Dunbar was not calculated to enliven the nation. Poor bleeding Scotland—bleeding at every pore! The curse of alienated kings, of traitor nobles, and of English aggression, had fallen heavily on thee!

In those years, many a mother wept for her slaughtered son, and many a maid for her lover dead.

Yule came, but all the hearty merriments of old had been swept away as relics of paganry. We had snow covering the mountain and glen as of old; we had the cold leaden sky, the copper-coloured evening clouds, the starry nights, the ice-sheeted lakes, and the frozen linns; but yule was no longer the happy and hospitable yule of our brave forefathers, with all its kind and noble associations. Christmas had been proscribed and banished by an act of the Scottish parliament, and the uproarious Lord of Misrule had been attainted as a traitor; so burning nuts on the glowing hearth, eating spiced cakes, singing a merry carol, or kissing a pretty maid under the mistletoe, were all voted popish, and punishable by law. Whether these things appertained to Rome I cannot say, being but a plain soldier; but *this* I know, that our Scottish people were kinder, heartier, and merrier of old, when palms and bays decked every market cross and village church, and men grew glad, they scarce knew why; when the yule log blazed on the ruddy hearth, and the red holly berries hung in the old castle hall, where the great baron shared with the poor wayfarer his Christmas cheer, and the good things God had given him; when the guisards went merrily from door to door, with costumes quaint, and joyous songs; when harper and minstrel made every roof to ring as they joined in the Christmas carol, and, blowing lustily, the gallant piper marched with lordly stride before the great boar's head, soused on its giant platter; and when the board was bedecked with wastal cakes and holly leaves; the yule pie of everything, with its goose in the centre, flanked by gigantic Christmas candles; then came the song, the dance, the jest, and the warm Scottish welcome, even to a feudal foe—for all the land vibrated with kindness and joy, from the silver Tweed to the savage isles of Thule. Such was yule among us, when the solemnity of religion and the warmth of right old hospitality, with a thousand time-honoured associations, were blended together, to make the day and festival the most important in the Christian year.

All this was swept away, never to return; no remnant of the
olden joy remained, save in the solitary hall of some sturdy old
cavalier like Sir Henry Lennox, who *would* surround his baron
of beef with mince pies and popish yule doughs; who would still
spice his tankard of sack, or wassail bowl of ale, with nutmeg, sugar,
or toast, and who obstinately adhered to the fashion of his
fathers; and laughed the more, because, in town and hamlet,
and on the frozen highways, men went abroad with sullen visages
and their bonnets pulled defiantly over their beetling brows, and
were never without their sword and Bible.

So passed our yule, and so dawned the first day of the new
year, 1651, with all its promises, its hopes, and fears upon the
world. All Europe was hailing it with joy; but we had made
up our minds to be sulky, and received it as we had done the
yule, in sullen silence, or with the quavering of psalms; while it
would have been as much as any little urchin's ears were worth
to have sung the old rhyme—

> Largess! largess! largess hey!
> Largess on this New Year's day!

This day was to witness the coronation of the king; and as
this is a season when, in our northern hemisphere, the distant
sun rises at eight A.M., and sets at four in the afternoon, our
regiment was mounted, under arms, and in marching order, on
the North Inch of Perth before daybreak. Old Hackiron called
the roll by lantern-light; it was a cold bitter morning, and we
had not sufficient heat in our bodies to keep the white hoar frost
from powdering our helmets and breast-plates. To give the
approaching ceremony more solemnity and effect—and, moreover,
as the enemy had established his head-quarters in Edinburgh—
the coronation was to take place in the venerable palace of Scone,
where a king had not been crowned since the time of James I.;
and for this place we marched about sunrise, with trumpets
sounding, kettle drums beating, swords drawn, and standards
flying, accompanied by a vast concourse of people, and by a
number of nobles, ladies, and great officers of state, on horseback,
in sedans, or in gilded coaches drawn by four or six horses each,
and surrounded by bands of armed outriders. All these poured
out of the fair city by the Brig-of-Tay Porte. The old bridge
having been swept away by the flood of 1625, all this multitude
crossed the stream by boats or the great wooden float, while the
whole road from Perth to Scone was thronged by thousands.

I had but one thought that morning: Flora Campbell was at
Scone, and I had a chance—a slender one, certainly—of beholding her again.

Willie Linn rode by my side, and knowing well what was
hovering in my mind, he spoke often to me of Dora Lennox,

and his wish that the war was over, that he might settle down in his quiet old manor-house of Linn, on the Almond, and bring home the heiress of Lennox as his bride.

"Happy rogue!" said I, "how I envy your success, your security, and that perfect love which casteth out fear."

"Were I to speak of Lady Flora——"

"Do not, I pray you, Linn," said I, hastily; "why speak of her, when to love is forbidden me?"

"Take courage."

"Nay, I can never hope to call Flora mine; and yet, Linn, if you knew how I love her——"

"'Tis a craze, my dear gossip and comrade. Would you have the Lady Flora Campbell to ride on a baggage wain? Why, zounds! Harry, you dare not even be her *friend* while this hatred of the earl and Lorn lasts."

"True—true," I responded, bitterly; "I dare not."

"Then why think of love, my poor Harry?"

"We cannot control our hearts."

"Nay, I think we can—yea, curb them, too; even I do this unruly quadruped of mine, when it kicks the flank files."

"In inspiring me with this unhappy passion, the very Fates seem to have conspired against me!"

"Not at all, friend Harry—the Fates, Mademoiselles Clotho, Lachesis, and Atropos, never troubled themselves in the matter. You conspired against yourself. What the devil tempted you to love *her*, of all the women in broad Scotland? But beware, lest in seeking to love you in return, Flora only coquettes with you."

"Hear me, Willie," said I, lowering my voice, as the soldiers were close in front and rear of us; "to be the slave of a hopeless passion may seem unmanly, and a mode of converting life into a curse, but when I know the interest I possess in her heart—the place I have in her thoughts—it is hopeless only because of her house's hostility; and when I think of this, and of her brother's hateful smile——"

"It must seem hopeless enough then, by all the furies! for her house is one that extinguishes the throne itself."

"But to yield her up tamely, knowing what I do, would be the act of a fool—a coward——"

"Of course; yet it were wiser, dear Harry, to avoid her, and fly the dazzling temptation."

"Wiser in me, and happier for her—better for us both, perhaps, that we should never see each other more; yet my heart glows at the hope of seeing her to-day. Oh, Willie Linn, you who are successful and beloved cannot know how weak, how futile, and how vain are the resolutions of one like I—more-over——"

"Front form troops!" cried Count Ogilvie, cutting short all further conversation, as he wheeled round his curvetting charger; "gentlemen and cavaliers, dress each your troop by the standard."

"Left form," cried each captain in succession, as the standard came up, and the leading threes of the front rank halted, the whole moving up to the left of them, till the troops were formed; then a flourish of trumpets was given, aud the Black Dragoons were in open column.

We now found ourselves in front of the palace of Scone.

CHAPTER XLIX.

THE PALACE OF SCONE.

THE day was clear, cloudless, and sparkling; the deep blue sky had not a vestige of vapour floating on it; and the winter sun poured his bright rays on the vast expanse of landscape surrounding Scone; on the slope of the Tay in the foreground, on the environs of Perth—the city with its spires and the vale with all its woods; on the upheaved ridges of the mighty Grampians covered with snow; for snow lay everywhere—pure, white, spotless snow, even on the Tay, which wound a sheet of ice between black groves of leafless oak, and darker forests of the mountain pine.

In the hollow of that gentle acclivity which slopes upward from the Tay, stood the palace of ancient Scone, hallowed alike by history, tradition, and antiquity, by reality and romance, with all its battlements and sunlit pinnacles glittering in the hoar frost. With something of melancholy interest I surveyed the time-worn *façade* of that venerable mansion, which for more than a thousand years has been consecrated to religion and to Scottish royalty. A gleam of the past had fallen upon it.

Scotland, since 1603, had been, most fatally for herself, deprived of the kindly influence of a resident court, by the departure of the selfish James VI. to England; and her palaces were abandoned to ruin and decay.

A thousand old memories of the dark and middle ages serve to hallow Scone, which, in the earlier days of the Scottish monarchy, shared with many other places the favour of being a regal residence; and at a more remote period, when France was Gaul, and England was a Saxon colony, our kings were crowned amid barbaric pomp on the Stone of Fate—the Pillow of Jacob —on which is inscribed the prophetic legend, said to be fulfilled in 1603:

BE SURE, O SCOTS! WHERE'ER YOU FIND THIS STONE,
IF FATE FAILS NOT, THERE FIXED MUST BE YOUR THRONE.

The ancient abbey of the Holy Trinity and St. Michael, in which it was enshrined, and which adjoined the palace, had fallen into ruin, and disappeared; but its boundary wall, which enclosed twelve acres, yet remained; and within this was now a great concourse of persons. The church of St. Colme, in which King Alexander I. buried his queen, the beautiful Sybil, had passed away; but in its place, David Murray, Lord of Scone, had built a new church on the Moat-hill close by; and from its portal to the palace gate, the cavalry were drawn up in a great semicircle and in double ranks, to salute the royal procession as it passed from thence, after sermon, to the great hall of the palace.

The royal standard of Scotland waved on the ramparts of the palace, and a brigade of artillery under General Wemyss were drawn up in front of it. Every battlement and window was crowded, every tree bore its load of urchins and icicles, and from the dense crowd assembled in rear of the serried ranks of the horse and musketeers, the breath arose like steamy vapour in the frosty air. The scene was very gay; the plumage and glittering accoutrements of at least three thousand troopers were there, with the splendid equipages, coaches, horses, and sedans of the great officers of state, while over all rose the masses of the palace, the rude round tower of Kenneth II. rising from the vaults of the Kuldees, the great square keep of Alexander I., the banquetting hall of William the Lion, and the gate of David II., the more florid additions of the Stuart princes contrasting with the grim dwelling of the race of Alpine. Yet it was a plain old palace, meant for those primitive ages when our queens, like the dames of great barons, were not ashamed to be thrifty housewives, and to carry the keys of their cupboards and trunks by a golden chain at their girdles.

In the older part of the palace, the furniture came from an age beyond the memory of man, being black, massive, and strong, as if formed for a race of giants, the chain-shirted Scots who fought at Northallerton, and routed the victors of Hastings; or crusaders who followed Douglas to Theba and St. Louis to Damietta. In the more modern chambers was a bed of orange-coloured damask satin, which belonged to James VI., and another of crimson velvet, flowered by the hands of the queen his mother and her dames of the tabourette.

"Der tuvyl!" said Captain Augustine, striking his gauntletted hands together, as the column halted; " 'tis as cold to-day as ever we felt it on the Vistula, under Marshals Ruthven and Klinkenspuhr."

"Ah, that was indeed a winter, when we routed the Poles," added Drumstanchel; "there were ten of old Leslie's cavaliers frozen to death there."

"What regiment is that?" I inquired, as six troops of lancers, accoutred in close casques, back and breast-pieces, with guarde-de-reins, sword, pistol, and cartouch-box, and with the royal colours streaming from their pikes, rode up all jingling and glittering, threes abreast, and formed close column of squadrons in front of us.

"'Tis Lady Lothian's regiment," said the Master of Oliphant.

"How—her ladyship's?"

"Because the earl commands the Lancers, and the countess commands the earl," replied Linn, with one of his hearty laughs.

"Robert Lumsden, his lieutenant-colonel, is a brave fellow, and paid for every step of his rank, in his own blood under Gustavus," said Count Ogilvie; "but the Countess of Lothian——"

"Plays primero o' nights with the king," said Oliphant, "and has won a marquisate for her husband, say the gossips about court."

"*Bon Dieu!* as we used to say in the Mousquetaires Gris, but it *is* cold, and this coronation sermon is devilish long!" exclaimed Somerville.

As we formed line from the church door to the palace gate, by order of old Marshal Leven, who was riding about, baton in hand, and armed *à la cuirassier*, we gave the place of honour to the king's Life Guards; and with our splendid equipment and sable chargers, we did not consider ourselves second to any regiment of horse in the army. But having many of my own adventures to relate, I must hasten over those historical events which are known to all.

The Reverend Robert Douglas, an aged minister of Edinburgh, lately a chaplain to the Scottish troops in Sweden, now moderator of the General Assembly, and who was said by scandalous tongues to be a son of Mary Queen of Scots and George Douglas, born in Lochlevin, preached the coronation sermon, his text being the crowning of Joash, 2 Kings, chapter xi., and the king yawned heavily until it was ended.

The royal procession then came forth, preceded by the trumpeters of the Life Guards, blowing a triumphal march, and mounted on splendidly trapped and high stepping horses, and escorted by the Foot Guards under Lord Lorn; while the cannon thundered from the palace park, the people cheered, the bells rung, and the kettle drums beat as the cavalry lowered their standards.

Preceded by Sir James Balfour of Denmyline, Lord Lyon,

king of arms, and the heralds and pursuivants in their tabards· by a long train of halberdiers, bluegowns, ministers, and elders; by Field Marshal Callander, and the staff of the army, all glittering in lace and steel; by the twelve knights of the thistle, wearing the broad green riband, collar, and insignia of the most ancient order, and by their dean, secretary, and usher of the green rod; preceded by the Laird of Scotscraig, master of the robes; by the Earl of Loudon, lord chancellor; by the six commissioners of the treasury; by all the lords, barons, and members of Parliament, in their robes; by Sutherland, the lord privy seal; Balcarris, the secretary of state; Cassilis, the lord justice general; the Duke of Lennox, great chamberlain; and all the great officers of state; *the king* came forth from the church door, and every heart thrilled with loyalty and delight, for within that hour he had renewed the solemn league and covenant.

The veteran Earl of Eglinton bore the spurs.

Ludovick, Earl of Crawford, the famous Spanish general, bore the beautiful sceptre of James V.

John, Earl of Rothes, bore the sword of state.

Argyle carried the crown on a purple cushion, and I saw his eyes twinkle like grey glass as he held it up at times to the people, who hailed it with louder plaudits as the *only diadem* in Britain, as Cromwell had destroyed the regalia of England.

Charles was habited in the scarlet robes of a Scottish prince, and walked on foot under a canopy, bowing and smiling to the people, with pleasure that "the coronation of Joash" was at an end. On his right was the Earl Marshal, on his left the Lord High Constable of Scotland, and four earl's sons, the Lords Montgomery, Newbattle, Erskine, and Mauchline, bore his train. Six others carried the canopy.

A long and glittering train of grooms of the bedchamber, equerries, cupbearers, with the master of the jewel house, clerks of kitchen and closet, halberdiers, foot guards, pages, and other followers, closed the rear of this procession, as it disappeared into the quaint old palace by the low arched gateway of David II., which was covered with the glories of stone carved heraldry.

A few officers from each regiment were present at the ceremony of crowning the king; and as the kind count, our colonel, chose me as one of the fortunate few, I followed him into the great hall of the palace.

As we pressed through the crowd, old Drumstanchel said, in a whisper,

" I have some rare news for you, count."

" Well."

" 'Tis said the king is to marry a daughter of Argyle."

The count's brow grew black, and mine flushed and throbbed.

"A daughter of Argyle, indeed!"

"The Lady Flora."

"If he does, by God's wrath I'll join Cromwell!"

"Nay—nay——"

"Or return to Germany, and seek foreign service again."

"Beware."

"I would never serve him more, my good Drumstanchel. Any man's daughter in Scotland, but *his*, would I gladly hail as queen. Oh, when will that black debt between us be settled?"

"Little knoweth the great earl that his dreaded creditor is so near him."

"He deems me with the dead; yet I shall live, I hope, to see his head chittering on the same scaffold to which he has brought many a brave cavalier. And this rare news of thine, comrade——"

"Came from the president of the privy council, and old Galloway, Lord Dunkeld, the master of requests."

And here this strange conversation, which they had maintained regardless of my presence, and every word of which was torture to me, ceased.

CHAPTER L.

THE CORONATION.

WE found ourselves in the vast and stately hall of Scone, through the painted gothic windows of which the noonday sun poured down its chastened light upon a magnificent spectacle. In this gigantic apartment, the walls of which were hung with portraits of kings, and with old tapestry, red, blue, green, and gold, woven by two of our princesses, the Countesses of Brittany and Flanders, and the oak roof of which sprung aloft from grotesque corbels, we saw the young king seated on a throne under a regal canopy, with his dark eyes sparkling, and pride apparent in his flushed cheek, and in the very pointing of his mustachios. The nobles of the land were all in their places around him, in their gorgeous robes, with their swords, coronets, and glittering orders of knighthood.

The officers of state surrounded the throne, and Count Ogilvie mentioned to me the Earl of Hartfield, who wore a silver key, as constable of Lochmaben and hereditary steward of Annandale; Hay of Bewlie, Earl of Carlyle and Lord of Souly in Yorkshire, the first Scot who ever bore an English title; the Laird of Caskieberry, master general of the ordnance, who lost a hand at the storming of Newcastle; the Marshal Earls of Leven, Forth, and Callander, with their cuirasses covered by

Danish, Swedish, and Imperial orders of knighthood; and Sir Patrick Murray, Lord of Elibank and Governor of Carlaverock, one of the few *noble* Scottish nobles, who opposed Argyle and others in the infamous surrender of Charles I. to the English.

Two galleries overhung the hall; one was filled with black-coated divines; the other with ladies of the court, among whom I soon discovered Flora Campbell, seated beside the well-rouged Lady Lorn and the laughing Dora Lennox.

Flora looked calm, placid, and beautiful; she was sparkling with diamonds, they flashed on her brow, on her breast, and among her hair. Her bare shoulders shone like snow in the sunlight which streamed through a window behind her. She saw me not, however, for her eyes and thoughts were fixed intently on the face of the young king. This was but natural; yet, when I remembered the conversation of the captain and count, my heart was wrung with jealousy; and I was in no way soothed by seeing her stoop over the gallery occasionally, to smile or bow to the Laird of Ardmohr, to whom the common rumour had hitherto affianced her.

"What courtier is this—he in the prodigious collar of *point d'Espagne?*" asked the count, touching me on the shoulder.

"Which, my lord count?"

"He with the weazel face and crooked chin—now he speaks with Argyle."

"'Tis the lord clerk register, Sir Archibald Johnstone."

"*He* a courtier," said Linn, laughing; "with that long sword, he looks, by my soul! like a grasshopper with a pin stuck through it."

"He is a villain who leagues with the enemy!" said I, in a husky whisper, as I remembered the packet of letters.

"Beware, Harry," said the count, "you are somewhat rash and bold in speech for this place and presence." And then placing his hand in the hilt of his sword, this cavalier of fortune, whose continental rank was not recognised in Scotland, pressed near the throne.

"Who is this Count Ogilvie—this colonel of horse, who carries his head so high and jostles here?" asked Argyle of Warriston, in an offensive and too audible whisper.

"Who is he?" faltered the little clerk register.

"One whose fathers bore a coronet on their shields when the house of Argyle were but Lairds of Lochawe," replied the count in a stern voice, as he drew himself up with inimitable hauteur, and his eyes flashed with the fire of long-concealed and concentrated hatred.

At that moment there was a flourish of trumpets; the king had sworn the coronation oath, and all our hearts swelled when we heard him call on Heaven to register the terrible vow—"*by the Almighty and eternal God who liveth and reigneth for ever, to keep inviolate the laws, privileges, and rights of Scotland.*"

Argyle then lifted the crown from the table, and while the trumpets sounded again, he placed it on the head of Charles, saying—

"Receive this crown, which one hundred and ten kings of Scotland have worn untarnished by conquest, and unstained by crime—God keep it so!"

"A noble sentiment!" said old Drumstanchel, whose heart was brimming with loyalty.

"I would that other lips had uttered it," added the count, in the same low voice; and now the king stood before us on his throne, crowned, girt with the sword and spurs, the sceptre in his hand, and the ruby ring on his finger.

When I gazed on Argyle, the second actor in this imposing scene, I could scarcely believe him to be the same man whom I knew to be Cromwell's sworn ally and concurrent. He now closed his hands in prayer, and I could not for the life of me say whether he had more the aspect of a visionary or a knave; and now the Reverend Robert Douglas exhorted Charles to be constant and true to the national covenant, expatiating on the falsehood of James VI., who had violated it, and thereby brought troubles on his race; and quoting Jeremiah and Nehemiah, warned him to beware, lest God might so cast him out of his lap and heap plagues upon him. Then followed a long, long prayer, during which the king solaced himself by gazing with a critical eye at the ladies in the gallery; and after all the nobles had sworn allegiance to him and kissed his left cheek, the ceremony concluded by the divines singing the twentieth psalm. Then once more the brigade of artillery poured their thunder on the frosty air, while two hundred infantry drummers, assembled in the palace yard, made every chamber shake as they beat the old Scots march, and the people rent the sky with cheers for a prince in whose name and person were united all the memories of a glorious past, and in whose veins mingled the blood of the Bruces, the Stuarts, and the line of St. Louis.

On that day, from more than a thousand parish kirks, the prayers to the throne of God arose "for Scotland's covenanted king!" Alas! the simple-minded people foresaw not the time when this volatile monarch would repudiate his tremendous vow with as much facility as he had sworn it.

CHAPTER LI.

THE REBUKE.

By order of Marshal Leven, the Black Dragoons were quartered in the town of Scone, and shared with the Guards the honour of guarding the palace and person of the king.

The rumour that the latter was to marry Lady Flora Campbell spread like wildfire, and nothing else was spoken of. Heaven alone knows how it originated; but it excited great discontent among the high cavaliers, and cost me many a bitter hour.

Notwithstanding the enthusiasm of the people and the splendour of the court, the coronation seemed but a dreary affair, owing to the gloom shed over it by the clergy. Instead of the usual new-year festivities, we had sighs, groans, fasts, sermons, and prayers without end, till I am certain the young king in his heart cursed us covenanters and our Treaty of Breda, which brought him among us; but now ensued a terrible affair, which eclipsed even the coronation and the battle of Dunbar.

In the palace of Scone there was a certain damsel named Annie Wilson, daughter of mine host of the "Cat and Bagpipes" at Glasgow; a plump, merry, black-haired and bright-eyed lass, on whom the eyes of various divines had loured dubiously, for "her carriage was averred to be far from discreet."

Now it chanced one day that the Reverend Robert Douglas, while strolling about the palace, peeped in at a lower window thereof, and perceived the said Annie Wilson seated on the knee of a gay young cavalier, who wore a laced mantle, and who kissed and toyed with her in such an ungodly fashion, that Mr. Douglas blushed up to the crown of his steeple hat. His reverence averred that he saw the cavalier kiss the maiden many times, while she displayed rather more than usual of her plump neck and pretty ankles; moreover, she pulled the moustaches of the gentleman, and many unholy manifestations of mutual good will passed between them. The righteous wrath of the pious moderator was roused; he lifted up his eyes and groaned; then he struck the casement with his hand, and the damsel fled; but the cavalier came furiously forward with a hand on his sword, and lo! the terrified presbyter discovered in this ungodly ruffler his sacred majesty the king, who bade him begone to the devil for a troublesome fool!

Full of horror at what he had witnessed, the divine hurried to the lord chancellor, who referred him to the secretary of state, who referred him to the lord justice general, who in turn referred him to the president of the privy council. Messages were despatched, and the commission of assembly, the ministers of Perth and Scone, were convened in a trice. All the divines mustered about noon that very day in a chamber of the palace, with their black cloaks, white bands, and conical hats, to deliberate upon "the terrible fact;" and after long prayer and deep meditation, the guilty monarch was duly summoned before them to be rebuked, "and to purge himself of his ungodliness."

Wearing my buff coat, gorget, and plumed beaver, as I happened to be that day officer in waiting upon his majesty, I was desired to attend him, and it was thus I became cognisant of all that took place; and I was malicious enough to feel delighted by the incident, and thankful to the prying divine who had drawn the eyes of the righteous upon it.

"After this scandal," thought I, "Flora, so gentle, so proud, and so pure, can never think of *him*."

So overweening were the clergy, that every man they could collect was present to hear their rebuke bestowed upon the hapless king, who had hitherto replied to all their grave remonstrances by a joke, or by saying—

"'Pon my honour, gentlemen, you would deem Cato himself impure, and Brutus corrupt."

The room into which we were ushered was a gorgeous one, situated in the older part of the palace, which had been decorated anew in the time of James VI. The walls were covered with oak panels with flutings or bent scrolls, indented at the top and bottom, in the French style. The ceiling was panelled and enriched by heraldic devices. The arms of Scotland surmounted the breastsummer of the fireplace; and reliques of remote Scottish royalty long preserved in Scone decorated the painted walls. Among these were the gilded armour of Malcolm I., the sword and lnrich of Constantine IV., and the gigantic battle-axe of Donald VII. The room was crowded by severe-eyed and darkcloaked divines; many of them were old and white-haired men, wearing black calotte caps; but the most prominent were the king's accuser, with Zachary Boyd and Robert Traill. There were also present many nobles, gentlemen, and courtiers.

In a chair of carved walnut, which had belonged to his ancestress Mary of Lorraine, sat the young king, whose swarthy face, surrounded by a black curling periwig, wore an expression of drollery and provocation. He looked very handsome in a doublet of violet-coloured velvet, on which gleamed the diamond star of the thistle, and across which he wore the broad green riband and gold badge of St. Andrew. The English Garter encircled his left leg, and with his gold-hilted rapier, scarf, and beaver with its white ostrich feather, he seemed the beau ideal of a rollicking cavalier.

"As we are colonel of our own regiment of Guards, I suppose

we may be pardoned having a warlike aspect," said he, twirling his moustaches; "or would your reverences prefer that I shaved off these appendages?"

To this no one vouchsafed any answer; so while the king yawned, shifted each leg over the other, and alternately bit his lips with anger and fun, all the particulars of his misconduct in many instances were recited with aggravating minuteness, by an old minister who was the mouthpiece of the commission, and who sternly rebuked the king, in the name of the universal kirk, and wound up by warning him "to beware o' women, for they had ever proved the cause of man's destruction, from Eve down to that lascivious limmer, Annie Wilson!"

"I have heard you with an immense amount of patience, sirs," replied the king, angrily. "Now tell me, am I less a king of Scotland than my ancestors? If not, why does this kirk commission dare to school, to tutor, and to govern me?"

"To me, it appears," said Marshal Callander, "that a king should be governed by God alone."

"The voice of the covenanted kirk is the voice of the Lord!" said Zachary Boyd.

"And he who will not hear it, let him be as a publican and sinner," added Mr. Robert Traill, in a deeply intoned voice.

"I would at least beg o' your most sacred majesty to remember one thing," said a sly-looking old divine, with a rubicund visage, who was author of "The Scottish Soldier's Last Bullet, or the Balme of Gilead,"—"that is, if I dare be so bold as advise——"

"Well, sir," said the king, sharply, "and what would *you* advise?"

"That your majesty would at least ha'e the wisdom to close *the shutters* when similarly engaged on a lower apartment."

"By my father's soul, but I love thee!" cried the king, with a shout of ungodly laughter, in which Oliphant and many of us joined. "Thou art the frankest fellow here," he added, shaking the old minister's hand.

Every reverend brow was knit; but Charles never forgot this old presbyter, or his advice, saith scandal. The king was now reminded that he must relinquish his attempt to introduce dances, especially the courtly galiard or cinq-pace, which was a heinous crime; and was also admonished that he must attend less to pell-mell and primero, and attend more to matters of kirk and state.

"State!" reiterated Charles; "the devil! Would you have me to sit all on the moat hill of Scone, like Kenneth II., in this frosty weather too; or like my other ancestor, St. Louis, at Vincennes, dispensing justice under an oak? So we must practise ascetic virtue, eh?"

"Assuredly, sire," replied the moderator, severely.

"But your dreary lectures, your solemn prayers, and sullen sermons are more than enough to put poor virtue to flight."

"Sire, this irreverence——"

"Reverend moderator, your restrictions are intolerable!" said Charles. "Zounds! the only slave in Scotland has usually been its king. 'Pon my soul, I wish some folks whom I could name, with their devilish long faces, only knew what it is to be king for a single day! I assure you, gentlemen, I should not care a rush to relinquish the trade to-morrow, and enlist as a soldier. *Your* fellows seem happy the live long day, Count Ogilvie."

The count merely bowed, for the light demeanour of the king was evidently mistimed, as he had to deal with men who would brook no trifling.

"I would warn your majesty to beware of this irreverence to the ministry of God's kirk," said Zachary Boyd, with grave severity. "But three days ago, we saw you crowned our king —yea, a covenanted King of Scotland. Beware, O sire! lest like he on whose fated brow we last saw yonder diadem shining, ye listen to the tongues of the ungodly, for they are next unto the whisperings of prelacy or popery—that which stinketh as an abomination in the nostrils of the Lord! Beware, I say, O king! for though thou art but a boy, the hour of reckoning cometh, when a dreadful voice will demand an account of those things which have been committed unto thee; for then, for 'by our fruits shall we be known.' Beware, I say, of the backsliding of your fathers, and remember that pure religion may reign in the lowly edifice as well as in the proud cathedral, though we praise not the Lord by kists fu' o' whistles, by shalms, and viols, nor clothe ourselves in lawn sleeves and gilded vestments — the empty ceremonies, the dregs of druidism, and the rags of pagan Rome!"

"Ye say well, my reverend brother," added Mr. Traill, of Elie; "and I doubt not your precious words will sink deep into the heart of our royal hearer."

The "royal hearer," gave his shoulders a very perceptible shrug.

"Moreover," resumed Zachary, warming himself into the fag-end of some old sermon, "my brethren, the accursed brood of Pharaoh——"

"Stay, stay, Mr. Boyd," said the young king, laughing; "be gentle with our royal Egyptian; for doth not history tell that our fair realm of Scotland was named so, from his daughter Scota?"

In short, they could make nothing of the merry king, and the assembly dispersed; but although he laughed, and was also gracious and polite, the fact of being publicly rebuked, sank deeply and bitterly into his heart. He had swallowed the covenant, but he could not digest the affront. The black-eyed Annie Wilson was now to feel the vengeance of the kirk, but she had mysteriously disappeared, aud was nowhere to be found; yet Linn and I knew that she was secreted in the Lord Oliphant's house in Perth, where the Master his son now resided.

"'Fore George! 'tis a hard life this!" said the king to Count Ogilvie, as the meeting dispersed. "What a world it is! Why cannot these meddlers leave me alone, and why cannot I live in peace in my own fashion? The poorest peasant may do that, while I, who am a king, am rebuked by the assembly, reprehended by the parliament, bored by the privy council, and bullied by the nobility. Now may the great devil take the Treaty of Breda! I was happier at the Hague, in exile, than here in the palace of my father, compared with whom, I am daily told, that Nero was a saint aud philanthropist. I'll e'en take old Davie Leslie's advice, and march into England, where I do not think these prosy kirk remonstrators will follow me; and if I cannot beat Cromwell, James II. and James IV have shown me how a King of the Scots should die."

A momentary glow of enthusiasm spread over the face of the young king as he spoke.

At that instant, Lord Lorn came up to me with a lofty air, and said to me,

"You are the officer in waiting upon his majesty?"

I placed my hand in the bowl-hilt of my sword, and drawing myself up, said,

"By what right do you question me?"

"As colonel of the Foot Guards, and your superior officer."

"To the point, my lord—to the point, and quickly!"

"You will please to remain without—in the anteroom, or in the great hall, until you are required."

Choking with passion (for I was bound to obey him), I was about to make some furious rejoinder, when Count Ogilvie said,

"My Lord Lorn, he who has trod firmly on the field of battle may well do so on the polished floor of a palace. If my clansman, Lieutenant Ogilvie, cannot show, like your lordship, the title-deeds of lands aud baronies, he has at least scars won in defence of Scotland; for her poorest sons are ever her bravest and *most true*. Your insult is uubecoming and unjust, sir!"

I thanked from my soul the stately count for his comeraderie and his stern eye, his martial air, and sparkling orders abashed the imperious Lorn, who drew back a pace.

"Count, I came not here unbidden," said I, gently.

"I am assured of that, Harry; but remain in the great hall till his majesty requires you."

I gave Lorn a terrible glance, and striking the pommel of my sword with my right hand, withdrew. Even Flora was forgotten in the revengeful glow that filled my heart at an insult so unmerited.

CHAPTER LII.

MORE UNMERITED CONTUMELY.

In a few minutes after all this the king, with the suite who had been present at the late remarkable scene, adjourned to the great hall to loiter and promenade, as the weather was so keen without that every window was coated with hoar frost.

"I hope your majesty will continue to bear these matters philosophically," said the count to Charles, who was laughing and jesting.

"Bah, count—who ever heard of a king that was a philosopher?"

"It would certainly be miraculous," retorted the count.

"And the age of miracles has departed, though my mother Henrietta Maria says nay. You are a plain-speaking soldier, count. Those prosy clerics would require an Admirable Crichton as their king—yet even he danced, diced, drank wine, and loved a pretty girl occasionally. Now, on my faith, Patrick," he continued, turning to the Master of Oliphant, "I think I shall surprise them all some day by turning virtuous."

"Virtuous!" reiterated Oliphant, laughing.

"Yes—does it surprise you?"

"It would at least be something new—but I am convinced——"

"Now, Oliphant, I shall have a great respect for you who are convinced—as I never yet was *convinced* of anything."

"'Tis well the reverend moderator hears not your majesty."

"Damn him!" muttered Charles, stroking his moustaches, "I shall not forget the favour he did me this morning; but rid us of Cromwell, gentlemen, and I will bridle the exuberant zeal of these divines, and teach our Scottish ladies that the sun rises at Holyrood and sets at Scone. The whole year shall be one round of jollity and gay amusement—but you are not about to leave us, lord earl?" said Charles, raising his plumed hat as old Marshal Leven made a farewell bow.

"I return to Perth, please your majesty, where I lodge me with my kinsman the lieutenant-general in Gowrie House."

"A place of bad augury, marshal—nay, nay, you shall stay here."

"Are there not earls enough in Scone?" asked the aged vete-ran, smiling.

"Any one may be an earl—even Earl of Leven," replied the flattering king; "but *one* alone could be general of the armies of the covenant. Nay, you sleep here, and posterity will long point to the chamber where slept the saviour of Pomerania and the conqueror of Wallenstein."

"This flattery would make an old mousquetaire blush," said Leven, as he gave a bow of acquiescence. "There was one earl whom I would fain have seen here to-day—Henry of Findourie, an old and faithful servant of the king your father."

"His attainder should be reversed, but Argyle——" hesitated Charles.

"Would join Cromwell dared we do so," said Leven.

"I served with Findourie, then an exile in Low Germany, and I pledge you my honour your majesty has no more faithful subject —but what matters his faith? His estates are gifted to Argyle, and Findourie House is the tocher of the Lady Flora Campbell," said Count Ogilvie, who was about to add something more, but kissed the king's hand and retired abruptly, as Argyle, with his daughters Jane, Mary, Anne, and Flora, all fair and beautiful women, entered the hall, and Lorn with his lady almost imme-diately followed.

"That woman Lorn hath an infernal memory," whispered Charles to Oliphant.

"How, sire?"

"Whenever I attempt to kiss her, she reminds me of her husband."

"All mere art," said Oliphant; and as the two groups mingled, five times the white plumes of the king swept the floor as he greeted the ladies of the Argyle family and stooped to kiss their hands.

The face and form ever present in my imagination and my prayers were before me now.

Flora dared not—or, alas! cared not—to bestow a glance towards my end of the hall; but Lady Lorn gazed at me repeat-edly. Her nose was *retroussé;* her cheeks were well rouged; her mouth was expressive of finesse and circumspection; her beauty—she was very beautiful—was of a vulgar cast, yet the king admired her greatly, and was suspected of such a *penchant* for her as would have ensured his sacred majesty another rebuke, but the name of Lorn sufficed to shed a holiness over everything.

Much laughter and gay conversation, of which the young king was the centre, ensued; and at times I perceived Argyle looking repeatedly towards me.

"Oh," said the king, carelessly, "'tis my officer in waiting—a brave fellow, Count Ogilvie says."

My heart leaped, for I could see that Charles was thanked by
smile from the beautiful lips of Flora—thanked for praising
me; but turning, he whispered something in her ear, a manœuvre
which dashed all my joy, for his merry impudence might lure
him great lengths with one so charming.

The ministers thought the king immoral, but we gentlemen of
the sword thought his majesty had a right divine to choose his
own morals, and that we should run any man through the body
who said nay.

The king, Lorn, and Ardmohr drew somewhat apart from the
glittering group, and cast their eyes frequently towards me. I
felt assured that I was the subject of their discourse, and burned
to know the purport of it; I disliked exceedingly the steady
stare of the king, for the eye of royalty lowers to none. I was
not kept long in ignorance, for raising his voice Charles said—

"So, sir, *you* are the young officer who allowed the enemy to
pass through Callander Wood, and who conveyed Cromwell's
letters to Edinburgh Castle? So—so, sir! 'tis thus we are
served," he added, and turned his back on me with an expression
of anger and contempt as he left the hall. Lady Lorn also gave
me a lofty glance as she swept past after him; but she who had
spat in the face of Montrose might easily sneer at a poor subal-
tern of horse; and as they all retired from the hall, my heart
swelled to bursting. The words, the look, and aspect of the king
withered it up within me; but I felt no anger at *him*, for it was
to Lorn and Argyle I owed this shame so undeserved.

"It is one more item in the great amount of hatred that
gathers in my breast," said I, pressing my clenched hands upon
my temples; "but, O Heaven, when will the day of reckoning
come?"

A soft hand touched me; I looked up, and met the gentle eyes
and pallid face of Lady Flora.

CHAPTER LIII.

HER face was more than usually colourless, and she was excited.

"I have stolen back a moment from these people, Mr. Ogilvie
—to say, to express, how I deprecate the cruel remarks to which
you have been subjected."

I know not what I answered; but I said something, and kissed
her gloved hand more than once.

Her interest charmed and her sympathy confused me; but she
became placid and calm the more I became agitated—I verily
believe I trembled.

To her graceful beauty—her best inheritance from twenty chieftains of the house of Argyle—she added that exquisite delicacy of complexion which we find only among carefully-nurtured women, who from childhood have never been visited too roughly by the sun, the rain, or wind; and she realised the vague vision formed long ago in boyish days of the woman I would wish to love me; and now she was before me, speaking in her own gentle tones, and apologising for her imperious brother's hostility, and I had not a word to say—at least, little that I remember now.

By her side bounded Corrie, the great Scottish hound, with his neck begirt by a silver collar, at which hung a circular bell. The dog leaped and fawned upon me; and I remembered to have heard him growl or show his teeth whenever Ardmohr approached his mistress.

"Do you understand me, sir?" said she, bending her kind and trustful eyes upon me; "do you understand me when I say, beware of Lorn and of my father, who have conceived a deadly hatred against you. My father's heart, alas! is like an adder in its shell," she added, weeping at the painful admission.

"I have no words, Lady Flora, to thank you for this generosity—to bless you for this confidence; yet I have much to say, if you—that is——"

"But many ears and many eyes may——"

"But where, unless in the palace garden——"

"Among the snow?"

"True; but one interview might take a load from my heart—a load that bears it down."

"Nay—nay, Mr. Ogilvie," said she, presenting her hand, "we must never meet again."

"Never!"

"Interviews will only end in our own ruin and misery," she continued, trembling violently.

"Ah! Lady Flora," said I, knowing that her thoughts were wandering to our last meeting in the garden at Lennox tower, "hear me, I implore you!"

"You have my warmest, my dearest wishes for your success and happiness in life," she continued, as we both became more and more agitated—"ay, my heartfelt prayers!—what more can I say? but—but——"

"The rumour about the king's marriage, you would say."

"With whom?"

"With—with you, Lady Flora."

"Oh! absurd; can *you* think of such a thing?" she asked, with cheeks and brow that burned.

"Then there is Ardmohr."

"Alas!" said she, as her tears fell fast. I felt assured that

was some fatal interest attached to that name, though Flora
did not perceive that her admissions were full of the happiest
inferences for me.

"Flora—ah, pardon me!—Lady Flora, I would say, we march,
rumour says, for England next month, and, it may be, to meet
another Dunbar. Oh! Flora, so gentle and forgiving, to leave
you with the conviction that I may never see you more——"

"Better a thousand times had it been that we had never met
—never known each other," she sobbed, covering her eyes with
her handkerchief; "much had now been spared us."

How these words thrilled through me—how I trembled!
Flora had almost avowed that I was not indifferent to her—that
she loved me—yet I dared not press her to my heart; I dared
not even kiss her brow. I felt as one in a dream. But suddenly
she recollected herself, and mastered her emotion.

"And you are going?" said she, placing her hand in mine—
for this earl's daughter was artless as a peasant girl.

"Yes, Lady Flora, far away—for so says Count Ogilvie. Our
absence may be for months—for months prolonged to years—as
an arduous struggle is before us, and in all that time we may
never hear of each other. But oh! Flora, be assured that the
impression made upon my heart by you, will still be there if I
survive to return from the battles of the king. Death may, but
time cannot, destroy it. You smile—and sadly, too. You think
I speak more like the student I was than the soldier I am.
Well—well, dearest Flora, may you smile often and happily when
I am gone, but think of me sometimes, and believe——"

I had now found language enough, but a step disturbed us.
Flora turned away with terror. I saw before me two bright
eyes, and a bosom veiled by rich white lace: a touch of a deli-
rately-gloved little hand, and the vision was gone—but need I
say that the king's unmerited contumely was forgotten now?

"Joy, joy!" thought I; "the horizon of my fortune is
brighter than ever."

The footsteps drew near, and Oliphant, muffled in his long
velvet mantle, with his plume drooping over a looped-up beaver,
approached me.

"Zounds! I've disturbed you, my friend," said he; "a brocaded skirt and red-heeled shoes—a court lady! By Jove,
Harry, you are in luck to-day. Pardon my interruption—but
beware of the kirk commission; and, moreover," he added, sinking his voice, and drawing closer, "beware of the Campbells!"

"Which Campbells?—who?" I stammered.

"Argyle, Lorn, and Ardmohr."

"Your meaning, Oliphant?"

"I heard them talking very significantly of some one, whom I immediately knew could be no other than you.   In the first place, I heard the earl say, 'You did right, Lorn, in desiring that jack-feather to withdraw, for I saw the lover in his frippery, and doubtless he thought that Flora would be present.'   (My poor Harry! you see how wise Linn's warnings are.)   'Did you not mark his step, how light it was?—his eyes, how they roved about?—his locks are curled and his moustache twisted up— every point and knot trussed to perfection; by the God of Israel, sirs, we must mar alike this presumption and finery.'"

"But no name was mentioned," said I, growing pale with mingled emotion.

"Listen.   'Malediction!' said Ardmohr, 'who are we, to let this bramble remain untrampled in our path?   Had that thrice sodden ass, Duncan, the skipper, done his duty, our spark had now been hoeing sugar in Virginia, or had his ribs picked long since by the Cannibal islanders.'"

"A pleasant suggestion the latter," said I.

"Now, comrade Harry, when you bethink you of what happened when we were youths in Glasgow, can you have a doubt as to whom they meant?"

"None; but I am alike forewarned and forearmed," said I, through my clenched teeth.

"But remember, these are not enemies who will openly assail you, sword in hand, in fair daylight, but will stab you in secret by sure and legal weapons, which a brave and generous fellow can neither parry nor perceive   They have made the king your enemy; but I can soon alter *that*.   Ride over to Perth to-night, and sup with me; Linn and Drumstanchel will join us; we'll have a roast capon, some grilled findons, and a stoup of Bourdeaux.   Come before the portes are shut, and we'll talk over matters.   Carry her off when you choose, Harry, for my house in Perth, and our castle of Aberdalgie, are alike at your service as a place of retreat."

He was gone as suddenly as he came; but his words had rolled the clouds of midnight on my sunny sky of an hour.

Without Flora, life I felt was less than worthless—yet it seemed that Flora never could be mine.   Almost heedless of the gap that yawned between us, I had dreamed on, amid visions and delusions; but visions fade and spells are broken, when reason and reality come home upon the heart to chill its enthusiasm.   So it was with me; and when I saw the realities of our position—the doubts that involved the future, the certainty that though loving with success, we were loving without the hope of a happy result, and that even if I won this idol, on which I had lavished all my secret love and tenderness, and on which I had garnered up my heart—I, a poor lieutenant of horse, had not a temple wherein to enshrine it! Oliphant's offer was generous; but how long would his poor tower of Aberdalgie withstand the thousands Argyle could march into Strathearn? Thus, in the bitterness of my heart, I could not help exclaiming, " Would to heaven I had been shot at Dunbar, or sabred at Restalrig, or that I had never been born!"

CHAPTER LIV.

THE KING'S ESCORT.

THE winter still slipped quietly away, and save rumours of that pestilence which desolated Edinburgh, and caused such a mortality among Cromwell's troops, that their dead bodies were rolled in blankets, and interred by twenties on the links and sands of Leith, we heard nothing that disturbed us in Perth-shire.

If the great Argyle and the gentlemen of his house had really on the *tapis* a plot against an individual so obscure as your humble servant, it was kept very quiet, and I performed my military duties at the palace of Scone; but seeing Flora seldom, and never having an opportunity of speaking with her, as when riding abroad she formed usually one of the brilliant suite which accompanied the young king, who loved to see about him as many beautiful women as possible. And though we heard the rumour of her marriage to the king of these realms revived occasionally, I could listen with placidity, and smile with the comfortable assurance of one who knew better; but when gossips again began to link her name with that of Ardmohr, I had always some trouble in maintaining my composure; and when-ever she left the palace, this Colonel of Musketeers generally rode by her side. On these occasions she never seemed to observe me, and I knew that she dared not acknowledge one whom her kindred had proscribed, and whom her youngest brother, the little Lord Neil of Ardmaddie, a flippant page, had twice contrived to splash, by curvetting his horse in the streets of Perth.

This distant adoration was somewhat humiliating, yet it was better than total separation, for absence from Flora was in-tolerable to me. The day of St. Valentine, the priest and martyr of fabulous antiquity, in honour of whom friends and .overs still exchange presents and offerings, and when we are told the birds are wont to couple, passed unmarked, like any other festival of the olden time. Blustering March whirled the last year's leaves across the fertile Carse of Gowrie; and now came

April, when the mild and silvery rain patters on the bursting leaves, the thick gummy buds of the balsam poplar are expanding bright and green, and the yellow Lent lilies fade, to give place to the virgin lily which blooms on the first day of May. It was spring, the season of joyous anticipation and happy promise, when we exult that surly winter has fled to the frozen north, when the earth teems with verdure, and the young leaflets, the tender grass, the yellow cowslip, and the purple violet glisten in the warm sunshine.

Glad to escape from those sermons and rebukes which for every petty fault and flirtation hung over his head, like the sword of Damocles, the king gladly embraced a suggestion of Marshal Leven, that he should visit the fortified places on the north side of the Forth. My troop was detailed as his Majesty's escort, and we had a rough ride at his heels, through half-a-dozen counties. He was accompanied by a brilliant train, among whom were the Duke of Chatelherault, K.G., the Earls of Argyle, Lothian, Eglinton, the Master of Oliphant, and Lord Newburgh of the Life Guards, KT., and master of the horse.

We visited the garrisons of Stirling and Inchgarvie, and the fords of Forth were ordered to be fortified by redoubts and cannon. Thereafter, we visited Burntisland, the provost of which had begirt the whole town with walls and cannon; then Crail, and next St. Andrew's; at all of which Charles received the keys from the provosts on bended knee, while flags were flying, bells clanging, and cannon pealing from porte and parapet, while loyal addresses were given with due admixtures of scripture, and the market crosses ran with very sour wine.

At Strughter, the king was royally feasted by the venerable Earl of Crawford, the same gallant peer who perished so obscurely in the wars of the Fronde. His residence was so crowded by wearers of stars and garters and their liverymen, that at night I could get no better couch than my horse's stall, and at meal-times there was such a prodigious fuss and swagger, that being neither lord nor lacquey, I was glad to content me with such beef and beer as were issued to the troop.

Unfortunately, the Lord Spynie, muster-master-general of the forces, was absent;—at all events, we were all short of that ready cash of which other great men, as well as the Black Dragoons, have often felt the want; thus Somerville, our cornet, and I would have fared badly when his majesty rode by Dunotter—where we had a garrison—to Aberdeen, where not even the Apostle Paul would get a stoup of ale or a crust of bread on credit, had he been forced to ask it; but the Master of Oliphant's bearing, so cavalier-like and swaggering, with his thick moustache, laced doublet, and loftiness of manner, bore all before it, and we had roasted turkey, broiled beef, stewed veal, canary, Bourdeaux, and Burgundy—the best that the hosteller of the "Bon Accord" could turn out; and on his demurring about credit, the Master swore at him, *à la cavalier*, as "a villanous taverner, a dirty dribbler, who frothed his beer by soaping the tankard, limed his sack to make it sparkle in the glass, and yet never omitted his prayers o' nights or his psalms in the morning."

"A thousand devils!" added Somerville; "when I served the King of Denmark, we had three words in Bremen—*take, burn,* and *cut*—signifying, take their money, burn their houses, cut their throats; and these three words were the war-cry of Tilly's men at Magdeburg."

This kind of bearing, together with an occasional box administered to the tapster's ears, made Boniface glad when our trumpets blew *boot and saddle*, and think himself well paid by the Master's note of hand on his father's baillie; yet he hinted that he "would infinitely prefer money, if any of the noble gentlemen could give it."

"But my note is as good, host o' mine," said Oliphant; "my purse is a lucky one, being made by a tailor's seventh son; yet it keeps Lent sometimes, like a good prelatist, and now hath but a largesse for the servants."

The king's tour occupied only five days; thus, when we halted in Perth, our horses were considerably cut up, for we had gone a great distance.

"By my faith, sirs," said Colonel Somerville, who was well up in years, "this rough ride has well nigh worn me out."

"Tush," said old Drumstanchel, "behold how fresh I am."

"Thou hast more mettle—more bottom," said I.

"Yea, and more belly, too," replied Drumstanchel, simply, for a few months in winter quarters at Perth had caused the honest captain's paunch to expand so much, that he could scarce mount without assistance.

I had scarcely dined in my billet in Scone, when I was despatched with a cornet, two sergeants, and forty troopers, to Anstruther, by order of Sir John Smith, the commissary-general, to escort to Perth fifty waggons, containing the cargo of an English storeship, the *Tilbury*, which had been captured by the captain of the *Bass*, on the 11th of January, and confiscated in the name of the Duke of Albany, Lord High Admiral of Scotland. Among her stores were 10,000 pairs of shoes, 6000 pairs of jackboots, 6000 cavalry saddles, 5000 red coats, 40 tons of London beer, and (as I afterwards read in the *Mercurius Scoticus*) as much biscuit, &c., as would have served the English army for three months. But more desperate work than escort duty was now before us.

CHAPTER LV.

THE MARCH.

BEFORE daybreak on the 18th July, I was roused from a sound sleep by hearing our trumpets blowing *to horse* in the streets of Perth, where we were then cantoned.

I sprang from bed, threw up a window of my billet, which was at the corner of the Water-vennel, and heard the hoarse voice of our sergeant-major, crying,—

"Black Dragoons to horse! saddles and boots! saddles and boots!" as he rode through the streets *cap-à-pie*, and the shrill blare of the trumpets woke the silent echoes.

"What is the matter?" I asked of an officer who was cuirassed and helmeted, and leading his charger by the bridle; "are you Captain Augustine?"

"At your service, lieutenant," answered the husky voice of the German; "and the sooner you harness, the better."

"Wherefore?"

"Gott bewahr! don't you know that Cromwell has crossed into Fife, under the cannon of Inchgarvy, to cut off our supplies. Our advanced guard of horse hath marched already, under Sir John Browne of Fordell, and we follow with the foot under Lieutenant-General Holbourn of Menstrie, for so commands the Marshal Earl of Leven. Gott in himmel! Lieutenant, we may have some sharp work before night."

In ten minutes I was accoutred in back, breast, and head pieces; Carlourie brought our horses, and we galloped to the North Inch, our place of arms, where all the cavalry ordered on this service were fast mustering; and where the count and Sir William Keith were superintending the formation of the Black Dragoons, who came spurring in from every quarter, while drums beat and trumpets twanged in the startled streets of the fair city.

The summer sun was yet far below the eastern hills; the waning moon shone cold and pale in the west; between green inches and greener woods, the Tay rolled down a white and milklike flood, under the leaden sky of the morning. The vane of St. John's spire was glittering in the growing light, and I gave a farewell glance towards where Scone lay sleeping among the copsewood. Flora was there—with her sweet face on its laced pillow, and little wotting, perhaps, that I was now riding forth to a battle from which I might never return. The mighty chain of mountains which form the Highland frontier were already tipped with light; but the valley of the Tay was dark and gloomy. In the calm atmosphere voices of command, as troops were mustered and squadrons formed, rang sharp and clear. Swords clanked, spurs and bridles jangled, the artillery rumbled through the echoing streets, and the brisk rat-tat of the infantry drums, and the shrill pibroch of the Macleans, evinced how all were ready and on the alert; and every heart beat high with hope to recover all that we had lost at Dunbar by treason and by bigotry.

Our trumpets and kettle-drums struck up "General Leslie's March;" the squadrons broke into sections, and the cavalry, brandishing their swords and waving their standards, poured through Perth; and as the sun rose above the hills of the Tay, the whole column of General Holbourn—horse, foot, and cannon —crossed the Earn, and marched rapidly south, along the old Roman road that passed through the Wicks of Baiglie. We were all in service order; every horseman, without distinction, carrying three pecks of oats at his saddlebow, and a threve of straw trussed up behind him. The Black Dragoons formed the rear guard, and as we filed over the brow of the last eminence, I looked back to Perth and the valley of the Tay, which lay basking in the glow of the summer sun. Further off lay Scone. .

I had won her heart, true! But without rank or wealth— without other subsistence than a scanty and desperate one, carved out by the sword in stormy times, could I take advantage of her confiding love, and urge upon her a union which would prove her own ruin and my destruction? Her family would have thought no more of putting me to death, if it suited them, than having a red deer shot for dinner. Now I felt bitterly the a suit, even if successful, may bring less happiness than a hopeless one. I could remember being more light-hearted when the success of my love was doubtful, and I felt like one who had done a guilty thing in winning the love of Flora Campbell.

These and similar reveries were occasionally interrupted by Corporal Bezabel MacSnaffle, who on the line of march was wont to solace his perturbed spirit by singing a psalm; but not being able to compass the higher notes, he *whistled them,* which had a ludicrous effect; the more so as he wetted his lips at times with the contents of a flask, which he carried in one of his holsters.

The Black Dragoons mustered six hundred and fifty officers and men. We had lately obtained many stout recruits, and a fine remount of horses; but in our hasty advance ten of these, belonging to my own troop, had their wind broken by being ridden after drinking on coming from grass. As a proof that the sermonising of the winter months had not been without effect, I observed the road strewed with dice, cards, &c., which our infantry had thrown away, believing that such matters were certain to attract bullets ; yet I know that Charlie Carlourie, of our troop, had a ball turned by a book of profane songs in his pocket ; while old Corporal Cuthbert MacLennan was shot dead through a psalm book, which he carried in the same place.

"Overton's regiment was the first to cross the Forth, though a boatful of men sank by a shot from Inchgarvie," said the count, as a group of officers surrounded him at our first halt, in Glenfarg.

"Hah—Overton's," said Oliphant. "'Sdeath! Thurlow is in that regiment—the very man I wish to meet, Harry ; so, so— we may chance to decide by the rapier which of us shall have the pretty Harriet Morton after all."

"But her brother—the worthy Master Anthony, is also in that regiment ; and it might prove awkward to mistake one musketeer for the other," said Linn.

It was the noon of a beautiful day, when, after a sixteen miles march, we arrived at Kinross, and saw the lovely loch, with its castled islet, shining in the setting sun, at the base of a steep hill ; and here the terrified people urged us "to push on, for God's sake, as the whole English army were crossing the Forth at the Queen's Ferry."

Our spirit was high, and our trumpets rang merrily by hill and glen, while the rattle of the infantry drums rang sharply up from many a wooded hollow, and helmets flashed, and colours waved—the old blue flag of Scotland, with its snow-white cross —as the column wound on its way to the foe.

The scenery of Fife—happy, fertile, and industrious Fife !— was beautiful and varied, with copsewood, rock and hill, lake and stream, grey baronial keeps, and quaint old village kirks. The wild roses and the honeysuckle perfumed the air, as they matted the roadside in luxuriance ; bright streams flashed among the dark woods, and the shouts of happy children greeted us as we trooped past the cottage doors.   Many an old man waved his bonnet to us, and many a mother held up her little son, in the hope that he too would one day be a soldier, to fight for Scotland's kirk and king—for it was an age when the Scottish matron was not second to those of Sparta in heroism and love of country ; and we thought exultingly how dear and beautiful was the land we were marching to protect, as we descended the verdant hills, through shadowy glens, or dense woods of red-stemmed fir and waving beech, towards the Firth of Forth.

Lieutenant-General Holbourn, though sluggish usually, had strangely resolved to attack the enemy that night ; but the wiser or more patriotic Sir John Browne represented the absur- dity of engaging fresh troops with those who were wearied by a thirty miles march; thus we halted and bivouacked on the margin of the Kelty Water, just where the road enters between the steep side of Benarty and the hills of Cleish, while our out-picquet or *perdues*—a troop of cuirassiers—occupied the bridge of the Orr, about a mile in our front.

CHAPTER LVI.

THE BATTLE OF INVERKEITHING.

An hour before daybreak the Lowland drum and Highland pipe summoned our infantry to their ranks, and they commenced their march in the twilight of the summer morning towards the enemy. We—the rear-guard—did not march till sunrise; and after a careful examination of arms, ammunition, and spur-leathers, testing every belt, buckle, and strap, we advanced at a rapid trot, and eager to attack the foe, as this movement into Fife was intended to turn the left flank of Leslie's position at the head of the Forth, and cut off the king's supplies.

Cromwell, with Overton's regiment fourteen hundred strong, and a few squadrons of cavalry, had crossed from Lothian on the 17th of July, and landed at the Cruicks of Inverkeithing, a promontory which runs into the Forth—the same ground on which the Jews prayed leave to found a new Jerusalem, or city of refuge, in the days of Alexander III., but prayed the Scottish king in vain. Cromwell threw up a small redoubt, and then returned to Edinburgh; but immediately sent over Lieutenant-General Lambert, with two thousand five hundred horse and foot. These were attacked by the gallant burghers of Inver-keithing, and a conflict ensued among the rocky hills which overlook the ferry; many lives were lost, but the English secured a position on the sloping ground at Hillfield, with sweyne feathers, and cannon in front of the infantry, and cavalry on the flanks.

Crossing Cowdenheath, and passing the Cross-gates, as we descended from the high ground, we saw beneath us the aged burgh of Inverkeithing, with its spire and quaint old streets, the man-sion wherein Queen Anabella died of a broken heart, and, about a mile to the westward, the weather-beaten castle of Rosythe, a huge square tower, grim and destitute of ornament, connected with a mainland by a drawbridge and causeway, and jutting out into the calm blue river, far along the shining surface of which its gloomy shadow was cast by the morning sun. Cromwell slept a night in this old keep, which had a peculiar interest for him, as, in an upper chamber of it, his mother, a daughter of Sir Robert Stuart, was born.

The midsummer morn was brilliant; light silvery mists were rolling along the slopes of the sunlit hills of Lothian, the opposite woods of Baronbougle, and the yellow shore beneath us, and all along that coast, so green with verdure or grey with ribbed volcanic rock. Bright, blue, and waveless, the Forth rolled away towards the German sea, round many a hazy bluff and rocky headland. The odour of wild flowers floated on the breezy air. Afar off, the dun hills of Clackmannan reared up their massive cones, and all nature was beautiful, as if she wore her brightest garb before those whose eyes might soon close on earth and sky for ever; for, natheless this repose and placid loveliness, it was the morning of a bloody battle.

The boom of cannon pealed across the sky, and we heard the sharp rattle of the volleying musketry; white smoke curled in ridges along the green hill sides, and steel flashed through it; and we soon saw our troops engaged in close conflict with the enemy.

"On, on, for God's sake—spur! spur!" cried several wounded stragglers whom we passed bleeding by the wayside; for being the rear guard, we were the last to come up and engage.

The adverse lines of Scottish and English infantry were now so close upon each other, that, tossing aside their muskets, the wild battalion of Macleans had flung themselves like a torrent, sword in hand, upon a regiment which had in its front a stand of sweyne's feathers. Over this they fired in stern security, and mowed the clansmen down. But still the brave Clan Gillian strove to wrench away the miniature stockade, and again and again rushed with tumultuous shouts and flashing swords, like human waves that had rolled back upon themselves only to gather fresh strength and fury. While closing up our battalions of infantry, the Foot Guards, the regiments of the Lord Duffus, Lawers, and Ardmohr, poured in their fire, ceaseless as the roar of a cascade, drowning every other sound save the crash of the field-pieces. The fallen strewed all the ground in front of the English line, and in rear of our own, which was advancing.

"Form squadron!" was now the order as we debouched from the road, upon a piece of waste muirland. It was done at a trot; then we formed line at a gallop, and waited a favourable moment to advance, the count fixing his keen eyes on the struggle below, where we saw the English battalions, three deep, looming darkly through the smoke that rolled along their front.

"See how the cannon bowl down the Foot Guards and Ardmohr's musketeers!" exclaimed some one.

"Like nine-pins," said I.

"'Twould matter little to you, Harry, if two lieutenant colonels we wot of, are struck off the roll to-day," said Linn

" But see, sirs—the English Horse are making a flank movement. Hobson's Dragoons——"

"Hobson—a malison on him!" cried Oliphant. " I have a little piece of business to settle with him, and hope to conclude it satisfactorily to-day."

At that moment a cavalier galloped towards us, brandishing his sword as a signal for us to advance, and our whole line vibrated with impatience.

" 'Tis the major-general—Sir John Browne, of Fordell," said several voices.

" Advance, count," cried he; " we have not a moment to lose; the struggle is desperate. I have had three horses shot under me already."

" By Heaven, Sir John, you'll ruin the king in re-mounts," said the count. Then turning to us—" Unsheath—away with your oats and straw—cut away the forage—forward, quick, trot!" and ere the last squadron leader had repeated the order, we were riding over the open ground, and treading down numbers of our own dead and dying.

Sir John Browne, an expert and skilful officer, united us to Cassilis' Cuirassiers, who had already suffered severely, and led us at a furious gallop round an eminence, to menace the English left. Passing through the hollow which is threaded by Pinkerton Burn, we were about to wheel again into line, and spur up the slope, to rush down on Lambert's exposed flank, when a loud neighing of horses rang above us, and six pieces of cannon appeared, as they wheeled round on the brow of the hill, and poured a terrible fire of small shot upon us. Then they were instantly withdrawn, to make way for a column of infantry, for our movement had been foreseen; and rumour said, that our *own* commander, Lieutenant-General Holbourn, informed the enemy of it, by means of a speaking-trumpet!

" A thousand thunders! Close up—close up!" cried Captain Augustine, whose troop were first disentangled from the burn, the bushes, and their own dead, and rushed up the hill. We all followed, in great confusion, and endeavouring to form line as we rode on. Oh, it was a wretched malheur!

The fire of Overton's regiment mowed us down fast; but seeing that we would soon be upon them, they fell back, and then, with a shout of fury, we found ourselves on the crest of the eminence.

A moment we paused to breathe our horses, and our cheer rang loudly in the morning air, when closing our files, we rushed on, with the count in the centre of our line; but the cuirassiers of Cassilis were all mingled with us, and Sir John Browne had also taken his place among us, such was the pell-mell confusion of our attack. When close upon the foe—so close, that all our swords were flashing in the air, and each trooper was keeping his charger well in hand, though pressing forward by the leg and spur to meet the mortal shock, a sheet of red flame burst along the line of stern faces in our front. We were amid a cloud of smoke, and a raking volley of balls whistled through us; but the uniform velocity of our ponderous line bore down the regiment of Overton. In short, although his front rank of pikemen met us in the usual manner, we passed over them like a whirlwind, and cut down more than four hundred of them; while Sir John Browne drew off the flank squadrons to attack the cannoneers, who were retreating with horses at full speed, the count, with the remainder, made arrangements to surround the survivors of Overton's battalion, who had formed a rallying square, and opened a fire on our rear.

An English officer, who was running to reach them, was intercepted by me; he fired a pistol full in my face, but missed his aim. Then Oliphant made a blow at him with his sword; but perceiving that he wanted an arm, allowed him to pass.

" Thanks, Master of Oliphant," said he; " I am Anthony Morton, of Durham, and thus repay the shot you gave me on Lanchester Moor."

And levelling a second pistol, he shot the brave and noble Master through the heart! Oliphant fell from his horse, and was dragged in the stirrup across the field, and through Pinkerton Burn, by his terrified charger; but before Morton could regain his own ranks, I clove him to the chin, and Sergeant Glanders put a ball through him.

By our advance, and the confusion consequent thereto, we had completely turned Lambert's left, and were on the point of cutting off Overton and his guns—a movement which would have gained the day, for it was nobly seconded by the clan Maclean, who fought like incarnate devils, when Holbourn, who commanded, actuated by some unaccountable timidity or premeditated treason, fell back from Hillfield, upon the opposite bank of Masterton, leaving us in danger of being surrounded by Alured's fresh brigade of horse; but closing our files, we made a reckless rush down hill.

" Forward, my brave Black Dragoons!" cried the count; " fear nothing, and trust to your swords and the shield of Omnipotence! Fall on!"

As we encountered Alured's heavily-accoutred regiments there was a momentary conflict of great desperation, and many of our best men went down never to rise again. Major-General Browne was taken prisoner; and after we had broken through,

Linn, who was rendered desperate by the untoward events of the day, wheeled round his horse, and rushed alone upon the enemy.

"Come back, Linn," I cried, "come back; for all cur troops have given way!"

"I will rather die than live to tell Dora of another Scottish defeat!" replied this brave enthusiast, who again plunged head-long into the storm of battle. I saw his sword flash once, twice, aye thrice, as the dark mass of Alured's dragoons opened and closed around him; then his helmet and plume went down, and I saw no more of poor Willie Linn. At the same moment my horse gave a terrific bound, as some wretched puritan, with the name of God on his lips and hell rankling in his dying heart, passed his sword into it, and almost disembowelled the poor animal. Away it bounded, and rushing against a fauld-dyke, fell heavily, crushing me by its weight. In vain I strove to free myself, and called to our wounded stragglers for aid, as I lay by the wayside, but none cared to assist me.

Two officers, accoutred *à la cavalier*, rode up; they were Lord Lorn and Ardmohr, and with shame—yea, sorrow, I write it—they cruelly plunged their horses over me. The hoof of one struck my head; my helmet failed to protect me; and just as ten pieces of Scottish cannon, with horses at full speed, the heavy wheels crashing over stones, bushes, and the bodies of slain and wounded, swept past, I became senseless, and remember no more of that most unfortunate and ill-fought battle of the 20th of July, of which I can give no detailed account, nor is any necessary here.

General Holbourn of Menstrie shamefully betrayed his trust, and the people of Inverkeithing assert* that he stood on the East Ness and conferred with Lambert through a speaking-trumpet. He was accused by the count of treason before the parliament at Stirling; but though it was not proved, he resigned his commission, for the united voice of the army condemned him.

We had the Lairds of Balcomie and Randerston, with sixteen hundred men, killed and wounded; twelve hundred were taken prisoners, with sixty stand of colours, fifty-two drums, and several bagpipes. Major-General Sir John Browne, overwhelmed by shame and grief, died in the citadel of Leith, a prisoner in the hands of Monk, who interred him among his ancestors in the kirk of Arngask, with all the honours due to his rank and bravery.

Nearly the whole clan of Maclean perished before they could prevail upon their venerable chief to quit the field, and, standing like a tower amid the storm of bullets, swords, and pikes, he saw all his sons—the stately six—die before his eyes,

* To the present day.

as each came up with sword and shield to defend his chief and father, who expected to be succoured by Holbourn, and left not the field until five hundred of his surname—the noble clan Gillian—choked Pinkerton Burn with their corpses, and dyed the whole stream in its course to the Firth with their hot Highland blood.

When the last of his sons fell before him, the aged chief threw away his sword and muffled his head in his plaid, exclaiming—

"My sons—my sons—my six, so fair and true! God of our fathers, why sparest thou me?"

Of the Black Dragoons three hundred were killed, wounded, or taken; but of all, I most deeply regretted poor Linn and Oliphant; the latter was lying dead not far from the brother of Harriet Morton; thus the bluff Captain Thurlow of Overton's regiment, was now without a rival for her hand. When I partially recovered from my insensibility, the sun was setting on that field where the shadow of Death was hovering.

The gloom of evening deepened. The hills were growing dark, and heavily I closed my eyes as night descended on the dying and the dead.

CHAPTER LVII.

NIGHT AMONG THE DEAD.

THE calmness of the descending dew revived me; when the placid moon of a soft summer night sailed through the clear blue sky, and the hour was so calm that the little fairies—if fairies indeed there be—might have heard the blue-bells ringing on the gentle wind that came from the eastern sea. I was still weak and incapable of motion. My head, aching and heavy, buzzed like a belfrey; and my horse, now quite dead, lay above me, a load from which I was quite incapable of freeing myself.

Poor nag! he had escaped many a bullet; but now he lay stiff as a bronze steed, with a pool of blood around him, and his fine nostrils wet with the large tears that had oozed from his eyeball in his death agony.

The scene swam round me. I thought my head was fractured; and while the image of Flora came before me, there came with it a tiger-like longing for vengeance on her brother for the dastard deed of the past day. Remembering that I dared not risk being taken prisoner by Cromwell, I attempted to move, but agony compelled me to relinquish the effort. A wounded musketeer of the Foot Guards, who lay near me, implored aid and water.

"If I move," said I, "I shall die."

"Wad to God that I micht dee, for my agony is mair than mortal!" sighed the poor man, and soon after he had his wish

accomplished; for over that field rode the destroying angel in all
his terrors.

The battle-ground presented a frightful scene of slaughter. The
mountain burn was choked with men, who had fallen there, or
rolled down into it; and there they lay, pell-mell, among muskets, pikes, swords, drums, havresacks, and wallets; and there
many were shrieking to the rest "to kill them, for God's love,
and end their misery!" Elsewhere they lay in long rows or
heaps, just where the shot had mowed them down—motionless
and still, with upturned faces, fixed and ghastly eyes; others
were crawling and writhing, legless or armless, and all plastered
and disfigured by powder, dust, and gore; but enough of this,
for every field is alike where men fall under shot, shell, and steel
—pierced, cut, and wounded everywhere and everyway.

I remarked that many died between the night and morning,
at least before daybreak—the coldest hour of the twenty-four;
and with dawn came the flies to torment the wounded, and to
batten in their blood; and that strange miasma which rises from
the bodies of the newly slain, pervaded the field, when they grew
rigid, and the pools of gore congealed under the rising sun; but
I anticipate.

About midnight I saw two men moving near, and believing
them to be plunderers, as one bore a lantern, I lay still, as if
dead, and scarcely dared to breathe. They drew nearer, and I
perceived them passing the lantern across the faces of those who
lay in their way. One carried his sword drawn, for I saw its
blade gleam occasionally, and both were cloaked and muffled.

"He was lying here about, with his horse killed over him," said
one whose voice I knew.

"But if your horse's hoof really struck him, as you say, it
must have finished him—and we have had a ramble for nothing,"
replied the other.

"Natheless, I should like to make sure," said the first, with
an oath; "and even were he headless, I would pass my sword
through his body, to be certain—for 'tis long before the de'il
dies at the dykeside."

I was startled by these terrible hints, for now I recognised
the voice of Colonel Campbell of Ardmohr, who bore the
character of a cruel and unscrupulous chieftain—half heathen
and half hypocrite. The other was Captain Thurlow!

"Faugh! 'tis a scene of horror," said the latter, "and I don't
like the errand. I have served a long apprenticeship to war,
Ardmohr. I have ridden through ten battle fields, and spilled
my blood in four of them——"

"Enough of this boasting, Thurlow—help me to search."

"I think I should know him well enough—but what is your
devil of an Ogilvie like?"

"Like ?"

"I mean, what manner of man ?"

"A lubberly lout—black haired and pale."

"All are pale enough here to-night, God rest them."

"Pale, with a black moustache—the scurvy hound—I should like to send his head to Lady Flora, as the MacGrigors sent the head of Ardvoirlich to *his* dame."

"Oho—there is a lady in the case as well as—see, there is some one."

"Where ?" asked Ardmohr, quickly.

"Beside that dead horse."

"'Tis one of the Foot Guards, minus a limb."

"On the other side."

"A poor little fifer, torn in two by a cannon shot. Let us seek this beau coq by the burnside; and I would we found his friend, Count Ogilvie of Mariburg, here. I am suspicious of that fellow; he is too proud to serve either a German kaiser or a Scottish king; and Argyle has some strange misgivings anent him. He will give *our party* some trouble yet, as Montrose did; and as for his lieutenant——"

"He knows so much of your plots, that *the earl* would give more than Cromwell for his head," said Thurlow; "yet, damme, I don't half like this work, sir !"

The lantern disappeared as they descended to the burnside, and left me, yet I saw the rays of light flashing upward from the hollow at times. That Ardmohr was searching for me, with murderous intentions, I had not a doubt. Oh, how my breast swelled with rage and bitterness at the thought.

"The villain ! the traitor !" I exclaimed; "God restore me to strength, and one day I shall unmask thee ! *Beau coq ?*" I repeated, over and over again; "now do I know the villain who deceived me at Callander Wood, for such was the phrase he used, and the voice and figure were those of Ardmohr."

My emotions almost choked me. I struggled desperately to free myself from my horse, but in vain. I believe that I became delirious for a time, and talked and threatened aloud; but the paroxysm passed away as morning dawned, and the sun arose in the blue midsummer sky; while the mountain erne winged his way from the woods of Dunfermline, across the ensanguined field; and it was strange to see the yellow butterfly floating, and the honey bee humming over the sharp pale faces of the dead.

With morning came many women—the mothers, wives, and sisters of the soldiers—to search among the slain; and their sobs and outcries mingled with the moans of the dying, for such were the sounds that had now succeeded the roar of yesterday's conflict.

Alas! there came none to look for *me!*

Many hovered near me, pale and wan with watching; the mother with her silver tresses, the wife with a babe at her breast, and the sister with her snooded braids; and there they wandered over that scene of carnage, with hair dishevelled, blanched cheeks, and bloodshot eyes, searching with agonized hearts for these beloved forms they only dreaded to find; and then, when found, an upbraiding cry went up to Heaven as they sank to earth beside the dead.

"A Black Dragoon!" exclaimed a voice near me.

"It must be he—my son—my Charlie—the last o' three these waefu' wars have left me!" shrieked a female voice, and an old woman, clad in a cloak and curchie, leaning on the arm of an older man, who wore a square-tailed coat with enormous pockets, hobbled with his staff towards me.

"'Tis an officer, Elsie; look at his black plume and golden scarf," said he; and the old woman uttered a cry of joy, and passed on, while I gave a sigh of misery.

"But there is life in the puir gentleman yet," said she, pausing. "Oh, sir, sir, ken ye aught o' my son; he was in Drumstanchel's troop?"

"His name, gudewife?"

"Charlie Carlourie, an honest, brave, and pious lad," said the mother, clasping her withered hands.

"Rest assured that your son is not on the field—at least, so far as I know."

"Oh, sir, ye ken him then!" said she, trembling; "he is the last o' three we have lost in war—but Thy will be done, O Lord!" she added, raising her eyes to Heaven, while her husband uncovered his silvered head; "for if I had three mair, they should all gae forth to fight for our covenanted king."

"A wounded trooper assured me, sir, he saw our Charley fall," said the father, who was old and bent with years; "be composed, dear Elsie," he sighed, as the woman wept anew; though this day maketh our hearth for ever desolate, His hand hath not fallen heavily on us alone. Puir Scotland; our men gie their bluid, our women their tears, and our preachers their prayers for thee, yet all availeth not!"

"Argyle!" muttered I.

"My puir son," resumed the mother; "well didst thou honour thy father and thy mother, yet thy days were not long in the land."

The grief and resignation of this old couple touched me.

"Are ye sairly wounded, sir?" said the old woman, passing her hands tremblingly over my brow; "a mother's heart may be yearning for thee this day, even as mine yearneth for my son."

"Alas! I have never known mother or kindred," I said; "nor is there one in all the land to weep for me! But take courage," I continued, as the old man, though frail, feeble, and in grief, endeavoured to assist me from under my horse, "I saw your son in the ranks, just before my charger fell with me."

"Blessed be your words," said the mother; "but may I humbly ask your name, gentle sir?"

"Harry Ogilvie, lieutenaut, by the king's grace."

"Our son's master!"

"The same—Charlie Carlourie is my faithful servitor!"

These words seemed to endow both father and mother with fresh strength; they drew me out, and sore, benumbed, stiff, and scarcely able to drag one leg after the other, I rose from the field, over which one party of Overton's musketeers were collecting the spoil and trophies, while another party were interring the dead.*

The old man took off the saddle, holsters, and housings of my horse, which were rich and valuable; he gave me an ample plaid to throw over me as a disguise; I tore the plume from my helmet, concealed my gold scarf to show as little of the officer about me as possible; and, propped between him and his wife, endeavoured to reach a thicket, beyond which their cottage lay.

As we crossed the field, I saw Captain Angus Dhu Maclean, a son of Duairt, lying dead with a skene dhu clenched in his teeth; and there was clutched in his hands an enormous gled, which, by the last effort of expiring nature, he had crushed, just as the hideous bird was in the act of tearing his flesh. Like his five brothers who lay dead near him, he was riddled by bullets.

A little apart from the many bodies that lay in every imaginable posture of agony, just as they had died, Englishman and Scot, in heaps across each other, I saw an officer of the Scottish Foot Guards, in a polished cuirass and white scarf, over whom a lady was stooping. Whether this person was his wife, his love, or sister, I know not, but there was something in her stupefaction that moved me. Her eyes were red and inflamed; her cheek ashy pale, and, though young, it was furrowed by tears and grief. I write these things plainly and simply, just as I saw them, and as they impressed me.

She took the slain man's passive hand in hers, and strove to raise it—alas! it was too stiff already. She kissed his dead face many times, and smoothed the clotted hair on his brow; she cut off a lock, and placed it to her lips and bosom, and then tied a tress of her own auburn hair round the dead man's hand.

* Old people at Inverkeithing still point to the plain, and say "it was like a *hairst field wi' corpses*"—meaning a field strewn with sheaves of newly-cut grain.

" 'Tis the young Laird of Randerston Tower, and the lady is his wife—Hartshaw's daughter," whispered the old man. "Go Elsie, to her assistance, and leave me wi' Mr. Ogilvie."

Near the lady were the puritan soldiers who buried the dead. They were laughing, talking, and smoking, or singing dreary psalms. She uttered a cry of despair as they approached her, and, pausing, leaned for a moment on their shovels. A deadly pestilence had been brought by the English into Scotland; the summer air was full of infection; and the orders, in both armies, immediately to inter the slain, were rigidly executed; she em-braced the body by the feet as the Englishmen drew it gently away, but the moment she fainted, it was flung into the deep trench, and others were heaped upon it.

It was a strange sight; all those men who had never spoken, and never met before in this world, heaped in one common grave, and taking their eternal rest together. I was in a mood for moralizing, and turned away with a sickened heart, leaving Elsie to attend the young widowed lady of Randerston.

CHAPTER LVIII.

THE COTTAGE.

THE dwelling of the old carle, Carlourie, consisted of little more than two apartments—a *butt* and a *ben*—having a clay floor and thatched roof full of swallows' and martins' nests, with a duck-pool in front, and a kail-yard behind. A green and sheltering hill sloped up to the north of it; to the south lay green knolls and broomy hollows, beyond which appeared the blue Forth and the grey battlements of Rosythe Castle, with black columns of smoke always ascending from its chimneys; for there Colonel Overton and Captain Thurlow had taken up their quarters, which made the vicinity anything but pleasant for me; and I often saw them galloping their horses along the causeway which con-nects the castle with the land; however, these worthy enforcers of independency and the Lord's word erelong betook themselves elsewhere.

Here had Simon Carlourie dwelt in peace for three quarters of a century, devoting all his energies to the cultivation of kail, as his wife devoted hers to her wheel. It would be impossible to detail the kindness I received from them; thus I recovered rapidly, and became so far convalescent, that I could assist the old man in hoeing up his kail, or sit with him at the door in the sunshine, to watch the passing ships, which still sailed for the ports of Norway, Holland, and Sweden, fearless of the cannon of

Admiral Blake, who hovered in the North Sea, prowling alike for the vessels of James, Duke of Albany, high admiral of Scotland, and those of their high mightinesses the States General, against whom the English bore a hearty grudge.

I had been severely bruised and crushed by the fall of my horse; in some places my skin was all the colours of the rainbow; but the decoctions and simples of Elsie Carlourie—who was never tired of asking me about her son and expatiating upon his merits—soon removed my ailments; as she, like old women generally in Scotland, was an expert mediciner—too much, so, perhaps, for her own reputation, for having cured two persons whom the barber-chirurgeon of Inverkeithing had nearly poisoned, that worthy practitioner threatened to have her indicted for witchcraft.

The last of the dead had been long since buried; the ruts of the artillery wheels, and the hoof marks of the galloping squadrons had disappeared from the velvet turf; the last remnants and relics of the fray—the broken blades, muskets, pistols, and iron balls—had all been gleaned up, and under the soft showers and the summer sun, the grass looked fresh and green as of old, and it was sprouting on those hideous mounds—those barrows of the slain—that lay by Pinkerton Burn, which ran clear and pellucid as ever, with the brown trout lurking in its deep shady pools, and the pale drooping willow, the pink wild rose, and the white water lily kissing its shining surface; and no one who gazed on the silent field, or the quaint grey burgh that lay beyond, with its snug old-fashioned streets, could have believed that *here*, three weeks ago, a bloody battle had been lost and won; and that, in the sunny hollow below, so many gallant men had given up their souls to God, at the sword's point and the canuon's mouth.

In the solitude of old Carlourie's cottage, I heard but occasional rumours of passing events, but they were such as made me long to rejoin the poor remnant of the Black Dragoons; with them to make another effort in the cause of my country. Seeing that I was restless, and longing for intelligence, the old man was wont to take his staff and walk daily into the adjacent town to glean up news for me; and daily he brought me some that were of interest.

Five days after the battle of Inverkeithing the king, finding his position at the head of the Forth rendered precarious, by Lambert turning his left flank and entering Fife, had marched to invade England with all the Scottish troops that were not in garrison—viz., eleven regiments of horse, twenty battalions of infantry, and a train of artillery, with fourteen field-pieces—in all, twenty thousand men. With these he hoped to rouse the English cavaliers—but hoped in vain. Being entirely in Cromwell's interest, with that anti-national party which, in *all ages*, has existed in Scotland, Argyle, now a marquis, protested against this southern march, and so far incurred suspicion of disloyalty, that Charles would have committed him a prisoner to one of the royal castles, but for Lady Flora's intercession.

"'Ods fish!" said he, "I can refuse nothing to lips so beautiful; they would lure St. Anthony himself!"

So the army marched, and the new marquis, like a diplomatic spider, was left to spin his webs at home.

"And I am little better than a prisoner!" I exclaimed, bitterly, on receiving this news.

"But the Black Dragoons are not with the army, sir."

"How?"

"They are in garrison at Dundee," answered old Carlourie; "where colonel the Laird of Bewhany commands, while Marshal Leven, with a body of troops, hovers in the Howe of Angus."

The Scottish host entered England on the 6th of August. The king, as generalissimo, threw a garrison into Carlisle, of which he made Sir William Livingstone, of Westquarter, governor, and then he advanced through Lancashire, driving the enemy before him, thus confounding Cromwell, and rendering that general's recent success less than useless.

Leaving General Monk with a column to maintain the cause of republicanism in Scotland, and work in concert with Argyle and Warriston, Cromwell prepared to follow the king without delay. He first attacked the little town of Burntisland, which is remarkably situated on a rocky peninsula, and was begirt by walls and towers. The bold Burntislanders defied him; but he threw in such a shower of shot and shell from the steep green hills which overhang the Kirk-toun, that the provost, a dealer in stone-ware, was sorely discomposed by the rattle of these bitter almonds among his crockery, and told his people that "Cromwell was a loon, wi' whom it was kittle wark to warsle;" so he agreed to capitulate, on condition "that the main street of the burgh should be paved, and a road made thereto." To these curious terms Cromwell promised, by the mouth of Captain Thurlow, to accede, and he faithfully fulfilled them; after which he pushed on to Perth, *en route* destroying Fordell, the seat of poor General Browne, then dying of wounds and grief at Leith. He bombarded Perth for a night, and, after a sharp defence, it was surrendered by Grant of Balhagils, the lord provost. Then Cromwell united his forces to those of Lieutenant-Generals Lambert and Harrison, and leaving Scotland for ever, vigorously followed the march of our army into his own country.

Thus were matters standing in the first week of August, when

I flung aside the *Mercurius Scoticus*, in which I read these startling details, and astonished the gudeman Carlourie, by a brisk effort to march across the room and test my strength. I felt that now I must be up and doing. I was almost well; my money was nearly spent, and I could no longer linger in idleness, but must hasten to rejoin. I shook off my fit of the doleful dumps as I progressed towards recovery; being too much of a soldier, I hope, to remain long depressed, my spirit always rose, and I became buoyant and full of hope, after a casual prostration, from poverty, sickness, disappointment, or any other evil of my chequered career.

I cleaned and polished my accoutrements till back, breast, and head pieces, steel gloves and gorget, sword-blade, spurs, and pistols, shone like new silver. I prepared all my housings and trappings, and commissioned my host to procure me a horse, suited alike for battle and for ordinary riding. I was all eagerness to begone, and thought of nothing but my departure, when one night, as we were talking over it, after the good people with whom I lived had concluded their frugal supper and their usual prayers, and when we were just beginning to be drowsy in the heat of the bogwood fire, which made the delft plates on the rack, the pot-lids, and the pipeclayed hearthstone glow with warmth, a hand was laid hastily on the pin by which the door was fastened; the collie erected his bristles, and grimalkin crept closer within the warm ingle, as a knocking followed, and a voice cried,

"Open!"

"Wha tirls the pin at this time o' night?" asked the host.

"'Tis I, father—Charlie, your son."

In a moment more, my trooper sprang in, and threw his arms round the necks of the old people, after which he turned to me.

" *You* here, sir!" he exclaimed, astonishment getting the better of respect; "*you* in my mother's puir cot!"

"As you see, Carlourie; and by my faith, trooper o' mine," said I, "it is better to be here, than buried in yonder trench by the burn side, where so many hundreds of our men are lying."

"Heaven be blessed, you are still spared, sir. It was a rough day's work, that 20th of July! I have been a prisoner among the English. I was fettered to the brave young Laird o' Linn—God rest him!——"

"Was he not killed in the battle?" I asked, hastily.

"No, sir."

"Is he dead, then?"

"You shall hear, sir; but sorely am I fatigued—I've travelled on foot frae Stirling since morning."

"Frae Stirling—frae Stirling a' the gate," cried the anxious mother, drying her tears, bustling about, and producing cheese, bannocks, and a jack of Lammas ale, with a piece of cold meat from her corner almrie; "my puir bairn, you'll be well nigh famished!"

"Famished—de'il a bit, mother," responded her "bairn," who stood six feet three inches in his jack-boots, and had on a sorely-splashed buff coat, and rusty regimental head-piece, indented by many a cut and blow; "the de'il a bit; I had a gude feed as I passed through the Broad Wynd this morning; there was a regular banquet spread there for a' that chose to come; and the cross-well gushed out wine and ale by turns."

"Whence this joy," asked his father, "at such a time, when war and pestilence are in the land?"

"It was a brave banquet, given by Argyle, in honour of his new patent as marquis."

"So the earl can find time and spirit to rejoice thus, when the king's throne is crumbling, and his country is torn by intestine broils and foreign invasion!" thought I.

I had ample food for bitter reflection, and dreamily heard the garrulous trooper, who informed us that he was on his way to join the regiment at Dundee; but had taken the liberty to make a little detour, for the purpose of visiting his parents.

"This is fortunate, Charlie," said I; "we shall travel together. But I am impatient to hear about the Laird of Linn."

"Puir Linn!" said the soldier, sighing as he wiped his bristling red moustaches, and pushed aside the cleanly-picked bone and empty flagon. "I have a sorrowful tale to tell, sir."

With this preface he related their mutual adventures, which I now give in my own words, in following chapters.

CHAPTER LIX.

THE LAIRD OF LINN.

THE last cannon-shot fired by the English had killed Carlourie's horse, and he was taken prisoner by Alured's dragoons, before he could free himself from the stirrups of the fallen steed. He was then driven into a field where all the prisoners were collected and surrounded by the musketeers of Monk and Overton, with cocked matches. Here all the officers were either manacled or tied by cords, each to a private; for such were Cromwell's orders, in the spirit of republicanism, to degrade the king's commission and level all ranks; and thus it was, that he had marched the late Duke of Hamilton and Chatelherault, a Knight of the Garter and lieutenant-general, to London, on foot, and handcuffed to a sergeant—old Hackiron by-the-bye—when that noble was taken prisoner in 1648, on the Scottish army marching into England, to relieve King Charles I.

By this arrangement, it was Carlourie's lot to be fettered by the left hand to the lieutenant of his own troop—the young Laird of Linn. They were secured together by two iron loops, through which was an iron bar, closed by a padlock.

Linn had also been knocked off his horse and taken; but, save a slight cut or two, was well, strong, and furious with anger at the indignity to which he was subjected. The prisoners were immediately marched towards the North Ferry for embarkation, that they might be sent to England; but all the fishermen along the Fife coast had either fled with their boats to the Lothian side, or scuttled them; thus great delay ensued, as only one or two craft could be found fit for service.

As the prisoners—twelve hundred in number—musketeers, troopers, and pikemen, officers and drummers, all disarmed and stripped of their belts, cuirasses, and trappings—all disconsolate and crest-fallen, crowded like a herd of cattle along the beach, the exulting puritans guarding, with matches cocked, and hearts so full of joy in the Lord, that they made the air resound and the rocks echo with hymns and psalms in honour of Him who had vouchsafed a victory to the sons of Jacob, a great coach, covered with carving and gilding, with a top like a Christmas pie, large glass windows, and panels gay with coats armorial, was seen descending the steep road towards the landing-place. It was drawn by four smoking horses; before it rode an old cavalier in a broad plumed beaver and calf-skin boots, strapped up to his girdle. Like his two mounted servants, he had long holster pistols and a swinging broadsword, while the coachman had a carbine slung across his back.

Preceded by this advanced guard, the coach approached the pier, and a mob of puritan soldiers, relinquishing their psalms, uttered a shout, and scampered off to plunder it.

"Beware! on your lives, beware!" cried the stout old cavalier, unsheathing his great spada, and making his horse capriole right among them; "beware! for we have the pest, the plague among us!"

At this terrible warning, Overton's musketeers, who had begun ominously to handle their firelocks, paused, and the coach was stopped.

Linn, who had recognised Sir Henry Lennox, became much excited, and, undeterred by cuffs and blows from the butt-end of muskets, forced his way towards the coach, dragging Carlourie after him.

" Zounds!" exclaimed the old baronet, " is it thou, my son, whom I see a prisoner?   Gude kens, but sore misfortunes never come alone.   Our dear Dora——"

" Is with you, is she not?" exclaimed the lover, who was about to open the coach door, when Sir Henry grasped his arm, saying, with a broken voice,

" For God's sake beware, Willie; there is ower mickle stir already.   She is there, but ailing deadly—*the pestilence hath stricken her*, and we are hurrying home, for no house will receive her.   Heaven be about us!"

A faint and feeble sound was heard in the recesses of the vehicle—it was the voice of Dora, inquiring, or confirming what her father said; but the noise made by the armed soldiers around them drowned the gentle accents of the sick girl.   All now shrunk back, for the very name of " the pestilence," which was then ravaging England, and was desolating our border counties, and in a few years after nearly destroyed London, carried terror to every heart.

" And no house will receive her?" faltered Linn.

" Not one; every door is closed against us."

" Curse on the cowards!"

" One man pled his wife who was sick, another his bairns, a third something else, and so we are e'en going home to the auld tower at the foot o' the Pentlands, Willie, where I would to Heaven I saw you and her, as I saw ye ere these woes and wars began, linked hand in hand, and smiling happily.   I have got new gates to the auld place, and a brass mortar before the bridge —so if Cromwell comes up the glen, I am ready for him——"

" Heyday! what prankling, ruffling gallant is this who stops the way with his gilded wagon?" asked Captain Thurlow, pressing roughly forward.

" I am Sir Henry Lennox, of that ilk," said the baronet, touching his beaver; " and were my years as few as thine, I would teach thee to respect a white-haired man, thou ruffian bully.   Clear the way, you flea-lugged hypocrites; or, waladay! I will through some of your briskets in a twinkling!"

" Damn it, old cut-and-thrust, give us none of your hard names, or we shall fling this great rattle-trap of thine into the water!"

" Beware! sir," said the old baronet, trembling with passion; " it is the coach of my lord, the Marquis of Argyle—you may see his arms and coronet on the panels—lent me kindly to convey home my daughter—my poor child! whom Heaven hath chosen to afflict with the pestilence."

" Pestilence!" reiterated Thurlow, in an altered voice; " and this is the coach of Argyle?   Oho! he is our best friend in Scotland, and to meddle with his wares would bring Noll about our ears.   You wish to cross the river—where the devil will you get a boat?   We have only three, and they are full of prisoners."

Old Sir Henry, who glared at the Englishman with eyes that would have slain him if glances could kill, now lost all temper, and swore "by every hair in his moustachios" (which were of great size, *à la cavalier*), that he *would* have a boat, even should men die for it; and ordered his servants to unsheath their swords, though not less than a thousand horse and foot were drawn up in line upon the pier.   How the matter would have ended there can be little doubt; but the arrival of a coarse, dark-looking little man on horseback, wearing a large flapped hat, enormous calfskin boots, and a wide-skirted scarlet coat, caused a veritable suspension of arms.

"Who the devil is this now?" growled the old baronet, eyeing him with stern contempt; "some brewer of Huntingdon!—some leatherseller or butcher of Nottingham, not worth a tester, perhaps!"

"Neither butcher nor brewer, sir, but Lieutenant-General George Monk, at your service," said the little man, with an ironical scowl under his broad hat.

"Lieutenant-General, indeed! I should never have thought it," responded Sir Harry, who found his hatred too exuberant for concealment.

Monk's arrival was a lucky event, as that worthy pillar of in-dependency, impressed either by the appearance of Argyle's coach or by the advantage of placing a pest-stricken family on the south side of the Forth, as he was now to campaign on the north side thereof, ordered a way to be opened towards the beach, and a large boat was surrendered to the use of Sir Harry and his people; who, after no small trouble, embarked his lumbering coach, with the horses, baggage, big boots, holster-pistols, and carbines; and slowly the freight was pulled by eight unwil-ling oarsmen across the narrow strait of two miles, through which the river rushes with considerable force.

"Give these loons your parole, my lad," said Sir Harry, on leaving Linn; "and if you have not the ready, I will be good for it to any amount; so we'll expect you at Lennox to-morrow."

Roughly held back by the armed guards, who respected their own safety more than the emotions of any lover under the sun, poor Linn, with an agony which may be conceived, saw the great coach which, like a funeral catafalque, bore away Dora, of whom he had seen nothing but a thin, wan hand, which once or twice was feebly raised against the glasses as if she were essaying to open them, but had failed through illness and inability.

Meanwhile the prisoners were being ferried across in boat-

loads, all crowded together without distinction, officers and privates mingled; and all the former who were not severely
wounded were, as I have said, manacled to their men. Linn
watched, with strained and eager eyes, the waters of the ferry;
and, in the hazy summer sunshine, saw the great lumbering
coach dragged by its switch-tailed horses up the opposite shore,
from the landing-place at Newhall, and disappear over the hill.
Then his excitement could no longer be restrained. The conviction that his beloved and light-hearted Dora was stricken by that
terrible and mysterious plague—that she was ailing, sinking,
dying perhaps, while they were hopelessly separated—he a prisoner, and she unable to approach him—fired his soul with grief
and passion at the thraldom and disgrace of being manacled like
a criminal to a trooper of his own regiment.

"Dora, Dora!" he continued to mutter, and wrung his hands.

People have now almost forgotten the pestilence which in those
days desolated the land.

It first came from England in 1645, and after abating in its
virulence, was again brought into Scotland by Cromwell's invading army. It lurked long in the dark wynds and narrow
closes of our cities, before it burst abroad to desolate the towns
and villages of the Lowlands, where the efforts and prayers of the
people proved alike ineffectual in arresting its progress. All the
ancient acts of James II. for suppression of the pest were revived
and rigidly enforced; but still it spread from hearth to hearth
and from door to door; the healthy and the strong, the weak and
the feeble, sank alike before its baleful breath, and the denizens
of entire streets and districts were swept away. In Edinburgh,
carts traversed the city after nightfall to bear off the numerous
dead, who were rolled in blankets or whatever came to hand, and
interred in pits on the burghmuir, near the chapel of St. Roque,
a saint famous in Hagiology as the protector of the pest-stricken,
and whose fame had survived the Reformation. In Stirling they
were flung into pits, irrespective of age, sex, or rank, near the
well of St. Ninian. The town council held their meetings in a
park beyond the walls, and the sheriff-muir was covered by a
tented camp of the infected.

The parliament dispersed; every burgh closed its gates against
all but its own inhabitants, and even they were thrust forth if
they became infected; while their goods and gear were consumed
in flames, by order of the provost, or "the smeikers and
cleanziers" whom he appointed. This scourge had somewhat
abated before the battle of Dunbar, but the terror of it was yet
strong in the minds of the people.

Pale with sorrow and apprehension, crushed in spirit, and subdued in bearing by the consciousness of his helpless position,

and the danger overhanging his dearly-loved Dora, the young Laird of Linn sought the blustering Captain Thurlow, who, as senior officer of Overton's regiment, actively superintended the embarkation of the prisoners—a forlorn and sorrowing band. He soon found him loitering near the beach, where he was looking about with that provoking air peculiar to some classes of his countrymen, who, in their ignorance of foreigners, vote everything *not* English decidedly bad and wrong.

"Sir," said Linn, "I presume it is needless to acquaint you that, like yourself, I am an officer, and bear the king's commission ?"

"Your being handcuffed, as I see, is the best proof of your being a king's officer," was the blunt response; "but what of that ? I bear the parliament's commission, which is of more value than a king's t'other side of Tweed."

"I am a gentleman," said Linn, making a severe effort to restrain his anger, for the hand that was at liberty was twitching to grasp the bull-like throat of the nonchalant parliamentarian; "I am William Linn of that ilk, a lieutenant in the king's Black Dragoons, and am willing to give my parole of honour with a sum of money for my liberty."

"Impossible !" said Thurlow, doggedly.

"For Heaven's sake hear me, sir; my estate is small, though it has been in my family for ten generations—it yields me 300*l.* a year; I will give you a bond over for a year's rental and my solemn parole for two days' leave."

"I assure you, sir, it is beyond my power—aye, or George Monk's either," replied Thurlow, whose rudeness gave way before the sad-eyed earnestness of Linn; besides, he was perhaps thinking of Harriet Morton; "it is the young lady in the coach who interests you; well, I assure you again, on my word as a plain man and honest fellow, that I would trust and give you leave sans bond or bribe for any length of time if it lay with me; but unfortunately I am no more my own master than you, Mr. Linn."

"I will even give your lieutenant-general my parole not to serve against England during this war."

"Nonsense," said Thurlow, becoming gruff again; "you leave this to-morrow with Blake, if his ships come round."

"And for where, sir, may I ask ?"

"London Tower in the first place."

"And in the second ?"

"Virginia or the Dutch colonies. All these prisoners taken to-day will share the fate of those taken at Dunbar last year——"

"Starvation and death ?"

"Oons, man, no—they shall be sold as slaves to the planters."*

* Fact

" By the God of heaven, I will pistol every English puritan
I lay hands on !"

"*After* this you freely may," was the taunting reply.

" I am a Scottish man, and am no more amenable to the acts
of your English parliament than to those of the Turkish divan."

" So thought King Charles—yet we made him shorter by a
head. Every man who serves his son, be he Englishman or
Scot, if taken in battle sails for Virginia, and that is all about
it—so, sir, your servant."

With these words, Thurlow turned and left Linn with his companion Carlourie, who, having no love affair to deepen the desperation of his case, was solely concerned about himself, and looked
forward with blank dismay to the prospect before him; for the
English puritans, in their mode of conducting the contest, set at
defiance all international law as regards prisoners of war.

Linn thought not of himself, or what he might endure; his
whole soul was centred in the idea of Dora ill and sinking under
the terrible pest. He longed to be stricken with it too, that he
might share her sufferings, and be free to perish with her, if
Heaven willed it so. Every action of her life, every charming
turn of her manner, every endearing remembrance, every beauty
of her person, every petty pique and lover's quarrel, every darling
hope of which she was the object, were now revolving in his
mind; and in fancy he saw her writhing and wasting under this
loathsome visitation—a source of terror even to those who loved
her most.

Bewildered by these painful thoughts, he furiously strove to
free his hand from the iron fetter; for now the sun had set;
night was approaching; and though he and Carlourie were left
a.nong the last of the prisoners, he resolved to make a vigorous
effort for freedom.

" Carlourie," said he, " can you swim ?"

" Like a wild juke, sir," was the ready reply.

" Will you make one brave effort for freedom ?"

" Troth will I, sir—a dozen of them."

" Well—think of what I say. The night will be dark, or
nearly so, before we are embarked; let us watch when the boat
is just above Inchgarvie, then we will fling ourselves overboard
and swim for the island—our garrison is still there, under Captain Roy, of Duffus' regiment."

" Are you certain, sir ?"

" Mahoud, man !" said Linn, angrily; " did you not see the
Scots flag flying on the keep all day long ?"

" True, sir—but I heard some rumours of the castle being
taken; and mairowre, its batteries never fired on the English
boats."

"How could they, when these same boats were full of Scottish prisoners?"

"True, sir—but how can we swim if fettered by these iron bracelets?"

"We shall make the effort. I will rather drown in the Forth, Charlie, here before our own doors as it were, with the chance of being graved in Scottish earth, than linger out my life as a Dutch or English slave, and go at last to feed the worms of a foreign shore. Let us bide our time—we may again be free men—yes, before the moon sets to-night, and ere she is renewed, I may write a receipt for politeness on the fair smooth Saxon hide ot yonder rascal Thurlow!"

As Linn had foreseen, before their turn for embarking came, the red western gloaming had faded into night; the moon, white and silvery, which hung above the chain of the Pentland mountains, was occasionally shrouded in vapour that sailed across the dark blue sky. The surface of the river had become opaque, and the shadows of the little island castle which guards the strait, and those of every rocky ness and wooded promontory had melted into night, when the heavily-laden barge, with at least forty prisoners, Captain Thurlow, and twelve musketeers with cocked matches, seated six at the bow and six at the stern, was pulled away from the pier of the North Ferry, and with its head pointed somewhat up the river, to stem the downward current which there runs like a mill-race, shot out into the mid channel.

On the river the night, though a summer one, seemed to be darker than on the land; and now a gauzelike veil obscured the placid moon for more than an hour.

The boat was sturdily pulled, but at every stroke of the oar the impetuous current swept her nearer the castled islet, which loomed in large and dusky outline as they approached the middle of the passage, for the Inch is an oblong rock in the centre of the river, which here narrows to two miles and a half in breadth. Linn's heart throbbed more rapidly as the distance lessened between him and this rock-built tower, and as the moment drew nigh when the grand attempt would be made, when matches would be blown and bullets shot—bullets which might kill or wound them both. Then came the terrible reflection, that if *one* was killed or disabled the other would be sure to drown with him; for being fettered together, each had as it were two lives to risk and to lose.

These thoughts occurred for a moment to Linn; Carlourie was watching his eyes, and intently awaiting the signal to spring over. Another stroke of the oars would have brought them in a line duly west of the castle, when one of the Puritan musketeers uttered a shout of surprise and terror, for close by a large

seal or sea-calf 1aiscd up its round black head with long whiskers
and gleaming eyes, that looked straight at him.   Several others
had seen it, and a clamour of tongues ensued; and while some
exclaimed   that it was "a Scots sea monster—a devil—a
leviathan," and urged the oarmen to pull away, others insisted
on their pausing, and began to blow their matches and handle
their muskets.

The splashing of the oars, the swaying of the boat, and
the clamour of tongues at this juncture, was fortunate for our
two comrades.

"Now," said Linn, "now or never!" And they both went
head foremost into the water; and not a man of all those who
crowded the boat either observed or missed them, so intently
were all gazing after the seal, which had been swimming up the
river.

The fetter which secured the left hand of Linn to the right
hand of the soldier, caused them to make but an ineffectual dive;
thus they rose almost immediately to the surface—fortunately,
however, more than a pistol-shot distant from the boat. They
then struck out, and swam sturdily to reach the rock; and if the
fetter impeded, the river at least seconded their exertions, for in
less than two minutes they were swept close to it by the current,
and found themselves among the surf that chafed the rock, on
which they obtained a footing, breathless, and gasping with
excitement and immersion. They then turned to look at the
boat, which was again under weigh with its now silent freight,
and with its oar-blades flashing in the moonlight.

No voices rang upon the still, calm flow of the river, and no
alarm was given.

"Strange," said Linn, "we have not yet been missed!"

And now they clambered up the rocks towards the little
fortress which crowned the isle and towered above them, dusky,
grey, and spotted by lichens like the long and narrow wedge of
basalt on which it stands.

———

CHAPTER LX.

INCHGARVIE.

On this islet, which is very small, as its Celtic name implies,
stands an ancient tower built by Dundas of that ilk, in the days of
Flodden field, to defend the passage of the strait.   The Inch is a
mere rock, without verdure, though a few weeds and shrubs
grow in the clefts and crannies, and it is all but inaccessible,
though a flight of steps, hewn into the basalt by the French
arquebusiers, who garrisoned it under the Regent Duke of

Albany, led from the gate to the place where the castle boat was usually moored.

At the commencement of the war, a detachment of twenty musketeers of the Lord Duffus' regiment had been placed in the tower as a garrison, under Captain Roy of Aldivalloch, a brave, stout fellow from the braes of Anchindoune, and, moreover, an experienced soldier, who had served in a brigade of Walloons under the German emperor, and left an eye on the upper Rhine and a leg on the plains of Westphalia, and who had accepted this solitary command to be away from a gay and jilting wife.

When summoned by a party of Cromwell's troops under Overton, a day or two before the late battle, he had replied by a shower of shot; but perceiving at least three hundred men under Monk coming off in boats from the east Ness, he blew up the magazine, spiked his iron guns, and escaped with his party into Fife by means of their boat. The tower was garrisoned by the English. Thus we may imagine the sensations of the anxious Linn and the exulting trooper, Carlourie, when, after thundering confidently at the gate, they found it opened by a musketeer of Monk's regiment—no other than our old acquaintance, Private Zerubabbel Meek, in his square-tailed brick-red coat, and a broad white collar under his astonished visage—for visitors were doubtless of rare occurrence at a solitary tower which rose almost sheer from the edge of the water. So now, in ten minutes after levanting from the boat, they found themselves prisoners again to Sergeant Melchisedeck Makepeace, who with Corporals Fight-the-good-fight-of-Faith Twaddle, Goliah Gander, and twelve other choice musketeers of Monk's regiment, occupied the tower!

They were immediately seized and confined in an upper chamber—the same in which Patrick Panater was imprisoned by Albany, and in which he composed his " Valiados," in 1516, in praise of the heroic exploits of Sir William Wallace.

" Rascal!" exclaimed Linn, losing all temper.

" Didst thou speak to me, friend?" snuffled Corporal Twaddle.

" Yes, sirrah."

" Then thou hadst better keep a civil tongue in thy head, lest we gag 'um with a drum stick."

" Why did you keep the Scottish flag flying all day?"

" To deceive ships and boats," replied the Puritan, with a grin, the only approach to a smile which ever appeared on his square, stolid visage; " for such was the order of Captain Thurlow."

" Captain Thurlow—who is he?"

"Governor of this castle of Inchgarvie for the Parliament of England."

"Some rascally cut-purse or London cloak-snatcher, I suppose?"

"Thee hadst better not tell him so, when he cometh, for verily we expect him on the morrow," responded the corporal; "so beware, I say, for if thou smitest him on one cheek, he is not a man to turn the other; yea, yea, as Paul saith——"

"Hypocrite, begone, lest I trounce thee!" exclaimed Linn, furiously. Again the Puritan grinned, and retired. During the night, the crest-fallen prisoners heard the sergeant expounding, Corporal Goliah Gander responding, and various musketeers singing psalms, while the odour of sanctity, beer, and tobacco, pervaded the tower together.

At last the various indications of the spirit ceased, and not a sound was heard, save the ripple of the river against the rocks, the screech of the ugla (as the owl is named in Fife), or the sighs and impatient ejaculations which escaped the overcharged bosom of William Linn, as his restless imagination portrayed the form of Dora—his "dear little droll," as he was wont to name her—in the last stage of the deadly plague; and as in all his motions, fits, and starts, our bewildered lover was quite oblivious of his being fettered to Carlourie, that honest fellow's patience was sorely tried, for not being a lover, he had a faculty for sleeping like a dormouse, united to a great love of repose. Thus he found small comfort in the honour of being fettered to Linn, who wished to walk about all night, and who remained awake till day dawned on the hills and river, and the morning sun shone cheerily through the grated windows of the stone chamber.

Then Corporal Goliah appeared with breakfast, and told them that they had permission to ramble about the tower and rocks until Captain Thurlow came, but would be instantly shot dead on making the least attempt to escape.

Under other circumstances, Linn might have smiled at the liberty thus afforded, for in its area the tower was not much larger than a good-sized room, and nearly covered all the rock, leaving little more than a rabbit might scramble over without falling into the water. So, like two terriers coupled together, the officer and private passed the long summer day drearily enough, either on the tower-head or on a pinnacle of rock, gazing at the beautiful coast which lay a mile or so distant, shrouded in haze and copsewood, revolving a thousand impracticable plans of escape, while a hawk-eyed sentinel, with his musket shouldered, walked to and fro on the bartizan above, keeping a watchful eye upon them, as the only objects which he had to guard.

Several days passed; Captain Thurlow never came; no boat approached the little fort either with messages or provisions, for the Laird of Aldivalloch had unwisely left an ample store of the latter; but many barges laden with troops crossed the ferry southward, as Cromwell was collecting all his spare forces to follow up the king's march. Carlourie grew weary, and Linn became sick at heart, for he knew no more of what was occurring on the mainland. than if he had been at the bottom of the sea. The Puritans passed their time in alternate feasts for the body and the soul, and in mutually imbibing draughts of inspiration from the scripture, from each other's discourses, and from the ale barrels of Sir John Smith, the Scottish Commissary-General. Having frequently found that the soldier who rejoiced in the cognomen of Zerubabbel Meek was less morose or more accessible than his comrades, Linn and his companion — they could never be apart—approached him one evening when he was a sentinel.

His eyes were fixed on the Queen's Ferry, but his thoughts were evidently wandering Zionward, if one could judge from the loudness of his prayer, as if he was to take heaven by a stormy torrent of expostulation. Linn interrupted this clamour by touching him on the shoulder.

"Back, friend," said he; "lest I anoint thee with the butt of my musket."

After some judicious praise, Linn promised solemnly to pay him down fifty sterling pounds if he would assist them to escape.

"Nay, nay," replied the Puritan, through his nose, as he marched to and fro, with musket shouldered, his sword and bandeliers clanking; "get thee behind me, Satan, and tempt me not."

"A hundred pounds then; hear me, good fellow," said Linn; "a hundred will I give, by the king's head and my own sacred honour."

"Nay, I tell thee nay," snuffled the incorruptible Zerubabbel; "I would not free thee for a Scottish earldom. Lo you! through the Lord's grace I am one of Monk's regiment."

"Art sure you will resist all I may offer?"

"Yea and verily; for, as Master Gumble, our chaplain, saith again and again,—because we are like unto the nobles of Hisrael oom Deborah loved, and of oom she singeth in the book of Judges."

"How so?"

"Verily—because like them we peril our lives on the 'igh places of the field—yea, verily, do we."

"Damn thee, and thine intolerable cant," cried the exasperated cavalier, grinding his teeth.

"Friend Scot, swear not; 'tis bad for thee," replied the immoveable musketeer; "the gospel——"

"To the dogs with law and gospel, if their expounders are to be such prickeared curs as thee!"

"Werily, friend, thy tongue leaveth thy discretion a long day's march behind it," said the Englishman, as he quietly turned from Linn, who, in his own mind, could not but applaud the faith of the soldier who resisted a bribe, for which, though so small, many a Scottish peer and placeman would sell king, country, and honour, as many a black page in our history remains to attest. Linn turned away in despair; and now the seventh day slipped into night.

"*Seven* days!" thought Linn; "by this time Dora must either be well or——"

He dared not add, even to himself, the terrible words "dead and buried;" but he *thought* them, and anxiety preyed upon his heart, till a stupor took possession of him; and the poor trooper, Carlourie, grew as weary of his companion as of his own confinement.

On the seventh day, as they sat on the rocks, Linn as usual buried in reverie, Carlourie roused him by an exclamation of satisfaction, and displayed some plants which he had culled from the clefts of the basalt.

"What are they—some weeds—eh?"

"Weeds that will set us free," said Carlourie, laughing.

"Free—how? and how dare you laugh?" said Linn, angrily.

"They are poison—rank poison; my mother, who bydes at yon burn side (puir body! I can see her lum reeking frae here!) kens a' manner o' plants and simples; and I have seen her make cosmetics o' this for the Lady Rosythe a hundred times."

"'Tis the sleepy nightshade," said Linn, examining the plants, the stalks of which were about two feet long, with light green leaves, and large black berries, insipid to the taste; "you would counsel suicide to end our troubles?"

"Do you think I am daft, sir?"

"Buchanan mentions in the seventh book of his history that it is a soporific; but, if taken in quantities, will make men mad."

"And, mind ye, that he adds how, in auld King Duncan's time, hundreds o' years ago, Macbeth destroyed the Danish army at Perth, by sending them provisions and liquor drugged by the juice of this sleepy nightshade."

"I remember—but what of it? The berries are poison—suck them if you will; but leave me in peace," said Linn, relapsing into apathy again.

"Listen to me, sir," said Carlourie, gathering the berries and carefully selecting the seeds; "listen, and I will tell you a tale that was told me by auld Duairt's henchman, the night before the battle of Inverkeithing—a story to the very point, too."

"Go on—I am too petulant, my good fellow ; but pray forgive me ; I have cares of which you know nothing."

"Far away in the north, on the coast of Caithness," began the trooper, "stands the auld ruinous tower of Achaistal, upon a high rock above the sea, and cut off from the land by a drawbridge and fosse. This strong keep was built by a valiant warrior, John Beg, the second son of Nicholas, Earl of Sutherland, who lived in the days of King Robert II.; thus what I am about to relate occurred many hundred years ago. In these times, Caithness and Sutherland were sorely infested by robbers, stout rievers and armed limmers, who ravaged the whole country, and were a terror to the peaceful ; for they were wild men who cared little what they did, and never tholed steering. It is on record that once, in a fit of anger, they roasted a bishop alive in his own kitchen ! A hundred or so of these rough lads, armed with sword and bow, axe and dagger, came down from the wilds of Assynt, and arrived one night at the tower of Achaistal. Finding the drawbridge down, they swarmed into the hall, just as John Beg was sitting down to supper with his wife and bairns, and rudely demanded food in the first place, plenty to drink in the second, and a sum paid down as blackmail in the third ; threatening, otherwise, to plunder the house, carry off the cattle, and put the laird's head on the platter beside the haggis he was supping on.

"' Had I expected sae muckle gude companie,' said John, with a dark look, ' I would have been *better* prepared ; but as you've come for pot luck, ye maun een tak what we can gie.'

"Summoning his seneschal, pantler, and butler, he ordered a sumptuous entertainment ; a cow was killed, flayed and turning before the kitchen fire in a trice, while strings o' turkeys, geese, pouts, pigeons, rabbits and hares, were sputtering and browning in the gravy. A grand feast was served up an hour before midnight ; and the best in the cellars—the runlets of wine, bombardes of ale, and demijohns of usquebaugh, were set abroach ; and furious grew the uproar of the midnight banquet, while the blaze of red pine torches, and the roaring fires in kitchen and hall, shone far over the darkened sea, and lit the peaks of Maidenpap and Scaraben.

"With a laughing mouth but a scowling eye, John Beg was master of the revels ; but the wild mountain men, as they dipped their rough beards in the greasy platters and bowls of brown ale, knew little that every morsel they had eaten, and every drop they drank, were poisoned by the juice of such berries as these—the deadly nightshade : thus, long before morning glinted on the Ord of Caithness, every one of them lay stretched in deep and snorting slumber on the floor of the hall. The feast was over; the feasters were quiet enough now; but where was John Beg?

"He with his seneschal, butler, pantler, and serving-men— aye, even his wife and bairns, were working hard below, filling the entrance of the hall and the lower chambers with straw, timber, hay, and brushwood, while others placed everything moveable and valuable on board of a great birlinn at the mouth of the Berriedale water. When all was completed, he fired the lower chambers, locked the iron gates, and, with his curse, flung the key into the ocean, while his people destroyed the drawbridge.

"The fire rushed from chamber to chamber, and from story to story, in broad, red and wavering sheets or in forky flames; John saw them leaping from the roofs, and blazing in yellow torrents from the grated windows, as his birlinn bore away with all her sails spread, for the coast of Sutherland, leaving every robber to be scorched to cinders.

"John Beg never returned; and though he became ancestor of the Sutherlands of Berriedale, his castle has remained a ruin since then, and masses of burned wood and charred bones are yet found among the calcined walls."

"A plague on't!" said Linn; "what is all this devilish story of robbers and a ruffian chieftain to me?"

"It is a parable, as Coporal MacSnaffle would say."

"A parable! speak out—I am in no mood for riddles."

"Let us gather the berries, and serve these English loons here in Inchgarvie, as John Beg served the robbers in Achaistal. Faith, this auld tower in a blaze, wi' these fat southerns bir-selling here like greasy crail capons on a griddle, would be a brave sight for the Queen's-ferry folk!"

"No," said Linn; "we have failed to corrupt these honest fellows—let us not stoop to murder them."

"Murder here or murder there," said Carlourie, losing his temper; "I would have pistolled every mother's son o' them the other day at Inverkeithing. You are unco fashious, Mr. Linn; this is a clear case of eating a cow and worrying at the tail."

"And how do you propose to drug these military saints, for I have no objection to merely drugging them; then seizing their boat and attempting to escape."

"Now, sir, you become reasonable, and meet me half way. Aldivalloch left six tuns of gude Lammas ale in the tower, and the sergeant, his corporals, and men spend half the day in mulling the ale to wet their prayers, which seem but dry work. The third cask was broached in their guard-room this morning, and it is half drunk already. Now a few handfuls of these berries and leaves dropped through the bung-hole, will set them all dosing in less than an hour."

"A brave thought, Carlourie; once in the boat we are free!"

said Linn, who, like his companion, had so often faced death and danger, that they had no longer any terrors for him; for when we risk life often, as every soldier must, on service, we value it only as a gambler does his cash, and less perchance, for use lessens alike danger and marvel.

The two being fettered together proved a great impediment to each other, in every motion which required care and stealth; yet they contrived not only to drop a quantity of these berries—the fruit of the belladonna—into the barrel of ale which those worthy diffusers of the Gospel and gunpowder had hoisted into their apartment for greater convenience, but the adroit Carlourie, while pretending to mull a little ale for himself, actually dropped some into the kettle which the musketeers were constantly using. The soporific effects of this potion were soon visible on all who partook of it; for the corporals Twaddle and Goliah Gander, with five of their men, sank into a profound slumber, which the sergeant and five others, who were occupied elsewhere, escaped. One of the former was Hezekiah-accepted-of-Islington, who was posted on the tower-head, and to whom the whole safety of the petty fortlet was intrusted. Poor Hezekiah was soon buried in sleep, and lay against the parapet of the bartizan, dreaming perhaps of the pretty village of Islington, and hearing the bells of Canonbury and the voices of home.

On seeing this result the two prisoners, who had been anxiously watching him, hastened below, to find all there in the same drowsy predicament.

It was evening now; a faint light stole through the grated window into the vaulted tower, and as it fell on the pale and upturned faces of the sleepers, a chill came over Liun, and he shrank, with proper horror, from the idea that they *might* be poisoned; but Carlourie had not an atom of compunction in the matter, and was wholly intent on freeing himself from the company of his superior officer, whose moody and wayward fits had bored the worthy trooper beyond all expression.

Having secured, as he said, " a sword from one of the seven sleepers," he inserted the blade thereof into the padlock of their fetter, and, by a vigorous wrench, opened it as easily as he would have done an oyster-shell; and then they both threw up their arms with an emotion of joy on finding themselves free.

Linn seized a musket, and uttering a shout of triumph and derision, they rushed from the little tower and sprang into the boat at the rock-stairs, just as the last vestige of the sun's disc sank behind the Ochils, and a blaze of light flashed along the waters of the river, which rushed tumultuously round the western extremity of the isle.

" Dora, Dora!" thought Linn; " this night will I behold thee, if still in life, my beloved one! Slash through the boat's painter," cried he, as Carlourie struggled in vain to cast off the moorings; "slash it through, if that sword has an edge."

The blade gleamed in the western glow as the trooper dealt a furious cut at the tough rope on the gunnel, but failed to sever it.

"Hew, hew for Heaven's sake, hew!" cried Linn.

"Come back, ye sons of Moab; on your lives come back, lest ye perish!" cried the deep, bass voice of Sergeant Melchisedeck from the tower-head, where he was kicking and cuffing brother Hezeckiah in a most unbrotherly way; "I was placed here by the Lord and the Lord General to be as a pastor and governor over ye, and ye shall not escape from your bonds, ye accursed Levites."

"To the devil with thee, for a blasphemous kite and rebellious spawn!" cried the cavalier, levelling the musket, and firing straight at the Englishman's head. The latter never winced an inch, but held up a cold 24-pound shot, and crying, in his sing-song voice,

"Come back, I say, ye foul Egyptians, or by the glory of Jerusalem, I will hurl ye both into the abyss of hell!"

The fugitives uttered a shout of derision, as the painter was severed and the boat shot away from the rock!

Then there was a whizzing sound, a crash, and the heavy iron shot, directed by a strong hand and unerring eye, soused through the bottom of the boat, and swamped it; thus, in a moment, Linn and Carlourie found themselves struggling with the rapid waters of the Forth.

<hr>

CHAPTER LXI.

EVERY BULLET HAS ITS BILLET.

THEY would have struck out for the opposite shore but it was a mile and a half distant, with a tremendous current pouring through the narrow strait; and now the sergeant and his five soldiers, who had *not* partaken of the drugged liquor, opened a fire of musketry upon them, and they were fain to get close under shelter of the rocks and tower, where they were again seized, and feeling more crest-fallen than ever, were about to be subjected to very rough handling, when a large boat filled with Puritan officers shot round the western point of the isle, and was steered straight to the landing-place, where the coxswain caught an iron ring by the boat-hook, and held on with all his strength, lest the current should sweep the craft away. Several officers, in those large plain hats, square-tailed coats, and enormous boots worn by the English army, landed, and the sergeant, in evident consternation at their arrival and the recent occurrence, thrust the prisoners rudely, and with a hearty malediction, into their old chamber, and secured the door.

Wet, dejected, and miserable, they gazed at each other for a minute, as if they could scarcely realise the events of the last five minutes.

"Baffled—baffled again by a trick of the devil!" said Linn, in sorrow and anger: "so has failed a chance of freedom as fair and brave as ever happened to captive men! Why, in the fiend's name, did you not slash that infernal rope sooner, and put us beyond reach of that round-headed ruffian's shot?"

Carlourie grumbled an oath, and emptied the water from his boots; but he listened patiently to the angry remarks of Linn, who lost all command of himself, as he thought on "the chance of escape lost," as he repeated, "lost, lost for ever," and considered that but for the obstinacy of the boat-rope, or the bluntness of the sword, they might now have been free, and treading on the shore of West Lothian.

"We shall look like a couple of arrant blockheads, on appearing before this canting halberdier again."

"To be cleeked together again; 'od, sir! wi' ane so dowie and waefu' as you, I like that least o' a'!"

"Hush—some one comes; let us put a bold face on it, for I never knew modesty gain a man anything in this world."

While they were speaking, the door was unfastened and thrown open by the pious but half-tipsy Sergeant Melchisedeck Makepeace, whose tyrannical leer inclined Linn to box his ears; but now there was a clanking of iron scabbards, of steel spurs and heavily-heeled jack-boots, and three Puritan officers entered. In one they recognised the boisterous and peremptory Captain Thurlow, who, unlike his brother soldiers, never quoted Scripture; but when in an ireful mood, damned alike the prophets and the patriarchs.

"Harkee, sir," said he, shaking his clenched hand in Linn's face "you are a pretty man as ever stood in jack-boots, so I would not like to see you come to mischief; but mind your game, lest you be check-mated. I have heard of your offers; but think not to bribe English soldiers with your outlandish Scots money —it won't do, sir lieutenant—no, damme!"

"Silence, Thurlow!" said another officer, who was plainly attired in a buff coat destitute of lace, a rough beaver, calfskin boots, and had rather a vulgar cast of face, with keen dark eyes, and a large nose; "be silent!" he reiterated, striking his cane on the ground; "this language doth not become a dweller in the tents of Israel, nor a soldier whom the Lord hath bidden to uplift his banners against the mighty Let us not judge harshly, but have mercy upon the fallen, for we in turn may also fall. Let us deal gently one with another. What have you to say, Lieutenant Linn, that thou and thy fellow here should not be brought to the drum-head and shot, and thereafter flung into the river, for this second attempt to break from the wardship of my soldiers?"

"I have an answer which would suffice any soldier in Christendom, who knows the custom and practice of war. As a prisoner, I was refused alike the privilege of ransom and parole; as an officer, I was treated worse than a felon; as a gentleman, I was manacled and disgraced, without crime or reason; hence I sought to free myself at all hazards, and am resolved to make the attempt again. Thus much for myself. For my companion, he is blameless and simple——"

"Aye, simple as a lawyer," sneered Thurlow.

"For him I crave pardon."

"For yourself?"

"Nothing! I would scorn to ask for soldier-like treatment from the banded demagogues of England."

"Do you know me, sir?" asked the dark man, changing colour.

"No!"

"No matter—I know thee, and saw thee at Dunbar, where bravely thou borest thyself, on that day so glorious to the children of the Lord."

"And who are you, that dare assume your canting regicides are the chosen of the Lord?"

"I am Oliver Cromwell," replied the other, quietly.

"Cromwell!" reiterated Linn, with a thunder-struck air.

"At your service, sir."

There was a pause, then Oliver said—

"Confess that your rash speeches are a temptation of Providence, when by one word I could send you and this poor soldier into eternity! It is written, thou shalt not yet die," he continued, resuming the cant which suited him but ill; "I give thee life and liberty, as well as the life and liberty of thy companion; but I must receive the parole of both, that neither will serve against England during this war—or until exchanged for some of the prisoners taken from us in Stirlingshire. Go—the Lord be with you."

Linn made several efforts to speak; but a cloud—a confusion had fallen upon him; for the coolness, gentleness, and kindness of this remarkable man, who seldom omitted an opportunity of personally conciliating the nation from whom his mother sprung, had confounded and bewildered him. Besides, the thought of Dora, and of rejoining her, swelled Linn's breast with gratitude for Cromwell's generosity.

As soon as he rallied a little, he politely thanked the English

Lord-General (as he was termed), but that personage merely replied by a wave of his gloved hand, as much as to say, "Enough—for this sort of thing wearies me;" and desired Thurlow to get ready a boat to convey the two Scots to the other side of the river. "Ill luck hath attended this my first visit to your little government, Jack Thurlow; but before these captives leave us, they shall see a sample of English discipline, such as we mete out to soldiers of the Parliament, who sleep upon their posts, and are derelicts in duty. Lead on to the tower-head."

On the small area formed by the paved bartizan of the tower, the sergeant assembled his slender garrison of twelve men, in the soft twilight of the summer evening, when the hills were growing dark and dim, and when the river lay blushing around each promontory and isle like a stream of purple wine, tinted here and there by riplets of ductile gold, as it chafed on the yellow beaches and wooded rocks; and there the musketeers stood in silence leaning on their firelocks, while an impromptu court-martial, composed of three officers, sat in the little hall below, and the stern Cromwell walked to and fro with his gauntletted hands behind him, his broad hat drawn over his keen and sullen eyes, his wide boots and large sword clanking heavily. He paused at times, and gazed fixedly either westward, to where the shining river wound away and was lost in the hazy obscurity cast on it by the shadows of evening and the mountains; or eastward, to where its waves, widening to an ocean, mingled with those of the German sea, and where some white speck—a sail—at the far and faint horizon, alone indicated where sky and water met. But he never bestowed a glance either at the little rank of musketeers, who never took their gaze off him, or at Linn and his companion, who stood near, uneasy, irresolute what to do, and longing anxiously for the moment that would find them stepping ashore.

At last the three officers ascended to the platform, and one of them (Captain Thurlow) handed a written document to Cromwell, who perused it, and while doing so, repeatedly bit the point of his right glove, and retaining the latter in his teeth as he drew his hand out of it, affixed his signature to the paper, and said, in a firm but intoned voice,—

"Sergeant Melchisedeck Makepeace, take the sword and bandoleers off our erring brother Hezekiah-accepted, and bind his hands with a cord : for lo! it is written that he shall die, by sentence of a court-martial, for sleeping on his post."

"Yea and verily," snuffled the sergeant, relinquishing his halberd and hurriedly disarming the musketeer, who heard these terrible words without a muscle of his face exhibiting the most trivial discomposure.

"The Lord has accepted me—blessed be his name! I am ripe and ready to be gathered from the vineyard," said the poor man, with a deep groan.

"Harkee, drummer," said Cromwell, to a tall and hollow-eyed youth; "what is thy name?"

"Maccabæus Pure-in-heart," replied this military minstrel, with a salute; "I perform, moreover, on a wind instrument called a fife, and am a sweet singer as any in the House of Jacob."

"Set down thy drum, Maccabæus, and bring hither a set of dice and a Bible; be quick, brother, for the evening weareth apace, and darkness cometh down on the waters."

The drum was placed before the rank of musketeers, the Bible and dice-box were set thereon. The brief proceedings of the court were then read, and the prisoner was sentenced to be *shot*. He heard it without emotion.

Prayers were said by an officer; a psalm was sung, and the sergeant approached to bind up the culprit's eyes, when Linn sprang forward, saying—

"Spare this poor fellow; he is in no way to blame. 'Tis I alone. I drugged the liquor by which he was impelled to sleep on his post; and if an example must be made, General Cromwell——"

Here the stern eye and upheld hand of that formidable person imposed silence upon the young cavalier.

"I give thee praise, O Scot, for this candour and generosity," said he; "but the prisoner, by drinking on his post, and sleeping thereafter, transgressed the rules of discipline, and imperilled, it might be, the safety of the garrison intrusted to his care. Silence, young man—we may not, and must not be interrupted."

"I have picked up five pounds in sterling money, in the way of contribution among the Scots," said the prisoner, placing the money on the drumhead. "Will any dweller in the tents of the chosen take a cast of the dice with me for his life? *Every bullet hath its billet;* if I lose, the money is his."

"It is just," said Cromwell, "for such, indeed, is the rule of our English discipline, brother Hezekiah; but who here will peril his precious life to save that of a drunken soldier, who sleepeth when he should watch well?"

"I will, lord general," said Zerubabbel Meek, stalking forward, with his musket recovered; "verily if thou wilt give me leave, brother Hezekiah, and let the five pounds be mine if thou losest, I will throw with thee."

"Corporal Gander, do thou throw for me," said poor Hezekiah of Islington, with a sigh.

Twice the dice were rattled in the box, and twice they clattered sonorously on the drumhead.

Zerubabbel threw cinq-quatre, and escaped.

"Verily, brother, thou must die," said he, with a sympathizing groan, as he pocketed the cash, and buttoued his breeches carefully.

"What, in the fiend's name, tempted thee, Zerubabbel, a good man in Israel, to peril thus thy life?" asked Cromwell. "Suppose thou hadst thrown alms ace, and lost?"

"Sir, I have hazarded my life in battle against the Scots many a time for *eightpence* per day, and might well do it now for *five pounds* a minute."

"Gallant pay, by all the Furies!" said Captain Thurlow.

"Yea, verily, sirs," said private Meek; "nothing ventured, nothing won."*

Such scenes were of daily occurrence in the English army, and, consequently, Cromwell beheld this unmoved.

In ten minutes after this, the report of six muskets rang sharply in the summer twilight, and pealed among the naked rocks and windings of the shore, rousing the black erne and the wild sea-mew from their secret nests, and making the fishers at the ferry, as they sat on the shingly beach, or at the doors of their thatched cottages, mending their brown nets, turn their eyes with wonder to the little island castle, where the white English flag hung drooping on its staff; where a light cloud of blue smoke was curling upward and slowly melting into thin air; and where poor Hezekiah (*the accepted*, let us hope) was lying dead on his face—pierced by six ounce bullets, with the life-blood of his gallant heart running along the stone gutter of the time-worn bartizan.

Soon after, two boats shot from the fortlet, and were swiftly pulled ashore.

One bore the Lord-General of the English army, whose horses were waiting on the beach to convey him to Leith, where his troops were mustering to follow up the Scottish host, which had, as related, marched for England.

The other landed Linn and Carlourie on the beach near New-hall, where they wished each other joy of their mutual freedom and narrow escape. It was the gloaming now. Mouutain, wood, and river, were all growing dark, though the bright evening star sparkled amid the flush of the west, like a diamond among dusky amber.

* See *The Scout*, Aug. 2, 1654.

CHAPTER LXII.

THE DESOLATE HEART.

CARLOURIE, for the present, attached himself to the fortunes of Linn, who procured from the Provost of the Queensferry a pair of saddle horses, but with difficulty; for Monk, who, on the 26th of May, was appointed lieutenant-general of the English ordnance, had seized every available quadruped to drag the cannon and baggage of Cromwell's army, which left the kingdom by two routes.

Linn and his follower struck across the country in the moonlight; the woods of Baronbougle, the old bridge of Cramond, the wide, purple lea of Clermiston, the loch of Corstorphin, gleaming pale and silvery like an oval mirror, where the black ouzel swam and the solemn heron stalked; the rocks of Craiglockhart, and the willow graves of Auld-sauchton were rapidly left behind; and they soon saw the Leith sparkling at the bottom of the deep and savage *Corrie*, which gives its name to a parish, and passing the kirk, which was thatched with heather, and its little secluded burying-ground, where the *pest graves* lay thick and close under the sepulchral yews, they turned to the west, and traversed the narrow bridle-path which led to the tower of Lennox.

Linn soon saw its square, black outline rising between him and the moonlit sky, on the slope of the river bank; dark it looked, and huge and dreary. He remarked that not a light was visible at any of its windows, and that no smoke was curling from the square chimneys that rose in a sharp outline from its crowning cape-house of stone.

"On, on," said he, spurring his horse, as new and dark forebodings took possession of him; and one minute more brought them to the barbican gate.

It stood wide open—an unusual circumstance at such a time, especially with such a castellan as the old baronet, who, being a veteran, was wont to have watch and ward kept regularly in his little garrison, even in times of peace.

" 'Sdeath!" said Linn; " has the place been sacked by Cromwel! and his psalm-singing roundheads? Has old Sir Harry had his wish gratified by a siege at last? But the brass cannon, I see, still face the entrance."

They dismounted, and drew their bridles through the rings at the door. Then Linn paused for a moment to arrange his confused thoughts, which were all fear and anxiety, as he knocked loudly at the arched door of the tower that was never before approached without a challenge. It was of oak, studded with iron, and sounded hollowly: all remained quiet and still.

"Knock, Carlourie, like a kind comrade," said Linn, in a stifled voice, for brave and young though he was, the agitation of his nerves deprived him of all firmness.

The trooper gave the door a violent blow.

It was unfastened, and swung slowly open on its creaking hinges; and there could no longer be a doubt that the whole castle was empty.

What terrible event did this presage? Empty! Linn remembered how Dora had sprung forth to meet him, when last he was there with me; how her cheeks glowed with health and pleasure, how her eyes sparkled with love and vivacity, while all her magnificent hair hung floating on her shoulders. Poor Dora! every feature of the place was full of her memory, and Linn reclined against the wall in irrepressible agitation.

He recalled innumerable instances in which her gentleness, her playfulness and beauty shed a calm and pleasing influence over the rugged nature of the boisterous old baronet, and his rough household of scarred troopers and bronzed pikemen, drawing respect and love from them on the one hand, while she diffused refinement over them on the other; thus, when the bluff Sir Harry was in his greatest fits of passion—usually at the neighbouring baronet, Sir John Skene, of Curriehill, who, being a lawyer, kept our old warrior of the league in constant "hot water" by his pleas *anent* meithes, marches, multoures, right of forestry and commonty, till he was ready to expire of spleen, and a desire to raze the enemy's stronghold to the ground-stone—even then Dora, by a glance of her merry eye, a caress or a kiss on his brown cheek, subdued the old laird, who was too stout a Scotsman to be subdued by aught else under high Heaven.

"Have you a flint and a steel?" asked Linn, in a broken voice.

"Yes, sir," said Carlourie; "no soldier was ever without them."

"Then strike a light — strike a light, for I must learn whether war or the plague has brought silence and desolation on the home of the Lennoxes. Here is the nest—but where, alas! is my dove?"

The spark was struck and a light made with a pistol match twisted round a dry branch, which burned readily; and they ascended the stone stair which led to the hall, while the rats, who had held holiday, scampered before them in every direction. The echoes of their footsteps sounded hollowly and far off in the distant recesses of the vaulted stories, and smote heavily and painfully on the heart of the unhappy lover. The place seemed to be peopled by wavering shadows, as the gleams of their feeble light fell into the masses of darkness. The great hall was vaulted with stone, and had a dreary aspect as its roof yawned above them.

The ashes of a fire yet lingered in the ample grate, eddying and whitening in every current of air; while above them grinned the grotesque iron heads of the two fire-dogs. The favourite stag-hounds and wiry otter terriers of old Sir Harry slept no longer on the glowing hearth; but a wild and starved-looking cat glared and spat at the two visitors, as it sprang from place to place like an evil spirit.

The hall was desolate and chilly.

Sir Henry's large elbow chair, of crimson leather, still remained near the cold fire-place, and on its gilded knobs hung his bowl-hilted rapier, his gold-headed cane, and broad hat with its cavalier plume.

How bare and silent seemed the large oak table now! But around it Linn had often seen a circle of merry faces, and there he had last seen *me* sitting in sullen dignity *below* the salt; and all the old familiar household came crowding back upon his recollection; and he could well recal the hearty laughter, the loyal toasts, the merry camp songs and hunting chorusses of the leal cavalier.

" Sir—sir !" said Carlourie, aghast, as he lighted a candle which he found on a beauffet; " the pest—the plague has been here !"

" Good fellow—kind comrade, do not leave me yet," said Linn, in a smothered voice, as his eyes filled with tears; " come with me—this way—I will not detain you long."

Honest Charlie Carlourie would rather have followed Linn against a square of English infantry, or a battery of brass guns; but influenced either by sympathy or discipline, notwithstanding his horror of the plague, he accompanied his officer, who ascended to Dora's chamber; but there all was darkness and desolation, too !

On her toilet table stood a looking-glass and a rat-eaten candle surmounted by an extinguisher, and between these two a spider had spun his web industriously; hence it was apparent that many nights must have elapsed since that candle had been last extinguished. Dora's linnet was dead in its cage; ribbons and laces, dresses and ornaments, were scattered about. On a side table were numerous phials and cups, indicative of recent sickness and suffering; and a damp, heavy, and mysterious odour pervaded the apartment.

Linn felt his senses reeling.

Now for the first time he perceived that the chamber was hung with *white*, and that branches of rosemary were scattered on the floor.

Terrible convictions forced themselves upon his agonised mind, and he tottered towards her pretty bed, which had festooned curtains of pale blue silk, and a gilded roof. Where now was the pale and delicate cheek which had nightly pressed that downy pillow?

Alas, what was this?

The distinct impression—the awful *outline*—of a coffin remained yet on the damp coverlet of the deserted bed. Poor William Linn threw up his hands in despair, and Carlourie sprang forward, but too late, to seize him; for, heart-stricken, and alive only to the terrible present, and dead to the future, he flung himself upon Dora's bed and sobbed like a child.

CHAPTER LXIII.

THE PEST.

MORNING was beaming on the green Pentland Hills, and the summer mist curled from the woods of Redhall and Dreghorn, when these two men came forth from the desolate tower, and mounted their horses, which for the last four hours had been shaking their ears in the echoing court.

After Carlourie closed the ponderous iron gate, which was composed of welded yetlan bars, they rode rapidly down to the hamlet of Currie, which nestles in the wooded hollow near an ancient bridge, that spans a pool the depth of which has become a Scottish proverb. The gables of its grey slated manse, and the vane of the heather-roofed kirk, glittered in the sunshine; the dew lay deep on flower and tree; the young birds were spreading their winglets on the morning air; and the white smoke of the yet sleeping hamlet ascended high through the clear balmy atmosphere. At that early hour there was no one stirring, so Carlourie knocked at the door of a small change-house, which stands at the bridge end, and may yet be known by a grotesque face carved on each of its lower crowsteps. It wore the usual sign of a village shop—

"Dundee threid—Edinburgh breid, and new laid eggs, by me, Lucky Legget, Ail-browstar."

Repeated knockings brought forth the proprietrix, an old and wrinkled woman, clad in her curchie, with its long lappets, and her short-skirted gown.

"Eh, sirs—what is this o't? The Laird of Linn!" she exclaimed, wringing her hands with kindly commiseration.

"Aye, good Mother Legget, thou knowest me. I have been up the river side, at Lennox, and found only desolation. Where in Heaven's name, is Sir Henry, the laird?"

"God rest him! God rest him! He is in his grave in the kirkyard up the brae yonder," replied the carlin, wringing her hands anew.

"And Dora, his daughter?"

"Lying beside him—oh, woe worth the day!" she replied, in a burst of honest grief,—for all the people loved Sir Henry and his daughter.

"When did this happen, carlin?" asked the trooper,—for his leader's voice was gone.

"She died on the night they brought owre the ferry—yea, on the very night o' her down-settling at home did she pass awa. The old laird was stricken wi' the pest, as she died in his arms; and thereafter followed her to her last resting-place; and now they lie under the green sod side by side; but they died in the Lord, and in peace wi' our auld minister and wi' Curriehill too, though they could neer thole ilk ither in life. The servitors fled the tower, and none will venture near it, till the smeikers and cleanzears come to purify the place."

Linn had heard only the first part of the old woman's information. Leaving his horse, he sprang over the churchyard stile, and sought the burial place of the Lennoxes, which he knew well, as they had all been buried there since the knights of Malta lost the kirk and their possessions in the parish, under the queen regent, Mary of Lorraine. But I have so much of my own adventurous life to relate, that I must be brief with the story of poor Willie Linn.

Here he found the graves of the baronet and his daughter lying side by side, where the former may yet be known by a stone carved with a sword and the old French cross of Mount Carmel, on the south side of Currie kirk; and there he remained long in sorrow, prayer, and reverie—longer, perhaps, than my reader would believe; and he buried his head in his hands, for the brightness of the summer sun, and the merry song of a goldfinch from an old yew tree, fretted and distressed him. Stupefied by grief, he lingered while the sun rode high in heaven, and his heat drank up the dew; and while Carlourie drank his ale at Lucky Legget's, and yawned, marvelled, and blessed his stars that he was not a lover.

At last our trooper lost all patience, and approaching the cavalier, said kindly,

"Come awa, sir, come awa—we maun e'en gang back to the regiment and hope for happier times."

"I will never go back to the regiment, Carlourie—never!" replied the other, in a changed voice, and the kind soldier saw with alarm how pallid, wan, and trembling he had become—how his skin burned, how his eyes were sunken and bloodshot.

"Will ye ride hame, sir?" he reiterated.

"Home, comrade! I have no home but the grave—this grave, if possible, where *she* is lying."

Carlourie shrugged his shoulders, for he did not believe in all this; at least, he thought it "unco queer."

"Leave me, Carlourie," said Linn, in a faint voice, as his head sank on his hand, "leave me; I am faint and ill; my head begins to swim."

"I'll never leave you, sir, till I see you riding with your troop of the Black Dragoons."

"God bless thee, kind fellow," sighed Linn; "well—well, let it be as you will. Take me home; my house stands at the Linn on Almond side—any one will show you the way. Let us go."

Carlourie gladly placed him on horseback, and they rode northwards to Temple-liston, as in that parish the little estate of the sick lieutenant lay, in a beautifully wooded dell, on the banks of the Almond. As they drew near the old village, with its Temple-church and preceptory, which crown a lofty eminence, they found everywhere marks of the terror and desolation spread by the plague; many cottages were empty, and the people were in mourning, for in this locality the plague had hovered for five years past.

Striken by it. poor William Linn went home only to sicken and to die. Though welcomed by his old hereditary race of servants with open arms and the warmest welcome, no sooner did they behold his wan and sickly aspect, as Carlourie assisted him from his horse and conducted him to bed, than they all fled the place. for excess of terror deprived the people of all courage and humanity; and there, in the lonely house, with no sound to break its stillness but the rush of the Almond pouring over its rocky *linn*, the faithful trooper, unassisted and unseen, tended our gallant comrade, who rapidly sank, and expired before morning.

"That eerie, dreary night, sir, on whilk the you g laird de'ed, was to me the maist awfu' adventure I had gane thro'," said Carlourie. in whose eyes the tears were standing. "The sicht o' death on the battle-field produces neither awe nor fear, for *then* our bluid is up, and we are spurring sword in hand for glory and our country. But to witness a man deeing in a lanely and half-darkened room, at mirk midnicht, when there is nae sound near but his moans and the deed-rattle in his throat—or, as on that nicht, the bummel o' the Almond owre its stany bed—oh! sir, that is different a'together; and my crushed heart felt heavy as that gallant spirit passed upward to its God; the   the death-rattle ceased, his jaw fell, and I heard nocht but th wind as it soughed in the woods of Linn."

"Thou art a kind fellow," said I, "and this good faith shall not pass unrewarded."

Linn with his last breath had implored Carlourie to bury him beside Dora Lennox; but the poor trooper found the fulfilment of his promise impossible, circumstanced as he was then—alone, deserted by all, and an object of terror, as the companion and attendant of a pest-stricken man.

Like a good, pious Scot, he prayed for a time, and wrapping up the dead officer in the bedding in which he died, carried him with difficulty into the garden of the mansion; and selecting a place where the roses were all in full bloom and the blush of summer beauty, he dug a deep grave; therein he laid him, and the honest fellow wept as he covered him up.

Then he was about to go, but remembered that none might know where the last laird of the Linn was lying. He raised the hearthstone in the chamber of dais, and having been bred a mason in his youth, on procuring a chisel and mallet, he cut a brief epitaph upon the slab, which he placed over the lonely grave, and then retired.*

It was the noon of the next day before these labours were over, and without food or rest he toiled to complete his ghastly task. The moment it was ended he turned the horses into the fields, lest they might starve; unkennelled the dogs; and locking the door of Linn House, flung the key into the Almond, crying (with the true superstition of a Scottish peasant) on the river kelpie to keep it till the true owner come to demand it; and without waiting to see whether *a hand* rose from the stream to clutch it, he set off with all speed to visit his parents, and rejoin the Black Dragoons.

CHAPTER LXIV.

OUR RIDE THROUGH FIFE.

SUCH was the story of their adventures and my poor friend's fate, which Carlourie related to me in his own plain, earnest, and graphic way. It made a deep impression upon me, and some time elapsed before I could realize a conviction of Linn's death; for now, in him, and in the dashing Master of Oliphant, I had lost my two oldest and most valued friends—those who had known me from boyhood, and who had been true to me in those days of poverty, obscurity, and hard study, when such friendship was doubly dear to a poor and nameless student of St. Mungo.

However, the necessity of rejoining, left me no time for the

* The house of Linn, near Kirkliston, is now a mill, and its flower-garden the miller's yard; but the solitary grave of the young laird still remains with the inscription cut thereon by the faithful dragoon.

> *" Here lieth William Linn*
> *The rightful heir of Linn."*

availing sorrow; and on the day after Carlourie's arrival, we bade adieu to the quiet cottage of his hospitable parents, whom, to the best of my power, I repaid for their great kindness to me, and marched off for Dundee, where our regiment was then cantoned. I rode my new horse, a fine dark charger, with all the trappings of my old one; while Carlourie rode a pony or bidet, as our dragoons named those sturdy nags furnished by the Scottish government to carry cavalry baggage.

I felt well and strong, and with an emotion of joy inhaled the pure air of the summer morning, while my breast expanded with new anticipations and new hopes. As we descended into the Howe of Fife the sun rose, and along that magnificent valley his golden light was shed on many a baronial tower and snug farmhouse, on many a deep blue lake and wooded hill, and on many a burgh begirt by walls and gates that crossed the king's highway, and were kept by armed men and pointed cannon. At many a door sat maimed soldiers, the trophies of the English invasion, minus legs and arms, who waved their bonnets to us, and cried " God speed," in the name of kirk or king, as their loyal or religious sympathies inclined them most.

As we approached that thriving old burgh which stands in the vale of Eden, a place so pleasant and beautiful, that, when the royal family occupied Falkland Palace, the royal nursery was always at Cupar, I resolved to remain there overnight, as there was no ferry over the Tay after nightfall.

It was a day of unclouded sunshine, and the valley of the Eden lay smiling before me, with all its woods wherein our kings, in prouder days, followed the chase with mouthing hound and twanging horn, aud where the wild buck's bell rang up from the forest dingle. On one hand I saw the old tower of Scotstarvet, the seat of one who, in his time, was the poor scholar's bountiful patron; on the other rose the older dwelling of Scotland's greatest satirist; the green trenches formed by the French chevaliers of Chatelherault and d'Oysell, against the lords of the congregation; and farther off, the old spire of Ceres, throwing its shadow on the last home of the Lindesays and the Crawfords —on the quiet grave of that ferocious peer who crushed in his iron glove poor Mary's snowy arm, and forced her to sign the deed which tore our diadem from her brow;—and so, full of these memories of the olden time, I entered, by its west port, the venerable seat of the Stewartry of Fife, after being strictly questioned by an armed guard, near which I perceived four brass cannon and a mortar, for the burghers were all in harness. We rode to the Fife Arms, an hostel in the kirkgate; dismounted, and resigned our nags to the ostler and his peddies.

On the burgh-cross and the Tolbooth there yet hung the faded garlands of the 6th July, when the king was royally banquetted by the provost.

In a corner of the great common hall, my brother soldier and sat down at the same table to dine; for, in the kindly north, we had not yet completely imitated the English fashion of making inferiors eat at a separate board; thus the laird and his groom, the chief and his vassal, still drank to each other, clinked their cups together, sat at the same table, and filled their quaighs from the same black jack—at least in the secluded districts of Scotland.

We had a dish of roasted venison, with eggs, broiled in gravy, and a gallant jug of claret to wash them down with; but thi repast was barely laid, when there rode into the inn-yard a figure which I thought familiar to me.

This new arrival was attired in a black Geneva cloak, black smallclothes, square-cut clerical bands, and broad-leaved hat with a steeple crown; his elbows stuck out at sharp angles, and flapped like loose wings when his nag trotted; his hair hung lankly over his ears; his long lean legs almost reached the ground as they stretched over his saddle-bags and rough Galloway cob. In short, he was the Reverend Zachary Boyd.

"Welcome to Cupar, and to the ' Fife Arms!' " said I, shaking the hand of old Zach. (as we called him at college); " your servant, my worthy sir."

"Well met, Master Ogilvie," said he. " Verily, now, but this meeting is passing strange; for last night I dreamt of you."

"Something good, I hope?"

" Nay—that I assisted at your marriage—which, I sorrow to say, portendeth misfortune. Yet I hope we shall not separate in such a hurry as on that night when Thurlow, the wicked Levite, and his sons of Cain, came upon us, like wolves upon a fold. Oh, but you jinket them bravely! My gudes and gear suffered sorely tho'; every panel was shot through by pistol-bullets, and every bed and bolster pricked by sword-blades. Yea, there was one English Amorite, a sergeant with a happety leg, that nearly ran his halbert into me in the ardour of his search."

I pressed Mr. Boyd to share our dinner, and we all sat down together; but my dainty venison was cold as human charity before the preacher had ended the grace which he deemed necessary; but then we fell on, with clear consciences and a good appetite.

He was on his way to Alyth, in Angus, where the conventions of the parliament and kirk were met, protected by a body of troops under Marshal Leven (who had found himself too old to march a second time into England), and we agreed to travel together to Dundee. Perceiving that my reverend friend was much excited, and alternately full of many words, and then of deep thought, I asked what was the matter—if he had any evil tidings?

"Evil—no, but joyous tidings, which shall make every heart in Christendom rejoice. Have you heard of the wonderful manifestation of Providence among the heathens of the East—the barbarian Turks and infidel Moors?"

I answered that I had not; whereupon he drew from one of his capacious side-pockets the *Mercurius Scoticus* for the 29th of last month, and after taking a draught of claret, read, with the loud voice of one who sees something important, and with a preacher's peculiar intonation, the following paragraph:—

"They write from Aberdeen, that a letter from a Scottish Jesuit, to James of Jerusalem, the mass-priest who lurketh among the Grants in Murrayland, was intercepted by the Laird of Warriston, and found to contain these wonderful tidings:— About five months since, there were many barbarian Turks and blackavised Moors met together at a town called Mecca, in the mosque, or high kirk, whereof their false prophet hath lain for many years suspended between heaven and earth, by a loadstone, say the learned—by devilish agency, say the vulgar. The assembled heathens were all at prayer, when lo! there rang a clap of thunder, which shook the dome of the said mosque! The earth yawned in the centre thereof, and flames arose, with the shrieks and yells of the damned; and, awful to relate, the coffin sank slowly into the abyss of fire and smoke, and disappeared. The spectators fell on their knees, being struck with a deadly fear; and all in the land of the Grand Turk have rent their turbans, trampled on the crescent, and embraced the presbyterian religion. The Lord be about us! for of a verity it would seem that the day of doom is at hand!"

"Now what think you of *that*, sir?" said the divine, closing the little newspaper.

As Mr. Boyd evidently wished to believe this startling piece of foreign news, though it rested on no better authority than the letter of a poor Scottish Jesuit, whose calling made him abhorred by his own countrymen, I had some difficulty in explaining that I considered it only one of the many absurd stories that came among us from distant lands, of which we knew little, and with which we had no direct intercourse—stories but too readily received by our own people, who lived in a perpetual round of wonder; as nothing was spoken of now but omens, miracles, predictions, witchcraft, and bloody battles.

By this avowed heresy, I only drew upon myself a long oration on prophecy, flanked by copious quotations from the " Last Battel of the Soule," amid which Carlourie slipped away to look after our nags, and I finished another stoup of claret. On any of his favourite topics, the energy of Boyd was undying, for he was one of those enthusiasts who, when the covenant was sworn, had foretold that the Scottish drums should ring at the Flaminian gate, before the sword was sheathed in our ranks!

Next day, when we reached the Port-on-Craig, to take the ferry boat for Dundee, the weather was lowering; the Tay foamed upon the bar, and the wind blew stiffly from the north.

The want of a bridge at Perth caused this ferry to be much frequented; thus though the boat was a large sloop, she was destitute of deck, as the charge was trifling, James III. having ordained in parliament, in 1474, that " at the Port-on-Craig, one penny for a man, and for his horse, one penny," should be the fare; thus sixpence took us over, nags and all. As the village was without a pier, all embarked at the point of *the Craig*, or rock. The little craft was crowded by passengers, shepherds with their dogs, and women with baskets of ware and food. The mainsail and jib were set; the sloop was close-hauled, for the river here is two miles broad, and the wind was dead against us. As the sloop tacked, we had to stand by our horses' heads; the women screamed, the dogs barked, and the spray flew over us, and many poor sinners lay to leeward, where, as Mr. Boyd drily remarked, they " cast out the devils that were in them."

On landing, he took the road direct for Alyth, in Angus, while Carlourie and I trotted westward to Dundee.

CHAPTER LXV.

REJOIN.

THE industrious and flourishing seaport of Dundee was at this time surrounded by walls and closed by gates. On these were mounted nearly fifty pieces of cannon. The garrison consisted of the Black Dragoons, now reduced to little more than three hundred swords; two battalions of the Lord Duffus' regiment, each about six hundred strong; and a body of well-armed citizens, disciplined and commanded by the magistrates, who were determined to defend their town, which had long been the abode of ease, opulence, and manufacture. Their stores and shops teemed with goods from all parts of northern Europe; their wharves were filled with casks and bales, and shipping crowded their harbour.

The thirteenth hereditary Constable of Dundee, the Viscount Dudhope, K.T., was now absent with our army in England, as colonel of horse; but his deputy-governor, Robert Lumsden, of Bewquhany, a lieutenant-colonel in our service (though lately colonel of the Finnish Pistoleers in Sweden) was a brave and skilful veteran, in whom the people implicitly confided. Thus all was peaceful by the Tay. The Dundeans rose with the sun, set about their avocations with their proverbial industry, and, undisturbed by the distant din of war, and the rumour of battles lost and won, went to bed with their wives and little ones when the kirk bells rang at eve, and the town piper blew his pibroch at the cross.

The dealer in the Luckenbooths secured his door at one P.M., and retired quietly to dine; the opulent merchant dozed over his mulled sack, and old ladies made themselves comfortable with cant and cordial.

In those days, a journey from Dundee to the capital was a serious matter; it caused more preparation and thought than the march of the ten thousand Greeks; it occupied many days, and there were no small risks to be run, among robbers, bullying ferrymen, leaky boats, lame horses, and deep fords; and as there were no banks, as on the Continent, the merchant hoarded his gold in a strong box, and the thrifty gudewife knotted her good Scottish silver in au old stocking, or stored it away in kistneuks and pirlypigs. All was peaceful in Dundee, for the flame of war had not as yet scathed the shores of the beautiful Tay.

In the seagate we were recognised and welcomed by many of our comrades; among others, by Captain Augustine, who was standing at the door of an hostelry, smoking a meerschaum, rushed forth to shake my hand.

"Potstausend!" he exclaimed, "is it thee or thy double-ganger? Mein Gott in himmel, I thought thee buried on the field of Inverkeithing!"

"Nay, noble comrade," said I, laughing, "I am worth a day's pay and a dozen of dead men yet. But where shall I find the count, that I may report myself, as in duty bound."

He indicated the residence of our colonel, asked me to sup with him at his billet in the Bucklemaker's-wynd, to talk over the *slaght von Inverkeithing*, and then we parted.

The quarters of Count Ogilvie were in a handsome mansion known as Whitehall, a strong and vaulted edifice of some antiquity, which overlooked the Nethergate, and had occasionally been the residence of James VI., of the queen his mother, and of Charles II., when he visited Dundee, before crossing the English border. One of our troopers was on duty with his carbine before a door, the lintel of which bore the injunction, "Obay ze King James VI.;" and here I found our quarter-guard established under old Sergeant Hackirou

I was warmly welcomed by our dark and stately Colonel, and almost hugged by the rough old Laird of Drumstanchel, with whom he was seated over a bottle of sack, for they were inseparables. They then introduced me to a fine-looking old cavalier, who sat with them, as the Laird of Bewquhany, lieutenant-governor of Dundee. He was a bronzed and white-haired veteran, who wore on his breast the Order of the Tower and Sword, won from the hand of Gustavus, when leading his Scottish pikes across the Lech under the fire of seventy Austrian cannon. To this gallant soldier the kind count praised me in terms which I dare not repeat.

"Thou art a brave young fellow, I hear," said old Bewquhany; "join us at dinner to-morrow. I byde in the Seagate, and am a plain soldier. We shall have only a haunch roasted, mutton broth—*potage de mouton à la Ecossaise*, as we used to say in the Scots gendarmes. Bravo—we'll all dine together *à la Gamelle!* You know I served four years in the gendarmerie under Holbourn—he was premier captain then."

"An infamous traitor, whom I should have pistolled at Inverkeithing, for his betrayal of us and of his trust," said the count, irefully; "we arrived here sorely cut up and jaded, Harry, and utterly without food; but the musketeers of Duffus shared their rations with us."

"Aye, poor fellows," said Bewquhany, "they had each but one biscuit in his havresack, yet they were broken to share with the Black Dragoons."

"For which we gave them three hearty cheers," added Drumstanchel; "friend Harry, by the henekers! as we used to say in Friesland, 'tis quite a resurrection this! we were told that you were among the dead with poor Oliphant and Linn—brave souls as ever yielded to fate!"

"Told—by whom, captain?"

"By the Lord Lorn," said the count, handing me a long glass of wine.

"Lorn!" I gave a start, and controlled myself, yet not before the count's keen eye had observed the sudden emotion that name kindled within me.

"But I never despaired of you, Harry, and have kept a troop vacant, although Lorn (and he ground his teeth at the name) pressed me to bestow it on a kinsman of his own. But now that troop is *yours*. It was young Balcomies', but he fell at Inverkeithing with a ball in his chest. I will write at once to Marshal Leven anent it; he commands at Alyth, a few miles north of this."

"Is not the Lord Lorn in England with the king, and at the head of his regiment?"

Bewquhany and Drumstanchel twisted their grey moustachios, and laughed.

"Save his father," said the count, "there *never came a coward* of the Campbell blood, yet his lordship has deemed it necessary to remain behind, and leaving his lieutenant-colonel, brave Auchinbreck, to lead the foot-guards against the English republicans, is now with the estates at Alyth. Ardmohr's regiment is there also, for not one battalion in which the Marquis of Argyle has family influence was marched southward with the king."

"An ominous circumstance," said Bewquhany.

I thought of Lady Flora, and these pointed remarks brought a blush to my cheek.

I was billeted near Augustine, in the Bucklemaker's-wynd, and two days after my arrival received my commission as captain, with the privy seal of Scotland, like a broad waxen pancake, appended thereto; so now, by the fortune of war and the count's favour, I found myself ritt-master of the third troop of the king's own regiment of Black Dragoons.

As the corps was much reduced by the result of the late unfortunate battle, the count, who had won a high reputation as a cavalry officer in Germany, kept us constantly at drill, being determined by skill and discipline to make up for lack of numbers. Equitation, and the use of the pistol and carbine, he pressed particularly upon us.

"The first," he would often say, "is indispensable to the perfect cavalier, in order that, being able to govern his charger by the aid of his legs and bridle-hand, he may have the right at full liberty for using his sword, and be capable on all occasions of acting either alone or in squadron. Experience has taught me, noble comrades, that the fire of the carbine is always most effectual to the *left*, and that of the pistol to the *rear*; even the wild Croats never fire to the right with the carbine, or front with the pistol. Many a Finnish trooper and Swedish cuirassier I have seen them unhorse by a flying shot."

So expert was the count himself, that once I saw him, when at full gallop, bring down a crow by a single ball from a carbine. This was when we were drilling one day to the westward of the old tower of Blackness.

CHAPTER LXVI.

THE OLD OAK PEW.

On the first Sunday after my arrival, I went to church. Being anxious to hear the Reverend Colin Campbell, who was celebrated as a preacher, and who had served as chaplain in the campaigns against Montrose, I visited the east kirk, which was merely the chancel of the great church of St. Mary. It was crowded by wealthy and respectable burgesses, with their wives and daughters clad in Genoa taffeta and the best of Florence silk; the fronts of the galleries were hung with coloured stuffs, festooned and fringed, for the council, the hammermen, and the ancient fraternity of seamen. The pews were all of black oak, richly carved, and some bore the insignia of the nine corporations to whom they belonged, and pious legends, invoking blessings on the Lorimers, Baxters, Bucklemakers, and Bonnetmakers, &c.; and therein each craft sat with its deacon, who in virtue of his office wore the sword of a gentleman.

The bustle caused by the arrival of the provost, dean of guild, the four bailies and councillors in their robes, accompanied by their halberdiers and piper, and the clatter made by the hammermen, ascending an ancient stair, named *the king's*, since it was trod by Charles II., attracted the attention of the pew-openers so much that I was left to shift for myself; and after looking about for a few seconds, I assumed a seat in a spacious and comfortable pew, the old oak panels of which were richly carved, and the inside of which was lined with modest black cloth, in the puritan taste. I had barely done so, depositing my beaver, rapier, and gloves beside me, and my bible on the book board, when there was a rustling of silk, a sense of perfume, and a pretty hand was laid on the pew door; its proprietor had arrived!

I started up to make way and to apologise; but was stricken dumb when my eyes met the startled gaze of Lady Flora Campbell!

I felt the blood rushing to my temples, while she grew pale as death, and giving me but a slight bow, for many eyes were upon her, passed in and took her seat beside me. Irresolute, and full of confusion, I would have sought another place, as I dared not compromise her; but at that moment the church service began, and the psalm, in which all the people joined with tongue and heart, rang under those ribbed aisles, which in earlier ages had echoed only the solemn masses and Gregorian chants of our forefathers.

I was as one in a dream! The charm of sitting beside Flora, of hearing the rustle of her dress, and feeling it touch me again and again; the joy of hearing her low soft voice mingling with the singers; of hearing her lower breathing; of seeing her tremulous white fingers among the fluttering leaves of old Andro Hart's "*Psalme Buke* in Scottish Metre;" of watching one beautiful curl that fell from under her broad round hat upon her white and delicate neck, all combined to bewilder me; and for the pleasure of being there, I would have braved the fire of a whole English battalion.

How swift were the two hours I spent in that old oak pew!

I took no heed of the time or of the service; thus the Reverend Colin, whom I came especially to hear, had passed through the firstly, secondly, thirdly, and attained the fourth degree of warm latitude in his fiery discourse, before I became aware that even the psalm was ended. I had been conscious of one idea alone.

That Flora Campbell was beside me!

She trembled from time to time; and I knew that she was endeavouring to lead her timid thoughts to God, and to forget that one who loved her passionately was by her side; but the flush at times that crossed her white and slender neck, assured me that such oblivion was denied her, and made me sigh and tremble in turn. Dear, dear and gentle Flora!

At that time I forgot her father's wiles, her brother's hatred, and the interest—not a kind one, certainly—taken in my fate by her lover, Ardmohr, when I lay wounded that fatal night on the field of Inverkeithing.

Perceiving that the fair daughter of his chief was present, the Reverend Mr. Campbell (who had been shorn of his ears by the wild cavaliers of Montrose, at Inverlochy) conceived it incumbent to weave up praises of the great MacCallum Mohr with his discourse; and I could perceive how the timid Flora quailed and trembled, as all the eyes of the congregation fell upon her, while her clansman held forth in the following manner, pausing only to prime himself by an enormous pinch of snuff.

"Yea, my brethren, despite the malice of the malignant cavaliers, whose hearts are black as the blackness of hell; despite the wiles of the blasphemous sectaries, and the sneers of the unlawful engagers, Argyle is one who standeth at his post, as the most faithful centurion in the hosts of Israel! Nobly hath he done his part in rousing the people of this covenanted kingdom to resist the innovations a mansworn king would have made in the worship our fathers framed; and Jacob hath no truer son than he, who hath stood as our tower of strength amid the sea of blood that for twelve years past hath drenched the Scottish plains! Oh, accursed be the tippets, the cornered caps, the copes and cassocks of the Babylonians—the badges of that antichrist who brought this mischief among us! Woe be to those who ransacked Jerusalem, Ephesus, and Crete to adduce proofs that proud prelacy existed in the primitive kirk, and who blasphemously appealed unto Timothy and Titus in support thereof. Did not James VI. say—'Give me but the making of judges and bishops, and the law and the gospel shall be as I please?' But the Scotsman said NAY, and taking his sword and bible, ascended into the mountains. Down, then, with all pre-latists, for the horns of their mitres are like unto those of the beast in the Apocalypse! We have girded up our loins and unsheathed the sword, and NEVER shall it go back to the scabbard until prelacy and sectarianism are alike swept away, the ark of God restored, and the glory of the temple revived. But lo! the Philistines are upon us—they have smitten us in battle; yet it shall never be said while there remaineth one leal-hearted Scot in the land, that the church of his fathers—that fair pile cemented by their blood—shall be cast down, and Zion trod beneath the cloven hoofs of the blasphemous puritans. To the grindstone with your swords; up, up, I say, for Scotland's kirk and king!"

The eyes of the people kindled; their cheeks flushed; their whole souls seemed to follow his words, which were full of fire and energy, and many a sword was grasped; for his language was well calculated to rouse the passions of his hearers, and may be taken as a fair specimen of the preaching that was then heard every Sabbath in more than a thousand parish pulpits throughout the realm of Scotland.

Within a year after this, the voice of our fiery preacher was hushed, and he lay at rest in the south transept of that venerable church. It was remarked by certain evil-minded cavaliers, that on the occasion of his *last* sermon, a curious animal, somewhat like a black tom-cat, perched itself on the canopy of the pulpit; but of this I can say nothing.

Sermon over, the congregation began to disperse. I assumed my beaver, gloves, and sword, and held the pew door open for Flora, bowing almost to my boot tops as she tripped down the aisle.

"Oh, why did you come here?" she asked, in a low and hurried voice. "Oh, Mr. Ogilvie, was it kind or just of you?"

"By my soul, Lady Flora, I conjure you to be assured that I knew not of your being in Dundee, or that yonder pew was yours. I am not so presumptuous as to thrust myself thus publicly upon you."

"Oh, if my father—my brother——"

"I know their hostility; but neither are in Dundee, I trust."

"No; the marquis—he is a marquis now——"

"So I am aware."

"If he had been with me to-day?"

"'Sdeath, don't think of it."

"Most fortunately he is at Inverary, and Lord Lorn——"

"Is with the estates at Alyth."

"And I am but waiting his return, to travel westward with him into Argyleshire."

" Dare I hope that I shall see you again ?"

" Alas, no," she answered, in an agitated voice ; " yet, oh, Mr Ogilvie, I never again expected to hear your voice."

" Lady Flora !"

" The—the Laird of Ardmohr told me that you were slain at Inverkeithing."

" 'Tis no fault of his that I escaped the carnage of that day, and the horror of the subsequent night ; and if that life, dearest Flora——"

" Leave me—leave me, for Heaven's sake ! here comes my little brother, Neil, from the Cross Kirk, to join me, and *we* dare not be seen together."

I bowed, and mingled with the people, while she hastened away, accompanied by her brother, the little Lord of Ardmaddie, whom I remembered at court as a page who deserved to be well switched for his petulance. I followed, with anxiety, at a little distance, to discover where they resided. She passed along one of the oldest and principal streets of the town, and disappeared through an archway.

" What street is this ?" I asked old Drumstanchel, who at that moment joined me.

" The Argylegate—or Overgate, which you will; the count hates the name so much, that he will ride a mile round rather than pass through it."

" Has the marquis property here ?"

" Yes; that mansion with the carved windows is his, as well as the house that pertained to the Earls of Findowrie in the Seagate; 'twas there he feasted Charles royally, only a month or so past."

I reconnoitred the arch, which was closed by an iron gate. A coat armorial, bearing the arms of Argyle, surmounted it. There I loitered mauy an hour, afterwards, but neither at the gate nor at the window was Flora ever visible. I became a constant attender at church ; and though the young Lord Neil came in his laced cloak and plumed beaver, with a hawk on his wrist, Flora was, or pretended to be, ill—at least, she came to church no more.

A few weeks glided quietly away. We heard neither tidings of the estates at Alyth, of the king's army in Englaud, nor the operations of Monk in Scotland ; but a time was coming !

On a Sunday eveuing I was sauntering slowly along the Argylegate, having passed and repassed the well-known windows of Flora until I could no longer do so without arresting the attention of the many armed and insolent lackeys who hovered about the archway, when the sound of voices in altercation attracted me as I was about to withdraw ; and, on turning, I perceived two of the provost's officials, sturdy halberdiers, dragging towards the Tolbooth a poor little mannikin, across whose back there was slung a large fiddle.

Recognising my former acquaintance, Jock of the Lodge, I interposed in his behalf, and the myrmidons of the magistrates, who stigmatised as vagrants all who "made music," or absented themselves from church, released him and retired.

The poor, half-witted deformity, whose wrath, terror, and loquacity had been great, was very profuse in his thanks, and was so grateful that he almost wept on seeing me.

"'Od, sir, I told them owre and owre again wha I was, for I thocht a'body kenned puir Jock; but they seem to hae queer ways o' their ain in Angus here. I've ta'en to a wandering life syne the puritan pockpuddings burned my bit lodge on the muir, and barried the Lowdens. I have fiddled my way through Fife, and owre the water to Dundee. I have been happy and blythe, but never sae blythe and happy to see a kenned face before. Oh, Mr. Ogilvie, there are nae friends in this world like auld friends?"

"And I owe you a brave guerdon, friend Jock, for that letter you brought me to the moss of Dunmore, in the midwinter time."

"Guerdon—hoots, havers, sir! that is naething between you and me," said the poor dwarf, erecting his uncouth figure, with his long beard hanging before him, and his prodigious fiddle behind, exciting the astonishment of all who passed us.

"But where got ye that letter, Jock?"

"From Argyle's bonniest bairn at Lennox tower, where I've played many a merry rant to the auld knicht in the hall, and spent mony a happy hour."

"Oh, Flora," thought I; "then I judged correctly, as to whence that unavailing warning came! How generous and how kind! But whither go ye, Jock?"

"Hame wi' you, sir."

"With me!"

"Just sae, for I would rather be among soldiers than among saints, and I fear there are owre mony saints in Dundee, for an honest carle like me to win his bread among them. Let me byde wi' you, sir; I am easily up-pitten, and can tak' onything ye like to gie; a bone to pyke, a bit bannock and cogue o' milk at meal-times, and a sleep on the door-mat at nicht, is a' that puir auld Jock hath a richt to look for in this world, and he'll sing and play rants and reels to the Black Dragoons as lang as bow and fiddle will hold together."

I found no mode of ridding myself politely of this absurd appendage to my small establishment, without hurting his feel-

ings; and knowing well that this mannikin was intensely sensitive, and moreover petulant and revengeful as an enraged
brownie, I e'en brought him straight to my billet, where his
aspect discomposed my worthy host (an old bucklemaker) so
much, that he was about to arm himself with a bible, while the
gudewife and her little ones retreated to bed, and Captain Augustine uttered such a roar of laughter, that Jock began to lose his
temper. Setting down his fiddle with a bang, he shook his large
knotty fist in the face of the German cavalier, while his grey
eyes gleamed like those of a snake.

"Mein Gott," was Augustine's exclamation; "'tis a devil of
the Brocken—a gnome of the Harz mountains."

The captain then apologised and appeased Jock, whose figure,
so stunted and dwarfish in stature, with its huge head, ample
beard, and grotesque expression, surmounted as it was by a prodigious and overshadowing bonnet, and then the fiddle that was
slung across his squat misshapen body, realised the gnome of
some old German legend, and scared the soldier into respect.
We shared our supper with the mannikin, and he told us many
strange, droll, and occasionally horrible stories, for his small
modicum of brain was wild and unsettled. Then he played his
fiddle to admiration, and sang his strange songs, and before the
close of next day had established himself as the peculiar pet of
the Black Dragoons.

———

CHAPTER LXVII.

THE PLACARD.

ONE day when passing along the Argylegate (my usual place of
lounge), I perceived a crowd of yarn-spinners, bonnet-makers,
and other persons, collected near the well-known mansion. They
were laughing and listening to the sound of a violin. Then I
could detect the shrill cracked voice of my friend Jock, and
pressing forward in the midst of the circle, I obtained a glimpse
of his broad bonnet, under which his short right arm was wield-
ing the bow that sawed away upon the stomach of the large
brown violin.

The people seemed greatly taken by his marvellous aspect, his
skill in the instrument, and the strange words of his song, one
part of which I remember was a conversation with a crow—

" The corbie sat in the corbie's heugh,
Crouping as if he wad dee;
O when shall I get meat enough?'
Quo' that corbie black to me.
· When Morgan, Monk, and Overton,
Hang on the gallows tree,

And the bells shall ring, and the lasses sing,
  By the lady well o' Dundee.'
The corbie croaket loud to hear,
  And wi' a gurly screigh quo' he,
' I aye was fond o' weel fed cheer,
And the ribs o' an English musketeer,
  Are the best o' meat for me.' "

At this moment several gentlemen broke roughly through the crowd. They were gaily attired in laced mantles, broad collars, plumed beavers, and buff boots; even the scabbards of their swords were blue or crimson velvet. They ordered the poor minstrel to "begone to the devil with his rabble rout, and to cease that hideous noise." Then one of them bestowed several severe strokes of a hunting-whip on the poor creature's shoulders.

Pressing forward, I at once interfered to protect poor Jock, who slunk behind me, his eyes gleaming with rage, and I found myself confronted by Lord Lorn, Ardmohr, little Lord Campbell, and others of their party. The two former gazed at me with undissembled rage and astonishment, for they evidently deemed me dead at Inverkeithing. I remembered the midnight search *for me* on that disastrous field; I felt that the moment to redress my wrongs had come; and forgetting Flora, all—everything but vengeance, pale with fury and nerved by righteous anger, I stood before these proud insulters.

"Stick them a', captain!" screamed Jock; "skewer them a', like red herrins on a withy!"

"Is this the conduct of gentlemen," I asked; "to scourge a poor old creature who cannot defend himself? Which of you, sirs, dared to use his whip?"

"Aye—which?" cried the people, who all sympathised with me.

"Come, come, clear the causeway," said Ardmohr, laying a hand on his sword; "beware, my beau coq—my gay fellow, or this may prove unpleasant for you."

(*Beau coq* and *gay fellow!*)

"Villain," cried I, thrusting him back by my clenched hand, as I again recognised the voice and phraseology of the man who deceived me by the false order near Falkirk; "have I discovered, at last, the traitor of Callander Wood?"

He grew very pale, but did not draw.

"What does this fellow mean?" asked Lord Lorn, with an air of proud disdain and cool surprise; "is he mad or drunk to brawl thus with us, in open day, and in the face of the people?"

"My Lord Lorn," said I, "I crave the honour of a few words apart with you."

"You!—what can *you* have to say that these gentlemen, my friends, may not hear?"   Y

" You will regret it, should I speak before them."

" 'Sdeath, sir—who am I?" asked Lorn, loftily.

" Heir of the Marquis of Argyle—our would-be dictator."

" Very well, sir, very well; one rascal was hanged, and another lost his head for saying this. Look to your own neck, fellow! But who are you, sir?—I know nothing about you."

" I am Captain Ogilvie of the Black Dragoons, and I insist on a private meeting—at least a few words apart with you."

" Come to me when I am more at leisure."

" This assumed disdain defeats your purpose," said I, with intense scorn. "Of what is your lordship afraid? You have your rapier—so have I."

Seeing that I was not to be baffled, and that inevitable disgrace would fall upon him, he drew aside with me, and while his eyes gleamed like two white stones, and his voice become husky with suppressed hatred, he asked,

" Now, sir, in the name of all the demons, what do you want?"

" Merely to make arrangements for returning *this shot*, which I received from your lordship's pistol at Dunbar, and to repay a cruel attempt to trample me to death on the field of Inverkeithing."

" You are mad or mistaken, sir," he replied, becoming suddenly cool; " besides, the Lord Lorn can only fight with his equal, and you assuredly are not so. I presume (he added, rejoining his friends) that fighting is your object?"

" Consider again, my lord," said I with a withering smile; " I am not now the poor boy whom you and others strove to kidnap in the streets of Glasgow."

" Away, away! I do not fight with nameless beggars."

" You know my secret, traitor, and son of a traitor ; from your heart will I wrest it!" I exclaimed, drawing my sword and losing all command over myself. " Here I brand you, as false to your country, a traitor to your king, and a consorter with the English brewer! Draw, draw, lest I kill you undefended."

" Separate them—separate them!" cried Lord Campbell.

" Tak ye tent, lest ye win the reddin straik!" exclaimed Jock, and here the people rushed between us. Lorn was drawn by Ardmohr within the archway of his own mansion, and I was dragged away by the Captains Drumstanchel and Augustine, who at that moment came up; otherwise I know not what fatal end this affair might have had, for passion rendered me blind to everything but revenge.

I rushed away to a printing-house, and demanded pen, ink, and paper, wherewith to write; and in two hours thereafter, there appeared on the burghcross, on the church-doors, on the barrier-portes, and at the corners of the principal thoroughfares of Dundee, the following notice :—

"I, the undersigned, a captain in the king's own regiment of Black Dragoons, hereby proclaim Archibald Lord Lorn, Colonel of the Royal Foot Guards, an arrant coward and poltroon, in so far as he inflicted many deadly wrongs upon me, and yet declines to accord the usual satisfaction with sword or pistol, according to the custom of gentlemen, and the rules of honour. — H. OGILVIE."

As I walked through the streets, this bold placard stared me everywhere in fair round capitals; it greatly soothed and appeased my wrath; but, on becoming calm, I reflected on what Flora's emotion would be, on hearing that I had so bitterly reviled and so publicly exposed the timidity of her eldest brother. Oh, that I could but obliterate *her* image from my mind for twelve hours, I exclaimed; for it seemed so strange and unnatural to hate one, and so deeply love the other!

This affair caused a pretty hubbub in Dundee.

Lorn had now no alternative but to fight me, or lose his good name for ever; but before his mind was made up, whether to risk the danger or the shame, his kinsman, Colonel Campbell of Ardmohr, who was a brave but unscrupulous man, sent me a message, saying, "that as it was derogatory in the son of his chief to meet me, *he* would in person volunteer to accord me the required satisfaction."

I was with the count in his quarters, and a number of our officers were with us, when Colonel Campbell of Lawers brought this message on the part of his clansman.

"So he refuses to fight me because I am nameless?" said I, with gloomy joy. "Well, so be it; I accept of his substitute, for I meant to have him paraded at all events. Fool that I was, to save Lorn's life in the Torwood of Stirling!"

"There is but little chivalry in remembering that act," said Lawers, with a haughty smile; "to reproach a brave man with such a service, Captain Ogilvie, is to insult him."

"Your rebuke, perhaps, is just, sir," said I.

"You will also be aware, sir, that in maligning my kinsman Ardmohr, you make me your enemy?"

"And though by meeting you I may have to fight some other Campbell, I take your hint, sir; the moment Ardmohr measures his length on the sward, I shall be at *your* service. You will tell the Lord Lorn, that though accepting his substitute, I still assert that his imaginary rank gives him no privilege to wrong me, and that having done so makes us *equal;* thus he is bound by every tie and code of honour to answer and to satisfy me in person."

To this Lawers, a fine-looking Highland soldier, vouchsafed no other reply than to throw down the leather glove of Ardmohr and lift up mine. He then retired with Captain Augustine to make arrangements for our meeting.

I felt happy and joyous. A mountain seemed to have been taken off my breast; for in meeting Ardmohr, I was only meeting a rival—one whom I had long viewed with hostility; but, if I encountered the brother of Flora, I would do her a life-long injury, and lose alike her love and esteem for ever.

"Ardmohr is a Campbell," said our colonel, whose dark face became yet darker with fiery joy. "They are a brave and a proud race those Campbells; but God alone knows the hatred I have to all their kith and kindred."

"So if you put a bullet through his pineal gland, you will do the count and mankind in general a special service, Harry," said Drumstanchel.

The fiery energy of one usually so quiet as the count surprised me; but I knew not then the cause of his deep emotion.

"I have but one regret in the duel," said I; "it is, to draw against a Scotsman this sword, which I have never before unsheathed but against the natural enemies of my country."

"Tush," said Drumstanchel, "if that be all, my bully boy, I will send you an old case of rapiers that were never drawn against aught but Austrians and Poles, Turks and Tartars."

Captain Augustine soon returned; the preliminaries had been easily adjusted. We were to meet next day on the north-side of the hill of Dundee, at noon precisely, attended each by three friends, and having only our swords and two brace of pistols.

CHAPTER LXVIII.

AN ACCUSATION.

ALTHOUGH duelling was expressly forbidden by those "Acts and Ordinances of War" which Marshal Leven had drawn for the use of the Scottish armies, on the plan of the *Swedish Discipline* of the great Gustavus, we were compelled, by the more powerful code of honour, to infringe them and risk their penalties, which, in a nation so military as ours, no man would dare to enforce. At least, so some of us thought. Duels and brawls with sword and dagger were matters of less remark than a cloudy day or a sudden shower, for we set small store on human life, and danger only gave it a little zest or relish, just as sugar may to sack or pepper to a broiled bone.

Augustine and I talked over the matter as quietly as if it was

a hunting party we projected, and after supping with a good
appetite, we made a bowl of hot whiskey punch; and while the
unlucky Jock played to us on his huge fiddle, we idled over chess
and primero, till my German fell fast asleep on an arm chair,
and I was left to ponder and think alone.

I fixed my eyes on the glowing embers, and sank into deep
reverie.

I longed for morning with a most unchristian and unrighteous
desire for revenge. Oppressed or awed by the catastrophe of
which his minstrelsy had been in some measure the innocent
cause, poor Jock sat silent in a corner, crouched down behind his
fiddle, one hand was placed around it, the other grasped his bow;
and with wild, glaring eyes he watched me inquisitively, since I
had carefully loaded, primed, and prepared my holster pistols,
and thereafter laid them on a side buffet for the pretty little
affair of to-morrow.

I was seized by a desire to see once more the abode of Flora,
and to watch the extinction of a nocturnal lamp, which I fondly
believed lighted her bed-chamber. Full of this idea, and intent
only on its gratification as a species of farewell to her, unto
whom, if I was perhaps little then I might be still less on the
morrow, I left my billet, passed up the Bucklemaker's Wynd,
and, well muffled in my cloak, sought the marquis's mansion in
the Argylegate, with its arch rich in heraldic sculpture, and its
row of fantastic dormer gablets standing in sharp relief against
the sky. Its whole façade was enveloped in darkness. The
solitary lamp which I had watched for so many nights burned
there no longer; and though I had no other certainty than a
lover's fancy that it lighted the sleeping room of Flora, the chill
of disappointment fell heavily upon me.

For more than an hour I loitered there, gazing at the darkened windows, with my heart full of Flora, and her name on my
lips; at last I turned to go, but my attention was arrested by
the flash and report of a pistol within the court-yard. Then
followed the baying of a hound, and the tinkling of a bell, and
I remembered Corrie the constant attendant of Flora.

What could all this portend?

I approached the iron gate and shook it; but it remained fast,
bolted and barred.

A cry from within came faintly to my ear; but this might be
fancy, or the wind moaning under the hollow archway. On
moving away, some one muffled in a horseman's cloak came
roughly against me.

"I crave your pardon, sir," said he.

"Sir, the fault was mine," said I, bowing.

"You are late abroad, Captain Ogilvie," resumed the other

"see that you meet us betimes on the morrow;" and unlocking a wicket, he passed in and left me.

I recognised the voice. He was Colonel Campbell of Lawers, my recent visitor, and the second of my antagonist. Annoyed at being found by him loitering in the neighbourhood of the Argyle mansion, I hastened back to my billet, drank off a huge goblet of wine, threw myself upon a bed, and was soon in a profound sleep.

I lay long thus oblivious of coming trouble; but just as day was breaking, and its dim light stealing among the dark and narrow houses of the Wynd, I was roused by loud and authoritative voices in my chamber, with the clanking of halberds and the trampling of feet. I leaped from bed to find myself surrounded by a dozen of rough-looking fellows, muffled in plaids or capotes; some of them carried lanterns, others halberds, staves, or swords.

"Zounds! what the devil is the matter?" I asked.

"Yes — potstausend! have you come to storm the house?" demanded Captain Augustine, who appeared in his shirt and small-clothes.

"Eh, sirs—oh, sirs—dearie me, sirs!" howled the gudewife of the billet.

"Here's an awfu' business to happen in a Christian land!" apostrophised the buckle-maker, her gudeman, scratching his head and surveying me with fear and perplexity.

"Are you all mad! Speak—what the fury seek you here?" I exclaimed, snatching up my sword; upon which I was immediately seized by many strong hands, from whose gripe I struggled in vain to free myself.

"There is some mistake here," said I, quite breathless with rage and surprise.

"No mistake at all, sir," said one, whom, by his gold chain, I recognised to be a magistrate.

"Who are you?" I demanded, furiously.

"Baillie Mylne, of Mylnefield, senior magistrate of Dundee?"

"And this band of housebreakers?"

"The town watch."

"And why am I thus assaulted in my quarters? 'Sdeath, fellows, this is hamesucken and felony. Colonel Campbell!" I exclaimed, on perceiving the Laird of Lawers forcing his way towards me; "what is the meaning of this new outrage."

"No outrage whatever, sir," he answered, gruffly; "it simply means that you are arrested."

"For what purpose?"

"Committal to prison."

"Of what am I accused?"

"Murder," he replied, with a withering scowl from under his broad beaver.

"Murder!" I reiterated, in a voice that scarcely seemed my own, so thunderstruck was I.

"Aye—well may your tones falter, fellow," replied the Laird of Lawers, "for murder it may prove to be; as yet, 'tis but the attempt to assassinate."

"You are all mad, I think. Assassinate who?"

"Colonel Campbell of Ardmohr," he replied. "He was shot by a pistol-ball not ten yards from where I met *you* prowling at midnight, and almost at the same moment. This pistol, which is marked with *your* initials, and the fellow of which is now lying on that buffet, was found near him; and if further proof is wanting, the half-burned wadding, which was found in his doublet, proves to be a portion of a letter, the remainder of which has just been found by Baillie Mylne in the pocket of your coat. This accumulation of proofs would hang a whole brigade; so truss your points, and prepare to march. Away with him, Baillie, to Dudhope."

I was overwhelmed by all this. One of my pistols was assuredly gone; and in my pre-occupation of thought I had certainly, when loading them, used the warning letter which dear Flora had so kindly sent to me when at the Moss of Dunmore.

"Here is some new and infernal complot!" said I, looking round with pride and scorn. "Jock—where is that idiot with the fiddle? Could he——" but Jock was nowhere to be found; so turning to the proud, resentful, and suspicious Laird of Lawers, I asked, what object, he thought, I could possibly have to gain, by the committal of such an outrage.

"Merely to avoid a more honourable mode of meeting my friend and clansman in the morning," replied the colonel, drawing on his military gloves, and placing *my* pistols in his girdle, to be produced as evidence against me elsewhere. "In your hands I leave him, Baillie, while I ride to Alyth, anent a court-martial. Away with him to Dudhope; and woe to Dundee if its burghers allow either a rescue or an escape; for we have in the Howe of Angus two regiments of Campbells, who will not leave one stone of the burgh standing upon another."

With these comfortable assurances he left us.

Carlourie, my servant, had disappeared, taking with him his sword and pistols. There was little doubt in the Baillie's mind, that he had hastened to rouse my troop; and, fearing a consequent rescue, this party of the town watch, which consisted of the captain, lieutenant, ensign, sergeant, and twenty burgesses of the Bucklemaker's quarter, barely afforded me time to dress, when they hurried me into the street, and in the grey daylight of the early morning, while the soldiers of the garrison and the inhabitants of the town were yet all a-bed, I was conveyed to the Castle of Dudhope, and there made a close prisoner under a guard, as the provost and baillies believed that the Black Dragoons would have stormed the Tolbooth to free me, had I been committed there to ward.

I leave the reader to imagine all I felt under this new and terrible accusation!

Divested of sword and trappings, shorn of my pride, and smarting under unjust obloquy and suspicion, I sat in one of the stone chambers of the Castle of Dudhope, and saw the far expanse of the Tay rolling between its fertile shores, and studded by vessels and craft of every description; the busy town on its margin overshadowed by the giant tower of St. Mary, all shining in the noon-day sun, and as my eye wandered over the brilliant prospect, I could not realize the truth of my position—that I was a prisoner—accused of a frightful crime, and, with all my innocence and pride, I felt how feeble was all I might urge against the accusations of such potent enemies as mine.

The clock of the old castle tolled twelve, slowly and monotonously. I counted every stroke.

"Noon! at this very hour I was to have measured swords with Ardmohr on the green and sunny slope of yonder hill; and here I am a prisoner!"

Agony wrung my heart at these thoughts, to which the regular tread of the sentinel outside my door was the only and jarring response. The galloping of horses drew me to the window, and I saw several cavaliers with plumes and mantles waving, dash up to the castle gate. These were all officers of the Black Dragoons, to come condole with me; and the Count, Drumstanchel, Augustine, Somerville, and our adjutant, Sir William of Ludquhairn, were among them.

Their presence and injunctions to put a bold face on this new misfortune, as my innocence must soon appear, lightened my heart, and I soon learned only to regret that anything should have interrupted my hostile interview with the intended lover of Flora Campbell. Ardmohr was not dead; the ball had wounded him dangerously near the left lung, but hope was entertained of his recovery. As for the real culprit, we had no doubt who *he* was.

It was but too evident to us that the idiot fiddler, taking advantage of my absence, had stolen one of my pistols, and sought Ardmohr at an hostelry which he was known to frequent; that he had dogged him from thence, and, animated by revenge for the horsewhipping bestowed upon him, had shot the colonel just as he was entering Argyle-house by a private entrance, as he resided there, and there he was found bleeding with my pistol beside him, just where the half-witted assassin had flung it down.

But Jock had fled, and not a trace of him or his fiddle were to be found in Dundee; and how were we to make out our view of the case before a court that had such heavy proofs accumulated against me? I felt myself in the hands of the Philistines; and, notwithstanding the assurances of my comrades at Dudhope (where sergeants, corporals, and soldiers, even to little Tom the trumpeter of my troop, came to visit me), I was no sooner left alone for the night, than my old prostration of spirit, varied by occasional gusts of unavailing wrath, regret, and bitterness, returned upon me.

"What does Flora think of all this?" was my constant question to myself; "surrounded as she is by my enemies, and hearing their story alone, may she not be readily taught to abhor me? And may not a sympathy for his sufferings win her heart for Ardmohr?"

I left nothing unthought of that could serve to torture me in my imprisonment, which was close enough, although I had not the least idea of escape. Being innocent, and assured that sooner or later the truth would come to light, I longed only for the day of trial, and my longing was soon gratified; for when enemies so powerful as Lorn, Lawers, and Ardmohr, were leagued against me—men who had the ears and attention of all the civil and military authorities—men whose influence in the state was overwhelming when compared to that of a penniless, or landless young captain of horse—men who had already sentenced me in their own hostile hearts, and long foredoomed me to disgrace and destruction, the order for a court-martial was soon procured from the field-marshal commanding the king's troops at Alyth; and, though the principal evidence, Ardmohr, was unable to attend (being still under the surgeon's care), the military tribunal was ordained to assemble in the castle of Dudhope, at nine o'clock in the morning of the third day after the attempted assassination.

CHAPTER LXIX.

THE COURT-MARTIAL.

On this eventful morning I was up betimes, and long before our trumpets blew reveille, or the lark was winging his way aloft, for I longed to have this misfortune at an end, and to know the worst.

From the barred windows of my chamber I watched the lagging sun. It was a morning of one of the last days of August, and the dawn was beautiful. Before me lay the great river, rolling down in the blaze of sunshine from the mountains of the west—winding between yellow sands and bright green woods.

its shores teeming with fertility and every natural loveliness. Along the hills of Fife the mists were rising, from the verdant cones and rough grey rocks, the waving woods of Leuchars and Balmerino. It was a spacious prospect of flowering meadow and ripening cornfield, of foliaged coppice and flowing river, mountain-peak and busy burgh-town; of ships and fisher-boats at anchor or under sail, with the glorious August sunshine beaming over all, and everything was full of light, of life, and happiness around me; yet I turned away with an impatient sigh, to count the minutes till the court would meet in Dudhope Hall.

This old castle is situated on the southern slope of the beautiful hill of Dundee, and occupies a fine terrace near the base. It consisted then of merely the square donjon, or watch-tower and turrets, which had been built by David the Crusader, the brother of King William the Lion, and which a hundred and fifty years after, formed (with the adjacent barony) a part of the marriage-portion of Prince Edward Baliol and the niece of Philip of France, the beautiful heiress of Valois and Anjou, with whom he received 25,000 livres de Tournois, a few of which were spent in repairing this said Castle of Dudhope.

Exactly as the bells of Dundee rang nine, the court-martial opened its proceedings in the great hall; Marshal the Earl of Callander, Knight of the Thistle and Colonel of the Red Regiment of Horse, and twelve other officers, formed this (to me) imposing tribunal; and by the mal-influence of the Lord Lorn, it was chiefly composed of officers belonging to the regiments of Lawers and Ardmohr—men who were his clansmen or kindred by blood. Before such a tribunal, I could expect but little mercy.

After they had all been sworn on the Bible "duly to administer justice according to the *Acts and Ordinances of war*, framed for the better government of his Majesty's forces by sea and land within the kingdom, isles, and dependencies of Scotland, without partiality, favour, or affection," &c.; it was with a leaping sensation in my heart I heard the voice of the Marshal Earl say, "bring in the prisoner!"

Divested of sword, scarf, and belt, I found myself in presence of this hastily-constituted court, in the hands of which were my life, and that which was dearer to me—honour, the poor man's sole and best inheritance.

On the black oak table lay the Bible, old Leven's "Acts and Ordinances of War," various volumes of French and Swedish discipline, with pens, ink, and paper for the judge-advocate and clerk of court, who recorded the proceedings. At the head of the table sat that fine old soldier of the Thirty Years' War, Marshal Callander, with the silvery tresses and fifteen orders of knighthood which covered his gilded cuirass, beaming in the flakes of sunshine that were shot in long and misty rays through the deeply-embayed windows of the ancient hall.

The six officers on each side of the table were old gentlemen of good family, and were men who had seen much service against Montrose, the English, and Imperialists. Most of them were well bronzed, and all wore military decorations—all at least save two, the youngest, who were lieutenants in the musketeers of Lord Duffus, and being subalterns, sat with their heads *uncovered,* for in the Scots service, in all points of etiquette, we closely imitated our old allies the French.

As there were *thirteen* officers in the court, I foresaw that a rigorous sentence—death, perhaps—was contemplated, for I was accused of brawling, duelling, leasing (a Scottish legal term) and attempting to assassinate a superior officer.

The court was crowded by my comrades; but notwithstanding their presence and sympathy, and my sense of innocence, my spirit could scarcely bear up against the unmerited humiliation to which I was subjected, and the atrocious accusation, which had sunk so deep into my heart, which was ever a sensitive one, on all points of honour.

I pled, of course, " not guilty," on which all the Campbells present exchanged glances, and curled up their mustaches, so much as to say,

" We shall see that, my fine fellow !"

One whispered to the president,

" Is not this the young officer whose neglect caused our friend the Brewer to surprise your castle of Callander ?"

" Sir Colin of Lundie, he was deceived," said the Count, sternly ; " and that affair has nothing to do with the accusation of to-day."

Here I met the proud and bitter smile of Lorn, who was the first witness summoned. My heart swelled with suppressed passion ; to calm myself, I gazed upon his features, and strove to trace a resemblance to Flora, but failed.

I will not trouble my reader with a recapitulation of all the proceedings, or the long statement made to the court, or the many acts of Parliament cited against me, to prove me guilty of maligning the Lord Lorn and his father the marquis, when in my anger I stigmatised the former as " a traitor and the son of a traitor ;" to prove also that I had been guilty of an act of insubordination in drawing upon one superior officer and forcing another to accept a challenge; that I had been guilty of cowardice in shrinking from the duel, and to avoid it, had basely, cruelly, and wickedly wounded — mortally, it was believed — Dougal Campbell of Ardmohr, colonel of a regiment in his Majesty's service.

All the martial ordinances of Europe, past and present, were ransacked against me; the Roman law, that "all contumacy in a soldier against his leader was a capital offence," was not forgotten. Tacitus and Germanicus were cited against mutineers, who, according to them, "forfeited all rights of citizenship;" the laws of Cæsar concerning those who wounded a brother soldier with a sword or other weapon; and then the Scottish Articles of War, and the Dutch discipline, were quoted to show that mutineers must be hanged, beheaded, or shot; nor was the act of James VI., passed A.D. 1600, omitted, whereby "it was statute and ordained, that no person, in time coming, without the king's permission, should fight any single combat under pain of death; the provoker to suffer a more ignominious death than the defender, at the pleasure of his Majesty."

From the mass of Roman law quoted in this redundant document (which by its length and mysteriousness had great weight with the court), it was evidently the production of a Scottish advocate; and, indeed, I afterwards discovered that it was framed in Lorn's house, by Sir Archibald Johnstone of Warriston, and a notary of Dundee. Being opposed to two such legal pundits, and left, moreover, to defend myself, I was often far from being cool and collected.

"Harry Ogilvie," said the Count, repeatedly, "it is easier to say than to unsay; therefore, my friend, be wary and be cool."

I was soon borne bown under a mass of evidence, flattened out by legal quips and quiddities, or confounded by an avalanche of hard technicalities, which had no connexion with military law.

To do him justice, I may mention that Lord Lorn gave a true account of the street brawl and subsequent challenge.

Captain Augustine was then called, and being duly sworn, was compelled to depone, that after having seen me load my pistols he fell asleep, and on waking, found that I had gone out.

Colonel Campbell of Lawers, a short, thickset man, with a bushy red beard, and short, sharp, and decisive voice, deponed that after supping with the Laird of Bewquhany, on returning through the Argyle-gate he heard a pistol fired; that thereafter he met *me*, and close by lay Ardmohr, bleeding from a wound; not a yard from him lay a pistol initialled H.O., the neighbour of which was found in my possession, and that Ardmohr exclaimed—

"Oh, Lawers, the villain has shot me!"

"Who?" asked Lawers; "mean ye Captain Ogilvie?"

Upon which the wounded man gave a groan, that could signify nothing else than *yes*, and then fainted.

Again all the Campbells curled up their whiskers, and looked at me with eyes the reverse of friendly. Then my pistols were laid before the court, with their balls and the fragments of the wadding, which were fitted to the remains of Flora's anonymous letter; the chain of evidence was declared complete in all its links, and the court was cleared. All that I could adduce against this mass of misfortune had gone for nothing. I felt my heart sink, and deemed my fate as sealed; and such also seemed the conviction of my friends, so far as I could read in their faces.

There was a long and rather stormy debate, for I believe that the old field-marshal and Lord Duffus' two lieutenants were my friends; a whole day passed away, and in my solitary chamber in that strong fortlet I heard nothing of what passed. On the second afternoon the brief proceedings were handed to me, and by the light of the setting sun, which streamed through a barred window, I read my fate in the following document, which I here transcribe verbatim :—

"At a General Court-martial held in the Castle of Dudhope, on the Tuesday, the 29th of August, by order of Field-Marshal the Earl of Leven, of which Field-Marshal the Earl of Callander, Lord Livingstone and Brighouse, Knight of the Thistle, and all the Swedish and Danish orders, Colonel of the Red Regiment of Horse, was President, Captain Henry Ogilvie, of the Black Dragoons, was tried on the following charges,—

"I. Mutiny in drawing on a superior officer, Colonel Campbell of Ardmohr.

"II. In forcing him to accept a challenge to fight him in single combat with sword and pistol.

"III. In accusing the Lord Lorn, Colonel of the King's Foot Guards, with treason.

"IV. By wickedly and maliciously slaying, or attempting to slay, the before-mentioned Laird of Ardmohr, Colonel in the King's service, by a bullet from a pistol, in the Argyle-gate of Dundee, on the 25th instant.

"Of all these charges the Court found the prisoner guilty.

"*Sentence.* The Court do therefore adjudge him, the prisoner, Captain Henry Ogilvie, of the said Regiment of Black Dragoons, to be brought out on the parade of all His Majesty's forces in Dundee, at the Magdalene Yard, on the third day from this date, there to have his sword broken and his sash trampled on, and thereafter, at 9 A.M., he to be shot to death by a platoon of twelve musketeers.

(Signed)   "CALLANDER, *Field-Marshal.*"

" Confirmed, LEVEN,
   "*29th August*, 1650."

As I read this document a shudder came over me, and for a moment the light left my eyes; I thought of Flora's sweet sad face, and then the smile of Lorn came before me in fancy, as this cruel sentence was read to the troops, and methought I saw his upper lip, which was so very short, disappearing under his pointed nose, thus imparting something peculiarly bitter to a visage which was sufficiently sardonic.

The light of the west and the shadows of the prison bars faded away; the sun sank behind the Perthshire mountains; the stars twinkled out one by one, and were reflected in the darkened bosom of the Tay; but still I sat there in the recess of the window, lost amid a sea of thoughts; too deep, too sad, and too terrible for utterance or committal to paper.

A little white spot lay on the table, and was painfully visible even through the darkness of that stony chamber.

It was my sentence of death!

CHAPTER LXX.

DUDHOPE.

On the third day from "this date!"

Already two of the days were gone, and to-morrow I was to die!

My reflections were alternately fierce, resentful, and sorrowful —exceedingly sorrowful.

Alas! what availed a thousand protestations of innocence against a judgment so harsh, and before judges so influenced and so resolved?

To what end had all my enthusiasm, my love of military glory and my native land, my pride in her institutions and her honour, my ardour and my honest wish to gild a humble name by honourable exertion, now brought me?

Here they ended in ignominy, disgrace, and a death to be suffered at the hands of my brother soldiers. I must own to feeling for a time emotions very repugnant to the true principles of religion, and unsuited to the terrible situation in which my desperate fate had placed me. I upbraided Divine Providence with the wrongs and sufferings heaped so unjustly, as I thought, upon me. My heart was swollen and my breast teeming with bitterness; my firmness and my faith were sorely tried; patience and charity had been practised without reward, while hatred and calumny rode triumphant, and trampled me in the dust.

In what, I asked, have I wronged these men, that they should pursue me thus? Whence the origin of this malevolence—this mysterious hatred, in which they had ever tracked me out from place to place, laying snares and pitfalls in my path?

The idea of attempting to escape never occurred to me, for I had no other idea than to meet the death to which they had devoted me courageously and manfully, as became a soldier and cavalier; to die with my face to the fatal weapons, and to give the word of command myself firmly and loftily, as whilome I had given it to the same men on the battle-field, and to fall beside my coffin with my last breath asserting my innocence.

It was as well that the idea of avoiding this catastrophe by flight never occurred to me, as the castle of Dudhope, in addition to being garrisoned by a company of Duffus' regiment under Roy of Aldivalloch, was watched by some well-armed followers of Lorn and Ardmohr, who would have shot me without the least compunction.

The emotions of a poor devil under sentence of death are very different from any that ever occurred to him before; and though I escaped that terrible doom—else the reader had never had the good fortune to enlighten his mind by the perusal of these pages —and though many years have passed since then, I can recal every thought and emotion of that epoch as clearly, distinctly, and painfully as if they had first thrilled through me but yester-day.

No light was brought me that night; perhaps the thrifty seneschal at Dudhope considered that a man who was to die so soon might contrive to do without a candle; at least I had none, and I never missed it.

Into the dark chamber one strong ray of silver light glared through the barred window, throwing the shadow of the yetlan *grille* (which the apertures of a Scottish house were never without) in strong dark lines upon the floor; for high in the wide blue sky the full round moon of August was sailing in her glory, steeping in a flood of light the hills of Fife and Angus, the towers of Dundee and the broad surface of the Tay, the ceaseless course of which rolled on between rock and wood, sandy shore and sunken shoal, to mingle with the sea that washed the dykes of Holland.

As I sat that night in my guarded chamber, all the incidents of my short life passed in review before me like a moving scene, out of which old faces looked and smiled at me. The struggles of my youth, the obscurity of my boyhood; the poverty and mortification of my student days; my efforts, success, and enthu-siasm as a soldier; the love of her I was losing for ever, and dying by her brother's malice. The brave and noble friends I had lost—Oliphant and Linn—oh, how much I missed them now! —my hopes so fatally crushed and blighted, and my name loaded by obloquy. I was consigned helplessly to death, without one hope of vengeance against Fate!

To-morrow would come—that terrible to-morrow—and long ere noon, night, noon, and morning would be all the same to me. The world would be unchanged; but one poor unit would be a partner in its cares no more.

To-morrow would come—to-morrow and to-morrow! The great march of events would continue; but my place in the ranks of life would be supplied by others, and its great battle would be fought without me. As the night wore on, I became more composed, and, oppressed by the load of my own reflections, sank beneath them, as it were, beneath a sea, and fell asleep.

From this happy state I was roused by a sob close by me. Starting I listened, believing that my ears had deceived me. No—it was repeated.

"Who is here?" I asked.

"Carlourie, sir."

"Is it possible?"

"Aye, sir—I got leave to keep you company—till—till the morning."

"My poor fellow! and were you sobbing?"

"I think so, sir."

"What! a great six feet *sabreur* like thee? Tush, Carlourie, this will never do; be a man and a soldier. Tell me, what are the Black Dragoons about—what do they think or say of all this?"

He told me that the sympathy for me in the regiment was very strong; that not a man believed me guilty of firing at Ardmohr, and that the troopers had leagued together to resist any attempt by ballot or selection to furnish a *firing party* from their ranks, for not a man would level a carbine at me; and the rumour went, that the musketeers of Duffus being mostly Redshanks—but here Carlourie's emotions got the better of him.

"And the count," said I, "and Captain Augustine; where are they that they do not come to visit me?"

"They, with the Laird of Drumstanchel and old Sir Robert Lumsden of Bewquhany, were all at Alyth, conferring with Marshal Leven about me, and using all their influence to have a new trial; but no tidings had come from the Howe of Angus, and to-morrow at nine A.M. I was to—die.

"And the Lord Lorn," I asked, "what of him?"

"Is believed to be at his own house in the Argyle-gate, where he keeps Ardmohr guarded like a close prisoner."

"Why?"

"His lordship kens best; none of his race ever did aught without having a good reason for it."

I had one more to ask for—Flora.

But of her Carlourie could tell me nothing.

I now begged that faithful fellow to attend to a few memoranda which I pencilled on the fly-leaf of my Bible, aided by no other light than the rays of the brilliant moon, which streamed through the deep stone embrasure upon me.

I bequeathed my pistols to the colonel as a memento; my sword to rough old Drumstanchel; my horse and its trappings I left to Augustine, who, as a soldier of fortune, was poor. All else—clothing, arms, and my arrears of pay—I left to my servant Carlourie, whose attention I particularly directed to Flora's ring, begging that, after death, he would not let me be deprived of it by the provost-marshal's men, but would see me placed in my coffin, and so watch over me till all was ended—till the green sods were battened down by the sexton's spade.

All this he promised in a broken voice, while pressing my hand in his; and then a long silence ensued. So much were we absorbed by these last little arrangements, that we did not perceive the door had been opened and two persons admitted, until the lamp which one of them bore flashed upon our faces.

I looked up, and met the massive visage, and square, awkward figure of Zachary Boyd, on whose arm leaned a lady, masked and muffled in a cloak; but, oh! no disguise could veil that beautiful form from me, and my heart seemed to fly to my head as I sprang forward, so full of joy and gratitude, that these words only escaped me—" Dearest Lady Flora!"

CHAPTER LXXI.

LIFE—LOVE—FORTUNE.

"This is kind—most kind!" said I, pressing the huge bony hand of the divine, and raising to my lips the passive fingers of Flora, whose features were pale and colourless, and whose eyes were dim and bloodshot. By her side stalked as guard her rough Highland staghound, which leaped and curvetted caressingly around me.

They sat down in silence, and each looked to the other, so much as to say, "Will *you* speak first?"

Flora's face was calm, thoughtful, and placid; but the divine's ample visage expressed vast importance; and in the twinkling of his eyes, under their shaggy brows, methought I could read more of kindness and joy than of sorrow for my fate.

"Alas!" said I, as he laid on the table a copy of his "Last Battel of the Soule in Death." "what fanaticism is this? Are you come to smile at the ruin that has fallen on me, deeming it a proof that Heaven scourges with the heaviest afflictions those it loves best?"

"No, Harry, I have not come on this errand, but——"

"I know all you would say, my dear sir," said I, with calm bitterness. "In the spirit of Him who preached forgiveness of injuries, peace, and goodwill unto all men, you would desire me patiently to endure every wrong, and meekly to submit to every injustice. Let them put me to death if they will. Do not weep, oh! dearest Flora; to-morrow I shall be far beyond their reach; to-morrow I shall be as if I had never been; my place will be void, as it was before I was born—as it will be a hundred years hence. Stunned as I am by my sudden calamity, by the bitter certainty that the fond hopes and brilliant plans of years are crushed for ever now, it is no easy task to cultivate blessed charity and forgiveness, yet I forgive both Lorn and Ardmohr the evil they have done me, and shall die at peace with them and with all mankind. You see, my dear sir, you have nothing left to urge."

Touched by this Christian spirit, tears rolled over the rough cheeks of honest Zachary Boyd, and his large jaw was contorted in the efforts he made to conceal an emotion of which he felt ashamed; but the graceful and generous Flora sprang forward, while her cloak fell back, revealing to the dusky lamp her pale and beautiful face, her white teeth and flashing eyes, as she clasped my right hand and arm, and pressing them to her breast, said joyously, while presenting me with two sealed documents,

"Oh! Harry, who would not love you, who are so gentle and so good! We have come to relieve you from shame, sorrow, and captivity—aye, Harry, to reprieve you from death; to restore you to honour; to give you to life, fortune, and the love of those who—love you," she added, retiring a pace, and permitting my hand to drop, as if she had betrayed herself too much.

"We came neither to preach nor to exhort, Harry," said Mr. Boyd, patting me on the shoulder; "but you run on at a deevil of a rate, man, and clean take the office of minister out of my hands. But joy to thee, Harry Ogilvie, joy!—these papers will save thee! Within the last two hours, it hath pleased the Lord to take unto Himself the Laird of Ardmohr, whose dying confession we leave in thy hands, together with this other sealed paper, which we were to give to none but you or Count Ogilvie, of Mariburg."

"Count Ogilvie is here," said a firm voice; and my stately colonel, whose entrance with Augustine and Drumstanchel had been unheard by us in our excitement, approached. "Those accursed Campbells have been too strong for us, my poor clansman, Harry. God help thee, boy! The Marshal Earl of Leven is inflexible; he refuses a new trial; so there is no hope for thee but in the Lord."

"And most kind hath His manifestations been this blessed night," said Zachary Boyd, raising his eyes, and taking the trembling hand of Flora, who, awed by the presence of the Count, implored him to lead her hence, for she was agitated, too confused and humiliated to remain. "Farewell, sirs; to-morrow will disperse these solemn clouds, and bring us all together in happiness."

"Happiness!—the chiel's mad!" said Drumstanchel.

"Mein Gott!" added Augustine; "is this a time for joy?"

"*His* daughter here!" exclaimed the Count, in a voice hoarse with sudden passion; "a child of Argyle! Now, by all the gods, what new mystery is this?"

"These papers will explain, sirs. Be wary, be watchful, and pray ye; for lo! great joy and gladness are coming with the morrow," replied Zachary Boyd, leading away Flora, whose tremulous hand I kissed with excessive agitation and perplexity as they retired.

"Joy!" continued the Count; "he speaks of joy on the morrow, when Monk is on the march through the Carse of Gowrie, when Leven loiters on the braes of Angus, and when we must begin the duties of the coming day by slaughtering one of the king's bravest officers. What meaneth all this mystery—this visit and these papers?"

"The confession of Ardmohr," said I. "He died within the last two hours, certifying my innocence."

"The confession of Ardmohr!—the last dying words of a Campbell!" said the Count, with a strange laugh, and he threw down his beaver and gloves. "A light—a light there, one of you; trim the candle in that rascally lantern. The papers, Harry—the papers!" and tearing open the seals, the Count read the first, which ran as follows:—

"I, Dougal Campbell, of Ardmohr, colonel of a regiment of musketeers in the service of his most sacred majesty, Charles II., whom God long preserve, and captain of the Castle of Gloom, for the right honourable my very good lord and chief, Archibald, Marquis of Argyle, finding my last hour approaching, and being willing to die in peace with all mankind, make this solemn confession, which, in the great agony with which it has pleased God to afflict my mind and body, I would have made earlier, to save the life of an innocent and much-injured youth——"

"Meaning you, Harry," said Drumstanchel.

"—But for the seclusion in which I have been kept by one who is now absent——"

"Meaning Lorn," said Augustine.

z 2

"Right," said the Count, grinding his teeth; "but pray do not interrupt me in this fashion."

" —One who is now absent, and who wished me to die without divulging the painful and important secrets which follow.

"Too much devotion to the will, desires, and ambition of my chief, the present Marquis of Argyle, and too much zeal for the glory and aggrandizement of his house, have hurried me into acts of wrong and vengeance, and led me to commit or aid in the committal of crimes on which I now look back from this my painful deathbed, with wonder and with horror!

"To this end I served him blindly at the Ford of Lyon, where our project to divide the kingdom of Scotland into two republican dictatorships was discovered by the Laird of Fintray and the Commissary of Dunkeld; but our influence was too strong, and they perished beneath it on the scaffold, as liars and perjurers!

"In this spirit I served him bravely in his wars against the late Marquis of Montrose, and prevailed upon the wretched Laird of Assynt to betray this immortal soldier (after the battle of Invercarron) for forty bolls of meal!

"In this spirit I wickedly urged the betrayal of his late Majesty to the English at Newcastle; and have trafficked, intrigued, and consorted with Cromwell, to further the purposes of Argyle; and for the same end, I aided him with all my followers, without scruple, remorse, or pity, in those desperate forays made by the Campbells against the Grahames of Montrose and the Ogilvies of Angus.

"In early life a deeply-rooted hatred had grown between Argyle and the Earl of Findourie. They were students at the same university, and competitors for the same prizes in literature and the lighter sports of the ring, the fencing-court, and the butts, in all of which Findourie proved himself the victor; and once they nearly came to blows with their swords, when at a great archery meeting on the Links of Musselburgh, where Argyle lost, and Findourie won, by a truer aim, the silver arrow of the burgh.

"Hostility waxed more bitter in the heart of Argyle, on his cousin, Marion Crawford of Drumstanchel, whom he had long loved in vain, becoming the Countess of Findourie. He declined to be present at her marriage, and shutting himself up in his Castle of Gloom, brooded on schemes of vengeance. From that hour he left nothing undone to compass the ruin of Marion's husband, the young earl, who had once, in a gust of boyish anger, taunted him with his obliquity of vision and ungainly figure.

"Findourie, a high and enthusiastic admirer of episcopacy,

had been reared among the Ogilvies and other cavalier clans on the Braes of Angus, and he was open, chivalric, and reckless to a fault; but Argyle, gloomy, morose, and cautious to the verge of cowardice, had been educated according to the strictest rules of the kirk of Scotland, as established at the Reformation.

"In politics they took opposite sides, and lost no opportunities of thwarting each other in the parliament and privy council (of both of which they were members) and everywhere else, in public and private; but the influence gained, held, and wielded by the cool, subtle, and resolute Argyle was overwhelming, compared to that enjoyed by the more open, unsuspecting, and soldierly Earl of Findourie.

"Thus were they situated in the year 1625, when Charles I. succeeded his father, James VI., in the two British crowns, and in the ungracious task of attempting *to force* on the Scottish people those innovations in religion which, in his latter years, this weak monarch had projected so fatally for his family. Urged by Argyle, *then* sincere and true, the Scottish clergy petitioned Charles against the articles of Perth, by which the introduction of bishops, organs, &c., had been authorized; but they received a stern denial. This was attributed to the Earl of Findourie, who was then in London with his young countess, having accompanied the new Queen Henrietta from France. Symptoms of discontent appeared in Scotland, and the people justly began to arm. Then the king rashly wrote to Spottiswood, Archbishop of St. Andrew's, desiring him to *enforce* the new order of episcopacy. Of this fatal letter, the lynx-eyed Argyle discovered his foe Findourie to be the bearer.

"A storm broke forth in parliament; a new administration was appointed at Edinburgh to appease the clamour of the people; Findourie was proscribed by the Scottish Estates, and his titles and baronies declared to be forfeited. He fled tc Austria, and entered the service of the imperialists, where, as an officer of horse, he won the highest civil and military honours, while his ancient earldom in Angus was bestowed upon Argyle; and his countess, an outcast with her infant son, sought shelter in the house of her brother, John Crawford, of Drumstanchel, in the Middle Ward of Clydesdale.

"The proprietor, with most of his men, was then abroad, serving as a soldier of fortune, under the Duke of Friedland; thus the countess was sole mistress of his mansion for two years, during which she lived in great seclusion, and made arrangements to join her husband at Vienna, as soon as the health of her son, a sickly child, would permit her to travel.

"Meanwhile, Argyle, still pursuing his old feud against the proscribed earl, laid many plots to get this child into his power, with the revengeful intention of concealing it for ever from the parents, or destroying it; and this task he committed, alas! to me.

"I was then in my twentieth year, reckless and full of zeal for my chief; I came down from the wild mountains of Argyleshire to the middle ward of Clydesdale, with a band of armed followers, and on a dark night in the year 1632, surrounded the old tower of Drumstanchel, which stands on the edge of a dark and solitary ravine, a sequestered place, far from succour and assistance.

"Being young and inexperienced, it pleased Heaven that I should go somewhat too noisily about the intended outrage; and thus, while blowing up the barbican gate by a petard, happily afforded the terrified countess an opportunity to escape by a postern wicket, mounted on a fleet horse, alone, and bearing in her bosom the little child which was the object of our search.

"We burst in, slew several of her domestics, and forced one, with our swords at his throat, to reveal which way his lady had fled. He pointed to the path down the glen; the horse-hoofs in the snow told the rest. We shot him through the head, set the tower on fire, and the flames, which soon wrapped it in one huge and wavering sheet, served to light the path, as, with ten armed and mounted men, I followed the poor fugitive, who fled towards Glasgow, past the orchards and ruins of Blantyre Priory, past Dechmont hill, by the braes of Cathkin, and across the Clyde; for she dared not tarry at Shawfield, which was the house of a Campbell.

"Amid the falling snow, the darkness, our confusion and ignorance of the way, one by one, my followers sank behind, though the distance was short; but the dame we followed was bold and desperate as a mother may be for the safety of her child. She was nobly mounted; and escaping all our pistol-shots, galloped furiously on, and was leaving me, her only pursuer, far behind, when she entered the streets of Glasgow.

"Midnight was past now, and on that dark winter night all were abed, and no succour abroad in the streets; for the heavy and blinding snow-flakes were falling fast and thick on the sleeping city and its frozen river.

"I frequently lost sight of the countess, but saw her again, looming before me through the drift, like a noiseless phantom, as the deep snow deadened the noise of her horse's hoofs.

"'Now I have thee!' thought I, triumphantly, as her horse slipped and sank heavily, just as we entered the desolate and deserted High-street; but skilfully and boldly disengaging herself from the fallen steed, she snatched up her child, and uttering shriek after shriek, rushed along the street, and franticly essayed the entrances of the different houses; but every door was barred, and the barrier-gate of every wynd and close secured; and on she fled, fear and despair adding to her strength and energy.

"Three bounds of my foaming horse brought me upon her, just as her hand reached the huge iron bell of the old college gate.

"'The child!' said I, hoarsely—'the child!'

"Her cries redoubled, and her grasp upon the infant was firm as steel. Steps approached from within; and, blind with wrath and fury, I barbarously and most pitilessly ran my sword through her heart, and killed her!

"May God in His mercy forgive that act of woe!

"Her hot blood, as it gushed upon my hilt and hand, allayed the fever, the frenzy of the moment. I forgot the child, and fled to the mountains, fearing that the law, if it failed to touch my chief, might at least crush his miserable tool.

"I told him that the heir of Findourie was dead.

"All the domestics of Drumstanchel perished in the flaming tower, which was believed to have been burned accidentally. The dead countess, supposed to be an unknown wanderer, was buried in Glasgow near the cathedral wall, and there was an end for the present of her calamitous story.

"A few years afterwards, we discovered that her little boy, Henry, Master of Findourie, was reared and protected in the University of Glasgow. Argyle, who had procured a gift of all his father's estates, after burning 'the bonnie House of Airlie,' and ravaging the country of the Ogilvies, spared no pains to have him kidnapped and carried off, but the child eluded us. He grew to manhood; he became a soldier; and is now Captain Ogilvie, of the Black Dragoons. Still we have left no means untried to remove, to disgrace, and destroy him; and animated by a dread that he might one day discover and avenge the murder of his mother, I entered into those cruel and heartless projects with all my soul; but still God's hand protected him from us, and he continued to serve the king with honour and fidelity. And I hereby declare that the wound of which I am now dying was inflicted by the idiot, known as Jock of the Lodge, who shot me with a pistol, in revenge for my having horsewhipped him in the Argyle-gate of Dundee.

"How little I anticipated that this wound would prove my death, when I permitted a court-martial to condemn the innocent young Master of Findourie for that crime; and when I concealed from him the fact, that Count Ogilvie, of Mariburg—*whom I have long known and recognised, natheless his face so scorched and disfigured by powder at the storming of Munich*—is his father, Henry Ogilvie, Earl of Findourie, and Lord Ogilvie, of Fernkirk, at whose feet I now lay the king's most gracious pardon, restoring to him his titles, estates, and honours; a pardon granted on the day our army captured Carlisle, but which was intercepted by the Laird of Warriston, and by me concealed—a pardon granted as freely as I trust the Lord of Hosts and those I have wronged will accord their pardon and their pity unto me.

"DOUGAL CAMPBELL, of Ardmohr."

"I certify having written this document to the dictation of the above-signed, in presence of the Lady Flora Campbell.

"ZACHARY BOYD, Minister of the Gospel."

Such were the contents of this document, which filled us all with astonishment and joy.

Thus by a strange fatality—by some predestined working of the hand of Providence—the truth, though long concealed, had come to light at last; and by the same blessed guidance I had been led to enlist as a soldier in the regiment of my father, and in the troop of my uncle, bluff old John of Drumstanchel; and hence the mysterious principle of sympathy and affinity that drew their hearts to me.

Strange was the mixture of warmth, sternness, and old rankling sorrow with which they greeted and embraced me.

I laid before my newly-found relatives the little gold medal which had been attached to my neck, and on which had been inscribed the initials H. O. E. F. (Henry Ogilvie, Earl of Findourie), with the cognisance, a lion passant crowned and collared; the marriage ring with its two ruby hearts, and the lock of silky black hair, all of which the reverend principal had so kindly and carefully preserved.

These reliques, or proofs of my identity, moved deeply the brave hearts of the Count and Drumstanchel, who both kissed the braid with sorrow and affection.

"Poor Marion!" said my uncle; "unhappy sister! I remember weel o' thy bonny black tresses, and the winsome young face they shaded!"

"Look up, son of mine, and let me see thee," said the Count, raising the lamp, and fixing his keen sad eyes upon me; "fain would I trace somewhat of your winning mother in your features. Yes, yes, Harry, my boy; thou hast her dark eyes, and the same wan thoughtful brow. Oh, my God!" he added, bursting into tears, "this mysterious affinity of blood was the secret voice that spoke within me, and made me select thee as my favourite trooper among six hundred of our Black Dragoons!"

"Potstausend!" muttered Augustine, after a long pause, as a cannon pealed across the morning sky, for day had broken now.

Another and another followed.

"Monk approaches!" said Drumstanchel, with a kindling eye, as he assumed his heavy sword; "these are the three alarm guns."

"Yes—'tis the foe again," said the Count, placing the confession of Ardmohr and the king's pardon in his breast; "'tis Monk—daily have we expected him; and now again we are summoned to the field. Come, Harry, my son—this day you shall lead your troop against the enemy as the Master of Findourie. Our forefathers won their patent in the wars of King Alexander III., and please Heaven it shall be wet anew in the blood of that aggressive Saxon race against whom it seems to be the fate of Scotland to struggle for ever."

Ten minutes after saw us all spurring towards Dundee.

In my whirl of thought, the proud reflection that I was now Flora's equal was ever uppermost; but with the bitter conviction that it must be avowed to the shame of her father and her family.

CHAPTER LXXII.

THE SACK OF DUNDEE.

In the grey dawn, while the dew lay yet upon the grass and the shadows were dark, for the sun was below the verge of the German sea, our troops mustered, horse and foot, under their colours, in the ancient Seagate and market-place of Dundee.

"To your saddles, gentlemen," said the Count, whom I must now style Earl of Findourie; "fall in, and trust that Heaven will order all for the best."

Drumstanchel took a drop of comfort from a flask; MacSnaffle sought it in a drier fashion from the leaves of his Breeches Bible; Augustine quietly smoked his meerschaum; others were jesting and in high spirits at the prospect of coming to handy-blows with the foe again; and old Sergeant Glanders swore with the impatience of a true trooper as he called the roll of my troop, and threatened to batoon Carlourie, the last man who appeared.

Many of the inhabitants fled into the country towards Leven's position at the woods of Alyth, and one of those who left us was the Reverend Zachary Boyd.

"Blow your trumpets at the approach of the foe," said he, on bidding us farewell; "blow lustily, and they will yield—even as the walls of Jericho yielded and fell before the trumpet of Joshua."

But we had ceased to credit the vapouring prophecies of our preachers.

We—the cavalry—remained under arms in the Seagate, to act where we might be required; the horses were linked by troops, with the bits hanging at their breasts. The two battalions of Lord Duffus' regiment, with a strong body of trained citizens led by the magistrates, repaired to the walls, and stood by their gates and cannon. Many persons of the highest rank were in the town to make service against the enemy; among these were Francis Scott, the last Earl of Buccleuch; James, Lord of Auchterhouse and Earl of Buchan; with the Earls of Balcarres and Tweeddale; the Lords Ramsay, Elibank, Newburgh, and John Balfour, Master of Burleigh, with fifteen gentlemen bearing the rank of knighthood, and eleven landed lairds. All these appeared on the walls, in buff coat, cuirass, and burganet, sword and pistol, like good and brave Scots, to make service against our common enemy, to obey the orders of the governor, Sir Robert Lumsden, and to leave nothing undone to make a vigorous defence.

General Monk, whose cruel conduct during the Scottish campaign forms a contrast so strong to the gallantry and gentleness of his master, Cromwell, was a coarse and brutal soldier, mean in aspect and vulgar in manner, as we might well expect to find the spouse of Nan Clarges, a female barber of Dury-lane, and a woman of bad repute. Monk, the betrayer of his own party, and the deceiver of all, was a mere military cut-throat, without one quality of a superior order; cunning and wily, he was by turns the servile partizan of the English parliament, of the army, of Cromwell, and of the king, who despised in his heart the coarse musketeer, whose ignoble old age he gratified by the dukedom of Albemarle. But to resume.

He commenced his march from Stirling on the 12th August, with the horse regiments of Grosvenor, Berry, O'Key, Alured, and Morgan; a column of infantry, among which were nine companies of his own regiment (the future Coldstreamers) and nine of Ashfield's, with a train of battering cannon and mortars.

After halting for a night at Dunblane, he marched to Blackford, swam his cavalry across the river, which swept away a few scores of them, and then he marched straight to Dundee.

The gleam of arms on the green crests of the high ground to the northward, on the evening of the last day of August, announced the vicinity of the English; and we saw their white colours flying as the columns deployed and cannon were galloped into position above the town, which is commanded unfortunately by eminences, of which Monk took immediate advantage.

In Dundee everything was unusually still; the streets were thronged by men, armed, thoughtful, and gloomy; and weeping women mingled with them. Rumour was busy; the air was close and sultry, and an undefined murmur seemed to float through the picturesque streets of that quaint and antique town.

Accompanied by a trumpet, an English officer bearing a flag of truce was introduced to the Laird of Bewquhany, requiring him to surrender, on pain of having *all put to the sword.*

As he passed our column I recognised him to be the enterprising Captain Thurlow, who, after receiving a good glass of claret, was briefly dismissed, bearer of a blunt refusal, and a letter commanding Monk and his men to lay down their arms and surrender to the authority of his majesty the king.

To this no answer was returned; but, on the evening of Sunday, the 31st of August, Monk began to cannonade the town, from the walls of which forty pieces of ordnance replied. His first missile was a shell, the shrill whistle of which, as it passed above the Black Dragoons, made all look upward, and we saw the globe of iron curving over our heads. It crashed through the roof of a house in the Argyle-gate and exploded, blowing all the windows out. Soon after sunset every cannon, musket, carbine, and pistol were plying their missiles, as the English columns pushed their approaches nearer to the walls, on which nobles, gentlemen, burgesses, and soldiers all emulated each other in the defence; while a strong body of merchant seamen, from the ships in the Tay, made good service with their musketoons and ship-guns, under the command of one who deserves to be remembered with honour, George Ponton, a gallant skipper of Kirkaldy, who was killed about midnight.

The din of the double cannonade was deafening, while the sharp ring of the shotted guns and their concussion were stunning; the balls came bowling along the streets, hurling down chimneys, gables, and out-shots; the bombs were rolling off roofs, and bursting in the thoroughfares, lighting up their dark outlines, like sulphureous gleams, as they exploded to spread ruin and death in every direction.

In two hours after sunset, the whole air seemed alive with shot and shells; but the English did us more mischief than we could do to them, as the circle of the town presented a large mark, into which their projectiles could fall easily; while the old spire of St. Clement indicated a line for their cannon in the twilight to breach the northern wall. Amid all this infernal hurlyburly, while shot were crashing along the streets in every direction, and the sky streaked by hissing bombs and blazing carcasses shot from the mortar's fiery womb at every imaginable angle and degree, the Black Dragoons remained by their horses' bridles, spectators of the scene, and of the wounded and dying, who were borne from the walls to their own dwellings, or into the vaulted stores as places of safety. I trembled for Flora, and mentally prayed that in her huge mansion of the Argyle-gate she occupied a secure and vaulted chamber, where neither shot nor shell could reach her. Fain would I have gone to enquire for her, at all hazards; but in that time of imminent peril, when an assault was constantly expected, I dared not for a moment leave my troop.

So passed the last night of August.

Two hours before dawn, on the 1st of September, a lurid gleam, as if all Etna had flamed above the town and river, filled the air with a mighty flood of light, revealing the battered houses, St. Mary's giant tower, the dark figures and glittering arms of the besieged, and the deep columns of the besiegers, and then it passed away in darkness with a terrific explosion that shook the solid ground beneath our feet, and made all our horses rear and plunge wildly. It astounded friends and foes, and made the work of death cease for an instant.

"The magazine has blown up; an English shell has entered it!" cried Sir Robert Lumsden, as he galloped past.

"Unlink your horses—close your files, gentlemen, and prepare for action!" said the Count.

The explosion rang like thunder along the mountain side, and made the river roll in ripples on the shore, while the craft on its bosom were swayed to and fro by the concussion.

The great magazine had blown up, with all our powder and live shells, tearing down a portion of the northern ramparts, and hurling into the air great masses of masonry, beams of timber from houses and batteries, yetlan guns, brass mortars, iron shot, dead bodies, and living men, to descend in fragments on the streets and river, leaving a wide, chaotic gap, from whence arose gigantic clouds of smoke and dust, which overhung the town like a pall of death and destruction.

A wild hurrah in the distance announced that, under the cover of that dusky pall, the English were advancing to the new-made breach.

Led by Mylne of Mylnefield, their senior Baillie, a crowd of armed burghers rushed forward to defend it.

"You're an old man, Baillie," said the veteran governor, Lumsden, whose head was nearly as white as Mylne's; "leave to us this desperate task."

"Auld I am, 'tis true, Sir Robert, but I have my country, my king, and, mair than baith, my dear wife and eight bairns to fight for," replied the brave burgher, unsheathing his sword; but at that moment a shot whistled through the breach and killed him on the spot.

The English came on with great ardour, as Monk had promised them a general slaughter of the people, and twenty-four hours' pillage of the town.

Over the *débris* of the fallen walls, through a cross-fire of cannon, muskets, and pistols, in the grey dawn of that September morning, the fierce and fanatical regiments of Monk and Ashfield, mingling pellmell with the cuirassed dragoons of Alured and O'Key, cut a passage into the town with incredible bravery. Among them were a hundred and fifty English seamen, who beat down the Wellgate Porte by sledge hammers, and effected a double entrance, and amid a dazzling blaze of musketry, flaming carcasses, burning splinters, and a maddening din of shouts, shrieks, and orders, the living trampling on the dead and dying, slowly fought their way into the heart of the place.

Our troops and citizens met them with equal courage at the northern rampart. A scene of the most dreadful carnage ensued, and in a few minutes six English officers and five hundred and twenty Scots and Englishmen were lying dead in the breach, with Captain Hart, a brave fellow, who led Monk's stormers. There we lost Sir John Leslie of Newton, Baillie Browne, two ministers of Dundee, and twenty-two citizens of Edinburgh who served as volunteers, and all perished sword in hand around Sir Robert Lumsden.

The explosion of a smaller magazine in their rear, gave our people a temporary panic, of which Monk, at the head of six hundred and fifty chosen dragoons, hastened to take advantage, and falling on with sword and pistol, made good a passage into the town for his whole army; and now followed one of the most awful scenes of butchery that ever man had the misfortune to witness.

Declaring that he would rather die than surrender to rebels, Sir Robert of Bewquhany, with a small party of brave cavaliers, retreated to the church of St. Mary, and when it was stormed by Monk's musketeers, they retired into the great spire and defended it stoutly by sword and pistol, retreating from story to story till they were driven to the summit. Roy of Aldivalloch fought valiantly, but his wooden leg being broken by a halberd; he fell on the stair and was literally hewn to pieces.

Finding himself on the bartizan of the spire, the veteran governor at last surrendered his sword to Colonel Ashfield on promise " of quarter to himself and ten surviving friends, all of whom were wounded." The moment their weapons were taken they were all cruelly murdered and decapitated; and the grey head of the gallant Lumsden was spiked on the northern buttress of the steeple.

Savage lust, grinding rapacity, drunkenness, and unglutted murder, reigned supreme.   The air was loaded with shrieks for mercy from kneeling women, and little ones who clung to the legs and knees of the English soldiers.   With their cries mingled lamentations for the dead, the groans of the expiring, the hiss of flames, the din of hammers and clubbed muskets crashing through doors and windows; in short, the barbarity of the Croats at Magdeburg, and of the English at Drogheda, were now revived by Monk on Scottish ground, with unexampled horror.

Finding themselves surrounded, the two battalions of Lord Duffus' regiment, all brave, steady, religious, and veteran soldiers, laid down their arms in front of the townhouse, at the old Yarn-market, capitulating as prisoners of war; but in an instant, the merciless Monk opened a fire of musketry upon them from every quarter, and butchered every officer and man, not one being permitted to escape.   A similar slaughter took place in the Fish-market.   The streets ran ankle-deep with blood; it dripped from the stairs of the houses, and bubbled along the gutters.   Every house was broken open, and the work of pillage, fire, and slaughter went on the livelong day.

Upwards of two hundred females were outraged, and afterwards murdered; thirteen hundred men, and an unknown number of children, perished.   Amid this scene of carnage and of crime, for which the fiends in hell might have blushed, the blasphemous hypocrites of Monk, while raising to heaven their hands drenched in the gore of women and babes, were heard exclaiming—

"The Lord hath done this for the glory of England!   Lo! here is the kingdom of Christ!   Commit sin that grace may abound; for, lo! here are Zion and the sword of Gideon!"

Three days and three nights the carnage continued, nor did it cease until the 3rd of September, when Monk saw a poor infant in the Thorter-row, sucking at the gashed breast of its dead mother.*

This was the gudewife of Mylnefield, and at this lamentable spectacle (one of many such) even the soul of Monk, now glutted with slaughter, was moved to pity.   He drew off his saintly sectaries and others, and ordered a collection to be made of the plunder, which was sufficient to load the sixty Scottish ships he captured in the harbour.

All these craft, loaded to the hatches, were ordered to sail for England; but God was pleased to thwart Monk's avarice; for a storm arose, the sixty ships were dashed against each other, and

* In the place where the dead were buried, 200 skulls were found in one pit, in July, 1851.—J. G.

perished on the bar, where the deep sands of Tay swallowed up the spoil.

*   *   *   *   *

The reader will naturally inquire, " What were the Black Dragoons about during all these horrors?" In the hurry of events, I had almost forgotten the part we were destined to play.

As cavalry, we could be of but little service in defending the town, which was entered on two points—by the main breach and the Wellgate Porte; thus a confusion was caused among the defenders, who found themselves taken in front and flank; and I was in an agony of excitement lest the English would break into the Argylegate, or set it on fire by their shells and carcasses.

" Gentlemen and comrades," cried my father the colonel, " I see that all is lost; but we must save ourselves for the king's service. They are coming in by the breach and barrier, at push of pike, so we shall meet them on the spur at sword's point."

" Let us ride boldly at them," said Drumstanchel, " and, making a sally, cut a passage with sword and pistol to the Sidlaw Hills."

A fierce hurrah arose from the regiment.

The earl's order was no sooner conceived than we prepared to execute it; and how could I leave Flora behind in that sanguinary and flaming Pandemonium? As we filed along the Argylegate, from every part of which rang the voices of women, wailing and lamenting, as they rushed about with frantic gestures and dishevelled hair, many with their valuables, but many more with their little ones, each helpless mother with her brood, affrighted and bewildered, I saw, at a window of Argyle-house, Flora Campbell gazing, with pale face and tearless eyes, upon the terrible scene below, where the panic-stricken people wandered like a crowd of phantoms in the grey light of dawn, which struggled for mastery with the blaze of cannon and musketry, bombs and carcasses, the flames of burning houses, oil barrels, tar pots, and torches, that flared upon the quays and ramparts to direct the fire of the besieged from the gunplat-forms and batteries.

" For Heaven's sake, my lord and father," cried I, " tarry here for me one moment—halt, halt, my comrades, and rein up, for there is one here with whom I shall either escape or die !"

" Halt !" cried the Count, as I leaped from my horse, and tossed the bridle to Carlourie. " Harry Ogilvie—boy, art thou mad ? Is this a time to think of aught but a soldier's duty ?"

" Beware, Harry," added honest Augustine; " beware, lest you share the fate of Bewquhany !"

" I care not, if I share the honour," I replied; and rushed into the Marquis of Argyle's deserted mansion, the doors of which were open, and the spacious chambers of which were deserted by his servants.

"Flora, beloved Flora," I cried; "come to me—quick, quick! we have not a moment to lose—we are about to sally forth and escape!"

As I spoke, she rushed down stairs to meet me, and all agitated and terrified, placed her hands confidingly, tenderly, and trem blingly in mine.

"Oh, Flora," I exclaimed, "what a meeting is this? and such a night of horror and devastation!"

"Harry, Harry, I dare not stay; and yet in going with you, I may but cause new danger and sorrow."

"With thee, Flora, I could brave a thousand dangers and endure a thousand sorrows. Come, dearest, one horse shall bear us both; come, and let us leave the event to fate."

"To God!" said she.

"So be it then," I exclaimed, and pressed her to my heart. I wrapped my capote around her, and endued with new strength by the desperation of the moment, bore her down stairs like a child, and leaping into my saddle, placed her behind me, just as the impatient regiment trotted in heavy divisions of troops, twelve men abreast, towards the Wellgate Porte, through which the fine battalion of Overton was pouring in solid column with colours flying and pikes in front.

Half fainting, Flora clasped me by the waist, to which I girt her tightly by my scarf; I kept the bridle of my horse in my teeth, a cocked pistol in one hand, and my sword in the other; at the head of the leading troop and by my father's side, I rushed full upon the serried ranks of the English musketeers, who gave us a steady fire over the heads of their pikemen.

Like an iron torrent, our heavily-armed horsemen dashed themselves against the stand of pikes, and in a moment the human rampart was broken or hurled back in death and havock on their rear-ranks; and we were firing our pistols in their faces or hewing them down on every hand, as we fought our way through that living tide of desperate men, who were densely wedged in the narrow thoroughfare, all breathless, begrimed by powder and smoke, and covered by sweat and dust. One musket-shot pierced the sleeve of my buff coat, and grazed the arm of Flora; the plume was shred from my helmet by a second; my cartouch-box was dashed to pieces by a third; but escaping all, I pressed on with my troop, amid clubbed firelocks that were plied like flails, flashing swords, and a hedge of pikes.

With us it was the sure but silent carnage of the sword; skulls were cloven and bosoms pierced through burganet and breast-plate; and on we swayed, spurring, plunging, and fighting every inch of the way. Suddenly a shower of blows rang upon my head and shoulders, and I found myself encountered by Captain John Thurlow, who rode a wounded horse.

"Death be my lot, fellow, if I do not slay thee," he cried, while his grey eyes flashed with despair and ferocity.

Flora uttered a piercing cry as his sword flashed about me; but the Earl of Findourie ended the affair by standing in his stirrups, and giving him one tremendous blow. In a moment a pair of armed heels were in the air, and the bright helmet of the burly Captain Thurlow rolled in the dust to rise no more.

He was killed close by the Well of Our Lady.

A dreadful slaughter of our troopers ensued at the Wellgate Porte, where the half of Overton's men were cut to pieces as wo issued out and spurred up the slope towards the north, crossed the green plains of Fintray, passed the wooded glen of Claver-house, and wiping our dripping blades on our black horse's manes, retired, leaving Dundee—once the happy, the beautiful, and the opulent—a smoking mass of ruins drenched in the blood of its defenders.

CHAPTER LXXIII.

THE CASTLE OF FINDOURIE.

WE rode rapidly until the hills of Glen Ogilvie and Denoon were behind us, and the setting sun saw us slowly traversing one of the most beautiful districts on the Braes of Angus, among slopes where the blackberries grew so thick, that they dyed the hoofs of our horses' blue, and where the South Esk rolls from the Grampians to meet the German sea.

Now once again, as in the days of the Romans, nearly the whole of our Lowlands were overrun by foreign invaders: but the unconquered Highland clans held sullenly aloof, and from the hills that rose before us, looked scornfully down on a struggl in which, as yet, they had no vital interest, for their mountain chains have ever formed the limit of invasion, even as they bounded the empire and ambition of the Cæsars, whose rule we are told spread from the Euphrates on the east, to the Scottish frontier on the west.

We were traversing a wooded and rocky district, where the pines grew like a sea of dusky cones between the hills, the tops of which were rough extinct volcanoes, where crags formed by one once molten lava frowned above the hardy coppice.

The Earl of Findourie had ridden long in silence, and none of us knew where he meant to halt for the night.

Passing through a narrow defile which cleft the mountain

chain, and at the bottom of which a wild, impetuous tributary of the South Esk leaped and plashed from rock to rock, between banks covered by purple heather, wild thyme, and giant water-docks, a beautiful glen opened before us. Its sides bristled with rocks, and were shaded by chesnuts.

On a mass of columnar rock, the sides of which were tufted by solitary Scottish larches and silver birches, rose a strong, square keep, that towered above the dark pool of a mountain stream, and was flanked by four lesser towers connected by a rampart, all loop-holed for arrows or musketry. Its façade was steeped in warm red light, by the sun, which was setting behind the Grampians.

" Drumstanchel, behold !" exclaimed the Count, as he pointed to the old fortalice, with a proud and bitter smile, and shook the plume in his helmet.

Flora now rode another horse, and I drew near my father, who had treated me with marked coldness during all that long day's devious and undecided march ; for he was irresolute to which of the king's garrisons to repair.

Twice I approached to inquire the cause of his singular manner ; but instead of replying, he asked angrily,—

" What is this daughter of Argyle unto you, that you should cumber yourself in saving her ?"

" Could I leave her to perish—she who saved me, and restored me to you, by procuring the confession of Ardmohr ?"

" Nay, by my soul, not to perish altogether ; she seems so gentle, fair, and modest, too ; but I would rather owe a favour to the veriest churl in Scotland than to a child of this false Highland marquis—the Scottish Judas who betrayed his royal master."

" My lord and father," said I, imploringly, " I pray you do not speak so bitterly."

" I speak in bitterness because I speak with truth. Argyle—Argyle ! How many thousands of brave Scottish men have offered up their souls to God upon our battle-fields, to defend the honour, interest, and integrity of their country, while he and other Catalines, misnamed as nobles, are ever ready to barter all we have of honour and of name for English gold ?"

" My lord," said I, eager to change this subject, " know you the name of that strong tower which crowns yonder mass of rock ?"

" Yes, well do I know every stone of its walls," said he, sadly; " in that tower you were born, Harry, some two and twenty years ago. It is my castle of Findourie, from which I have so long been exiled and excluded ; but to which, my friends and comrades, I now bid you all welcome to-night !"

As the leading files of the regiment rode through the arch, with trumpets sounding and kettle-drums beating, I perceived there was carved above it the same coat-of-arms that my gold medal bore—the lion passant, crowned and collared; and the same initial letters for Henry Ogilvie, Earl of Findourie.

My heart bounded with joy and gratitude to Heaven, as I lifted Flora from her saddle, and bade her "welcome to *my father's roof!*"

CHAPTER LXXIV.

CONCLUSION.

I HAVE little more to add, for fortune had now been so kind to me, that, after winning the love of Flora, I could scarcely believe that greater happiness was in store for me.

We lived for some weeks in seclusion at the old tower of Findourie, and the whole regiment were quartered in it or around us, for many had health to recover and scars to heal, before we could again take the field. James Earl of Airlie, Patrick Earl of Findlater, the Lairds of Lonmay, Wester-pourie, Kinmundie, nverkeillor, and a score of other gentlemen of the surname of Ogilvie, came around us, to bid us welcome to our old paternal home, and assure us of their aid and alliance against the Campbells; but fortunately neither were needed.

The arrival of Mr. Zachary Boyd about this time was most opportune, as his quaint and friendly intervention alone was wanted to flatter the pride and soothe the asperities of the Count's disposition, and incline his heart, which was naturally warm and amiable, to love one who at present was hopelessly separated from her father, by all the neighbouring country being in possession of the enemy; and who had already said to me, while her cheek grew pale, her bosom trembled, and her fine long eye-lashes drooped,—

"Oh, Harry Ogilvie, if my love for you can in some degree repair the wrong my family have done you, take me to your heart—I am yours!" aud I pressed Flora Campbell to my breast.

"Verily, but my dream hath come true, after all; oh, what a marvel is here!" exclaimed Mr. Boyd, striking his huge hands together, as he interrupted us most inopportunely.

My life assuredly had hitherto been anything but a comedy and yet, like a comedy, my story must close by a marriage.

I regretted much that my old patrons, Mr. Zephaniah Boyle and Nehemiah Spreul, the sour-visaged Janitor of St. Mungo, were not present to witness how fortune had favoured me.

So, married we were—Flora and I—in the old castle hall o
Fiudourie, while my Lord Marquis of Argyle was fretting about
it in his stronghold of Inverary. Four fair Ogilvies of Airlie
were the bridesmaids, and Flora was given away by her devil-
may-care brother, Lord Neil Campbell of Ardmaddie, who turned
up about this time.

Mr. Zachary Boyd, with a suitable quotation from the " Last
Battel of the Soule," pronounced the nuptial blessing; and my
father—the dark count of other days—pressed my trembling
bride to his heart.

A banquet was spread in the court-yard, casks were set abrooch,
while the kettle-drums beat and the trumpets were blown; and
never was a merrier dance seen on the Braes of Angus than on
that October eve, when rough Drumstanchel, the soldierly Augustine, old Sergeant Hackiron, burly Gideon Glanders, even the
quaint MacSnaffle, and all the Black Dragoons, footed away in
the blaze of pine torches on the castle green, hand in hand with
the fair dames of the Ogilvie clan and the cottar lassies of Findourie; while Jock—the inimitable and inevitable Jock (who
also made his appearance)—sawed away on his enormous fiddle
to the air of " Fy, let us a' to the Bridal;" and the long-silent
echoes of our ancestral home rang with new merriment and joy
as many a deep carouse to " the fair mistress of Findourie" was
quaffed in good Burgundy or nut-brown Lammas ale, by the
flower of the old Scottish service, my brave comrades of the
BLACK DRAGOONS.

NOTES.

1. Concerning the Scottish prisoners taken at Dunbar, the relation given by the Master of Oliphant is not overdrawn. Among these unhappy captives were sixty officers, and Hesilrig, in his " Defence," admits that 1600 of their soldiers perished miserably. Among the charges brought against that ruffianly officer, after death, by Sir Jeffery Palmer, the English attorney-general, is one to the effect, " that he used the Scots prisoners taken at Dunbar in such a barbarous and horrid manner, that they perished of *hunger*, and were not admitted to have any relief." (Concerning this, see Mackinnon's " History of the Coldstream Guards," vol. i.)

2. The Scottish reveille, like the Scottish march, was remembered long after the Union. In 1714, " the grenadiers of the three regiments of guards, during their stay at Greenwich, pursuant to an order from his Majesty, are to beat the English and Scots reveillez alternately."—Letter from Secretary at War, 16th September.

3. An account of Captain Augustine's exploit in December, 1650, will be found in Balfour's " Annales," vol. iv., and in the " Memorials of Edinburgh Castle."

4. Scotland never possessed better organized armies than those equipped and disciplined by Sir A. Leslie, afterwards Earl of Leven, and Sir D. Leslie, afterwards Lord Newark ; and the cavalry of the latter would have done no discredit to the British service in the present day, in their bravery, efficiency, formation, and general armament. In Sir James Balfour's papers we find the following list of Scottish cavalry :—

" The division of the armey ot horse into brigades as they are to goe upon service. Stirling, 7th May, 1651.

" First Brigade, under Lieut.-Gen. Sir David Lesly—
   Earl of Rothes' regiment.
   Lord Brechin's regiment.
   Colonel Craige's regiment.

" Second Brigade, under Major-General Robert Montgomerie—
    Earl of Linlithgow's regiment.
    Earl of Dunfermline's regiment.
    Lord Cranstoun's regiment.

" Third Brigade, under Major-General Sir John Brown, of Fordell—
    Earl of Balcarris' regiment.
    Sir Walter Scott's regiment.
    Charles Arnott's regiment.

" Fourth Brigade, under Lieutenant-General John Middleton—
    Earl Marischal's regiment.
    Lord Ogilvie's regiment.
    Arthur Erskine's regiment.
    James Mercer of Aldie's regiment.

Reserve.

" Fifth Brigade, under Major-General Massey—
    Earl of Errol's regiment.
    Lord Drummond's regiment.
    Colonel Stuart's regiment.

" Sixth Brigade, under Major-General Wandrosse—
    Lord Mauchline's regiment.
    Lord Erskine's regiment.
    Lord Forbes's regiment.
    Colonel Innes' regiment.

" Seventh Brigade, under
    Duke of Hamilton's regiment.
    Duke of Buckinghame's regiment.
    Earl of Home's regiment.

" The king's guardes to be upon the right of the right winge."

Buckinghame was an exile in Scotland, but, like Cleveland and other English fugitives, was supported by the Scottish treasury.

THE END.

TWO-SHILLING VOLUMES.

MAXWELL, W. H.—*contd.*

168 Hector O'Halloran.
177 Captain O'Sullivan.
552 Stories of the Peninsular War.
570 Flood and Field.
591 Wild Sports in the West.

NEALE, W. J. N.

200 The Lost Ship.
341 The Pride of the Mess.
490 The Flying Dutchman.
599 Will Watch.
609 Cavendish.
877 The Port Admiral.
938 The Naval Surgeon.

REID, *Mayne.*

198 The Quadroon.
199 The War Trail.
725 The Scalp Hunters.
726 The Rifle Rangers.
727 The Maroon.
728 The White Chief.
729 The Wild Huntress.
730 The White Gauntlet.
731 The Half-Blood.
732 The Headless Horseman.
733 Lost Lenore.
734 The Hunters' Feast.
735 The Wood Rangers.
736 The Tiger Hunter.
737 The Boy Slaves.
738 The Cliff Climbers.
739 The Giraffe Hunters.
740 Afloat in the Forest.
741 The Ocean Waifs.
742 The White Squaw.
743 The Fatal Cord.
744 The Guerilla Chief.
954 The Bush Boys.
955 The Boy Tar.
956 The Desert Home.
957 Bruin.
958 Odd People.
959 The Forest Exiles.
960 The Young Yägers.
961 The Young Voyageurs.
962 The Plant Hunters.
963 Ran Away to Sea.
964 The Boy Hunters.
965 Gaspar the Gaucho.

RICHARDSON.

497 Clarissa Harlowe.
558 Pamela.
559 Sir Charles Grandison.

SCOTT, *Michael.*

SCOTT, *Sir Walter.*

642 Waverley.
643 Guy Mannering.
644 Old Mortality.
645 Heart of Midlothian.
646 Rob Roy.
652 Ivanhoe.
653 The Antiquary.
669 Bride of Lammermoor.
670 Black Dwarf & Legend of Montrose.
674 The Monastery.
675 The Abbot.
676 Kenilworth.
677 The Pirate.
678 Fortunes of Nigel.
683 Peveril of the Peak.
684 Quentin Durward.
685 St. Ronan's Well.
686 Redgauntlet.
695 Betrothed and Highland Widow
696 The Talisman and Two Drovers.
697 Woodstock.
698 The Fair Maid of Perth.
701 Anne of Geierstein.
702 Count Robert of Paris.
703 The Surgeon's Daughter.

SMITH, *Albert.*

113 Marchioness of Brinvilliers.
119 Adventures of Mr. Ledbury.
126 Scattergood Family.
270 Christopher Tadpole.
281 The Pottleton Legacy.

SMOLLETT, *Tobias.*

457 Roderick Random.
495 Humphry Clinker.
501 Peregrine Pickle.

SUE, *Eugene.*

507 The Wandering Jew.
508 The Mysteries of Paris

VERNE, *Jules.*

699 Adventures of Capt. Hatteras.
700 Twenty Thousand Leagues under
   the Sea.
704 Five Weeks in a Balloon, and a
   Journey to the Centre of the Earth.
986 The English at the North Pole.
987 The Field of Ice.
988 Voyage Round the World—
   Australia.

TWO-SHILLING VOLUMES.

TWO-SHILLING VOLUMES.

716 City of the Sultan. Miss PARDOE.
718 Through the Mist. J. HERING.
719 Tales of the Coastguard.
WARNEFORD.
720 Leonard Lindsay. ANGUS REACH.
750 Romance of Military Life.
W. RUSSELL.
751 Robber of the Rhine. RITCHIE.
752 The Polish Lancer. REELSTAB.
760 Jasper Lyle. Mrs. WARD.
762 Flower of the Forest ST. JOHN.
767 Thaddeus of Warsaw.
JANE PORTER.
807 The Hazelhurst Mystery.
818 Strafford. H. B. BAKER.
822 The Prodigal Daughter.
MARK HOPE.
841 Madge Dunraven. HARRIET JAY.
846 Miss Roberts's Fortune.
SOPHIE WINTHROP.
851 Mysteries of Udolpho.
Mrs. RADCLIFFE.
852 Romance of the Forest.
Mrs. RADCLIFFE.
854 The Children of the Abbey.
R. M. ROCHE.
862 Two Pretty Girls. MARY A. LEWIS.
863 Tom Singleton.
W. W. FOLLETT SYNGE.
864 Blair Athol. BLINKHOOLIE.
865 Beaten on the Post.
J. P. WHEELDON.

866 Too Fast to Last. JOHN MILLS.
867 Through the Cannon Smoke.
ARCHIBALD FORBES.
899 A Fool's Errand.
ONE OF THE FOOLS.
902 Tales of the Slave Squadron.
903 Jack Ashore.
977 Sir Edward Seaward's Narrative.
980 Olivia Raleigh.
W. W. FOLLETT SYNGE.
981 The Adventures of Robinson Play.
fellow.
983 The Doctor's Family. J. GIRARDIN.
984 Uncle Chesterton's Heir.
Madame COLOMB.
985 True as Steel. J. GIRARDIN.
994 Here Below. J. A. SCOFIELD.
995 A Woman's Glory.
SARAH DOUDNEY.
998 A Tale of a Horse. BLINKHOOLIE.
999 Ten Thousand a Year.
1000 The Diary of a Late Physician.
SAMUEL WARREN, D.C.L.
1001 Unspotted from the World.
1002 Bridget. M. BETHAM EDWARDS.
1004 The Secrets of Stage Conjuring.
HOUDIN.
1005 Chinese Gordon. A. FORBES.
1013 Romance of the Forest, The Italian,
and Udolpho, in 1 Vol.
MRS. RADCLIFFE.

AMERICAN LIBRARY,

At 2s. each, boards, paper covers.

18 Roughing It, and the Innocents at
Home. MARK TWAIN.
20 The Innocents Abroad, and the
New Pilgrim's Progress.
MARK TWAIN.
21 The Celebrated Jumping Frog, and
the Curious Dream.
MARK TWAIN.
22 Prose and Poetry. BRET HARTE.
28 Patience Strong. Author of

34 The Gilded Age, a Novel.
MARK TWAIN and C. D. WARNER.
36 Wit and Humour. JOSH BILLINGS.
37 Prudence Palfrey. T. B. ALDRICH.
40 Marjorie Daw. T. B. ALDRICH.
60 Other People's Children. Author
of " Helen's Babies."
63 Mr. Miggs of Danbury.
J. M. BAILEY.

FLORIN NOVELS.

Crown 8vo, RED CLOTH, price 2s. each.

LYTTON, Lord.

1 Pelham.
2 Paul Clifford.
3 Eugene Aram.
4 Last Days of Pompeii.
5 Rienzi.
6 Ernest Maltravers.
7 Alice; or, The Mysteries.
8 Night and Morning.
9 The Disowned.
10 Devereux.
11 Godolphin.
36 Falkland and Zicci,
37 Leila and The Pilgrims of the Rhine.
38 Zanoni.
39 The Last of the Barons.

LEVER, Charles.

12 Harry Lorrequer.
13 Charles O'Malley.
14 Jack Hinton,

DICKENS, Charles.

15 Sketches by "Boz."
16 Nicholas Nickleby.
17 Oliver Twist.
18 Barnaby Rudge.
19 Old Curiosity Shop.
20 Dombey and Son.

COCKTON, Henry.

21 Valentine Vox.

LOVER, Samuel.

SCOTT, Michael.

23 Tom Cringle's Log.
24 The Cruise of the *Midge.*

FERRIER, Miss.

25 Marriage.
26 The Inheritance.
27 Destiny,

MARRYAT, Captain.

28 Frank Mildmay.
29 Midshipman Easy.
30 Phantom Ship.
45 Peter Simple.
46 The King's Own.
47 Newton Forster.
48 Jacob Faithful.
49 The Pacha of Many Tales.
50 Japhet in Search of a Father.

COOPER, Fenimore.

31 The Deerslayer.
32 The Pathfinder.
33 The Last of the Mohicans.
34 The Pioneers.
35 The Prairie.

RADCLIFFE, Mrs.

40 The Romance of the Forest.
41 The Mysteries of Udolpho.

ROCHE, J. M.

42 The Children of the Abbey.

MILLER, Thomas.

43 Gideon Giles the Roper

ROUTLEDGE'S RAILWAY LIBRARY.
ONE-SHILLING VOLUMES.
(*2d. Postage.*)

AINSWORTH, W. H.

337 Windsor Castle.
339 Tower of London.
343 The Miser's Daughter.
347 Rookwood.
351 Old St. Paul's.
356 Crichton.
359 Guy Fawkes.
362 The Spendthrift.
369 James the Second.
372 The Star Chamber.
375 The Flitch of Bacon.
378 Lancashire Witches.
381 Mervyn Clitheroe.
384 Ovingdean Grange.
387 St. James'
390 Auriol.
393 Jack Sheppard.
673 Boscobel.
668 Manchester Rebels.
840 Beau Nash.

BURNETT, Mrs. Hodgson.

890 Dolly.
891 Pretty Polly Pemberton.
892 Kathleen.
893 Our Neighbour Opposite.
894 Miss Crespigny.
895 Lindsay's Luck.
896 That Lass o' Lowrie's
897 The Tide on the Moaning Bar.

COOPER, J. Fenimore.

1 The Pilot.
3 Last of the Mohicans.
4 The Pioneers.
6 The Red Rover.
7 The Spy.
12 Lionel Lincoln.
273 The Deerslayer.
274 The Pathfinder.
275 The Bravo.
276 The Waterwitch.
277 Two Admirals.
280 Satanstoe.
290 Afloat and Ashore. Sequel to Miles Wallingford.
292 Wyandotte.
296 Eve Effingham. Sequel to Homeward Bound.
298 M

COOPER, J. Fenimore.—contd.

307 The Prairie.
312 Homeward Bound.
314 The Borderers.
317 The Sea Lions
319 Precaution.
322 The Oak Openings.
325 Mark's Reef.
328 Ned Myers.
331 Heidenmauer.

CARLETON, William.

2 Jane Sinclair.
14 The Clarionet.
42 The Tithe Proctor.
140 Fardarougha.
141 The Emigrants.

DICKENS, Charles.

834 The Pickwick Papers
836 Nicholas Nickleby.

DUMAS, Alexandre.

180 Half Brothers.
435 Dr. Basilius.
438 The Twin Captains.
441 Captain Paul.
451 Chevalier de Maison Rouge.
463, 464 Monte Cristo, 2 Vols. (1s each.)
469 Nanon.
480 The Black Tulip.
506 Ascanio.
551 Isabel of Bavaria.
579 Beau Tancrede.
581 Pauline.
582 Catherine Blum.
583 Ingenue.
584 The Russian Gipsy.
585 The Watchmaker.
656 The Mohicans of Paris.
837 The Corsican Brothers.
966 Monte Cristo (complete).
967 Three Musketeers and Twenty Years After. In 1 Vol.

Dumas' Stories with Sequels.

427 The Three Musketeers. a

SHILLING VOLUMES.

AMERICAN LIBRARY.

A Series of the most Popular American Works, in Fancy Covers, 1s. each.

TWAIN, *Mark.*

1 The Celebrated Jumping Frog. Author's edition, with a Copyright Poem.
4 Roughing It (copyright).
7 The Innocents at Home (copyright)
8 Mark Twain's Curious Dream (copyright).
10 The Innocents Abroad.
11 The New Pilgrim's Progress.
46 Information Wanted, and other Sketches.

HARTE, *Bret.*

3 The Luck of Roaring Camp, with a Preface by Tom Hood.
9 Bret Harte's Poems (complete).
29 An Episode of Fiddletown.
39 The Fool of Five Forks.
51 Thankful Blossom.
65 My Friend the Tramp.
70 The Story of a Mine.
76 The Man on the Beach.
77 Jinny.

HOLMES, *O. W*

38 Autocrat of the Breakfast Table.
86 The Professor at the Breakfast Table.

ADELER, *Max.*

35 Out of the Hurly Burly.
50 Elbow Room.

EGGLESTON, *E.*

2 The Hoosier Schoolmaster.
17 The Mystery of Metropolisville.

VARIOUS AUTHORS.

26 Life in Danbury. DANBURY NEWSMAN.
42 Artemus Ward: His Book—His Travels.
43 Eastern Fruit on Western Dishes. P. V. NASBY.
48 Cloth of Gold. T. B. ALDRICH.
54 Some Other Babies, very like Helen's, only more so.
55 The Man who was Not a Colonel.
57 Dot and Dime.
61 That Husband of Mine.
69 The Queen of Sheba. T. B. ALDRICH.
72 Leedle Yawcob Strauss. C. F. ADAMS.
84 Prudence Palfrey. T. B. ALDRICH.
85 Uncle Remus; or, Mr. Fox, Mr. Rabbit, and Mr. Terrapin.

RECITERS and READINGS, 1s. each.

1 Carpenter's Comic Reciter.
2 Carpenter's Popular Reciter.
3 Routledge's Comic Readings.
4 Routledge's Popular Readings.
5 Routledge's Dramatic Readings.
6 Routledges Blue Ribbon Reciter.
7 Ready-made Speeches.
8 School Reciter for Boys and Girls.
10 The Temperance Reciter.

THE ANECDOTE LIBRARY, 1s. each.

1 Scotch Anecdotes. J. ALLAN MAIR.
2 Irish Anecdotes. PAT. KENNEDY.
3 English Anecdotes. TOM HOOD.
4 Theatrical Anecdotes. PERCY FITZGERALD.
5 American Anecdotes. H. PAUL.
6 Legal Anecdotes. JOHN TIMBS.
7 Naval Anecdotes.
8 Military Anecdotes.

HAPPY HOME SERIES.

In large Fcap. 8vo, Fancy Covers, 1s. each.

1 Grimm's Fairy Tales.
2 Andersen's Fairy Tales.
3 Edgeworth's Moral Tales.
4 Edgeworth's Popular Tales.
8 Sandford and Merton.

CHRISTMAS SERIES, 1s. each.

2 Acting Charades. ANNE BOWMAN.
9 The Dream-Book. MISS LAWFORD.
12 Sensational Dramas. W. R. SNOW.
14 Pippins and Pies.
    STIRLING COYNE.
16 Shilling Manual of Modern Etiquette.
17 Plays for Children. MISS WALKER.
18 Christmas Hamper.
    MARK LEMON.

19 Christmas Day and how it was Spent. LE ROS.
20 Children's Theatricals.
    J. KEITH ANGUS.
21 Ancient and Modern Magic. VERE.
22 Theatrical Scenes and Tableaux for Children. J. K. ANGUS.
23 Lazinella, and other Drawing-room Plays. W YARDLEY, E. L. BLANCHARD and others.

EVERY BOY'S LIBRARY, 1s. each.

By *JULES VERNE.*

In cloth.

1 The English at the North Pole.
7 The Field of Ice.
8 Five Weeks in a Balloon.
9 Journey to the Centre of the Earth.
10 Twenty Thousand Leagues under the Sea, part 1.
11 ————— part 2.
17 The Floating City; The Blockade Runners.
20 Voyage Round the World—South America.
21 ————— Australia.
22 ————— New Zealand.
23 From the Earth to the Moon.
28 Three Englishmen and Three Russians.
35 Round the World in Eighty Days.
37 The Fur Country, part 1.
38 ————————— part 2.

In stiff fancy cover.

5 Dick Rodney. JAMES GRANT.
6 The Boy Voyagers. A. BOWMAN.
12 Ernie Elton, the Lazy Boy.
    Mrs. EILOART.
13 Ernie Elton at School. Ditto.
15 Robert and Harold; or, The Young Marooners. F. R. GOULDING.
16 Holiday Camp. ST. JOHN CORBET.
18 Robinson Crusoe.
19 Swiss Family Robinson.

24 Two Years before the Mast.
    R. H. DANA.
25 Arthur's Champion.
    Rev. H. C. ADAMS.
26 Young Gold Digger.
    GERSTAECKER.
27 Story of a Bad Boy. ALDRICH.
29 Being a Boy. C. D. WARNER.
30 Archie Blake. Mrs. EILOART.
31 John Hartley; or, How we Got On in Life. C. ADAMS.
32 Joshua Hawsepipe. C. R. LOW.
33 Life of Nelson. SOUTHEY.
34 His Own Master.
    J. T. TROWBRIDGE.
36 Æsop's Fables, with 50 illustrations.
    WEIR.
39 Cousin Aleck; or, Boy Life among the Indians.
40 The Lost Rifle. Rev. H. C. ADAMS.
41 The Marooner's Island.
42 Evenings at Home.
43 Adventures by Sea and Land.
    MARIA HACK.
44 In Land and Ice Deserts. Ditto.
45 Travels in Hot and Cold Lands.
    MARIA HACK.
46 Boy Life on the Water.
47 The Chief of the School.
    Rev. H. C. ADAMS.
48 Boy's Book about Indians.
    TUTTLE.
49 Adventures among the Indians.
    F. R. GOULDING.
50 The Playground. Rev. J. G. WOOD.

RUBY SERIES, 1s. each.